NO LESS THE DEVIL

By Stuart MacBride

THE OLDCASTLE NOVELS

Birthdays for the Dead
A Song for the Dying
A Dark So Deadly
The Coffinmaker's Garden
No Less the Devil

THE LOGAN McRAE NOVELS

Cold Granite
Dying Light
Broken Skin
Flesh House
Blind Eye
Dark Blood
Shatter the Bones
Close to the Bone
22 Dead Little Bodies
The Missing and the Dead
In the Cold Dark Ground
Now We Are Dead
The Blood Road
All That's Dead

OTHER WORKS

Sawbones (a novella)
12 Days of Winter (a short-story collection)
Partners in Crime (two Logan and Steel short stories)
The 45% Hangover (a Logan and Steel novella)
The Completely Wholesome Adventures of Skeleton Bob (a picture book)

WRITING AS STUART B. MACBRIDE

Halfhead

NO LESS THE DEVIL

STUART MACBRIDE

BANTAM PRESS

TRANSWORLD PUBLISHERS
Penguin Random House, One Embassy Gardens,
8 Viaduct Gardens, London SW11 7BW
www.penguin.co.uk

Transworld is part of the Penguin Random House group of companies
whose addresses can be found at global.penguinrandomhouse.com

Penguin
Random House
UK

First published in Great Britain in 2022 by Bantam Press
an imprint of Transworld Publishers

A CIP catalogue record for this book
is available from the British Library.

ISBNS 9781787634909 (hb)
9781787634916 (tpb)

Typeset in 10/14.5pt Stone Serif ITC Pro by Jouve (UK), Milton Keynes
Printed and bound in Great Britain by Clays Ltd, Elcograf S.p.A.

The authorized representative in the EEA is Penguin Random House Ireland,
Morrison Chambers, 32 Nassau Street, Dublin D02 YH68.

Penguin Random House is committed to a sustainable
future for our business, our readers and our planet. This book
is made from Forest Stewardship Council® certified paper.

In loving memory of Grendel MacBride,
my constant companion, muse, and
very own little fuzzy serial killer

2004–2021

— the wolves in the woods —

O

Malcolm ran. One hand curled against his chest, the wrist swollen and aching, the fingers numb and almost black in the sickly yellow street-light. His other hand clenched around the strap of his tatty old rucksack. Ancient trainers squealing on the slippery cobbles as the rain battered down.

Breathing hard.

Teeth bared.

Tears blurring the shuttered shops and parked cars that lined Archers Lane.

Sobbing out the words as he tried to put as much distance as possible between himself and the wolves: 'Please God. Please God, no. Please, please, please, please, please . . .'

Behind him, a high-pitched howl echoed through the night.

'Pleasepleasepleasepleaseplease . . .'

At the end of the street, he hammered around the corner onto the Chanonry, feet skidding out from underneath him, sending him crashing into the boot of a rust-brown hatchback hard enough to set the car's alarm screaming. Lights flashing angry orange as he scrambled upright and staggered out into the road. Three o'clock in the morning and the houses on both sides of the road were in darkness: no one peering out their windows to see what all the fuss was about. No one to witness what was happening. No one to save him.

What was the point of bloody car alarms if everyone just ignored them?

He hauled in a breath and bellowed it out again. 'SOMEBODY HELP ME!'

A curtain twitched on the other side of the road.

Malcolm waved his good arm, the rucksack swinging like a grubby metronome, but whoever it was, they just let the curtains fall shut again.

'HELP ME, YOU BASTARDS!'

Another howl joined the hatchback's wails.

Oh God: they were getting *closer*.

He backed away from the car. 'Pleasepleasepleaseplease . . .'

There – just ahead – a big Range Rover coming towards him, headlights slashing through the rain. The driver would help. They *had to* help.

'STOP!' Malcolm lurched into the middle of the tarmac. 'PLEASE! HELP ME!'

The four-by-four didn't even slow down, just blared its horn.

'NO!' Jumping back, out of the way, but not quite quick enough. The windscreen caught his rucksack and sent it spinning from his hand to bounce off the roof of a parked Volvo.

The Range Rover slammed on its brakes, window buzzing down to let too-loud music *bmmmmtch-bmmmmtch-bmmmmtch* out, followed by a bug-eyed woman's face. 'IF YOU'VE SCRATCHED MY CAR, YOU'RE BLOODY FOR IT!'

'Please, you've got to help me! They're coming!' Malcolm staggered towards the car, good arm outstretched, dirty fingers reaching. 'Please, they're going to kill me!'

'Eeewww . . .' Top lip curled, she shrank away from him. 'GET AWAY FROM ME, YOU HOMELESS FREAK!' And the window buzzed back up again.

Malcolm was inches from the door handle when the car shot forwards, accelerating away up the Chanonry in a cloud of choking diesel fumes.

'THEY'RE GOING TO KILL ME!'

The flashing orange lights went out, and the hatchback's alarm fell silent.

Now the only sounds were his wheezing lungs, battering heart, and the rain's never-ending rattlesnake hiss.

A shrill laugh sliced through the night. It was answered by another howl – this time from the other side of the street, behind the Volvo, where Malcolm's rucksack had disappeared.

They weren't close any more: they were *here*.

And now they had his rucksack.

He backed away from everything he owned in the whole world.

Swallowed as the wolves growled from the shadows.

RUN!

Malcolm staggered towards the end of the street, where the tarmac ended in a row of bollards and a lone streetlight stood guard against the murky blackness of Camburn Woods.

The woods.

He could lose them there.

Miles and miles of twisting paths and abandoned buildings and trees and trees and trees.

His trainers splashed through a puddle that stretched the width of the road. Faster. Passing the bollards and in beneath the thick dark canopy of needles, branches, and leaves, following the tarmac path.

That rattlesnake hiss was muffled by the trees, the air thick with the heavy brown scent of mouldering forest floor.

Behind him: the sound of small feet pounded the track; laughter; snarling.

Malcolm gritted his teeth and *ran*. Pumping his knees and elbow. Breath wheezing in and rasping out. Wet trainers slap, slap, slapping against the path. Sweat, clammy between his shoulder blades. Razors slashing through his ruined hand and wrist.

A crossroads appeared up ahead. The signpost pointed left to Castle Hill Infirmary, right to Saxon Halls of Residence, but Malcolm went straight ahead, following the arrow for Rushworth House. For a count of five, four, three, two—

He made a sudden turn, ducking right, leaving the path and crashing into a waist-high sea of nettles. Running and stumbling through the undergrowth as darkness wrapped its arms around him.

Those little feet scuttered to a halt on the path, and a lone howl rang out.

A high voice followed it: 'YOU CAN'T RUN FOREVER, LITTLE PIGGY!'

And they were after him again.

No idea what the building used to be, but it was little more than a ruined outline now, buried deep within Camburn Woods – half its roof missing, the upper floor bulging out above the doorway, like a drowned man's stomach. Ready to split.

There wasn't much of a clearing: barely enough space between the trees to let the rain clatter down on the crumbling slates and whisper in the jagged brambles. Bracken reaching for him with wet green tentacles. That small patch of sky up above glowing a dirty orange-brown, giving off just enough light to make out shapes and outlines.

Off in the distance, something rustled and Malcolm froze – crouching beneath the searching branches of a twisted oak. Might be a badger or a fox? Or it might be the wolves . . .

The rustling got quieter and quieter, until he was alone again.

Thank God.

Malcolm clutched his knee with his good hand and let the breath whoomph out of him. Tears warm on his cheeks as he shuddered and moaned. Biting his bottom lip to keep the noise to a minimum. Hard to tell what time it was, after crashing through bushes and nettles and brambles and broom for what felt like hours, till the sound of the wolves faded behind him. Then creeping about in the gloom, guarding every breath in case it might give him away. And now he was here. Soaked and exhausted, but still alive.

It was a while before he straightened up, wiped his eyes on the sodden sleeve of his new jacket, then limped across the tiny clearing and into the house. All he needed was a quiet corner, somewhere out of the rain to lie low till morning. Somewhere the wolves wouldn't find him. Get his arse to Accident and Emergency, soon as it was safe. Maybe leave town with a pocketful of pilfered drugs and a zip-a-dee-doo-dah in his heart. Head south to somewhere warmer, like Dundee, or even Edinburgh. After all, when you were sleeping rough, one shop doorway was pretty much like any other. Oldcastle could go screw itself.

Wooden floorboards creaked beneath his torn, sodden trainers as he scuffed into the dark interior.

Wasn't like the city had exactly been good to him, was it? Thirty-four years old and what did he have to show for it? A shattered wrist, a crappy sleeping bag from the army surplus store on Weaver Street, and a manky backpack . . .

No. Didn't even have that any more.

The wolves had taken it all.

Everything except the half-bottle of Asda own-brand whisky in his coat pocket – which was about to get a serious spanking.

*

'Wmmmmphaaaaargh!' Malcolm's eyes snapped open in the darkness, face wet, water running into his ears and soaking into his T-shirt.

A little girl loomed over him, features lit from below like she was about to tell a ghost story. Her voice was posh and clipped – polished marble and cut glass. 'Here we go. Knew you were in there somewhere.' She couldn't have been more than ten or eleven, big blue eyes staring at him above her tartan facemask as she waggled an almost empty bottle of water in her gloved hand. 'Wouldn't do for you to miss the grand finale, would it?' She was dressed down in a baseball cap and hoodie – both advertising rival crappy pop bands. Tracksuit bottoms and a pair of mud-smeared Nikes. She'd tucked her hair away out of sight, but the freckles visible above her mask and those pale-orange eyebrows meant she was a redhead in real life. Gloves and a facemask: like the pandemic had never ended.

'Gah . . .' Malcolm scrabbled back against the wall, levering himself up till he was sitting. Wiped the water from his face with his good hand. The whisky's warmth leaching out of his bones, leaving that old, famil-iar, thirsty tremor behind. 'You can't just come in—'

'*Do* shut up.' She looked over her shoulder. 'Are you recording?'

A large boy emerged from the gloom. About the size of a vending machine, broad-shouldered, big barrel chest, an iPhone clutched in his blue-nitrile-covered paw. Couldn't see his mouth, because of the skull-print facemask, but the smile in his eyes was clear enough. He sounded even posher than she did: 'Indubitably.' One of those accents that boomed with privilege, private education, and a sheltered upbringing. 'Worry not, my dear Allegra; Hugo has got it covered.'

The girl, Allegra, glowered at him. 'Don't use our names, you *utter* nimrod!'

'Oh.' Hugo's shoulders rounded, eyes going all puppy dog. 'But there's no one else here, and this unfortunate gentleman will be dead soon, so—'

'You're recording this! Now our names are on the footage!'

'Ah. Yes. I see.' A nod. 'Quite right. *Mea culpa*. Stupid Hugo.' He fiddled with his phone. 'OK, I've definitely deleted that one. Let's try this again, keep it anonymous, and all that.'

Malcolm stared at the pair of them. 'Wait, what do you mean, "this unfortunate gentleman will be"—'

It wasn't the hardest slap he'd ever received, but it came out of nowhere, jerking his head to the side, leaving the edge of his mouth stinging.

A squeak of nitrile as Allegra rubbed at her slapping hand. 'Did I say you could talk?'

'You're bloody children! You don't scare me!'

'Oh dear. That's unfortunate, isn't it?'

'Aha! Yes.' Hugo inched closer. 'Most unfortunate *indeed*.' He reached into the pocket of his hoodie and pulled out a long thin parcel wrapped in newspaper. About eighteen inches long. 'Still, "The goat will bleat till its throat is slit." As my dear grandmama always says.' He unwrapped the newspaper parcel, one-handed, and a kitchen knife's long curved blade gleamed in the light from his phone.

Malcolm pushed himself further into the wall. 'You . . . don't scare me. I'm a police officer!'

Allegra shook her head, reaching into her own hoodie pocket. 'Not any more, you're not: they fired you years ago.' The hand came out, wrapped around the handle of a claw hammer. The one she'd used to wake Malcolm up two hours ago, when he'd been sleeping in the doorway of McCartney's Hair and Beauty, minding his own business and not bothering anyone.

Just seeing it made his swollen wrist burn and throb. 'You can't do this, it's—'

'Do you think we picked you at random, Malcolm? Because we didn't.'

'Fortune favours the prepared, old man.'

'We've been tracking you all day.' She flexed her gloved fingers around the hammer's grip. 'Don't you want to know how we found you tonight? Here? In the woods so dark and deep? All hidden away like a frightened little mouse?'

'If . . . if you go away now, you won't get into any trouble. I promise.'

Her voice jumped up a bit, taking on a saccharine lisp. 'Oh, you *poor* man, you look so cold in that tatty old jacket! Daddy says I can spend my birthday money on anything I like, and I'd like to help *you*!'

It's a frigid Monday lunchtime and Malcolm's in his usual spot, outside the train station, sitting cross-legged on his square of cardboard and his sleeping bag, a battered baseball cap on the pavement in front of him. Huffing a steaming breath into his cupped hands, trying to get some life back in his frozen fingers. Huddling in the threadbare coat he 'inherited' when Sparky Steve got taken off with the Covid. The coat with ragged cuffs, holes in the elbows, and a big stain down the back.

So much for the Super Scorching Scottish Summer the tabloids had promised. Since when was August colder than February? And people *still* said global warming was a load of old—

'*Excuse me?*'

He looks up and there's a pretty little red-haired girl, holding a bag from Primark that's almost as big as she is. Pigtails. Freckles. Tartan skirt. Blue school blazer with some sort of crest on the pocket, so her parents must be worth a bob or two.

He gives her his best I'm-so-pitiful smile. 'Got any spare change?'

'Oh, you *poor* man, you look so cold in that tatty old jacket! Daddy says I can spend my birthday money on anything I like, and I'd like to help *you*!' She holds the bag out towards him. 'It's so you don't catch your death.'

He pulls his chin in and frowns at her for a moment. Is she taking the piss? Playing 'Mock the Poor Homeless Bastard'? Is she going to scream 'Paedo!' at him if he goes anywhere near?

She places the bag on the pavement in front of him, then digs into her pocket and comes out with a tenner. Drops that in his empty cap. 'Now you can get something tasty to eat too!' All perky and helpful.

So Malcolm opens the bag and takes out a nice new padded jacket – one of the dark-red shiny kind that look a bit like a duvet with sleeves. Stares at it. Then at her. Then at the jacket again.

Licks his lips.

Feels actual tears welling up. He chokes the knot out of his voice for long enough to give her a mumbled, 'Thank you. It's . . . Thank you.'

'Put it on! Put it on!'

And Malcolm wriggles his way out of Sparky Steve's manky jacket and into the brand-new padded one. Warm and cosy and the nicest thing anyone's done for him for years. '*Thank* you.'

'I sewed a GPS tag into the lining. My companion here's been tracking you on his phone.'

'Like a veritable *bloodhound*. Keen of eye and sharp of nose.' Hugo raised the blade. 'And knife, of course. Mustn't forget the knife.'

Malcolm's back pressed hard against the wall. Voice wobbling. 'Please, I don't want to die . . .'

'I know.' Allegra patted him on the shoulder, her voice soft and kind. 'But sometimes that's just how life is: some people live happily ever after; some people get stabbed. Or strangled. Or battered with a hammer.' She patted the claw hammer's metal head against her gloved palm. 'Or torn open like a bloody envelope.'

'Please, you don't have to do this!' Tears made the dark little room blur.

'Or, in your case, an unfortunate mix of the above.'

'Stiff upper lip, old man.' Hugo held the phone out for a close-up. 'Nobody likes a cry baby.'

'*Please!* I don't—'

Then the hammer slashed down, and the world screamed its very last breath.

— bless me, Father, for I have sinned —

I

Right.

Michelle checked herself in the mirror again: make-up perfect, auburn waves hairsprayed into submission, bright smile without a hint of lipstick on her teeth. Cupping a hand over a huffed-out breath revealed a reassuring minty freshness, too.

First day on the job and she was good to go.

All she needed now was a customer.

There – the lanky middle-aged woman, scowling away at the shelves of painkillers. Black overcoat on over a red-and-white striped top, mousey-blonde hair that was *far* too long for someone that age, skin like blanched milk, and a strong chin with a dimple at its point. She'd clearly gone for the 'natural' look, and it didn't suit her at all. And those thick-black-framed glasses didn't exactly help. Still, it was *amazing* what a bit of make-up – properly applied by a newly qualified professional like Michelle – could do.

The woman plucked a packet of paracetamol from the shelf and clacked towards the checkouts on a pair of Cuban-heeled boots. Which meant she'd have to walk right past Michelle's station, completely unaware that her world was about to become a little bit brighter.

Michelle nodded to herself, keeping her voice low. 'Remember your training, Michelle, you've got this.' Then cranked her smile up another notch.

It was time to make a difference!

Lucy squinted one eye shut against the knife-sharp sun slashing its way in through the shop window. Sparking off the harsh white floor tiles, glass bottles, and jars, as if it was trying to stab its way right into her already throbbing brain.

It was too hot in here as well, the heating turned way up to depths-of-winter levels – even though it was only early September – transforming the overcoat she'd pulled on that morning into an instrument of torture. Only been in here fifteen minutes and already her top was sticking to her back.

'Excuse me, madam? Hello?' An orange-faced horror with too much blusher, drawn-on eyebrows, and a white smock top, popped out from behind one of the make-up counters, blocking Lucy's way. Holding up a palm-sized tub of something greasy. 'I know crow's feet can be *such* a worry for middle-aged ladies, but, great news, now there's an organic alternative to Botox!'

'Middle-aged?' Lucy glared at her. 'I'm twenty-six!'

'Ah.' The idiot hid the tub behind her back and snatched up a couple of lipsticks instead. 'Well, perhaps, with your *classical* pale complexion, I could tempt you to a *slightly* brighter lipstick? Bewitching Coral? Or Pink Brandy?' Pointing them both at Lucy's mouth. 'Because that shade's really *far* too insipid for you.'

'I'm not wearing any make-up!'

The fake smile faltered. 'Then . . . now's the perfect opportunity to start?'

'Gah!' Lucy pushed past her and stomped over to the queue for the tills.

Of course, the self-service ones were all out of order, so there was no option but to shuffle forward, inch by painful inch, past the newspapers, magazines, and low-sugar sweets – arranged to corral the punters on their miserable death march towards the counter. Which *clearly* should've been manned by three people, but had been abandoned instead to the care of a single teenager with a permanent sniff who scanned people's purchases as if she was doing them a huge personal favour.

Insipid? Crow's feet? Middle-aged?

Like that make-up-counter troll was a sodding oil painting, with her face like a constipated Oompa Loompa.

Cheeky cow.

Lucy kept her head down, avoiding the treacherous sunlight, her one open eye drifting across the publications: 'LOVE ISLAND STD THREE-SOME SHOCKER!', 'STRICTLY COME DRUGS RAID', 'MY SECRET

WEIGHT-LOSS HELL!', 'SEX-PEST POSTIE STOLE MY HEART & MY CAT!' The crappy tabloids were just as bad: 'RANDY RHYNIE'S "RUSSIAN ROMP" RUMOURS', 'MIGRANTS "SWAMPING NHS" SAYS HERO COUNCILLOR', and 'JOCK COPS CAN'T CATCH CREEPY KILLER'.

Which was a bit unfair.

Even if it was true.

That last headline sat above a grainy photo of an empty, dilapidated room – ragged holes in the floorboards, pale blotches bleached into the crumbling walls.

A smaller picture was set into it: Abby Geddes gazing out at the world with tired eyes, mouth drooping at the edges, short brown hair rumpled and unstyled. Almost as if she—

'*Hello?*' It was barked out in an imperious male voice, right behind Lucy, followed by a tut. '*Are you actually* in *this queue, or are you just browsing?*'

Tosser.

Lucy turned, nice and slow, straightened her glasses, and gave the gangly dick in the pinstripe suit a lopsided dose of the evil eye. Baring her teeth. 'You want to *repeat* that, sunshine?'

Pink rushed up from the collar of his shirt, flooding his cheeks, making it look as if his tie was tied far too tight. He stepped back. 'I . . . er . . .' Taking a sudden interest in his polished brogues. 'I was . . . It's your turn.' One hand coming up to tremble at the counter.

She nodded, then took her time, ambling over to the bored spotty teenager. Thumped her packet of paracetamol down on the till's stainless-steel weighing plate.

There was a pause. Some chewing. Then words slumped out on a wave of stomach-clenching spearmint, twisted into a strangled Kingsmeath accent: 'You want a Chocolate Orange? It's on offer, like. Buy one, get one half price, and that.'

'No.'

The till bleeped as the pills were scanned.

And then a smile bloomed across the girl's face, rearranging the pattern of blackheads and zits. 'Here, you're that woman, aren't you?'

Lucy dug the debit card out of her wallet. 'No.'

'Aye, you are: you're that detective sergeant woman. We learnt all aboot you, in Media Studies! You and that bloke, whatshisname, Nigel something-or-other. Black. Neil Black! That's the boy.'

The card reader chimed out the purchase and Lucy snatched up her pills. 'No, I'm not!' She marched off, heels hammering the tiles out onto Jessop Street, into the crisp morning air. Even if it was laden with the pale-blue scent of exhaust fumes as cars and vans rumbled by.

The Dunk raised an eyebrow as she tore her way into the paracetamol. He was barely taller than the post box he leaned against, with a plump little face besmirched by a thin goatee-soul-patch-and-moustache thing that didn't make him look anywhere near as much like Tony Stark as he clearly thought it did. He'd squeezed himself into his trademark black polo neck, with black jeans, black sunglasses, and a dark-grey leather jacket. A languid cigarette drooping from the corner of his mouth.

Let's face it, the boy was one French beret and a pair of bongos away from going full-on beatnik. But on the plus side, he'd done what he'd been told and got the coffees in.

The Dunk held out one of the two large wax-paper cups. 'Caramel latte macchiato with chocolate sprinkles.'

'Breakfast of champions.' She knocked back a couple of pills, washing them down with a sip of hot sweet coffee goodness.

He pursed his chubby lips. 'Have you *still* got that headache?'

'We're going to be late.' She strode off down the street – the Dunk struggling to keep up on his short little legs.

He broke into a semi-jog, drawing level with her shoulder. 'Only I'm pretty sure that if a hangover lasts more than two months, you should see a doctor.' He shook his head. Thinning a bit at the back there. Not very Tony-Stark-like at all. 'At the very least, cut back on the booze.'

'Very funny. You're like a modern-day Bernard Manning. And for your information, this' – tapping her forehead – 'is probably stress-induced. Caused by having to work with weirdos like *you* all day.'

A busker had set up on the corner, by the lights, dressed in a Hawaiian shirt, shorts, and flip-flops – a brave fashion choice for Scotland in September – warbling his way through a bland reggae cover of something vaguely recognizable:

> *'Your love's got me shivering, like a disease,*
> *I splutter and sweat, I go weak at the knees,*

Your love, it's infectious, and I'm just defenceless,
I'm burnin' up, baby, don't need no vaccines . . .'

Not exactly in the best of taste.

They bustled across St Jasper's Lane, nipping between a bendy bus and a grubby-brown Renault van, emerging opposite the King James Theatre with its elaborate yellow-brick-and-pink-granite façade, featuring lurid billboards for upcoming performances – 'CHRISTMAS PANTO: SKELETON BOB AND THE GOBLINS WHO STOLE SANTA, TICKETS ON SALE NOW!', 'CASTLE HILL OPERA SOCIETY PRESENTS: THE SILENCE OF THE LAMBS', and 'SIGN UP FOR SUPERSPANKYBINGOSWANKY-WEDNESDAYS! ~ BIG PRIZES *EVERY* WEEK!!!' Because, apparently, being classy was overrated and . . .

Lucy stopped outside a small newsagent with one of those fake sandwich-board things screwed to the wall by the door. 'CASTLE NEWS & POST: FAMILIES' FEARS AS HUNT FOR BLOODSMITH FALLS FLAT'.

'Sarge?'

A flush of heat spread across the base of her neck, creeping upwards as it turned into that horrible, familiar prickling feeling – as if someone was watching her. Snatching the breath in her throat, setting her heart rattling. But when she spun around, fists clenched, it was just the usual assortment of shoppers and tradespeople, going about their business. Both legal and otherwise.

Wait a minute, there *was* someone watching her from the other side of the road: a tall, thin man, with a big forehead surrounded by curly brown hair. Beard and moustache. Corduroy jacket, like a supply teacher. Small round glasses that hid his eyes, but not the bags underneath them. And he was just standing there, staring.

Like a weirdo.

A large white van drifted by, blocking him from view, 'HAVE YOU TRIED SCOTIABRAND CHICKEN MACSPORRANS YET? THEY'RE CLUCKING TASTY!' in a lurid typeface down the side, with a happy mother feeding her little boy something revolting and flattened-Dalek shaped. And when the van had passed, there was no sign of the man.

'Sarge?' The Dunk poked her arm. 'You OK, Sarge? Only you look like someone's just shat on your grave.'

'Never mind.' Probably just a pervert anyway. Wasn't as if the city didn't have more than its fair share. And as long as he stuck to staring, that was fine. Creepy, but Christ knew it was better than the alternative. Lucy strode off again, going a bit faster this time so the Dunk had to abandon his semi-jog for a full-blown scurrying run instead.

The wee sod puffed and panted at her side, cigarette bouncing along – spilling ash down his jacket's lapels. 'Seriously, though: who's Bernard Manning?'

'God's sake, I'm only three years older than you, I'm not your granny. Because, let's face it, if *I* was related to you, you wouldn't be so repugnantly ugly.'

'All right, all right. Thank you, Sergeant Sarcastic.' The Dunk dodged a couple of schoolkids who probably should've been in class at quarter past ten on a Wednesday morning, instead of hanging about outside a shuttered off-licence smoking fags. 'So, what do you think the big briefing's going to be about?'

'Probably giving us all medals and a bonus for doing *such* a bang-up job of catching the Bloodsmith.'

'Oh . . .' He drooped a bit at that. 'Well . . . maybe there's been a breakthrough, or something, you know?'

'You're probably right. After all, it's early days, isn't it? Only been after the bastard for *seventeen* months.' She took a left onto Peel Place. 'What's a year and a half between friends?'

Halfway down, O Division Headquarters loomed in all its brutalist glory. The big, red-brick Victorian monstrosity jutted out from the picturesque ivory-sandstone buildings that lined the street, as if the genteel terrace had suffered a prolapse.

'Yeah, but it's not like we haven't been trying, is it?'

'Seventeen months, Dunk. And we're no nearer than we were on day one.'

Lucy slipped out of the briefing room, closing the door behind her, shutting off the bored chatter of two dozen plainclothes and uniformed officers.

DI Tudor paced back and forth along the corridor, face creased and taut at the same time, one arm hugging a stack of paperwork like a teddy bear, leaving the other hand free so he could chew at his fingernails. Tall and broad-shouldered, with a jet-black *Peaky Blinders* short back and sides that somehow didn't look ridiculous above serious eyes and salt-and-pepper designer stubble. In another life, he could probably have been a catalogue model – a rugged middle-aged man on a cold-looking beach somewhere, with his fake ash-blonde wife, both wearing matching chinos and rugby shirts: 'BUY TWO, SAVE £10!'

'You OK, Boss?'

He kept on pacing. 'Everyone ready?'

'Is something wrong?'

His mouth pulled out and down. 'They've put me in charge of the investigation. *Sole* charge.'

'Oh . . .' Lucy frowned. Bit her top lip. Nodded. 'That's not good.'

'Well, thanks for the vote of confidence, DS McVeigh!'

'You know that's not what I mean, Boss.'

'Apparently DCI Ross has more *active* investigations requiring his supervision, but, and I quote, "The High Heidyins have complete faith in my ability to bring Operation Maypole to a swift and satisfactory conclusion."' Tudor stopped pacing and covered his face with his chewed hand. 'I am so screwed.'

Hard not to feel sorry for the poor sod. 'So, first Superintendent Spence bails and lumbers DCI Ross with it, now DCI Ross hands you the stinky baby and does a runner.'

'Bad enough as it is, without you rubbing it in.' Tudor slumped back against the wall. 'Think it's too late to go off on the sick?'

Lucy shrugged. 'Maybe we'll get lucky and solve this thing?'

His face soured. 'Fat bloody chance.' Then Tudor gave himself a shake. Smiled the kind of smile that was meant to convey sincerity and sympathy. 'Listen to me, moaning on. I should've asked how *you're* doing.'

She froze for a couple of breaths, then mirrored his fake smile. 'Never better.'

'Only, if you need to talk or anything . . . ? My, you know, my door's always open, right?'

God, could this *get* any more awkward?

'I'm fine. Thanks for asking. Keen to get on with things: catch this bastard.'

'Yeah.' Tudor sniffed, then gave himself another shake, like an old spaniel coming in from the rain. 'Show no fear.' He pulled himself up to his full six-three and nodded at her. 'Come on, then.'

Lucy opened the door and he strode through, into the office, as if the world lay at his feet.

Amazing what a bit of self-delusion could do.

She followed him in.

Operation Maypole filled the big incident room on the third floor. Four mean, narrow windows punctured the far wall – separated by corkboards thumbtacked with memos and mugshots and crime-scene photos – glaring across the potholed car park behind O Division Headquarters to the boarded-up carpet warehouse that backed onto it. Vague hints of Camburn Woods just visible over the rooftops in the distance. Digital whiteboards lined the whole side wall, covered in notes and lines and boxes and process-flow diagrams. A small kitchen area was recessed into the grey rank of filing cabinets opposite the whiteboards, leaving the last wall to pinned-up actions and the kind of posters Police Scotland mistakenly believed were motivational, rather than deeply depressing.

The rest of the room was packed with cubicles, desks, office chairs, and DI Tudor's team – all two dozen of them. There were even signs hanging from the ceiling, marking out each specialist unit: 'HOLMES', 'FAMILY LIAISON', 'SEARCH', 'DOOR TO DOOR', 'INTERVIEW', 'PRODUCTIONS', and 'COMMAND'. Which had seemed like a good idea at the time, even if it bore no real relationship to the way things actually worked.

'All right, people!' Tudor thumped his stack of paperwork down on the table at the front of the room and the babble of voices stuttered to a halt. 'Thank you. I'm sure you've all seen the papers this morning.' He picked up a copy of the *Glasgow Tribune* in one hand and a *Daily Standard* in the other, holding them up so everyone could see the front pages. 'OLDCASTLE POLICE "INEPT AND FLAILING" SAY GRIEVING FAMILIES' and that old favourite: 'JOCK COPS CAN'T CATCH CREEPY KILLER'.

Someone at the back of the room booed.

'My feelings exactly.' The papers got dumped on the floor. 'As of today, I've been placed in sole command of Operation Maypole.'

A few of the older officers made eye contact with Lucy and winced at that, but they kept their mouths shut.

'I know it feels like we haven't made a lot of progress in the last seventeen months, but that changes *now*. Angus?'

One of the officers who'd shared a wince held up a biro in his podgy, hairy hand. He'd probably been clean-shaven at the start of the shift, but now his jowls were coloured a heavy blue-grey, tufts of black sprouting out of his shirt collar. Just a shame he couldn't grow any of it on his big shiny boiled-egg head. 'Guv.'

'Your team goes over the interview transcripts and witness statements. I want everything reviewed.'

A small grimace of pain, but Angus kept it out of his voice. 'Will do.'

'Emma? Your team does the same with our twenty-six ex-suspects. Have another crack at their alibis: see if we can't move a few of them back into the "might-be-our-killer" column.'

A middle-aged woman with an explosion of rusty curls and a hard teuchter accent nodded. 'Guv.' But you could tell she'd just died a little inside.

Then, section by section, Tudor handed out all the back-to-square-one assignments – trying to make it sound as if this was a real chance for progress, rather than a *massive* setback – and sent the teams on their way, until there was no one left but him, Lucy, and the Dunk.

She nodded at the whiteboard, with its list of ticked-off tasks. 'What about us, Boss?'

'I need you and DC Fraser to go over all the crime scenes again. Fresh pair of eyes. Start at the beginning and work your way through.' His smile slipped a bit. 'There has to be *something* we missed. Something that'll—'

A knock on the doorframe and a chubby PC stuck her head into the room. 'Sorry, Guv, but there's a visitor downstairs for DS McVeigh? Won't talk to anyone else. Says it's urgent.'

Tudor licked his lips. 'Is it about the Bloodsmith?'

A shrug. 'Like I say: he won't talk to anyone else.'

'I see . . .' Tudor's smile kicked back in again. 'Maybe our luck's about to turn after all?'

Or maybe it was about to get a whole lot worse?

2

Lucy followed the PC into the stairwell, making for the ground floor. 'This visitor: does he have a name?'

'Lucas Weir.'

Never heard of him.

They clattered around the landing and onto the next flight. 'And he didn't say what it was about?'

'Nope. Just that it was urgent. Oh, and someone's kicked the living . . .' She cleared her throat and they descended again. 'Sorry, Sarge. I mean: someone's assaulted him.' A smile stretched her cheeks, putting dimples in them. 'He didn't say that, though, I deduced it from all the bruises and things.'

Hark at Sherlock Sodding Holmes.

She held open the door at the bottom of the stairs, following Lucy into a corridor lined with yet more 'motivational' posters and the odd Health and Safety one too. Like the cheery black-and-red 'UNIVERSAL BLOOD & BODY FLUIDS PRECAUTIONS'. How could anyone fail to be buoyed up by that?

The PC pointed a chunky finger. 'Your man's in the Visitors' Room. Want me to come in with you, in case he kicks off or something?'

Yeah, because she'd be a whole *heap* of help.

'Thanks, but I got this.' Lucy marched down to the last room on the left, the one that lurked just inside the no-unauthorized-personnel-allowed part of Divisional Headquarters.

Lucy straightened the sleeves of her stripy top, knocked twice on the door, and let herself in without waiting for a reply.

She stopped, dead. Blinking. The smell was – bloody hell – it was like being attacked with a deadly weapon. The first thing that hit was the sharp piddly stench of clothes that hadn't dried properly, followed by the swift one-two of unwashed hair and rancid sweat. But the knockout blow was the eye-nipping reek of sour alcohol, wafting out on an upper-cut of halitosis.

The man responsible for the onslaught fidgeted on the other side of the scarred Formica table, his plastic seat creaking and groaning as he rocked back and forth. Scrawny was the first word that came to mind. Scrawny and stinky. Scrawny, stinky, and battered. In a grubby brown hoodie, left arm trapped from elbow to fingertips in a bright-white plaster cast. One side of his mouth was swollen like a bee sting; the eye above it wasn't any better, the skin a deep mix of blues and purple. The other eye bloodshot, the pupil dark and big and shiny. Nose hooked and dis-coloured, its bridge covered in surgical strips. More bruising on his knife-sharp cheekbones and pointed chin. His right hand fiddled with the toggles on his hoodie. Well, two fingers and a thumb did – his pinkie and the one next to it were taped together, as if he was practising his Vulcan salute.

But even under all that, he was instantly recognizable.

Lucy pulled out the seat opposite and sank into it, keeping her face still as granite. 'You told the officer you were "Lucas Weir". Want to tell me why?'

A sniff. 'It's my name now.' He'd managed to hold onto the posh Castleview accent, but the words came out soft and slurred and mushy, a gap showing where two of his front bottom teeth should've been. 'The court gave me it so *They* wouldn't . . . wouldn't find out where I lived.'

Clearly stoned. Either high on his own supply, or the hospital had given him some industrial-strength painkillers when they patched him up. Shame they hadn't given him a bath too.

Lucy settled back in her chair. 'So, how have you been?'

He dug into his hoodie's marsupial pouch, pulled out a crumpled-up sheet of newsprint, and dumped it on the tabletop. Holding one corner down with his cast so he could smooth the newspaper out with his thumb and two unbroken fingers. Tongue poking out of his mouth as they fum-bled their way through the task. Not easy when you're left-handed, and all you've got to work with are three digits on the wrong side.

It was the front page of yesterday's *Daily Standard*, the headline, 'KILLER KID SICKO LIVES NEAR PLAYGROUND', with a big 'EXCLUSIVE!' roundel, above a photo of the man sitting opposite. They'd clearly taken it from a distance, the image pixelated and grainy, catching him as he emerged from a corner shop. Smiling and unaware. Not knowing he'd been caught.

'Oh.' That wasn't good.

There was a smaller picture, inset into the larger one. This was the photo they'd used in all the news reports at the time, and the BBC documentary, and the appeal for more information, and then once a year on the anniversary of the murder. The photo of a smiling young boy with his whole life ahead of him. Glasses, strawberry-blond hair, freckles on his nose and cheeks. All dressed up for his primary-seven photo, in a white shirt and blue-and-red-striped Marshal School tie. The caption underneath it read, 'BENEDICT STRACHAN (11), TWO MONTHS BEFORE THE MURDER.'

A tear plopped onto the paper, turning it a darker shade of grey as it seeped into the text. 'You see?'

'I'm so sorry, Benedict.' Lucy reached across the table and placed her hand on his unbroken arm. 'You didn't deserve this.'

He nodded and another teardrop landed in the middle of the photo.

'Do you know how they found you?'

He shook his head, pulling his hand free to wipe the tears away. Voice ragged and jaggy as the crying started for real. 'I only . . . I only got out three weeks . . . weeks ago!'

Sodding hell.

Lucy turned the paper around and frowned at the introduction.

The *Daily Standard* **can exclusively reveal** that notorious killer Benedict Strachan (27) has been released from prison and now lives opposite a playground frequented by children as young as three years old. Residents in the leafy Shortstaine area of Oldcastle were horrified to learn that their new neighbour is a notorious murderer. 'I cannot believe they let someone like that out of prison,' said mum of three Angel Gardiner (25), adding, 'Life should mean life!' Karen Johnson (54) goes to the playground three times a week with her grandchildren. 'They should

bring back hanging,' she said. 'If you kill someone you should
not get to live. An eye for an eye, like it says in the Bible.'

Sicko Benedict shot to infamy sixteen years ago when he and
an unnamed accomplice brutally murdered homeless man Liam
Hay (31), who was sleeping rough in—

'They . . . they printed my *address*!' Benedict wiped his eyes again. 'I
can't . . . I can't go back there. What if They find me?'

'"They", who, Benedict?' She folded the paper and placed it off to the
side. 'The people who did this to you?' Pointing at his cast and his
bruises. 'Didn't they already—'

'No: *Them*!' The rocking back and forth got more pronounced, wring-
ing a tortured *wheeeeek-whonnnnng-wheeeeek-whonnnnng* out of the
plastic chair. 'Them. The Them that live in the shadows, controlling
everything!'

Ah.

There was stoned, and there was *stoned*.

Lucy softened her voice about as far as it could go, as if she was talking
to a small child with its foot stuck in a bucket of broken glass. 'Benedict,
I need you to tell me what you've taken, OK? Do you know how much
you've had?'

He sat forward, face creasing into a teeth-baring rictus. Probably got
a few cracked ribs under that grubby hoodie. 'They're everywhere and
They're always watching. They can see everything you do, everywhere
you go.'

'Did the doctors give you something for the pain? Did you take something else along with it? Something of your own?'

'No one suspects Them, but They're always there. *Always*.'

'I think you need to get some help, Benedict.' Reaching for his arm
again.

'WHY DO YOU THINK I'M HERE?' That one bloodshot eye wide and
watery and staring. Face flushed where it wasn't bruised. Little pink
flecks of spittle landing on the tabletop between them. Then he shrank
back. 'I'm sorry. I'm sorry. They . . . Don't let Them . . .'

She tried for a reassuring smile. 'Sometimes medication can make
people a bit paranoid, especially if they've mixed it with alcohol and
maybe cocaine? Heroin? Temazepam?'

'I'm not on jellies, OK? I'm . . . trying to warn you. They don't want me telling anyone what I know.' He was starting to talk a bit faster now, the words slipping and slurring. 'But They know you spoke to me in prison. I bet They read your thesis. I bet They know *all* about you.'

Maybe it was time to have a word with Benedict's Criminal Justice social worker? Get him enrolled on a rehab programme. Assuming there were any still open after the latest round of budget cuts.

'Have you talked to anyone about these feelings of—'

'LISTEN TO ME!' And the tears were back. 'Why does no one ever listen to me?'

'OK, OK.' She held up her hands. 'Why are "They" so interested in you? Help me understand.'

'*Because.*' Lowering his voice to a slurred whisper. 'Because of what happened when I was a kid. Because of what I *did*.' A grubby fingertip – poking out the end of his cast – came down to rest on the folded newsprint. 'They know everything.'

Or maybe he'd just become institutionalized? After all, Benedict had spent more than half his life behind bars – he wouldn't be the first person to emerge from prison unable to cope with the outside world. Maybe his subconscious decided he'd be better off getting locked up for paranoid delusions instead?

And while it wasn't exactly ethical to take advantage of him while he was in this state, there was one question still unanswered from that bloodsoaked night sixteen years ago.

Lucy didn't move. 'So they know who you were with, that night? The other boy on the CCTV footage?'

'Of course They know! How could They not know? Are you *insane*?' Benedict jerked around in his seat, setting the rubber feet scraiking across the grey terrazzo floor. As if checking for someone lurking over his shoulder. 'They know everything.'

'I could help you better if you told me who your friend was, Benedict.' Trying not to hold her breath as the silence stretched.

His mouth hung open like a battered gargoyle, showing off those missing teeth and the bloody gums they'd been kicked from.

Come on, come on.

Just give up the other boy's name.

You can do it, Benedict.

Please . . .

Then Benedict's one good eye narrowed. His mouth clicked shut. And he stood. Trying to scoop up the bit he'd torn out of the newspaper with the fingertips on his broken arm. And failing. He shoved his plaster-cast into the hoodie's pocket instead. 'I gotta go. I . . . Yeah.'

'It's just a name, Benedict, what could it hurt after all these years?'

'I've – got – to – go!'

Sod.

Lucy suppressed a sigh. Nodded. 'Can you at least tell me who beat you up, so we can arrest them?'

'Yeah. No. No one. I . . . I fell down the stairs.'

'Benedict, you don't have to—'

'I FELL DOWN THE STAIRS!' Then his shoulders curled forwards, head lowered, not looking at her any more. 'Can I go now? I *need* to go.' Sounding more like a scared eleven-year-old boy than a man of twenty-seven.

He fiddled with his hoodie's toggles again.

Fidgeted.

Chewed on his bottom lip.

Left leg picking up a tremor, till his heel beat a rattling staccato on the floor.

She'd lost him.

Lucy pushed her chair back. 'OK, Benedict. I'll see you out.'

And she'd been so close . . .

The moment Benedict was out through the main doors, he was off. Sort of halfway between a limp and a lopsided jog. Putting as much distance between himself and DHQ as possible.

Lucy stood there, one hand shielding her eyes from the sun, watching till he hurpled around the corner onto Camburn Road and out of sight.

Given the state he was in, probably wouldn't be long before he was either back in custody or Castle Hill Infirmary. Just had to hope it wouldn't be because of an overdose . . . Mind you, at least with his left hand in a cast, he wouldn't be shooting up any time soon. Not unless he'd turned ambidextrous in prison.

When she turned to go back inside, there was the Dunk, lounging against a low concrete wall, head buried in today's *Castle News & Post*, cigarette smouldering away between two yellowed fingers. He didn't look up from whatever article he was reading. 'Says here that Paul Rhynie's been handing out government contracts to firms owned by his mates. No tender process, no penalty clauses, no questions asked. He's the Business Secretary, for God's sake, how's that even legal?'

'Get a car sorted. I need to make a call.'

'Millions and millions of taxpayers' cash, spaffed into his buddies' pockets.' One last puff, then he pinged his dogend away. 'Makes you think we're after the wrong class of criminal, doesn't it?'

'Car, Dunk, as in "go get one."' She headed back through into reception.

The Dunk scurried in ahead of her, casting a leering look over his shoulder in the direction Benedict Strachan had gone. 'Your new boy-friend seems . . . nice. Not too keen on his aftershave, though: eau de wheelie bin?'

'And while you're at it: I need a copy of all the Bloodsmith crime-scene reports and victim profiles.'

'I mean, I know dating at your age can be tough, but you can probably afford to raise your standards a bit.'

'Car and reports. Now. ASAP.' She marched across to the security door, fast enough to make the cheeky little sod trot.

'Don't get me wrong, I know you ladies like to slum it every now and then, but Junky Jake there wasn't exactly—'

'You know' – she stopped, one hand on the keypad – 'I can always get another sidekick, Dunk.'

'No need to get all sniffy about it, Sarge.' A wee leer slithered its way onto his face. 'Especially given how bad your boyfriend smells.'

'Seriously: Mags is probably free, or PC Gilbert. Even Urpeth would do, at a push.' Lucy punched in the code and hauled the door open. 'I hear DS Smith's got space on his team: you could go work for him.'

The Dunk blanched. 'Come on, Sarge, joke's a joke!' Shuddering as the door swung closed behind him. 'That's a horrible thing to wish on anyone.' He jogged along beside her, down the corridor and into the stairwell. 'So, you going to tell me who Stinky the Loverboy is, or are you keeping it a secret till the church's booked?' Launching into the 'Wed-ding March': 'Dum, dum-tee-dum, dum dummm-tee-dooooo . . .'

Lucy paused on the first landing. 'And while you're at it, dig up every-thing we've got on Benedict Strachan.'

'Benedict Strachan?' The Dunk pulled his chin in, eyebrows pinched. 'Why do you want . . .' Then his whole face opened out. 'You're *kidding*! That was Benedict Strachan? *The* Benedict Strachan? Wow!' Staring back down the stairs, as if he could see through the walls of DHQ to watch her visitor hurple off into the distance. 'Benedict Strachan. Bloody hell!'

'Don't just stand there. Off. Go. Work.'

A low whistle. 'I always thought he'd be taller in real life.'

Useless.

Lucy headed up the stairs again. 'You're not working, Dunk.'

'So how come *the* Benedict Strachan is coming to see you, and only you, and it's urgent, and he won't speak to anyone else?'

Good question.

She frowned her way to the next floor. 'I did my MSc dissertation on "Children Who Kill" – dash – "The Role of Dissociative Personality Disorders in Non-Nurture-Related Psychopathy Resulting in Under-Aged Homicidal Acts".'

'Catchy title. Think I saw the film.'

'I interviewed Benedict a few times, when I was writing it. He was . . . troubled.' Bit of an understatement. 'Can you imagine growing up in prison? Eleven years old, behind bars, moving through the system till you're old enough to be locked away with all the other murderers.'

'Ah, *I* get it.' A nod from the Dunk. 'So, because you showed him a teensy bit of kindness, when he's known sod all but brutality and fear, he's glommed onto you. You're his good Samaritan. His bestest buddy. His confidante. His bosom friend. His—'

'Just get your backside off to Records. Then find us a car.'

The Dunk pulled a face. 'Sarge.' He turned around and trudged back down the stairs again.

She leaned on the railing, raising her voice so it boomed out after him. 'And make sure it's a *good* car this time – not some mobile skip half full of crap and takeaway wrappers. Something that's been cleaned in the last three years!'

Right.

Now she had that call to make.

3

'See, what I don't understand' – the Dunk steered their almost-clean pool car around the Logansferry Roundabout and onto Robinson Drive – 'is, if you did your dissertation on Benedict Strachan, how come you've never read his file?'

Outside, the industrial buildings on the left gave way to row after row of bungalows, with yet another business park rising up behind them. They'd probably looked quite cheerful in their day, but seventy-odd years had left their mark on the lichened pantiles and dirt-streaked walls.

'Hmmm?' Lucy flipped over to the next page: a statement from the bread-delivery man who'd discovered Liam Hay's body, halfway down an alleyway off Brokemere Street, lying face down, partially covered in cardboard, outside the side door to a manky wee shop called 'ANGUS MACBARGAIN'S FAMILY STORE'.

'And aren't we supposed to be making breakthroughs in the Blood-smith case?' Right turn, onto Morrissey Street, the bungalows giving way to tightly packed two-up-two-downs instead. A sigh. 'Not that we're exactly breakthrough-adjacent.'

'Did my dissertation before I joined the force, Dunk – they wouldn't let me anywhere near the official files. Had to make do with what was in the public domain. Well, that and whatever I could get out of Benedict.'

The next page was a photo of Liam Hay, lying flat on his back in the alleyway, after the paramedics had confirmed death. Not that it would've been a tough call to make.

The crime-scene photographer had captured the body in all its gory glory. Liam's stained corduroy jacket was punctured in at least two dozen places, its faux-sheepskin lining turned a dark shade of scarlet. His fleecy top, black shirt, and brown T-shirt were pulled up to expose the pale-blue skin of his belly, smeared with more red. The gash across his throat deep enough to let little glimpses of bone shine through the hacked mess. A sunken-cheeked face, fringed with a smear of greying stubble. Eyes open, staring out over the photographer's shoulder. Baseball cap half falling off.

Poor sod.

Lucy hissed out a long gravelly breath.

'Frenzied attack' barely began to cover what Benedict Strachan and his unnamed accomplice had done to Liam Hay. The next photo was even worse – a close-up of the stab wounds. Eighty-nine of them in total, most of them so deep that the knife's hilt had left its outline indented on the skin.

She turned the photo over, hiding the brutality. 'Not that anyone should take what Benedict says as gospel.'

The Dunk grunted. Stopped at the junction with North Moncuir Road, waiting for a couple of hatchbacks to growl past on oversized exhausts. 'To be honest, it's kinda surprising no one chibbed him in prison. Normally, you end someone famous like that? You get yourself a whole heap of respect from your fellow inmates and lauded in the right-wing press. If you're in for life anyway it's win-win.'

She got to the last page and frowned. 'Where's the rest of it? Witness statements, interview transcripts, productions, door-to-doors?'

'Dunno, Sarge. That was all Manson had. You know what Records are like, it'd take four years and a search party to find *anything* in there.' They pulled out onto the road, Moncuir Wood looming large on the other side. Reaching off into the distance as they followed the wee boys in their not-so-hot hatchbacks.

Lucy shut the Benedict Strachan file and slipped it into the rear foot-well. 'You would've been quicker taking the turning by Fife Street.'

'Don't like crossing a dual carriageway, you know that.'

'Such a baby.' She pulled out the other file the Dunk had signed for. 'Operation Maypole – Victimology Reports'.

He glanced at the manila folder in her lap. 'You know what I think? I think we've had seventeen months of getting nowhere, because they lumbered us with "Operation Maypole".'

'Uh-huh.' Lucy dipped into the file and came out with the Blood-smith's first victim.

'Everyone knows you don't reuse operation names, it's bad luck.'

'Uh-huh.'

Abby Geddes, twenty-four. Graduated with a BSc in Molecular Biology, ended up working in that big call centre in Logansferry Industrial Estate, opposite Homebase and Lidl. Way to go, post-Covid economy.

'Honestly, a quick google would've shown HMRC used it already. By the time we got the name, they'd sooked out all its mojo. Phuttttt: this operation name is mojo-less.'

'I said, "*Uh-huh*." That's code for, "You can stop talking now." '

Abby was still living at home with her mother and stepfather, because the call centre didn't pay enough for a flat of her own. No boyfriend or girlfriend that anyone could think of. No best friend or group of mates to hang out with. And no one at work had much to say about her, other than that she kept herself to herself. Liked reading romance novels and watching *Strictly*. So not exactly the life and soul of the party.

'That's why you should never reuse operation names. "Maypole" got wrung dry on a fifty-four-million-quid VAT fraud – and that was in 2007, back when fifty-four million quid was a lot of—'

'Dunk!' Lucy glowered up from Abby's file. 'Don't make me break out your rank and surname.'

'We're jinxed, that's all I'm saying. It's—'

'Detective Constable Duncan Fraser: hud yer wheisht!'

He made a dying-frog face. 'All right, all right.' Then pulled into a small lay-by at the side of the road, opposite Moncuir Park. 'We're here.'

Should think so too.

Lucy slipped the paperwork back in its folder and stuck the thing under her arm. 'Better grab a torch from the boot.'

'Ah . . .'

'You *did* remember to bring torches, didn't you?'

'Erm . . .' A sickly smile slithered its way onto that frog face. 'Define "remember".'

'Oh yes, I'm *so* glad I took you with me.' She climbed out of the pool car and into the sunshine. Turned her back on the park, with its duck pond and its trees and bushes and playground, marched across the road, and waded into the long, damp, yellowing, September grass. Seed heads sticking to her jeans, standing out against the darkening denim as last night's rain seeped through the material.

Making for the woods.

The Dunk huffed and puffed to catch up, struggling to light a cigarette as he jogged after her. The grass might've been thigh high on Lucy, but it was way up over his waist. He took his first puff, then held his elbows out at shoulder-height, hands curled inwards in front of his chest, as if he was doing a crap velociraptor impersonation, voice mumbled around his fag. 'Well, how was I supposed to know we'd need a torch?'

'You're right, I'm sorry, Dunk, I'm being unfair.'

He smiled at that. 'It's OK, Sarge, we—'

'After all, it's not as if Abby Geddes's remains were found in an abandoned building, buried way, way deep in the woods, is it? How could you *possibly* have guessed we'd need some way of actually seeing things when we get there? I mean, what are you, psychic?'

The chunk of waste ground ended in a riot of jagged brambles and bracken – glistening and dark green. Lucy stopped just in front of it.

Peching and heeching like a broken bellows, his black outfit clarted in grass seed and bits of leaves, the Dunk drooped to a halt at her side. 'Sorry about the torch, Sarge.'

She patted him on the back. 'Don't worry, you can make it up to me by forging a path through that lot.' Pointing at the soggy bracken.

'Oh' – he drooped even more – 'arse . . .' Then groaned and stomped into the undergrowth.

Gnarled grey tree trunks as far as the eye could see. Which probably wasn't all that far, given how closely packed everything seemed to be, here in the depths of Moncuir Wood.

The sun was a distant memory, shut off by a serrated canopy of pine and greasy oak, leaving everything shrouded in a gloom that cut visibility to twenty, maybe thirty feet? That dark-brown scent of mouldering vegetation *tainting* everything as the leaf litter broke down. Cold, too. It might've been a brisk September day, out there in the real world, but in here every breath turned into thin wisps of white as Lucy and the Dunk lumbered their way through the never-ending ranks of trees.

'Urgh . . .' His face had a shiny pink quality to it that suggested an imminent heart attack or aneurism. 'God, how . . . how much . . .

further?' He slumped against an old Scots pine and dug the cigarettes out of his leather jacket again. Sparking up. Sagging as a cloud of smoke headed for the canopy of leaves. 'You know this is a complete waste of time, right?'

Probably been going round and round in circles for the last half-hour. Be lucky if they weren't discovered in six months' time, wearing nothing but squirrel fur and mud. Assuming, of course, she hadn't eaten the Dunk by then. Not that he looked particularly appetizing, with his sweaty-beetroot face sooking on a fag as if it was the only thing keeping him upright.

'Would it kill you to at least *pretend* to give a toss?'

'Oh come on, Sarge, you know and I know this whole thing's a disaster. We're back to square one, because we haven't got a clue how to catch the Bloodsmith.' He howched up a gobbet of something brown and spat it out. 'Seventeen months, chasing our tails, going over the same ground, getting nowhere' – waving his cigarette at the woods – 'I'm *bored* with it. Aren't you bored?'

'He's killed five people, Dunk.'

'I know, but . . . Pffff.' A wee shifty squirm as he looked the other way, not meeting her eyes. 'Been thinking: maybe we should jump ship before this whole thing collapses? Cos that's why they dumped the whole thing on DI Tudor, isn't it? The High Heidyins want a scapegoat for when they declare Operation Maypole a useless farce, and it'll be on *our* permanent records too. Failure, failure, failure.'

'Don't be a dick.'

'We could be making a difference somewhere else, that's all I'm saying.' He hollowed his chubby cheeks, then hissed out a billow of work-shy smoke. 'Let someone else carry the can.'

She scowled at him. 'We're supposed to be—'

A *snapppp* rang out from somewhere behind her and Lucy whirled around, eyes raking the gloom.

No sign of life.

She dropped her voice to a whisper. 'Did you hear that?'

'Hear what?'

'Shhhh!' Lucy stood perfectly still, head cocked to one side, listening.

But the only sound was the Dunk's wheezy breathing.

Maybe it was just a dead branch, breaking under its own weight? Must happen all the time in a forest this size, right? Didn't have to be anything sinister. Nothing to worry about.

Yeah . . .

Then why did she have that weird feeling she was being watched again? Like spiders crawling up the skin of her back.

Lucy did a slow three-sixty, squinting out into the shrouded woods. No sign of anyone.

Been wandering about in here too long, that was the problem. Starting to see and hear things. Next stop: squirrel fur, mud, and Dunk tartare.

She pulled out her phone and checked the map again. The cottage they were after wasn't considered important enough to feature, and the satellite image showed nothing but a lumpy green sea of treetops. 'Why the hell didn't the search team put some sort of GPS marker on the place, so we could actually *find* it?'

'Cos they're idiots?' A rapid series of rasping coughs barked out of his gob, followed by another gobbet of brown and a grimace.

Well, there was no point just standing here, was there?

'Maybe this way?' She headed off, deeper into the forest with the Dunk wheezing along behind her.

The house, when they finally found it, buried away in the woods, couldn't have looked less like a gingerbread cottage if it tried. Its roof sagged, one gable wall exposed where the harling had crumbled away, the mortar missing between the rough lumps of sandstone it'd been built out of. Two small windows, devoid of glass, one either side of the gaping doorway, turned the building into a howling skull. A chimney breast should've poked up from each gable end, but the one on the left had collapsed at some point, leaving a ragged stump that played home to a trio of jackdaws – lurking shadows in the gloom. They stared down with glittering gimlet eyes as Lucy and the Dunk staggered into the dank little clearing out front.

There must've been a garden at some point, but all that remained was a bunch of straggly bushes and overgrown weeds, delineated by nothing more than the vague memory of a tumbledown wall partially consumed by ferns and moss.

'Oh, thank . . . thank God.' The Dunk grabbed his knees, bent over like a broken paperclip as his back heaved. Hauling in the breaths. 'Thought we'd . . . never . . . never get . . . here.'

According to the file, it had been a gamekeeper's cottage, back when most of Moncuir Wood was still part of Lord Dundas's hunting estate. A rough place, thrown together to house some bastard whose job it would've been to clype on anyone hungry enough to risk a backside full of buckshot in exchange for a rabbit to feed their starving family.

The Dunk let go of his knees and slumped back against a tree instead, wafting a pudgy hand in front of his flushed and sweaty face. 'One thing . . . one thing's for sure . . . the Bloodsmith knew where . . . this place was.'

'You're a wreck.' Lucy opened the Operation Maypole folder and pulled out the sheets on Abby Geddes again. 'Right: two years ago, fifteenth of October; Abby was seen leaving work at five past six by one Byron Moore. Byron said they were meant to go to the pub, but she begged off.'

'Oh, I remember Byron Moore – greasy as a chip pan. Me and Emma interviewed him, but his alibi was sound.'

Right: first things first. Lucy pulled out her phone, brought up the map, and added a GPS marker for the cottage. At least this way it'd be easy enough to find again. 'How long do you think it'd take to walk here from the call centre? Half an hour?'

'Yeah, if you didn't get lost in these buggering woods.' He pulled out an off-grey hanky and wiped the back of his neck. 'And even if you didn't, why *would* you? Not like it's a tourist destination, is it?'

True. 'Come on then.' Lucy clambered over what was left of the garden wall and picked her way across the uneven ground to the cottage. Its front door had disappeared at some point, leaving nothing but the rusty strap hinges behind, poking out from the darkness beyond.

The Dunk peered over her shoulder. 'Wow. Creepy. We going in?'

'No, Dunk, we came all that way to stand in this lovely garden, enjoying the view.' She killed the map on her phone and called up the torch app instead.

Its hard white circle swept across the doorway, pulling a crappy crumbling floor into view – rectangles of chipboard, with big rat-chewed holes in them. You could tell by the liquorice-coloured jelly-bean droppings that ran along the skirting boards. What little wallpaper remained was faded and peeling, unblemished by graffiti. Because who in their right minds would schlep all the way out here just to do a little light vandalism?

Lucy stepped over the threshold and the floor groaned beneath her feet. It was cold enough outside, but in here her breath came out in a cloud of bright white where it hit the torchlight, fading to a ghost, then gone for good. 'OK, so we can be pretty sure Abby Geddes didn't meet the Bloodsmith here. She'd never be able to find the place.'

Lucy swept her torch beam around a shortish corridor, leading off left and right. A closed door lurked at either end, three more doors on the wall in front of her, paintwork flaking and mouldy. A large hole in the flooring, showing off woodwormed joists like hollow ribs.

She picked her way along the outside where the chipboard butted up against the skirting board – just in case the middle bit gave way – inching closer to the hole. 'Did you get anything on CCTV?'

The Dunk stuck his head into the cottage. 'Can you smell that? Kind of nippy, sour, and widdly.'

'It's the rats. Now: CCTV?'

'God, I *hate* rats.' But he crept into the corridor anyway. 'Call-centre security cameras show her walking away from the front of the building about ten past six. Normally went out back to the car park, but her Ford Ka was busy failing its MOT at the time, so she got the bus that morning.'

Those joists didn't look particularly trustworthy – the pale wood was all crumbly at the edges and pocked with little black holes as if someone had thrown hundreds of darts at it. The first joist moaned like a dying dog when she put her foot down, but didn't collapse, so she tried the next one too. 'Business park?'

'Seems Logansferry Industrial Estate is in dispute with the company that's meant to maintain the security cameras. Haven't been working for two-and-a-bit years. Emma and me went through every company on the estate, but there's no footage of Abby Geddes walking past.'

Interesting. So, either she purposefully took a route that avoided CCTV, or she met someone who did. Or maybe she didn't show up walking on the pathways because someone gave her a lift?

The third joist complained even more when Lucy put her full weight on it, and so did the one after that. Little flakes of dry rot crumbled beneath her feet to fall away into the darkness.

'What about cars? Did you run plates for everything driving in or out of there from, say, half five to seven o'clock?'

One more creaking joist and Lucy was at the far door. She reached for the grimy Bakelite knob, then stopped. 'Dunk?'

'Ah. Don't know. We weren't doing that bit; Emma and me were on interviews.'

So worth chasing up, then.

Lucy pulled on a pair of blue nitrile gloves and turned the grubby handle. The door needed a couple of dunts with her shoulder – not easy while balancing on crumbly floor joists – but, eventually, its bottom edge scraped a squealing arc into the chipboard on the other side.

It was a small living room. Well, *dying* room would probably be more accurate, going by the crime-scene photographs. Environmental Health had been past with a big thing of trichloroethylene, and bleached Jackson Pollock spatters into the walls and floor, getting rid of any residual bodily fluids. Not that there would've been much left, not after all that time. A hollowed-out rectangle marked the middle of the opposite wall, where someone had ripped out the fireplace and mantel. Leaves and twigs made little drifts in the corners, mingling with the rat droppings. More holes in the floor, showing off the joists underneath, but this time wobbly lines scarred the chipboard sheets – where the Scenes Examination Branch had cut through them to get underneath. They'd nailed everything down again, but only just enough to stop some uniformed idiot going through the floor and suing. The room's single window had long ago given up its glass, leaving nothing behind but a rotting wooden frame.

Lucy tested her weight on the first segment of nailed-down chipboard. It shifted a little underfoot but seemed safe enough. Kind of. So she stepped inside and flicked through the file till she got to the pictures. Held the first one out, shuffling her way further into the room until it lined up with the real thing – creating her own little time machine of horror.

4

The photo was less graphic than others in the Bloodsmith collection, but only because Abby Geddes had lain here, undiscovered, until May last year. A seven-month-long all-you-can-eat buffet for the rats. What was left looked more like something from a World War One documentary than a contemporary crime scene. Abby's skull was tipped up on its side against the skirting board, no sign of her bottom jaw, ribs spread out across the chewed chipboard. The femurs were more or less where they should've been, but the pelvis had gone and so had all the fingers and toes.

A shattered jar sat between the radius and ulna of one arm, lid still on, the remnants of something dark sticking to the jagged glass.

Forensics identified it as Abby's blood.

There was more of it on the far wall: 'HELP ME!' spelled out in three-foot-high letters, dried to a thick burnt umber. The message didn't exist any more – erased by liberal application of trichloroethylene, but even though the super-strength bleach had removed all traces from the manky wallpaper, somehow the whole house still echoed with those two words, as if they'd been etched into the soul of the place.

The Dunk squeezed himself into the room. Pursing his lips as he looked around. 'Can you *imagine* dying someplace like this?'

There wasn't any reason to tiptoe, but Lucy did it anyway, picking her way over the patchwork boards to the largest hole in the floor. Peered down into the darkness. 'The rats took everything small enough to carry.' The beam from her phone's torch picked out churned grey earth at the bottom of the hole, peppered with more droppings. 'They only found about half the missing bits.'

'Maybe it wasn't the rats, maybe *he* took them.'

'He didn't take anyone else's fingers. Other things, yes, but not fingers. Besides, all the bones had gnaw marks on them.'

'Urgh . . .' A shudder. 'Did I mention how much I *hate* rats?'

She straightened up and frowned at the bleached wall again. ' "Help me". Do you think it was meant to be Abby talking? Is it her crying out, or is it him? Who are we supposed to save?'

'Tell you, that James Herbert's got a lot to answer for. Books gave me nightmares for—'

'Shhh!' Lucy switched off her faux torch and crept towards the hollow window. Keeping to the side, out of sight. 'Did you hear that?'

The Dunk froze. 'Is it rats? Gah . . . Please don't let it be rats!'

She honed her voice into a hard sharp whisper. 'Will you shut up and listen?'

He did what he was told, holding his breath.

There it was again: a rustling sound, like someone creeping through fallen leaves over rough ground.

The Dunk sidled up next to her. 'I can't hear anything.'

'Clean your lugs out: there's someone out there.'

He flattened himself against the wall on the other side of the window. Peered around the edge. 'Could be a deer, or a badger, or something?'

Lucy narrowed her eyes and stared out into the gloom. Letting her eyes drift out of focus so the trees, bracken, and brambles all merged into a green-brown mush. Not looking for shapes, just motion . . .

A flicker of tan-coloured fabric, and the rustling stopped.

Got you.

She slipped out of the dying room and picked her way across those crumbling joists to the front door, with the Dunk creeping along behind her.

The pair of them hunkered down beside the empty doorframe.

'Where we going, Sarge?'

'Ten o'clock: thirty, thirty-five feet away. He's slipped behind a Scots pine.'

A nod. 'On three?'

'Two, one.' And Lucy was out through the open doorway in a silent crouching jog. Skimming over the tussocked front garden. Hurdling the tumbledown wall. Glasses misting as they hit the warmer air.

The sound of puffing and panting boomed out behind her, then a strangled 'Shite!' and a crash.

She slithered to a halt, spinning around . . . and there was the Dunk, sprawled flat on his front at the end of a three-foot skidmark in the bracken.

He spat out a mouthful of pine needles. 'Go, go!'

Clumsy sod.

She was off again, making for the Scots pine. No point trying to be stealthy about it now – not with the Dunk going his full length. 'STOP, POLICE!'

Whoever was hiding behind the tree ran for it – the sound of snapping branches joining the *thump-thump-thump* of their feet. Going at a fair speed, too.

Lucy picked up the pace, elbows pumping, boots digging into the forest loam, huffing the breaths in and out, hands jabbing the air. Dodging between trunks, leaping over twisted knots of roots and lumps of vegetation. Ducking under low-hanging branches.

Trying to close the gap . . . and failing.

Whoever it was: they were *fast*. Leaving nothing behind but those flashes of tan fabric, glimpsed between the boughs of closely packed trees. Some sort of suit? No, the jacket was definitely a couple of shades darker than the trousers.

And what the hell was he doing in the middle of Moncuir Wood? Lurking outside the cottage where Abby Geddes became the Bloodsmith's first victim? No – no way there was an innocent explanation for that.

He crashed through a waist-high expanse of dead nettles, setting the grey stalks crackling.

Lucy gritted her teeth and smashed through them too, lungs burning.

Come on: *faster*.

He jinked off to the right, and she followed. Up a steep slope, feet slipping in the fallen leaf-litter, thighs aching, grabbing branches to keep herself upright and shredding her nitrile gloves in the process. Bastard was like a mountain goat, leaping up the hill as if it was barely there. Stretching his lead. Getting away. Disappearing over the crest.

Another push and Lucy scrambled to the top of the slope and—

'AAAAARGH!'

The ground fell away right in front of her, plummeting straight down, about twenty feet, to a mound of fly-tipped crap. Most of which looked very rusty and *very* sharp.

Her arms windmilled, hauling her shoulders and head backwards, feet slithering on the pine-needle floor. One hand grabbing onto the ragged branch of a dead spruce. Keeping herself from tipping over the edge onto the death-trap rubbish below.

Lucy pulled herself back to safety. 'Jesus . . .'

Where the hell did he . . . ?

She stood there, breathing hard, eyes scanning the forest.

There: on the other side of the hollow. A man. Curly brown hair with flashes of a high forehead. Corduroy jacket and chinos. Still running, and too far away to catch now. He slowed to a jog, then a walk. Looked back over his shoulder at her, showing off his beard and moustache. The light glinting off his small round glasses.

Son of a bitch.

It was the guy from that morning, the one who'd been staring at her across St Jasper's Lane. Had he *followed* them here?

He stopped for a moment and stood there, watching her watching him, then turned and disappeared into the woods.

She'd lost him.

The Dunk was sitting on the tumbledown wall outside the cottage when she got back. His expression wasn't exactly what you'd call happy. Anyone would think he'd just fallen flat on his face and ended up covered in dirt, mud, bits of pine needles, and smears of green. Could curdle water with that face, Tony Stark beard or not. A fresh cigarette glowered away in the corner of his mouth, the end slightly crumpled, as if he'd landed on the packet.

He picked a couple of needles from his filthy black polo neck. 'You lost the guy?'

Startling powers of deduction, there.

'Loving your new look.' Lucy snapped off what was left of her gloves and stuffed them in her pocket. 'Sort of like a Goth Worzel Gummidge.'

He held up his mobile phone, screen out. 'I've called the boss; they're on their way.'

'Not much point: he's long gone. Was off like a whippet with a fire-work up its—'

'Oh, there's a point all right.' The Dunk hopped down from his wall and stomped back towards the cottage. 'Trust me, Sarge, you need to see this.'

OK . . .

At the front door he pulled out his phone and fiddled with the thing till a circle of cold white LED light played across the manky hallway. But this time the Dunk didn't go into the dying room, instead he balanced himself on the exposed floor joists at the end of the corridor and hauled open the last door on the left-hand wall. It opened towards her, hiding whatever was inside. 'You're going to want to put on fresh gloves.' Then he disappeared.

She snapped on a new pair of nitriles, turned on her mobile's torch, and picked her way across the joists.

The door hid a narrow set of stairs that was almost steep enough to qualify as a ladder – its dark wood speckled with more tiny woodworm holes. Probably not the safest, then.

His voice echoed down from above. '*You coming?*'

'No, I'm having a nap.' The steps creaked and moaned beneath her feet, but they held as she climbed the half-dozen or so treads, until her head emerged into a semi-floored attic with a landing at the top of the stairs so narrow that the Dunk pretty much filled it.

The air was thick with the sharp gritty stench of rats and mildew, the only light filtering in through a narrow, cobweb-frosted pane in the roof. Most of the space to the left was open rafters and curled dust-grey loft insulation, but someone had erected a wooden partition just to the right of the stairs – with what looked like a wardrobe door set into it.

'Ready?' The Dunk took hold of the small metal catch and swung the door open. 'Better stay out here, though.'

It'd be tempting to say he was milking this, but going by the expression on his face, the Dunk wasn't enjoying it much.

Lucy climbed up into the loft space and squeezed past him. Peered around the wardrobe door.

Narnia had gone downhill a bit.

It was a cramped little room, with rough floorboards and a threadbare brown rug. A window the size of a shoebox graced the gable end, lifting the gloom just enough to make out vague shapes. Her torch did a much better job, revealing a collapsed metal bedframe, complete with rup- tured horsehair mattress; a steamer-style trunk, lying open for the spiders to decorate; and a dilapidated armchair that was missing a leg, tilted over to one side like a drunken pirate.

'So, what am I—'

'On your left.'

She swung her phone around and its light raked the water-stained coombed ceiling. At some point in the distant past, whoever lived here had nailed boards up between the roof joists, but the wood had rotted away in a couple of places, exposing the rags and straw stuffed in there for insulation.

And then her torch beam settled on what the Dunk's pantomime mys- terious act had been all about. 'Sodding hell . . .'

Two words were scrawled on the boards in three-foot-high letters. They'd probably been bright scarlet, once, but they'd dried to a coagu- lated brown: 'HELP ME!'

DI Tudor paced the length of the kitchen and back again, one hand squeezing his temples, the other gripping his phone to his ear tight enough to turn the knuckles pale as frozen butter. A wraith in the gloom. 'Yes, sir, I'm absolutely positive it *definitely* wasn't there before.' He stopped pacing to stare at the ceiling for a moment. 'Because we've got photographs of every room in the house, and the only wall the Blood- smith wrote on was where we found Abby Geddes's remains.'

The room had been stripped bare, leaving nothing but the corpse of a cracked Belfast sink, a couple of sagging shelves, and the rusted body of a long-dead wood-fired stove. Not too many holes in the floor, which made it perfect for pacing up and down, looking miserable, and talking to senior officers on the phone.

Lucy backed out and eased the door closed, leaving him to it.

An SOC-suited figure lumbered into the cottage, carrying a big square stainless-steel case as if it weighed as much as a small child. Then stood there, blocking the corridor while a couple of his mates kicked and shoved the attic door back as far as it would go – digging the Bakelite handle into the plaster wall – then forcing a brand-new sheet of sterling board down, creating a makeshift floor on the no-longer-exposed joists.

They gave their mate the thumbs up and he clambered up the near-vertical stairs and out of sight, taking his case with him.

Who knew, maybe they'd get lucky and find something?

Probably not, though.

Lucy slipped through the front door into the dingy clearing.

A quad bike and trailer were parked just beyond the garden wall, where a lone, large, pink-faced woman was wriggling her way into a rustling white Tyvek suit.

Lucy caught her as she was pulling a pair of blue plastic bootees on over her Dr Martens. 'I need a favour.'

'Oh aye?' Zipping herself up before plucking a facemask from its box. 'And is this favour legal?'

'Someone was hiding behind that tree, there.' Pointing at the Scots pine. 'If they've left fingerprints . . . ?'

She curled her lip. 'Fingerprints on *bark*? And what do you want for your second wish, a unicorn? World peace?'

'OK: DNA, then.'

'And you're authorized to approve the additional budget for DNA testing, are you? Cos this stuff don't come cheap.'

'Just . . . see if you can find something, OK?' After all, it wasn't as if Tudor was going to say no, was it? Not if it helped catch the Bloodsmith. Sod the budget.

The scene examiner puffed out her cheeks. 'Fine. But if they fire you for wasting resources, don't come whinging to me.' She finished getting suited up, then scrunched her way across the forest floor, taking a mini version of the big stainless-steel box with her.

Well, it was worth a try.

'Sarge?' The Dunk appeared at Lucy's shoulder, hands stuffed deep in the pockets of his bracken-streaked leather jacket. 'Boss says we should Foxtrot Oscar and go review the next crime scene.'

Lucy pulled her chin in. 'But we found the writing!'

'Yeah, he says we done good, but there's sod all going on here till FSSER have finished, so we might as well see if there's anything exciting lurking where Victim Number Two died. You know, cos we're on a roll.'

'FSS what?'

'Forensic Services Scene Examination Resources. It's what we're calling the Scenes Examination Branch this week.' He shrugged. 'You know what it's like.'

'What was wrong with "Smurfs"?' She frowned at the kitchen window – Tudor was just visible as a moving lump in the gloom, pacing back and forth again. 'Do we really have to go?'

'That's what the boss said.' The Dunk pulled out his phone and squinted at the screen, holding it just under his nose as he turned around three times. Then nodded, pointing off into the woods. 'Car's that way.'

'Bastard . . .'

5

Shaky Dave's Tattie Shack wasn't huge – just a small shed-shaped trailer with a fake-shingle roof and faux chimney. A couple of plastic seagulls perched on top, beaming down on the punters with a bonhomie that was, quite frankly, hard to believe while their real-life brethren stalked the tarmac like starving velociraptors. The Shack's side flap was levered up, forming a makeshift sunshade as the sweet-brown smell of baked potatoes oozed out into the sunshine, joined by the rustling-golden scent of chips and a delicious warm-green aroma of garlic.

Dave had parked his shack on North Esplanade, at the bottom end of Montgomery Park, where his clients could consume their tuber-based delights with a view across the river towards Dundas House and Kings Park, framed by neat little rows of Georgian terraces. All very genteel and civilized, even if the ugly bulk of Castle Hill Infirmary, looming in the background, kind of spoiled the view a bit – its tall twin chimneys spilling trails of white across the pale-blue sky as someone incinerated medical waste.

Lucy leaned against the guard rail, phone jammed against her ear, not doing a great job of ungritting her teeth. '*We* found the Bloodsmith's message, Boss. Us. Me and the Dunk.'

DI Tudor let out a long, breathy groan. '*So, you want to sit on your backside, watching the Smurfs do their jobs for the next three hours, is that it?*'

'No, but—'

'*The Chief Super's already called about a dozen times, wanting updates. Oh, and DCI Ross has just "popped by" to see how I'm getting on.*'

'Sod.'

'*Oh, yes, when things aren't going anywhere, they'll cut us loose to fend for ourselves, but soon as they think we're making progress? Bastarding vultures.*'

'Maybe—'

'*Which means I need you and DC Fraser, out there, digging up more break-throughs.*' A small bitter laugh. '*See if we can't solve this thing before the High Heidyins wade in and bugger everything up.*'

Her shoulders sagged, then she curled forward till the metal safety rail clunked, cool against her forehead. Staring down the grassy bank to the wide, iron-grey river. Sunlight flashed off the water's surface, sharp as daggers.

'*Lucy?*'

Wasn't as if she had any choice, was it?

'Yes, Boss.'

'*Good.*' Pause. '*And did you tell Denise she could swab a whole Scots pine for DNA?*'

'If the Bloodsmith really did write "help me" in the attic, then we know he's been back there at least once. Why not more? I'm not saying it was definitely him I chased, but if it was . . . ?'

A sigh. '*You* sure *you didn't get a good look at this man?*'

'Not enough to do an eFit – he was too far away. High forehead, beard, glasses, that's it.'

'*Fair enough. But next time you order DNA tests you clear it with me, OK? OK.*'

A little boat chugged past, bow forging a path through the water, dragging a curling V of white behind it.

'*Speaking of OK.*' DI Tudor cleared his throat in her ear. '*Are you doing . . . you know? I mean, the last couple of months have been . . . Lucy, you were doing so much better, I thought you'd put Neil—*'

'Don't even say his name!' She straightened up, mouth pinched, holding it all in.

'*It's just you've been . . . People are worried about you, that's all.*'

'I'm *fine*. Never better.'

'*Yeah.*' Tudor's voice softened. '*Only your therapist says you haven't been to see him for a while.*'

This again.

She twisted the phone upwards, moving the microphone away from her mouth. 'Boss? Hello? I can't . . . it's . . . reception. Hello?'

'And if you're about to go off on one about doctor–patient confidentiality, he didn't tell me anything about your sessions, just that you've missed your last two appointments.'

'Think . . . out of battery. Boss . . . Hello?'

'Do you want signed off on the sick, is that what you want?'

Damn.

Lucy gritted her teeth that bit tighter. 'All right, all right, I'll go see him. You happy?'

'Ecstatic. Then you can find me something that nails the Bloodsmith.'

The line went dead. Tudor had hung up.

'Perfect.' Because life clearly wasn't bad enough that a senior officer couldn't make it a whole lot sodding worse. She jammed her phone back in her pocket.

'Sarge?' The Dunk appeared at Lucy's elbow, in all his muck-smeared glory, holding a couple of cardboard containers, about the size of old-fashioned video cassettes. Each with a bamboo spork sticking out of it, pinning a raffle ticket in place. 'Shaky Dave was out of stovies, so I got you tartiflette. Which he says is kinda the same thing, only French. Gallic stovies. With garlic. Garlic Gallic stovies.'

'Thanks.' She pulled her spork from the cardboard and stuck it in the tartiflette instead, scooping out a creamy glistening mouthful.

'So, this bloke you chased: any clue?' The Dunk tucked one end of a paper napkin into the collar of his beatnik polo neck – as if it could get any dirtier – then stabbed a cheese-and-gravy-covered chip and popped it in his mouth. And immediately opened his gob like a howler monkey, panting out beef-scented breaths. 'Hot, hot, hot, hot!'

The tartiflette wasn't too bad, bit rich, but tasty with it. 'Never seen him before today.'

'Yeah, I know we did DNA and that, but it can't be the Bloodsmith, can it? Be a huge coincidence if he *just* happened to be popping by when we were there, right?'

The Dunk had a point.

'True.'

Another gravy-drenched chip got the howler-monkey treatment. 'Could be a reporter? Spotted us this morning and decided to tag along in case we found something juicy?'

Lucy shrugged.

The Dunk did a slow three-sixty, squinting at the Tattie Shack and parked cars. 'Probably lurking somewhere near, like a nasty little rat, creeping about, following us. And speaking of rats: which crime scene do you want to hit next?'

'Bruce Malloch.'

Victim number two.

Bruce Malloch's house was nestled halfway down a terrace of identical, narrow, yellow-brick two-up-two-downs in Blackwall Hill. Roysvale Crescent: a nice, respectable street, where the only way to tell one home from another was the colour of their front doors and the occasional shrub in the tiny gardens. Well, that and the fact number fifteen had spent three weeks appearing on the news and in all the papers. 'HORROR HOUSE OF BLOOD, SHOCK', '"BRUTAL MURDER WAS LIKE JACK THE RIPPER" SAYS TOP COP', 'SICK PSYCHO STRIKES LEAFY SUBURB'...

Still: nice view.

From up here, Oldcastle was laid out in all its tumorous glory. The crumpled-up-cardboard sprawl of Kingsmeath on the left, with its nasty little council houses and soulless tower blocks. On the right, the genteel Georgian streets of the Wynd and the fancy houses of Castleview. And straight ahead, down the valley and across the curling cul-de-sacs of Blackwall Hill to the twisted steel ribbon of Kings River. On the other side: Logansferry, with its harbour and industrial estates; Cowskillin, with its fifties post-war prefabs and the football stadium; Shortstaine, bloated and heavy with bland housing developments; and right in the middle, Castle Hill – Victorian streets twisting around each other, circling the huge granite shark's fin that broke through the valley floor, with the ruined castle perched on top – wreathed in its cocoon of scaffolding. The whole city brooding, and malevolent, and miserable, and oppressive.

AKA: home.

'You know what bugs me?' The Dunk dipped into his pocket and came out with an evidence bag. Tipped a shiny key into the palm of his hand. 'There's no consequences any more. Take that Business Secretary thing – millions of taxpayers' cash, *our* cash, going into Paul Rhynie's mates' pockets and nothing happens.' He unlocked the dark-green door. 'We're being robbed blind, but everyone just shrugs their shoulders and gets on with it.' The Dunk stepped back and wafted Lucy over the threshold. 'Whatever happened to accountability?'

She stepped into a hallway gritty-grey with fingerprint powder; mud and dirt tracked in across the no-longer-oatmeal-coloured carpet. The stairs leading up to the second floor were just as bad. Bruce Malloch's living room had a couple of movie posters on the wall: *Back to the Future*, *The Empire Strikes Back*, *Die Hard*; a black leather couch, faded a couple of shades where they'd tried to lift prints off it; big flatscreen TV; newish PlayStation; glass coffee table. All of which screamed 'bachelor pad'.

And loneliness.

'All that dodgy procurement wank during the pandemic – hundreds of millions spaffed away on PPE that didn't work, from companies owned by government cronies – just normalized it. That's why we get tossers like Rhynie.'

The Smurfs had covered Bruce Malloch's kitchen in fingerprint powder too. It wasn't quite as bright in here: some sunlight oozed through the frosted glass of the back door, but a roller blind obscured the window.

'Tell you, Sarge: people in power? They haven't got a clue what it's like to actually work for a living, so why *would* they care? Why *not* give your best chums, Quentin and Jacinda, a hundred-million-quid contract for doing sod all, or cocking things up? Why—'

'Dunk!'

He stared at her. 'What?'

'Any chance we could concentrate on the *actual* job?'

He pulled one shoulder up to his ear. 'Sorry, Sarge.'

'Thank you.' She flicked the light switch, but nothing happened. A couple more goes established that it probably never would, meaning Bruce Malloch's expensive kitchen toys couldn't shine in all their glory. Even then, what drew the eye wasn't the fancy-looking coffee machine, the Thermomix, sous-vide machine, or plethora of other gadgets, it was the huge dark-brown patch on the ceiling.

The Dunk stood in the middle of the kitchen, staring up at it. 'You'd think they'd've got rid of that by now.'

Lucy clumped up the stairs to a small landing. The bathroom door was open, showing off a tiled space just big enough for a toilet, sink, and shower cubicle. Master bedroom on the left, plain duvet crumpled on the floor, pillows scattered, drawers hanging out of the bedside cabinet, built-in wardrobes ransacked, clothes all over the place. Because God forbid a search team should tidy up after itself.

Which left the door straight ahead.

It opened on a small home office, wreathed in darkness. The vague outlines of a desk, swivel chair, and filing cabinet were just visible in what little light managed to work its way through the closed venetian blinds. Four monitors perched on arms above a beefy-looking laptop and ergonomic keyboard.

The carpet *scrunched* under Lucy's feet as she stepped inside.

'Bloody hell.' She pulled her chin in and clamped a hand over her nose and mouth. The whole room stank as if someone had left a handful of batteries and a packet of sausages on the radiator. For months. 'Dunk – open the windows, before we all choke to death!'

'Sarge.' He bustled over to the blinds and hauled them up.

Sunshine spilled in.

The search team hadn't bothered cleaning up in here, either. Those four monitors were spattered with little brown dots, dried and shiny like beetles. A leathery slick of coffee-coloured yuck covered half the desk, but most of it was on the carpet, like a huge puddle of mud had died there. Half a dozen black clumps marked where internal organs had been dumped outside the body. And on the wall opposite the window, those familiar three-foot-high letters: 'HELP ME!'

Worst of all were the drifts of shiny blue-black bodies. Flies. Had to be millions of them in here: born, lived, loved, and died on a dark-red diet of Bruce Malloch's blood.

Urgh . . .

Lucy raised her right foot and desiccated fly carcases tumbled back to the carpet. Which explained those scrunching sounds.

'Wow . . .' The Dunk hissed in a breath. 'And I thought the kitchen was bad.' Then he opened the window as wide as it would go, letting in blessed fresh air. 'Manky, manky, manky.'

Lucy handed him the folder as the stench dissipated a bit. 'Out loud.'

'Eh?' He turned it over a couple of times. 'You want me to *read* it to you? Haven't you already—'

'Rules for being a hotshot detective, number eight in an occasional series. You absorb more information when you consume it in multiple formats. Of course I've read the file – dozens of times. But now that we're here, standing in the actual crime scene, I want *you* to read it. Out loud.' She snapped on a fresh pair of nitrile gloves. 'Right now.'

'So how come we didn't do that back at Rat Haven Cottage?'

'Rule thirty-nine. Shake things up.'

'Detective sergeants are weird.' He rummaged through the folder and pulled out a chunk of paperwork much bigger than the one for Abby Geddes. Frowned at the top sheet, mouth moving in silence for a moment. 'Right, here we go: Bruce Malloch, thirty-five, software designer with Camburn Logistic Services Limited. Line manager reported him missing when he didn't come into work three days on the trot.' The Dunk shook his head. 'Imagine your *line manager* being the only one who cares enough to report you missing?'

'No family?' Being on the first floor afforded the room a miserable view of the narrow, overgrown rectangle of grass and plants abandoned outside the window. Could see into the next-door neighbours' gardens, too: wee kids playing on a swing set; dirty big Alsatian chasing its tail round and round and round; wannabe yummy mummy hanging out the washing in a strappy top that was two sizes too small for her . . .

'Next of kin's listed as one Shona Porter, ex-fiancée. They interviewed her: said she hadn't seen him since way before Christmas. And they found the poor sod's body halfway through April. God, it gets sadder and sadder, doesn't it?'

Suppose the surrounding houses explained why the search team had left the blinds down – didn't trust Bruce's neighbours not to let the press have a go with their telephoto lenses. Taking sneaky shots of the blood-spattered crapshow left behind, including the only clue O Division had managed to keep secret on this case: 'HELP ME!'

The Dunk went to park his bum on the edge of the desk, took one look at all the dried blood and stood up straight again. 'So, while Abby Geddes was the first *victim*, Bruce Malloch was the first one to be discovered. You want the psychological profile too?'

'Might as well.' Lucy frowned at the two words, daubed on the plain magnolia wall. A photo hung next to it: Bruce Malloch on the pitch at City Stadium, shaking hands with someone wearing a blue-and-white Oldcastle Warriors strip. Going by the way Bruce was grinning, whoever it was, they were some sort of big deal. As if he was meeting his hero.

The Dunk groaned. Then puffed out a breath. 'Who wrote this? It's like one big run-on sentence that's allergic to punctuation . . . OK. Blah, blah, blah, "insufficient evidence or incidents to be certain at this early stage, but markers at the scene suggest that our killer's primary motive was not to kill Bruce, but to create a dead body that would then allow our killer to live out his fantasy, making it a subcategory of necrophilia, even though there's no sign that the remains have been sexually interfered with, stripping the body implies a degree of voyeurism that may be used to fuel masturbatory fantasies later," deep breath, "which in conjunction with the message left behind, written in Bruce's blood, does suggest that our killer is probably from a dysfunctional home . . ."' The Dunk looked up from the report and grimaced. 'I can see why we pay these academics the big bucks. And here was me thinking normal well-adjusted people carve strangers up *all* the time. ". . . where parental or inter-sibling emotional affirmation were irregular features of his childhood, if they existed at all, causing him to internalize his need for that emotional affirmation . . ." Has this bloody psychologist never heard of a full stop?'

'Nope, and you've got three more pages to go.'

'Sod.' He skimmed through to the end. 'Hey: there's a summary at the back! "Killer is most likely an IC-One male," which doesn't exactly narrow it down, does it? Most of Oldcastle's white and northern European. Anyway, "IC-One male, late twenties to early forties, in steady employment, with a position of trust. He's not in a relationship, but when questioned will have had a string of one-night stands." Suppose that'll be him looking for "emotional affirmation" in all the wrong bedrooms. "It is highly likely that the individual will currently be reliving his kill and preparing to select another victim" – brackets – "assuming he hasn't already." Close brackets.'

'Not a huge amount of help, then.'

'Yeah.' The Dunk stuck the report back in the folder. 'But, to be fair, they only knew about Bruce Malloch, by then. Abby Geddes's remains didn't turn up till May.'

True enough.

He went back into the folder. 'You want to see the photos?'

'Not really.'

The Dunk produced them anyway, holding the things out as if they were infected. 'What bothers me is: how does our boy walk out of here without anyone spotting he's clarted head to toe in blood?'

Lucy puffed out a breath and accepted the proffered eight-by-ten.

It was a top-down picture of the room, in hideous technicolour. No skeletal remains here. Instead Bruce Malloch lay split open on the scarlet-sodden carpet: naked, head thrown back, mouth open, eyes half shut. One arm was hooked over the base of his office chair, the other lay out at ninety degrees to his body, hand curled into a loose fist – wrist slashed all the way down to the pale bone below. His legs were bent, knees splayed, the heels of his feet pressed together, like a frog in science class. Dark glistening coils looped out of his split stomach, draped across his thighs; a big chunk of purple liver by his left side; a slab of lung by his right.

She handed it back. 'Poor sod.'

'There's more photos, if you want?'

'No. I'm good.' Lucy shook her head. Swallowed. Stepped out onto the tiny landing.

Breathe normally.

Don't let the Dunk see.

Keep that tartiflette down, where it's meant to be.

The Dunk followed her, tucking the pictures into the file again. 'Next up: post-mortem. "Three blows to the back of the head caused cata-strophic damage to Mr Malloch's parietal and occipital lobe, but it is unlikely that death would have been instantaneous. The head wound is of sufficient severity to suggest that Mr Malloch must have been, at the very least, rendered incapable of independent movement, otherwise we would expect to see defensive wounds to the hands and forearms. Note this does not include the deep incision across Mr Malloch's left wrist as that appears to have been deliberate rather than as the result of any struggle."'

Just a photograph. That's all. Seen hundreds of pictures just like it. Attended post-mortems of victims who'd suffered much, much worse.

' "However, even if Mr Malloch was minimally aware of his surround-ings when his assailant began eviscerating him, the sheer volume of blood lost in the first few minutes of this procedure would have been sufficient to cause cardiac arrest. As such, it is unlikely that his heart was still functioning when it was removed." Urgh . . . See what I mean? The Bloodsmith would've been *swimming* in it. How come no one notices?'

So why this photograph? Why did *this* one make snakes writhe and knot deep in her stomach? Make her pulse thrum in her chest. Make sweat prickle between her shoulder blades. Make her hands tremble like someone in their nineties.

Maybe DI Tudor was right? Maybe it *was* time to go see her shrink again.

'Sarge? You OK?'

She nodded, kept her eyes on the stairs. 'Close the window, shut the blinds, and lock up will you, Dunk? I've got to make a call.'

6

She was putting her phone away when the Dunk shambled out of Bruce Malloch's house and locked the door. To be honest, the wee lad looked more than a little disreputable, with his black-and-grey outfit clarted in streaks of pale brown and dark green. As if he'd recently crawled out of a septic tank.

He slipped the key back in its evidence bag, then fiddled a slightly crumpled cigarette from the pack. Puffing away as he stared at her, one eyebrow raised. 'You sure you're OK, Sarge? Only you look a bit peaky.'

Lucy forced a smile. 'Think it was the tartiflette: all that cheese and ham and cream. Bit rich for lunch.'

'Knew I should've got you the potato and fennel galette.' He kicked his heels on the top step, smoking his fag. 'Where next? Craig Thorburn's closer, but if we're going in order of death it's Adam Holmes next.'

She edged around till she was upwind, because the smell of burnt tobacco definitely wasn't helping her roiling stomach. 'Neither – drop me back at my car, then you can go home and get changed. Don't get me wrong: I appreciate the hedge-backwards look as much as the next person, but *perhaps* not while we're on duty?'

The Dunk drooped. 'Yes, Sarge.'

Lucy waited till the Dunk and his pool car disappeared around the corner onto Siege Row, then unlocked her clapped-out, tiny, third-hand Kia Picanto. Which looked as if it'd been designed by Duplo. She sat there for a moment, then started the car. Might as well get it over with . . .

*

'I don't want to talk about it, OK?' Lucy stretched out on the couch, lying flat on her back, stockinged feet on the armrest. Staring up at the out-of-focus grey ceiling with its pipes and cabling ducts as her voice echoed back from the bare brick walls. Whichever idiot decided 'industrial chic' was a thing needed a good stiff kick in the testicles. Having to see a therapist was bad enough without feeling you were doing it in an abandoned business park.

But that was architects for you.

They'd stuck a single spotlight up there, casting its soft white glow on Lucy, the couch, and the coffee table, leaving the rest of the room bathed in shadow.

'Hmmmm . . .' Dr McNaughton had taken his usual position, in the chair, just outside the pool of light, reduced to an indistinct blur now she'd taken her glasses off. Not that he was much to look at: beard, slouch, cardigan, and far too much jewellery. The kind of man who wore signet rings and ID bracelets, chains round his neck and wrists so he rattled like Marley's sodding ghost. The kind of man who got off on being in charge of everything – asking the questions; making her talk about things she didn't sodding want to; making her *confess*; because if she didn't he'd report her to DI Tudor and get her signed off on the sick; revelling in his power over her. The kind of man who pretended to be a decent human being to your face, but stared at your arse soon as you turned around. Or, as they're more commonly known: dicks. *'And why is that?'*

'Maybe because I don't – want – to – talk – about – it.'

He gave that long-suffering sigh of his and let the silence stretch.

'Fine.' She slumped even further back into the couch and draped an arm across her eyes. 'I don't remember, OK? My mother died when I was little, my father couldn't cope, I went into care for a bit. Nothing special. You happy now?'

'And how did that make you feel?'

'Why do you think he cuts their hearts out?'

A pause.

Dr McNaughton shifted about in his seat, jewellery rattling away. Rings on his fingers and bells on his toes, and he'll be an arsehole wherever he goes. *'Lucy—'*

'The Bloodsmith – he cuts their hearts out and takes them with him. Even for Oldcastle that's messed up, right?'

Nothing came from the dick in the shadows, but a mild air of disappointment.

'We know he collects blood from his victims, but why the hearts?'

'*Lucy, it's important to address your feelings, if—*'

'You said I could talk about anything I want. I want to talk about this.'

Another sigh.

'You know what I think? I think . . . it's because even though *scientifically* we know "love" is nothing more than chemical reactions in the brain – dopamine, norepinephrine, phenylethylamine, vasopressin, oxytocin – we still say we love someone "with all our heart", don't we? A heart means love. It *is* love. And the forensic psychologist says the Bloodsmith's never had any in his cold, miserable life. So he harvests other people's.'

The blurry outline shrugged, setting his jewellery going again. Not a single word.

God, *why* did therapists always have to do that? Sit there like silent sodding lumps and expect you to do all the talking. What was the point of the bastards doing degrees in psychology when a pot plant could do the same job?

'Come on, Dr McNaughton, if—'

'*Lucy, we've been over this. Please don't call me Dr McNaughton, it's John, remember? John—*'

'I don't need to be your friend, *John*. I don't want to, either. Let's keep things professional, *Dr* McNaughton.' After all, it wasn't as if a first name was going to make him any less of a dick. 'So, the Bloodsmith's cutting their hearts out to fill the void.'

A pointed sniff huffed out behind her, and it was back to the silent treatment again.

This time, the pause stretched and stretched and stretched . . .

Lucy cleared her throat. 'Someone's following me.'

'*I see.*' Voice flat and non-judgemental. As if that didn't make him sound like a condescending prick.

'I'm pretty sure he started this morning, near St Jasper's. And the bastard was there in the woods: outside that cottage where the Bloodsmith killed

Abby Geddes? Did a runner when I challenged him. Male, mid-forties, curly brown hair, dresses like a geography teacher. Constable Fraser thinks it's a journalist, but what if it's *him*, the Bloodsmith?'

Another pause filled with passive disappointment.

She lifted her arm from her eyes and glared at McNaughton. 'You think I'm being paranoid, don't you?'

'*Lucy, it's simply not possible. You're projecting—*'

'I *saw* him, OK?' Putting a sharp edge into her voice. 'I'm not some sort of nutjob.'

The sound of a truck reversing *beep-beep-beep*ed away somewhere outside.

Motes of dust floated through the shabby spot of light.

A creak from the couch as Lucy turned back to glare at the ceiling instead.

The beeping died away.

Silence.

Dr McNaughton let loose yet another big jewellery-rattling sigh.

Lucy let her arm fall back into place again, shutting out all that industrial chic. 'But the idiots I work with are all, "Oh, are you feeling OK, Lucy?", "You've not been seeing your therapist, Lucy", "We're worried about you, Lucy."'

This time, the pause didn't feel artificial, it was more as if Dr McNaughton was trying to work out what to say. Which probably didn't bode well.

'*When someone's gone through what you have, it's normal to feel that way. Post-Traumatic Stress Disorder can make everything seem—*'

'I don't have PTSD.'

'*Are you still having flashbacks? Sweating? Nausea? Trembling? Blackouts?*'

'No.' And scurrying out of Bruce Malloch's house, trying to keep her lunch down didn't count. Nor did the shaky hands. Or the sweating . . . 'I have to go.' She sat bolt upright on the couch and stuffed her feet back into her boots. Snatched her glasses off the little table.

'*Lucy, what Neil Black did—*'

She marched for the exit, fists clenched, heels clacking on the concrete floor.

'*Lucy, don't go – I'm just trying to help!*'

Hauled the door open.

'Lucy, please, it's been so—'

And slammed it shut behind her.

Lucy leaned against the Kia's roof, one hand trying to massage the head-ache out of her temples while the other clutched her phone. Keeping her voice as upbeat as possible in the circumstances. 'We're doing every-thing we can, Judith, I promise.'

'It's just . . . the press coverage, they're saying all these things about the investigation being wound up.' A little wobble there, as if pain and gin didn't mix. *'We just want him caught, so we can bury our little boy. So we can . . . get his . . . get Craig's heart back.'*

Little boy? Craig Thorburn was in his thirties, for God's sake.

'I'm sorry.' Lucy took off her glasses and sagged forwards, till her cheek pressed against the car roof. Cool metal on warm skin. 'We're making progress. I know it's hard, but you have to be patient.'

'They said you're giving up!'

Bloody reporters.

'We're *not* giving up, Judith.'

A gull screeched somewhere overhead, making discordant harmonies with Lucy's headache.

The grumble of a distant diesel motor.

That iodine, seaweed, and dirty-clothes taint of the river.

'Have you talked to your Family Liaison Officer?'

'Urgh . . . What's the point? He never tells us anything.'

'I don't know what to say, Judith.' Lucy squeezed her forehead even tighter, but it didn't seem to help. 'I wish I could wave a magic wand and catch this guy, but it doesn't work like that. I promise, if I find some-thing, I'll let you know.'

'I need to bury my son!' And Judith hung up.

Lucy stayed where she was, slumped against the car roof. Opened one eye to make absolutely sure the call had disconnected. 'Shame you weren't so interested in the poor sod when he was alive, isn't it?'

DI Tudor was right: Lucy should never have given out her mobile number. But what was she supposed to do? Regardless of how screwed up Judith Thorburn's family was, the poor cow couldn't even grieve properly, not with the pathologist refusing to release her son's remains. And even if, somehow, Operation Maypole managed to catch the

Bloodsmith, there was no guarantee they'd find his victims' hearts. Maybe he threw them away? Or buried them? Or maybe he ate them? Dr McNaughton would have a full-on psychologist nerdgasm about that: absorbing the love. Very Freudian.

Urgh: Dr McNaughton.

It was better when he was just sitting there with his mouth shut, to be honest. OK, so the silent-therapist-I'm-only-here-to-listen act was a massive pain in the arse, but it was better than him opening his gob and making everything worse.

Still, at least this time he hadn't banged on about the id, ego, and superego the whole session. Cos God forbid anyone—

Her phone burst into its warbling ringtone, and when she opened her eyes a blurry 'UNKNOWN NUMBER' sat in the middle of the screen.

Brilliant. More crap.

She hit the button. 'McVeigh.'

A man's voice, lumpen with the weird half-teuchter, half-Oldcastle accent of someone from up north of Fiddersmuir. Banjo country. *'Aye, you the officer called us, the day, aboot Lucas Weir?'*

'Lucas . . . ?'

'No' his real name, like. But I'm in an open-plan office, so I'm being circumspect and that.'

Which could only mean one person: Benedict Strachan.

'Oh, *that* Lucas Weir. Yes.'

'Good. Mike Scobie, I'm his CJ social worker. That's "Criminal Justice", like, no' "Caffeine Junkie".' There was a little chortle there, as Mike Scobie laughed at his own crap joke. *'I've found him a placey to stay, in Kingsmeath. Have you got yoursel' a piece of paper? Cos here's the address: Fifty-Fower Stirk Road. It's a halfway house so he'll need—'*

'Hold on.' She raised her head off the car's roof. 'Why are you telling *me* this?'

'So you can get him ower there.'

Cheeky sod.

'Oh no you don't. Police Scotland aren't responsible for housing folk who've got out of prison. That's your job, not mine.'

'Thought you wanted to help.'

'I did: I called you. Have you got him on a rehab programme yet?'

A snort. *'You any idea how hard it is to get a place on one of those? I'd have more chance getting him on* The Great British Bake Off.'

Oh, for God's sake.

'He was eleven when he got banged up, Mr Scobie. *Eleven.* Wasn't even old enough to drink, but he's come out with a drug habit. That sound fair to you?'

There was a long phlegmy groan. Then a sigh. *'Fine, I'll see what I can do for the wee loon, but no promises. Seriously:* Bake Off.'

'Thank you.'

'I'd say you're welcome, but I'd be lying.' And with that, he was gone.

Lazy sod.

Lucy put her phone away, before it caused any more trouble. Got her glasses back on. Turned. And froze.

She was on the south side of the river, opposite MacKinnon Quay. But . . . ?

Sunlight glinted on the battleship-grey water. A handful of trawlers were tied up to the harbour wall, along with a couple of the smaller offshore supply boats too cheap to pay the Aberdeen dock fees. On this side of the river it was all red-brick processing plants, chandler's warehouses, lockups, and the kind of garages where you paid cash and didn't ask any questions. All of it rundown and grimy. Lots of boarded-up buildings with weeds growing out of their roofs and gutters, waiting for a demolition crew to put them out of their misery. Even the road looked depressed, its granite setts drooping into gutters rainbowed with oily water.

How the hell did . . . ?

Something crawled its way up her spine. Turned all the saliva in her mouth to sand.

What was she *doing* here?

Lucy stepped back from the car and something scrunched beneath her feet. But when she looked down, it wasn't dried-up fly carcases this time, it was a set of keys: a chunky silver one with 'DO NOT DUPLICATE' embossed on it; one that looked a bit like an anvil; a strange rectangular one with a wide head and no serrations – just dimples recessed into the blade; three Yales, each with a different coloured plastic cap; and one old-fashioned barrel key with some sort of crude lion's head stamped on its thick round bow; all bound together on a brass ring. Someone must've dropped them.

Should take the keys back to the station, stick them in the Lost and Found, so whoever lost the things could claim them.

She picked the keys up – cold in the palm of her hand. Jingling against each other as her fingers trembled.

And why did she have this weird, queasy feeling of déjà vu? Like she'd seen all this before, *heard* all this before, that every rib-constricting breath had already been breathed?

She leaned back against her manky little Kia.

Something else for Dr McNaughton to love: *Are you still having flash-backs? Sweating? Nausea? Trembling? Blackouts?*

No, of course she wasn't. This kind of thing was *totally* normal, wasn't it?

She didn't have PTSD, she'd just . . . spaced out for a bit. Everybody did it. Like driving home on autopilot and you get there with no idea what route you took or what happened along the way. Nothing strange about that.

Lucy bent double and grabbed hold of her knees. Did the breathing exercise they'd taught her. Everything was fine. Neil Black wasn't coming back. He wasn't lurking in the dark, waiting for her.

It wasn't real.

And slowly, breath by breath, she pulled it all back inside. Balled it up tight and stuffed it down. See? Didn't need any help. Could manage this perfectly well on her own.

She straightened up, pulled her shoulders back.

Dr Bloody McNaughton could go stick his . . .

Lucy stopped.

That feeling of being watched had returned, even stronger than before.

She spun around.

There – standing on the corner, twenty feet away, where the road played host to another row of crumbling warehouses. It was the man in the corduroy jacket. The one who'd been outside the cottage this morning. The one who'd got away.

Not this time.

7

There was no way the scumbag didn't know she'd seen him. And even though he had to be at least a decade older than she was, they both knew he was faster.

On foot, anyway.

Lucy yanked open her car door and jumped in behind the wheel. She cranked the engine into life and floored it. No time to waste fastening her seatbelt. Working up through the gears. Unleashing the mighty Kia's sixty-one brake horsepower as the engine roared like an angry chihuahua and the seatbelt-warning chimes rang out.

The man in the corduroy jacket ran for it, but not *away* from Lucy, towards her.

She slammed on the brakes, bracing herself against the wheel when momentum tried to evict her through the windscreen. But by the time the Kia had slithered to a halt, he was past. In the wing mirror, his reflection sprinted around the corner out of sight.

'BASTARD!'

She hauled the steering wheel around and slammed the car into reverse, setting the nose dipping as the tyres screeched on setts. Rising out of her seat. Swinging the whole thing around, then slapping it into first and putting her foot down again. Acceleration shoving her into the upholstery.

Maybe a seatbelt wasn't a bad idea after all?

She wrestled with it, one-handed – giving up when she hit the corner. Yanking the Kia around to the left, back end kicking out. More squealing tyres.

He was *already* a third of the way down the street and still going strong.

Jesus, that guy could run.

She hauled the steering wheel over, correcting the slide, then shoved the accelerator down hard, making the whole car *thrrrrrrrrrrrummm* across the uneven setts. OK, she definitely had him now.

Lucy pulled her phone out, holding it up at eye level. Well, she was already breaking the speed limit and not wearing a seatbelt, so what was one more road-traffic offence? Jabbing her thumb at the screen, unlocking it and—

'SHIT, SHIT, SHIT, SHIT, SHIT!'

A forklift truck wheeched backwards out of an open garage, front loaded down with a large black plastic crate, nearly as big as her whole car.

The Kia's tyres wailed again as she hit the brakes and wrenched the wheel to one side, her phone hand banging down on the horn and getting an apologetic *whreeeeeep* for its troubles.

Whoever was driving the forklift brought it to a juddering halt, swinging a fist in her direction as she roared by. It had the middle finger extended.

Couldn't return the favour, not without dropping her phone, so a heartfelt 'AND YOU!' would just have to do.

Up ahead, the guy in corduroy took a sharp left, ducking into a narrow ginnel between a dodgy-looking workshop and a dodgier-looking printer's. And there was no way even something as small as her Kia would get down it.

'ARRRRRRRRRRGH!' Lucy slammed the brake pedal to the carpet and the car skidded to a stop. She scrambled out, legging it across the pavement and into the gloomy narrow alley.

Cold wrapped its pale-blue tentacles around her.

She sped up into a proper full-on sprint, ginnel walls flashing by dark and damp on either side, speckled with green – doubt the sun ever made it this far – her Cuban heels clattering along, echoing back from those slimy bricks.

Where the hell was he?

A bunch of rusty leaflet-display stands sagged against one wall, abandoned and empty. Probably dumped there by whatever lazy scumbag ran the printer's.

A much narrower alley branched off to the right, behind the small forest of discarded stands, not much wider than her shoulders. That had to be the way he'd gone.

She barely slowed for the turn, heels skittering as she grabbed the corner to swing herself into the constricted space. Sped up again.

There he was – right ahead of her, disappearing through a grimy black door marked 'WIŚNIEWSKI DOBRE MIĘSO ~ TYLKO PRACOWNICY!'

Lucy surged forwards and barged through the same door, exploding into a large room, about the size of a tennis court, lined with stainless-steel panels. The tables and workbenches were stainless steel too – laden down with huge chunks of meat. Carcases hung from the ceiling on some weird track system. Brown tiles on the floor. And a lot of large burly men and women staring at her. All dressed in white from the hairnets and hats on their heads to the wellies on their feet. Blood-smeared aprons and butchers' jackets. And every single one of them wielded a massive knife, cleaver, or saw.

The whole place reeked of iron and fat and sweat.

The nearest woman slammed what looked like half a lamb down on the tabletop in front of her, setting it ringing like Satan's dinner gong. '*Hej! Tutaj nie można wchodzić!*'

Someone else joined in. '*Tylko pracownicy, ty głupia suko!*'

A fat man, slicing his way through a knee joint, jabbed his knife at her. '*Wynoś się stąd! To nie higieniczne!*'

No sign of the guy in the corduroy jacket.

Lucy hauled out her warrant card. 'POLICE! What is it . . . *POLICJA!* There was a man came through here – where is he?'

Almost as one, they dropped eye contact, shuffled their wellies, and went back to butchering meat.

'Come on: he was right in front of me! Where did he go?'

No reply.

'WHERE DID HE BLOODY GO?'

A door at the side of the stainless-steel room battered open, and in shuffled another man, all dressed in white, hat clenched in his stained hands, bald head shining in the strip lights. Eyes lowered. Voice heavily accented and dripping with deference. '*Proszę* . . . please, we do not want to have trouble, here. I have papers for everyone. Good papers. Proper papers. No one is being illegal.'

'Oh, for GOD'S SAKE!' Lucy kicked the nearest table leg and a muffled *clang* reverberated through the room, making everyone flinch.

He must've gone *somewhere*.

A walk-in fridge or freezer was built into the wall opposite the office. But when Lucy clacked over there and hauled it open, there was nothing inside but pork, lamb, and beef. Carcases suspended from hooks, boxes of meat on shelves. No man in a corduroy jacket.

There had to be another door – one the meat got delivered through. That manky ginnel round the back couldn't be the only way in and out. Fire regulations would never allow it.

'You.' She pointed at the man from the office, now working his cap around and around in his podgy fingers. 'Where's the main entrance?'

He let go with one hand and pointed at the far corner, where an opening was covered with wide plastic strips.

'Thank you. You've been *so* helpful.'

The man actually smiled at that, as if she'd been serious. '*Cała przyjemność po mojej stronie.*'

She shoved her way through the plastic strips – thick and clammy against her skin – into a small loading bay, with steps leading down to Plouviez Road.

Lucy stepped out onto the narrow pavement, glasses fogging up as they hit the warmer outside air.

By the time she'd wiped them on her stripy top there was no sign of the guy she'd been chasing. Not up the street, nor down it. He'd gone.

Let's face it, he'd had plenty of time while she'd been dicking about trying to get someone in the meat plant to help her. Could be in *Dundee* by now.

'Buggering *hell*.' It was meant to be a bellow of rage, but her heart wasn't in it.

The Dunk was waiting for her when Lucy pulled her ancient Kia Picanto into the car park, round the back of DHQ. He'd swapped his stained clothes for an identical black polo-neck-and-jeans ensemble, his dark-grey leather jacket looking mottled as if it'd been sponged down. A cigarette sending lazy curls of smoke to taint the afternoon air as he lounged against a not-so-clean patrol car with a cracked windscreen.

She pulled into the only spare parking spot in the place, climbed out, and locked her car. 'Don't you own anything that isn't black or grey?'

'It's called *style*, Sarge, look it up.' Voice flat as a concrete floor. 'Anyway, Forensics rushed through the analysis on that new "help me!" in the cottage. DNA matches: it's Abby Geddes's blood. No idea when it was painted there, though.'

'Bastard.'

'Total. They think he's probably been keeping it in the freezer.'

'So, definitely not a copycat, or a crank.' She sagged a little, ran a hand across her face. 'The guy from the woods – he was following me again, over by Queen's Quay. Chased him down Ksenofontova Avenue, but he cut through a meat-processing plant and got away.'

The Dunk's face pinched in around pursed lips. 'Bit weird. I mean, if you're a journalist after a story, why do a runner? Why not just ask for a quote, or, you know, offer a bribe for info, or something?'

'Thought we would've caught him on their CCTV, but all the sodding cameras were dummies. What use is that?'

'Unless he's not a journalist at all, and you were right the first time . . .' A frown. 'Thing is, Sarge, why would the Bloodsmith be following you? Is that not *way* too dangerous for him?'

True.

'Mind you' – the Dunk's eyes widened – 'what if he's scouting you out to be his next victim?'

'Yeah . . . Now I hear someone else say it, it does sound batwank crazy.' She pocketed her keys. 'Probably just some sort of pervert stalker.'

'Then we should *definitely* tell the boss. Never know what someone like that will get up to.' He hooked a thumb over his shoulder. 'Can do it now, if you like? It's only ten minutes till shift's over anyway; think we deserve a gentle wee coast till home time.'

'You still got that pool car?'

'Crap.' He slumped. 'I should've legged it while I had the chance.'

Yup. But it was too late now.

The pool car's radio popped and hissed as Lucy set it searching for something other than crappy boy-band pop music, finally clicking onto a woman's voice, doing her best to sound as if she didn't come from Kingsmeath. And failing. '*. . . bringing the death toll to eighteen, with more* *expected in the next few days.'* Pronouncing every word as if it was in a foreign language.

'God, I *hate* rush hour.' The Dunk eased their car forwards another length, keeping them an over-cautious four feet behind the Ford Fiesta in front, crawling along Kingside Drive in a queue of stop-start traffic that stretched all the way back across Dundas Bridge and halfway around Castle Hill.

'French police have shut all roads in and out of Avignon.'

'Mmm . . .' Lucy turned the page of the next report.

'Jason Spiers, CEO of biotech firm BoltronVitica International, has been cleared of murdering his mistress, TV presenter Chelsea Lipinski, at the High Court this afternoon.'

Adam Holmes, thirty-two, unemployed project manager. Got laid off from his job at an IT company a year and a half ago.

'Ms Lipinski, a former semi finalist on Strictly Come Dancing, *was dis covered in woods near her home, after being battered to death.'*

'I bet he did it.' The Dunk crept the pool car closer to the roundabout, keeping that four-foot buffer zone between them and the Fiesta.

The 'before' photo showed a slightly chubby bloke with a freckled forehead and dirty-blond hair in need of a trim. Round glasses. Serious face. Holding a hot dog in both hands as if it were an award of some sort that he'd never wanted to win. Heavy on the onion and ketchup.

A man's voice boomed out of the car speakers. One of those posh Scottish accents that dripped with wealth and pomposity. *'While I'm glad that the courts have finally thrown out this ridiculous case, I am deeply angered that the police have failed to make any progress in catching the monster that killed Chelsea.'*

'Oh, he *definitely* did it.' The Dunk drummed his fingers on the steering wheel. 'These rich bastards get away with everything.'

'My thoughts and prayers are with her family at this difficult time.'

The 'after' photo looked like a nightmare in dissecting class. Adam, stripped naked and flat on his back in a small family bathroom, head forced to one side by the toilet pedestal, left arm pressed to his body by the bath. Legs stretched out straight. Right arm bent at the elbow, the open hand thrown back, showing the deep wound across his wrist. Split from groin to throat and emptied out onto tiles that weren't black and white any more. The words 'HELP ME!' were reflected in the medicine cabinet's mirrored doors, above the sink, just over the shoulder of the blurry white figure in an SOC suit who'd taken the picture. As if they'd been snapping a macabre bathroom selfie for the world's most ghoulish social media platform.

Lucy turned the photograph over as something sharp burned at the base of her throat. She swallowed. Cracked the passenger window open an inch, letting in the fug of rush-hour fumes.

'Feeling OK?' The Dunk was staring at her, as if she was an injured puppy. 'I get all queasy reading in the car too.'

She nodded. 'Never better.'

'There was more criticism of Paul Rhynie at PMQs this afternoon, with the leaders of the Opposition, SNP, and Green Party all demanding answers to allegations the Business Secretary has awarded hundreds of millions of pounds' worth of government contracts to—'

'It'll be better when we get past Tranton Roundabout. Half these idiots will be cutting up Burns Road to the Parkway.'

'—without proper tendering processes, transparency, reporting, or penalty clauses.'

Lucy returned Adam Holmes' file to the folder. 'Why do you think he does it?'

'What, Rhynie? Cos all these politician bastards watched Donald Trump get away with bloody murder for four years, and they think, "If he can do it"—'

'Not the Business Secretary, the Bloodsmith.'

'. . . Prime Minister's complete support. Racing news and there's been a huge upset at Uttoxeter as long shot Mellbell Bing-Bong won the Alanna Knight Memorial Handicap Hurdles at one hundred and fifty to one—'

'Shut up.' Lucy turned off the radio. 'Can't hear myself think.'

'Why he cuts them open?'

'No. He does that to get the hearts. Why—'

'Yeah, but he doesn't have to make such a big production out of it, does he?' The Dunk shrugged and inched them closer to the round-about. Only three cars to go. A frown. 'Hold on, are we pretending we don't know about Jane Cooper and Craig Thorburn yet? Because if we're going to be all "fresh pair of eyes" about it, like the boss wants, we maybe should stick to the victims we'd know about if Adam Holmes had just died, instead of all the victims we actually *do* know about?'

'Did that make more sense when it was still inside your head?'

'Do you want to be fresh eyes, or don't you?'

A massive sigh huffed its way out of her. 'Fine, we'll be "fresh eyes".'

'You're in charge – I'm only asking.' The car grumbled forward one more length. 'No need to be sarky.'

A gaggle of teenagers skipped across the road, slipping between the slow-moving traffic. All spots and elbows and leggings with the knees ripped out of them.

The driver's window of the Fiesta buzzed down and a scrunched-up crisp packet sailed out into the sunshine. One of the teenagers snatched it up off the tarmac and bunged the packet back through the window. Following it up with what looked like a few choice mouthfuls of foul language and some rude hand gestures.

Good for her.

Still nothing from the Dunk, though.

'Stop sulking. I *said* we'll be "fresh eyes", OK?'

'OK.' Big squint-toothed smile. 'So, it's September last year and the Bloodsmith's on victim number three. He's had practice, right? He's done it twice already: he *knows* where the heart is. So how come he guts Adam Holmes like a kipper to get it? Took a chunk of liver away with him, too.'

True.

'What did the forensic psychologist say?'

'Can't remember. Something rambling and unpunctuated, probably.' They'd finally made it as far as the roundabout, and the Dunk wheeched them straight across, joining the queue of traffic on the other side. 'And you see the cut on the wrist? With Bruce Malloch he nearly took the hand clean off, would've been blood everywhere, like a fire hose, but look at the blood in the Adam Holmes crime-scene photos: it's not all up the walls, right?'

Lucy slumped back in her seat and groaned. 'We already *know* this, Dunk. By the time he kills Jane Cooper he's—'

'He's not killed her yet, remember? That doesn't happen till . . .' creases bunched up between the Dunk's eyebrows as that steam-powered brain of his tried to get the pistons moving, 'January next year. Four months from now.'

'Seriously?' Lucy puffed out her cheeks. 'This is a daft game; we can't just forget everything we know about the Bloodsmith.'

'Hey, it's your rule, remember? Thirty-nine: "Shake things up"?'

Might as well humour him.

Lucy pulled out the picture and risked another look.

The bathroom's tiled floor was *smeared* with blood, rather than drenched in it like Bruce Malloch's home office. And it looked as if it'd come from the bits that'd been emptied out of Adam Holmes – lying there in slippery sticky mounds . . .

Swallow it down.

Breathe.

There was blood in the bath, too. Arcing lines and little red dots. Because he'd got better at harvesting it. Not wasting so much. Learning on the job.

Her stomach lurched.

OK, that was more than enough.

Lucy put the photo away before her tartiflette made a guest appearance all over the dashboard. 'The papers are saying he's smarter than we are.'

'Not yet they aren't. They don't start printing that crap till October.'

'Seventeen months, Dunk, and we've got nothing but a bunch of dead bodies.'

Maybe the papers were right.

8

'Bit crappy, isn't it?' The Dunk locked their pool car and curled his lip at the small block of flats that blighted Ditchburn Road. Everything else was built in the local sandstone – nice homes with nice gardens, bay windows, two point four children, and a roses-round-the-door kind of feel. But Ruthkopf House was a four-storey abomination, clad in a mix of yellow panelling and strips of blackened wood. Like a massive Rubik's cube that'd gone horribly wrong. With a car park out front.

Lucy handed him the Operation Maypole folder on the way past. 'Flat Three F.' Then pushed into a small reception area.

Had to hand it to the developers: just because it looked ugly on the outside, didn't mean it couldn't look ugly on the inside as well. They'd gone for the sort of 'minimalist' approach that meant slapping a coat of garish paint on the bare walls and pretending that made the building stylish, rather than a nasty concrete warren stuffed full of as many flats as they could legally get away with.

The stairwell rang to the sound of Lucy's bootheels, all the way up to the top floor, while the Dunk puffed and panted along behind her.

Flat 3F was down a short corridor, the magenta door and lime-green walls fighting against each other in a headache-inducing contrast. A small plastic plaque was fixed to the doorframe: 'MR & MRS MYERS'.

Lucy knocked.

Waited, while the Dunk leaned against the wall – huffing and puffing, as if he was expecting one of the Three Little Pigs to answer the door.

Instead, it was an equally pink-faced man with a screaming baby cradled half over his shoulder, patting it on the back as it howled. He had a fairly impressive set of bags under his watery bloodshot eyes. 'What?' Not sounding all that welcoming.

Lucy checked the plaque again. 'Mr Myers?' Then pulled out her warrant card. 'Police. Can we come in, please?'

His mouth clenched like a fist. 'If this is about that wanker in Two G: he's lying. I never touched his bloody Majestic Wines delivery, *or* his Amazon parcels. He's the one you should be harassing, with his loud bloody parties at all hours!'

She put her card away. 'It's OK, we're not here about your neighbour, we're here about Adam Holmes.'

That got Lucy a blank look. 'Who's Adam Holmes?'

The Dunk pulled his chin in, doubling it. 'You're kidding, right? Adam Holmes? He lived here? In this flat?'

Still nothing.

'The Bloodsmith's third victim? He died in your bathroom, mate.'

Those watery pink eyes widened. 'He *what?*'

Lucy patted him on his unbabied shoulder. 'Probably best if we come in. You might want to sit down for this.'

The flat's bathroom was even smaller in real life. Only just wide enough to squeeze in a toilet and corner sink. Didn't even have a full-sized bath – you'd have your knees up around your ears if you tried lying down in it. The black-and-white tiles were still there, though it must've been hell getting all that blood out of the grout.

Lucy and the Dunk stood in the bathroom doorway while Mr Myers stomped around the living room, with his screaming baby over one shoulder and his mobile clamped to his other ear. Voice raised to shouting level, trying to compete with the screeching cries, *'NO, I'M NOT KIDDING, KAREN, THE POLICE ARE HERE RIGHT NOW. SOMEONE DIED IN OUR FLAT!'*

The Dunk held up the crime-scene photo. 'Right: it's a year ago, remember?'

'ACTUALLY, SCRATCH THAT. HE DIDN'T "DIE", HE WAS MURDERED!'

'Don't think it was this noisy last year, or someone would've reported it sooner.'

'YOU HEARD RIGHT, KAREN: MURDERED!'

'Come on, Sarge, focus.' He lined the photo up with the actual bathroom. 'We don't really know what happened with Abby Geddes, but Bruce Malloch was a complete mess. Blood everywhere. So, our boy tries something new.'

'NO, THE BASTARDS DIDN'T SAY ANYTHING ABOUT IT WHEN THEY SHOWED US THE FLAT. WE'RE RENTING A MURDER SCENE! I BET WE DIDN'T EVEN GET A DISCOUNT.'

'See?' The Dunk pointed at the body. 'This time he makes a precision cut in Adam Holmes' wrist. And does it over the bath, too. Much neater job.'

'OH, DON'T YOU WORRY; SOON AS THE POLICE SOD OFF, I'M GOING RIGHT OVER THERE AND TEARING A STRIP OFF THOSE LYING MONEY-GRABBING SCUMBAGS!'

'Still . . . it wouldn't be easy, getting all that blood into jars.' Hard not to imagine how horrible that would be – holding onto Adam's wrist while it pumped out every last drop it could, spattering across the white plastic bathtub.

A shrug. 'Maybe he used a funnel?'

'I WANT AT LEAST THIRTY PERCENT OFF THE RENT, BACKDATED TO WHEN WE MOVED IN!'

'Pathologist's report?'

'Hold on.' The Dunk dipped back into the folder. 'Right: this time it's two blows to the back of the head. Then death by something called "exsanguination". What the hell's—'

'He bled to death.'

'Well, why not just say so, then? Pathologists always got to show off, don't they?'

'WHAT?'

He went back to the report. 'Yeah, so basically Adam Holmes was *definitely* gutted after death. The heart was removed from the scene, as is our boy's wont, and then there's that six-inch chunk of liver he made off with.' The Dunk pulled a face. 'Reckon he's done a Hannibal Lecter?'

'THEY CAN'T EVICT US FOR COMPLAINING ABOUT SOMEONE GETTING HIS INSIDES RIPPED OUT IN OUR BATHROOM! HOW COULD THAT POSSIBLY BE LEGAL?'

'Hope not.'

'THEY SHOULD'VE TOLD US, IS ALL I'M SAYING, KAREN!'

He produced another sheet of paper. 'Want the psychological profile?'

'FOR CHRIST'S SAKE, CAN YOU NOT JUST SUPPORT ME FOR ONCE?'

Lucy turned her back on the bathroom. 'Can you imagine living somewhere like this?'

The Dunk did the same. 'Not exactly palatial, is it?'

'NO, KAREN, I KNOW YOU PAY "ALL THE BILLS", BUT I'M THE ONE STUCK AT HOME LOOKING AFTER BOSTON ALL DAY! I'M THE ONE SACRIFICING HIS CAREER!'

Two tiny bedrooms, a toy-sized bathroom, and a kitchen-living room that you couldn't swing a hamster in, never mind a cat. And it probably cost a fortune too, because let's face it, people in Castleview had more money than sense. Could rent somewhere twice the size in Blackwall Hill for the same price. Or buy a whole house in Kingsmeath. Mind you, then you'd have to live in Kingsmeath, and that wasn't exactly—

'Sarge?'

'Hmmm?'

'I WAS ON THE FAST TRACK FOR PROMOTION, KAREN!'

'Want to leave them to it?' The Dunk hooked a thumb towards the front door.

Definitely.

Sunlight kissed the buildings on either side of Ruthkopf House with gold, but left the block of flats as lumpen and ugly as ever.

The Dunk unlocked their pool car. 'Where now? And, in case you're worried, I definitely *won't* be disappointed if you say we're done for the day. Because it's after six. And we've got two more crime scenes to go, so we might as well do them tomorrow or we'll be here till midnight. And everyone else is off to the pub for Stan the Man's birthday.'

'He knows them, Dunk. The Bloodsmith knows them.'

'Sure?'

'He kills them in their own homes – he needs access to do that. Bruce Malloch in his home office, Adam Holmes in his miserly little bathroom. That's not stranger territory, that's someone you know.'

The Dunk leaned against the car roof. 'Maybe not. I come over to your house, and suppose I'm dressed up like a BT engineer, or a plumber or something.' Dropping into a mockney accent for, '"'Ello, guvnor, I'm 'ere cos we've 'ad complaints about the broadband being slow. Take us to yer router and I'll sort it aaart." Or, "'Ere, the building's owners are finally doing something about the crap water pressure, 'ow 'bout showin' us yer stopcock, darlin'?"' Then he mimed smashing someone over the head with a hammer.

Lucy made a see-saw motion with her hand. 'Risky. What if the potential victim wants to check your ID?'

'Ah . . .' His face scrunched up for a bit. 'Yeah, but it wouldn't be the first time, would it? Remember Eric Ratcliffe? Used to dress up as a council sewage guy and con his way into people's houses with that "there's been a cock-up at the pumping station and people are getting blowback off the effluent line" routine. How many women did he rape before we caught him? Six? Seven?'

'Nine.'

The Dunk b01nked his palm against the roof. 'There you go, then.'

Suppose . . . But it raised the unwelcome prospect that the Bloodsmith wasn't targeting his victims: he was picking them at random based on who was prepared to answer the door and let him inside. And that made him a *lot* more difficult to catch. But if he was working to a plan there might be something that connected the victims. Something that could be used to work out how these five poor sods came into contact with him. Something that could help catch the bastard.

Because God knew they needed all the help they could get.

The building's front door banged open and out strode Mr Myers, screaming child strapped to his chest in some sort of tartan papoose. 'OH NO, MR MCCREADIE, I'M COMING OVER THERE RIGHT NOW, AND YOU *WILL* BE THERE!' Stomping across the car park and off in the direction of MacMillan Road.

Yeah . . .

Lucy hauled open the passenger door. 'Back to DHQ. We're done for the night.'

'What are you still doing here?' DI Tudor leaned on Lucy's desk, brushing that floppy fringe out of his eyes with one hand. Probably thought he looked irresistible when he did it.

He was wrong.

Lucy pushed the ancient Police-Scotland-issue laptop away and rubbed at her eyes. 'Been working on an eFit of the tosser who's been following me. You recognize him?' Pointing at the screen.

A middle-aged face gazed back at them from the computer-generated image. It maybe wasn't the greatest likeness in the world – a bit of guess-work going on around the eyes and mouth – but it was the best she could do given he'd done a runner every time she'd spotted him.

'We're all off to the Bart. Stan's fiftieth, remember?'

'The Dunk thinks it might be a reporter, or a pervert, but I haven't seen the guy at any of the briefings.'

Tudor squinted at the image for a bit. 'Not ringing any bells.' He chewed his bottom lip. 'Lucy, you are taking *precautions*, aren't you? I know it can't be easy, being followed by a strange man, after . . . what happened.' He reached out and squeezed her shoulder. Held it there just a little too long.

She looked at his hand. 'Boss, are we having a "Me Too" moment?'

'No.' Snatching it back, as if it'd been scalded.

Better.

Now: change the subject before he really got going about Neil Sodding Black.

'How's Superintendent Spence and DCI Ross doing?'

'Don't, OK?' Tudor retreated a good six feet and leaned against a different desk, putting some safe space between them, but trying to make it look casual. 'They were all over us till they realized the new "help me" wasn't the massive breakthrough they'd thought it was. Why hang around for the hard work if a result isn't about to land, gift-wrapped, smack bang into their sodding laps?' Folding his arms and scowling at the nearest whiteboard. 'Bastards.'

At least if Tudor was feeling sorry for himself he was too busy to aim his corrosive sympathy in her direction. Still, it probably wasn't fair to leave him wallowing in it.

Lucy sent the eFit she'd been working on to the printer, then logged off and shut down her laptop. 'On the plus side, we're actually making progress. That's something, right?'

'Erm, Lucy . . .' Tudor picked at the desk with a bitten fingernail.

Oh God, it was Me Too time again. 'Actually, Boss, I'm—'

'It's just, if someone *is* following you, we can't rule out that it *might* be the Bloodsmith. And I don't like members of my team being put at risk.'

He dug into a pocket. 'Got this for you.' Then placed a cardboard box, about the same size as a cigarette packet, on the desk in front of her.

What if it was jewellery? Or something else inappropriate?

She didn't move.

'Well? Open it.'

Sodding hell. It *better* not be jewellery.

Lucy took a deep breath, picked the box up, and opened the thing. Blinked at what Detective Inspector Tudor had given her: a metal cylinder, about the length of her thumb, with a bright-red plastic top. Oh, God, was it a *vibrator*? 'Are you—'

'It's a rape alarm.' Then his cheeks flushed deep pink. 'Sorry. Didn't mean to . . .' Tudor cleared his throat. 'It's a personal-safety alarm. Normally they're about one-twenty, one-thirty decibels, this is one hundred and *fifty*. Got it from that dodgy high-tech shop in the Tollgate. And it's mono-directional – so you point the red bit at your assailant, pull the pin, and boom: loud enough to cause some serious pain. And possible permanent hearing loss.'

How romantic.

'Thanks, Boss.' She put it back in its box, then dumped it in her desk drawer.

'Just keep it on you at all times, OK? Unless you'd like me to assign you a babysitter, twenty-four seven?'

'Urgh . . . Fine.' Lucy took the alarm out of its box again and slipped it into the inside pocket of her overcoat.

'Good. Now: pub.'

'Actually, Boss, I'm just going to head home: soak in the tub.' She picked up the printout, then pulled on her overcoat. 'Been a long day.'

He stood there, head on one side, staring at her like a concerned parent. 'Are you *sure* you're OK?'

'I'm fine.'

He was doing the sad-puppy-dog eyes now. 'Lucy, it's—'

'All right, all right: *one* drink.' Turning on her heel and marching off.

But the first person who brought up Neil Black was getting punched in the throat.

The Dumbarton Arms was reasonably busy, for a change. In addition to the Operation Maypole team, a whole bunch of OAPs had taken up residence and were now busy getting tanked into happy-hour booze while a balding ponytailed freak set up the speakers, screens, and microphones on the little stage at the back.

The oldies avoided the far corner, where Lucy's fellow officers had made camp. Which was pretty sensible: crowds of off duty police could get a bit . . . *enthusiastic* with a drink in them. Every single member of Tudor's team was there, clustered into the booths, necking pints, talking far too loud, eating crisps, and slapping Detective Constable Stan Talladale on the back.

A cheery banner hung across the back wall, between the toilets: 'WEDNESDAY NIGHT IS KARAOKE NIGHT!' above '3 FOR 2 ON DRINKS* FOR SINGERS!!!' Because what wasn't to love about getting wankered and making a tit of yourself?

Hedgehog Dundee had a manky bar towel thrown over one shoulder, humming away to himself as he pulled yet another pint of Stella. Adding it to the collection lined up in front of Lucy. His long, straggly hair surrounded a bald patch the size of a dinner plate. Throw in a big round sweaty face, a manky goatee, sausage hands, and a physique that could best be described as 'lardy' – all wrapped up in a five-foot-two package of yuck – and he must've been beating the ladies off with a stick. 'May I just say that it's a pleasure to see you patronizing our establishment again, DS McVeigh.'

'And a white wine. Pinot Grigio, if you've got it; something that doesn't taste like drain cleaner, if you don't.' Not that it really mattered: she wasn't planning on actually drinking it.

'The usual, then.' He turned and plucked a large wine glass from the rack. 'I don't believe you've been in since . . . well, since that *thing* happened.'

Oh God, not Hedgehog as well.

She pulled her chin in. 'I don't—'

'I wanted you to know that everyone at the Dumbarton Arms was shocked and appalled when we heard what had transpired.' Filling the glass with a new bottle from the fridge. He placed it on the bar in front of her. 'This is a Domaine Rieflé-Landmann, Pinot Gris, Steinert, Grand Cru, Alsace, 2015. *Decanter* magazine rates it *very* highly. I ordered a bottle specially for when you came in next.' He held up a hand. 'On the house.'

She stared at the wine. Then at him.

Hedgehog stood there. Not moving. Not making a big thing of it.

And, technically, he hadn't used Neil Black's name, so maybe he didn't need punching in the throat.

Lucy licked her lips. Nodded. 'Thank you.'

Hedgehog nodded back. 'Bastard got what he deserved.'

Then why did it still hurt?

9

Lucy slipped her phone out and checked the time. Eight o'clock. A whole hour pretending she was into all this team-bonding bollocks: *surely* that was enough. No one could whinge if she left now.

That glass of Hedgehog's Pinot Gris sat untouched in front of her, joined by a forest of empty pint glasses, highballs, and tumblers that rattled like a crystal wind chime every time someone bumped against the table.

DI Tudor and Emma were up on the small stage, belting out an old Oasis number while a dozen members of Operation Maypole turned the little wooden dancefloor into an impromptu mosh pit – joining in on the chorus as the whole pub thrummed with the noise.

The Dunk was over by the bar, getting into it with a detective constable who looked as if someone had randomly applied Nair to a six-foot-tall baboon, leaving a bald head and Victorian set of moustache-and-mutton-chops behind. The pair of them leaning in close, jabbing fingers at each other's chests. Only the Dunk had to stand on his tiptoes to do it.

Should probably rescue him before she left.

Lucy emptied her wine into four or five of the abandoned glasses – just so Hedgehog wouldn't feel slighted that she hadn't drunk any of it – and slipped from the booth.

She waved at the birthday boy on the way past, but he was too busy wanging on about how much the final season of *Game of Thrones* 'sucked balls' to notice. Can't say she hadn't tried, though.

Whatever DC Johnson and the Dunk were arguing about, they shut up pretty sharpish as she approached. Forced on a pair of unconvincing smiles.

'SARGE.' Johnson had to bellow over a particularly rowdy bit of singing and stomping.

'STEVE. I NEED TO BORROW THE DUNK.' Then she grabbed her sidekick's elbow and steered him across the pub and out the door, into a blissfully quiet street, where the only noise was the ringing in her ears; every breath crisp and sharp, redolent with the scent of sizzling batter and vinegar that oozed out of Dougie's 'Famous' Chipper, just down the road; streetlights glowing warm yellow in the darkness.

'What can I do for you, Sarge?' He glanced back at the closed door, his face flushed and pinched. Then dug out his cigarettes, lighting one in his cupped hands and hissing out an angry cloud of jaundiced smoke.

'Just thought you needed a bit of a break from Steve Johnson, before you started throwing punches.'

'Johnson's a dick.'

'Massive. Want to tell me what you two were arguing about?'

'Nothing.' The Dunk pulled one shoulder up to his ear, then let it drop again. 'Just him being a dick. As per.' A sniff. 'You offski?'

'Been quite a day. Got a long hot bath and an ice-cold bottle of Pinot Grigio with my name on it.'

'OK.' His brow furrowed, mouth twitching behind pursed lips, as if he was wrestling with something in there. 'This guy who's been following you—'

'Don't worry about it. Can take care of myself, remember?' Then she dipped into her overcoat pocket and pulled out DI Tudor's rape alarm. 'Besides, the boss gave me this.'

'Good. Yeah. Right.' Nodding with each word. 'You're parked that way?' He pointed away down the road. 'Mind if I tag along for a bit? Johnson's getting on my tits and I figure a poke of chips and a walk will help.'

She loomed. 'I'm not some weak and feeble woman who needs protecting!'

'Yeah, I know that, Sarge. But Johnson's much bigger than me, and if I swing for him, he'll probably take my head off.'

Her old Kia Picanto scrunched onto the gravel driveway, headlights sweeping across the three houses on the other side of the road, leaving them in darkness as she killed the engine. Only three miles north of the city, but from here you wouldn't even know Oldcastle existed, if it wasn't for the dirty orange smear, reflected off the low clouds. The rest of it was hidden from view by Auld Dawson's Wood, lurking behind the homes opposite like a large dark beast. Its spines creaking and rustling in the wind.

Not that Ballrochie offered much to pounce on. A trio of farmworker's cottages, and the grieve's house – which merited a whole two storeys and a garage, because he'd been in charge and the lower classes needed to know their place.

Lucy grabbed her files from the back seat and let herself into the granite-and-sandstone status symbol. Locked the front door behind her and dumped her keys in a bowl on the sideboard. Hung her overcoat on its hook. 'Honey, I'm ho-ome.'

No answer, as usual.

She took off her boots and lined them up with the other pairs arranged on the rack in the hallway. Looked at the stranger in the mirror. Practised smiling at them, like her therapist always used to bang on about:

It's neuro-linguistic programming, Lucy . . . Smiling releases endorphins, even if you don't feel happy, Lucy . . . Smile and you'll trick your brain into feeling better, Lucy.

But then, like Detective Constable Steve Johnson, he'd always been a dick.

She gave one last rictus grimace a count of ten, then huffed out a breath. Sagged. And stomped off upstairs to change.

Her bedroom was smaller than Dad's, which didn't really make any sense. It was *her* house now: she could sleep wherever she liked. All she'd have to do was move his stuff out of the wardrobes and chest of drawers. Take it down the charity shop. Give the place a lick of paint. Buy some fresh bedding. Get herself a new mattress and pillows too. Easy.

Still, no point rushing these things.

Maybe after Christmas?

She swapped the work outfit for an old hoodie and pair of sweats. Turquoise Crocs rounded off the ensemble. Not exactly stylish, but who was going to see?

Next up: cup of tea.

Down in the kitchen, Lucy set the kettle boiling while she fished sliced white out of the bread bin. A bit stale, but it toasted up fine. Earl Grey, slice of lemon, toast with a smear of butter and Marmite. Crunching down on a darkly savoury mouthful as she wandered through into the living room, tea in one hand, files tucked under her other arm.

Twin couches sat on either side of the fireplace, their green leather looking a bit worn and shabby. A coffee table played host to a jar of markers and a carton of Post-its. The TV in the corner wasn't one of those modern flatscreen jobs, so a technical antique. And last but not least, the reason the curtains were always shut in here: her murder board.

The one back at DHQ was big, but nothing compared to this. It covered all four walls, stretching from just above the skirting boards to as high as she could reach by standing on a dining-room chair. Photos and notes and memos, crime scenes and post-mortems, transcripts and reports – all of it copied from the Operation Maypole files. And OK, DI Tudor would probably have a fit if he found out she'd taken all this stuff home, but at least she was trying, right? Sifting through the evidence, searching for whatever it was that'd been overlooked these last seventeen months. The thing that would identify the Bloodsmith . . .

She'd annotated everything with Post-it notes. Lots and lots of Post-it notes. Extra sticky ones, in every colour you could buy. Each one of them covered in dense splodges of handwriting.

There'd been a brief dalliance with red ribbons, making a spider's web between suspects and victims, like they did on TV and in the movies, but it was all a bit . . . melodramatic. That and it was a sod to move any piece without the whole thing unravelling. Ended up spending more time reweaving the red ribbon from point to point than analysing the evidence.

Victims took up the wall around the door, their 'before' photos in stark contrast to what the Bloodsmith had left behind – the crime-scene photos pinned up the wrong way around: images facing the wallpaper, so only their blank white backs were on show. Impact statements from their families were in the corner, each one treacly with remorse, and pain, and how loved the dead had been, even though most of them hadn't seen the victim for months.

Suspects were on the wall opposite, the fireplace making a dark-brown mouth in the middle. They'd all been interviewed, and they'd all been cleared.

Transcripts took up most of the wall facing the big bay window, while a forest of Post-its clustered on both sides of the closed dusty curtains. Theories, questions, thoughts.

And none of it had helped one single sodding bit.

Lucy settled onto the couch. *Her* couch. Not the one Dad always used – with the pinhole burns in the leather from those revolting cigars of his – but the one he'd reserved for her not-particularly-frequent visits.

Right. Just because the suspects arranged either side of the fireplace had been officially marked as 'no longer viable', that didn't mean she wasn't looking at the Bloodsmith right now. Because she *knew* she was.

'One of you bastards did it.'

Crunching her toast, sipping her tea.

The forensic psychologist's profiles might be breathless unpunctuated rambles, but the conclusions in all five of the reports – one for each victim – were the same. The Bloodsmith was a man, in his late twenties to early forties, with a vehicle, a position of responsibility, and no significant affection in his life.

Of course, that didn't mean he lived *alone*: he could be staying with an aged parent he had to care for, or trapped in a loveless marriage. Possibly because no decent human being could ever love a serial-killing piece of shit like him.

Which meant you couldn't rule out anyone based on that.

But if they had to have a 'position of responsibility', that eliminated seven of the suspects, leaving nineteen to deal with. Not much of an improvement, but it was a start.

What about the 'trying to establish an emotional connection by having a string of one-night stands' angle? Who would women sleep with, out of this lot?

Suppose that would depend on how drunk he got them.

Maybe six you'd take home with you, if you were in the mood. Another three would be possibles after a bottle of white. Two more, if you'd had a couple of gins before that, providing they had a good sense of humour.

And not a single one of them looked like the man she'd chased. Nor did any of the 'too ugly to shag' crowd.

Lucy finished her toast, wiped the crumbs off her fingertips, then rearranged the photos, putting her six potential killers in a row. Relegating the wannabes to a pile on the coffee table, pinned down with the fist-sized lump of blue-and-purple geode she'd got in a dead friend's will.

That left her with an architect, a self-employed accountant, a partner in a law firm, a junior doctor at CHI, a manager at the big Winslow's in Logansferry, and a member of the city council. Six potential killers, all with alibis for the nights the Bloodsmith's victims disappeared.

Need to go over all their statements and alibis again. Didn't matter that Angus and his team were already doing that – Angus meant well, but he couldn't think outside the box if you hacked his head off and chucked it in a vat of baked beans.

And she had one more suspect to add to the list.

Lucy headed back through to the hall, collected the printout of her eFit, and pinned it up with the other potential serial killers. Stepped back to frown at that slightly out-of-focus face. There was something . . . familiar about it. Not what you'd call classically handsome, but not *bad*-looking. There was maybe even something appealing about him, in a strange sort of way.

So definitely on the list.

Just a shame she had no clue who he was.

'Urgh . . .' Lucy rubbed at her gritty eyes till little orange and black spots burst behind her lids like fireworks. Yawned. Sagged. Sighed. Put her glasses back on. Took another swig of her fourth mug of tea. And squinted at the wall of victims.

They had to have *something* in common. But all five had gone to different schools; they didn't look anything alike; none of them worked in the same industry; they weren't the same sex; they hadn't belonged to the same clubs; they hadn't joined the same Facebook groups; they hadn't even followed the same people on Twitter.

She glanced over at the new eFit, gracing her suspects board. 'Why did you pick them? What was it about these poor sods that got you all hot and bothered?'

No reply.

OK, back to basics. Five victims: Abby Geddes, Bruce Malloch, Adam Holmes, Jane Cooper, and Craig Thorburn. Two women, three men. So, who said the Bloodsmith *had* to be male? Yes, statistically speaking, men were much more likely to murder other people, but that didn't mean women couldn't go on a homicidal rampage. As Oldcastle had proven over, and over, and over again.

Even the rambling forensic psychologist had hedged her bets on that one, hadn't she? All her profiles used the male pronoun when talking about the Bloodsmith, but she'd left herself a big chunk of wriggle room with 'Killer is most likely an IC-One male . . .' And 'most likely' wasn't the same as 'definitely'. So, why *not* a woman?

A smile spread across Lucy's face, followed by another jaw-cracking yawn.

Tomorrow, soon as Morning Prayers were over, she'd nab a HOLMES terminal and go through the actions: see if there was someone knocking about in the background who might be a good fit. With a bit of luck, if she came up with a viable suspect, there'd be no need to go schlepping around the last three crime scenes – she'd be off solving the case instead.

Lucy blinked.

Two.

Two crime scenes. Not three.

Yeah . . . She peered at her watch – nearly midnight.

No wonder she was too knackered to think straight.

Time for a quick soak in a lovely hot bath, and then bed.

It was going to be a big day tomorrow.

— tell me about your childhood —

IO

Lucy leaned back against the worktop, crunching her way through breakfast – toast slathered in butter, mashed banana, and salt – washed down with a big mug of black coffee. Outside the kitchen window, a pair of coal tits squabbled over the bird feeder, a cock pheasant strutting about on the frost-crisped grass beneath it, like a vile priest in his dog collar waiting for scraps from above. The sky: a lid of pale grey, bruised with darker clouds. All to the soundtrack of crappy pop music, crackling out of a radio that was almost as old as Dad's Neolithic toaster.

The awful song jangled to a halt, only to be replaced by some OTT idiot doing their best to sound like the world *wasn't* a lonely, miserable, and brutal place on a cold September morning. *'Hey, hey, hey! That was Mister Bones, and "Angela's Calling Me". What did I tell you, folks? It's a smasharoooooonie!'* Comedy honking noise. *'You're listening to Castle-wave FM, you lucky people; this is* Sensational Steve's Breakfast Drivetime Bo-nan-za; *it's seven o'clock and here's Gorgeous Gabby with the Naughty News!'*

Why was it that the world's biggest dicks were always so immeasurably proud of their dickishness and so keen to share it?

'Thanks, Steve. Westminster, first, and the Home Secretary has defended his handling of the latest migrant crisis as eighteen people are found dead, washed up on the Kent coast . . .'

Had to admit, the prospect of spending a couple of hours wading through the Home Office Large Major Enquiry System, looking for potential female suspects, wasn't exactly appealing. Might be an idea to draft in a bit of help. Spread the misery.

'. . . *facing prosecution. Polls have now opened for the hotly contested by-election for Thanet South, but the England-First National Party candidate, Rebecca Hughes, claims the vote's been "rigged" by "lefties and foreigners". Miss Hughes was expelled from the Conservative Party last year following a series of controversial tweets . . .'*

Lucy unplugged her phone from its charger and texted the Dunk:

> You like computers, don't you?
> How do you fancy a bit of IT shenanigans after Morning Prayers?

SEND.

After all, what was the point of having a minion if you didn't get them to do the boring bits?

'. . . *more allegations in the* Guardian *claim embattled Business Secretary, Puul Rhynle, has been having an affair with a member of the Russian embassy staff for over three years . . .'*

Anyway: time for teeth, then better get a shift on if she was going to make it into the office before rush hour kicked in.

'. . . *statement saying Mr Rhynie had the Prime Minister's complete support. The search continues today for Antonia Taylor. The eighty-two-year-old was last seen in Aberdeen on Sunday—'*

Lucy clicked the radio off. Did her teeth in record time. And was out the door in five minutes flat. Waterproof jacket today, boots, and a faded blue Oldcastle Warriors scarf that still carried the burnt-leather ghost of old cigars. She locked the door behind her, turned and . . . froze.

Stood there, on the gravel driveway, staring at her car.

'BASTARD!'

All four tyres were flat. Not just flat, *slashed*. And whoever had done it, they'd drawn a smiley face in the frost covering her windscreen too.

'AAAAAAAAAAAAAAARGH!'

Wait a minute . . . The smiley face – it hadn't iced over yet; the lines were still shiny and dark. Dripping at the edges of its mocking mouth and wide dot eyes. It was still fresh.

She clenched her fists. 'WHERE ARE YOU?' Turning slowly. 'COME ON, THEN! YOU WANT SOME OF THIS?' Thumping herself in the chest, like a silverback. 'DO YOU?'

The three cottages across the road still lay in darkness, curtains shut against the early-morning light. Auld Dawson's Wood looming behind them in all its malevolent glory. Nothing but the sound of magpies shrieking at each other.

'OH, YOU'RE A BIG MAN HIDING IN THE SHADOWS, AREN'T YOU?'

She stomped out onto the frost-paled tarmac, breath puffing out in angry misted lungfuls.

'WHERE ARE you . . .'

A man stood in the middle of the road, about two hundred feet away, just past the last cottage. Next to a red-and-white Mini, its pale exhaust pluming out into the cold morning air.

He wasn't doing anything. Just standing there. Arms hanging by his sides. Motionless.

It was the same supply-teacher-looking bastard she'd chased yesterday. Tall, thin, big forehead, beard, small round glasses, chinos looking crisp and freshly ironed beneath the corduroy jacket.

He raised one hand in a small wave, showing off his purple nitrile glove, then turned and squeezed himself in behind the wheel of the idling Mini.

'COME BACK HERE!' Lucy broke into a run, heels clacking, the drumbeat getting faster as she picked up speed.

But she got nowhere near. The Mini's engine growled and the wee car pulled away, leaving her in a cloud of bitter grey exhaust. Couldn't even get the number plate – he'd done something to it, making the registration unreadable. Probably smeared it with mud.

'AAAAARGH!' She slowed to a jog, then a walk, then stopped, right where the car had sat – twin black lines in the frost that faded away until there was no sign left he'd ever been there.

'Well, I don't know, do I?' Lucy hunched her shoulders as the van rattled its way across a cattle grid, setting all the dashboard trim vibrating. Engine sounding like someone had trapped half a million wasps in a washing machine on spin cycle, then chucked in a brick. 'Took me half an hour just to get this bloody thing started.'

The Dunk's voice was barely audible over the racket, even though her phone was turned up full pelt, wedged in between the steering wheel and the instrument panel. '*Yeah, but your tyres? Sarge, you live in the middle of Arse-Munch Nowhere, who the hell would go all the way out there to—*'

'Just tell Tudor I'm going to be late.'

The van grumbled its way up the hill, getting slower and slower, because Dad couldn't have bought himself a *decent* van, like a Ford Transit, or a Peugeot Boxer, or even a sodding Renault Kangoo, could he? No. *It's distinctive, Lucy . . . People smile when they see it, Lucy . . . There's nothing wrong with a Bedford Rascal, Lucy.* Take a wardrobe, paint it bright fuchsia, shove it over onto its side, then slap on four wheels, a windscreen, a sign saying, 'MCVEIGH & MCVEIGH ~ ARTISANAL BUTCHERS', add some happy, dancing, cartoon meat products, and that was her dad's Bedford Rascal.

'You get a good look at whoever did it?'

'Same dick who was following me yesterday.'

'Oooh, that's not good. If he's a stalker and he's been to your house—'

'Dunk, I can barely hear you. Tell DI Tudor I'll be there quick as I can.' Assuming the stupid van didn't fall apart before then.

It was hard to tell what was more worrying: that the guy who'd slashed her tyres had been following her for most of yesterday, or that he knew where she lived. Actually, no, it was definitely the latter. And there was no way he was doing all this for wholesome reasons.

First he slashes her tyres; what came next – her throat?

Well, he was in for a bloody shock if he tried.

Lucy drove through Blackwall Hill, then along Keirbarrie Drive – following the river west as a misty drizzle speckled the windscreen. Trying not to make eye contact with other drivers or pedestrians whenever she had to stop for traffic lights, because there was only so much humiliation one person could take in a morning.

Might not be a bad idea to get an alarm system fitted. Something with motion sensors. And maybe stop past the Argos on St Jasper's Lane and get herself a baseball bat.

She'd almost made it as far as Dundas Bridge when her phone launched into its ringtone and 'THE DUNK' appeared on the screen.

'God's sake.' She poked the green button. 'I'm going as fast as I can!'

He was almost shouting, the noise of a siren wailing in the background. *'CHANGE OF PLAN, SARGE, MORNING PRAYERS IS CANCELLED. IT'S THE BLOODSMITH: THEY'VE FOUND ANOTHER BODY. WE'RE ON OUR WAY NOW.'*

She sat up straight, seatbelt tight across her chest. 'Where?'

*

The Bedford Rascal lurched from side to side as it crawled along, every pothole rattling the suspension so hard it felt as if the ridiculous thing was about to tip over at any second. Trees crowded in on both sides, their branches intertwining, leaves overlapping, turning the rutted track into a tunnel.

A patrol car blocked the track ahead, parked sideways to make sure no one could get past, its blue-and-whites turned soft-focus in the drizzle as they swept across the trees. On the other side of it a couple of big police vans sat empty, squeezed onto the grass verge, along with a handful of unmarked vehicles, another two patrol cars, a Range Rover, and an SOC Transit.

As Lucy pulled up, a uniform emerged from the driver's seat of the patrol-car blockade, pulled on his peaked cap, and glowered his way over – one hand held up, palm outward to stop her.

'HOY, YOU! OUT OF IT!'

Lucy had to manually wind down her window, like an animal. 'Don't be an idiot, Tim.'

He lowered his arm, and a hideous smile broke across his lopsided face; crooked nose and uneven ears going pink in the cold. 'Morning, Sarge. What – and I mean this with the utmost respect – the living *hell* are you driving?'

'Where's DI Tudor?'

'Only, you know, all pink and rectangular like that, it looks a bit like Frankenstein's cock.'

'Frankenstein made monsters, not penises.'

That horrible smile widened. 'You've not read my erotic fanfic, Sarge. I'll email you a copy.'

'*Please* don't. Now: where's the boss?'

Tim hooked a thumb over his shoulder. 'Crappy wee cottage, thataway. Be warned, though, he's got the new Procurator Fiscal with him.'

Urgh.

Lucy struggled the window back up again, then climbed out into the drizzle. Pulled her hood up. 'Keys are in the ignition, if you need to shift it.'

'No offence, but I wouldn't be seen dead driving that.'

She squeezed her way past the knot of police vehicles; nodded at a pair of constables having a sly fag in the undergrowth, out of the rain; and followed the sound of voices to a forward operations centre – a boxy white caravan, sitting on its own, where a handful of uniforms were struggling their way into white SOC suits.

'Sarge.' PC Hill zipped himself up, then dug about at his crotch. Face still sporting a half-dozen-teenagers' worth of yellow-headed plukes. 'You joining the search team?'

'Looking for DI Tudor.'

'In there: Grandma's Cottage,' nodding towards a grey outline, about sixty feet away, just visible between the closely packed trees. Twin lines of 'POLICE' tape stretched from this side of the track towards it, marking out the common approach path. 'Better watch, though, he's got Spudzilla with him.'

'Yeah, Tim said.' Lucy helped herself to a suit from the box. Peeled it out of its plastic wrapping before performing the ungainly and undignified dance needed to pull the thing on over her boots and clothes without falling over.

The others got their masks and goggles on, then grabbed gloves and disappeared into the woods while she finished dressing. Double-gloving it, just in case. Taking a pair of blue plastic booties for later. Then followed the common approach path in beneath the canopy of pine and beech. Boots scrunching through fallen needles and decaying leaves. Kicking up that garden-centre-compost scent.

There wasn't much left of the building: two storeys of crumbling masonry not much wider than a double garage; the roof half caved in; no glass in any of the windows, just rotting outlines where the frames used to be. Looked as if a strong sneeze would bring the whole thing down.

Wasn't much of a clearing, either. The trees huddled close to the bulging stonework, three white-suited figures rustling about on their hands and knees as they picked through the loam.

Lucy signed into the crime scene, then leaned on the sagging wall by the door to pull on her booties. Stepped inside.

The cottage where Abby Geddes died might have been a dump, but it was the Ritz Carlton compared to this place. Most of the floor was gone, the walls hanging onto only the briefest scraps of mould-blackened plaster. Doors missing.

A little avalanche of cracked black slate spilled out from one of the downstairs rooms, and when she stuck her head in, drizzle drifted down through the gaping hole where the ceiling used to be. Leaving nothing but a two-storey void and a couple of crumbling joists between her and the ugly grey sky.

Yeah, sneezing *definitely* wasn't a good idea.

The other downstairs room must've had a bare earth floor, because now it was a sea of rosebay willowherb – the flowers drooping and pale. Raw stone walls. At least the roof was still intact on this side. Scuffed footsteps rattled down from overhead.

That would be their crime scene, then.

A narrow set of rickety stairs led upwards, towards the noise.

'Yeah, because that looks safe . . .'

Lucy picked her way up them to a small landing at the top with two doors leading off it. The one on the right was sealed off with a big X of yellow-and-black 'CRIME SCENE' tape, presumably to stop some idiot from walking through it and plummeting down onto the collapsed roof in the room below. The door on the other side opened with a haunted-house creak. Which was appropriate.

The unmistakeable, throat-clenching stench of rotting meat crawled out onto the landing.

'OK . . .'

Inside, three people in the full SOC get-up were standing around what was left of the man on the floor. One was taking photographs with a huge digital camera, its flash bright enough to sear the room onto the back of Lucy's skull. The other two had their heads together, the tall thin one having to bend down a fair bit to reach the short tubby one, voices little more than a murmur, as if they were worried about disturbing the dead.

And the body lying spreadeagled on the blackened floorboards was very, *very* dead.

Stripped naked and hollowed out. And going by what was left of his face, ears, toes, and fingers, the rats had been at him too.

Lucy huffed out a breath and turned her back on the remains.

There, on the wall beside the door she'd just come through, were the same two words they'd found with every dead body. 'HELP ME!' smeared in big, dark-brown, capital letters. So it was *definitely* their boy. The Bloodsmith. Nothing for five months, and now this.

'Where have you been since April . . . ?'

A sharp, posher-than-thou Morningside accent slashed through the foetid air. *'And what,* exactly, *do you think you're doing here? This is a* sealed crime scene!'

II

Lucy paused for a breath, pulled on a fake smile, and turned. 'Mrs Edwards.' A small nod. Then did the same to the other, taller figure in the SOC suit. 'DC Fraser said you wanted to see me, Boss?' Not *strictly* true, but the new PF didn't know that.

'Did he?' Tudor didn't sound convinced by her misquoting the Dunk, but he shrugged and went with it anyway. 'Oh. Right. Yes. I want you to put the crime-scene review on hold for now and get me everything you can on our victim.' Pointing at the remains.

'Yes, Boss. We got an ID?'

Mrs Edwards snorted behind her mask. 'Don't be ridiculous. Would DI Tudor need to ask you if he already knew who the victim was?' Frumpy, fat, stuck-up bitch. She placed a hand on Tudor's arm. 'Now, is there anything else you need to discuss with this *person*, Alasdair, or can we get back to work?'

Oh, it was 'Alasdair' now, was it? Add 'randy', 'hormonal', and 'deluded' to the list.

He visibly cringed. 'Sorry, Mrs Edwards. I need to go over an operational point with DS McVeigh.'

'Please, Alasdair, it's *Kim* to my friends.' Swear to God, she actually simpered a bit.

'Of course. Yes. "Kim".' Even covered from head to toe in PPE, Tudor looked creeped out. 'I'll just be a moment.' Then he marched from the room and out onto the tiny landing, beckoning for Lucy to follow.

She squeezed out after him and shut the door behind her.

Soon as she did, Tudor sagged against the wall, gloved hands covering his facemask and goggles, voice a low muttering growl. 'God, that woman is . . . challenging.'

'Not the word I would've chosen, Boss.'

'They couldn't have assigned us a reasonable Procurator Fiscal, could they? Course they couldn't.' He sagged even further. 'The Chief Super's barely been off the phone since we got here. Not to mention Superintendent Spence and DCI Ross crawling out of the woodwork like . . . rats. They couldn't wait to wash their hands of the whole thing yesterday, but now we've got a new body? Oh, *now* it's all "appropriate oversight", "high-level perspectives", and "watching briefs". Meanwhile muggins here will be neck-deep in the septic tank if it all goes wrong again.'

'Have we got anything for me to go on? Does our victim have any distinguishing features? Possessions?'

'You know, I had a "motivational" speech from Spence this morning that had me seriously thinking about going up to the castle and jumping.'

'Anything that would help at all?'

Tudor's head fell back to thunk against the old stonework. 'Still, look on the bright side, at least we've got another body. Maybe the Bloodsmith will have cocked up somewhere this time and we'll catch him?'

'Boss!'

'I know, I know.' He raised a hand, then let it flop down again. 'Can I not just enjoy one *teensy* little moan before I have to go back in there?'

She folded her arms, frowning at the closed door. 'Nothing for five months, now this. Thought the Bloodsmith was supposed to be escalating? Six months between his first two victims, five between the second and the third, then four, then three, and we're back to five again.' She tilted her head on one side, picturing the remains. 'Well, five minus however long he's been lying in there.'

'Maybe the Bloodsmith's been out of town?'

'Maybe. Or maybe he's bright enough to know he was getting out of control and reined himself in for a while? Can serial killers do that? Maybe that's why he's gone back to killing them in the woods? He's starting again.'

'No idea. Want to take it up with our behavioural psychologist?'

The one with the long rambling sentences? No thanks.

'Erm . . . I think it'll be better coming from you, Boss – what with you being in sole charge and everything. It'll carry more weight.' Quick, change the subject before he tries to pass the buck back again. 'I've been wondering about the fact we've been looking for a man this whole time. What if it's not?'

Tudor frowned off into the distance for a while. 'But the behavioural evidence analysis all says—'

'Yes, but it doesn't. It's all "he" this and "him" that, but nowhere does it actually say that the Bloodsmith's *definitely* one hundred percent male. I checked this morning.'

'Hmmmm . . . Worth a punt, I suppose. I'll get someone to look into it while you're identifying our latest victim. And before you whinge: no one's stealing your credit. Right now, my number-one priority is getting Procurator Fiscal Frisky off my back, ASA-frigging-P.'

Now it was Lucy's turn to sag. 'Yes, Boss.'

'I'll get Gail to send you any relevant pics, when she's finished taking them.' Tudor pointed down the stairs. 'Quick as you like.'

Lucy rolled her eyes, which probably wasn't all that effective through the safety goggles, then picked her way down the creaking wooden steps again.

Tudor's voice boomed out behind her. *'And see if you can chase up that bloody pathologist for me. Hairy Harry should've been here half an hour ago!'*

She kept her reply as quiet as possible as she stomped her way out of the tumbledown house. 'Yes, Boss. No, Boss. Anything you say, Boss.'

Tosser.

Back at the caravan, a huge man was hauling an XXXL white Tyvek suit on over jeans and a sweatshirt. He'd a bit of a tummy on him, but the rest looked completely solid, as if he'd been built out of breezeblocks. A bushy beard reached down to the middle of his chest, more salt than pepper. His hair was the same, held back in a thick grey ponytail. The kind of eyes that crinkled at the edges when he smiled. 'Well, well, well.' Those crow's feet deepened as Lucy took off her facemask and goggles.

She smiled back. 'Harrison.'

'If it isn't my favourite Detective Sergeant. How are you holding up?'

Not more bloody sympathy.

'DI Tudor's waiting not-so-patiently for you.' Hooking a thumb over her shoulder. 'And he's got our new PF with him.'

A shudder. 'Knew I should've let Teabag take this one.' Harrison tucked his beard into his suit and zipped it up. 'And tell me: the risible pink van thing, with "McVeigh and McVeigh" on the side. Is that . . . ?' Both eyebrows raised. 'Only I could do with half a pound of mince and some pork chops, if you're moonlighting. Mates' rates, as we're both in the meat trade?' The crow's feet were so deep now, his eyes had nearly disappeared.

Cheeky sod.

'Bye, Harrison.' She stomped off, drizzle misting her glasses as she made her way back to the clump of police vehicles.

The Dunk was lurking under a tree, by the side of the track, phone pressed to his ear as he puffed away on a cigarette. Who said men couldn't multitask? He looked up and grimaced at her, held a finger up. 'Yeah . . . OK . . . Yeah, right . . . Will do.' Then hung up. 'Sarge.' The Dunk ducked out from under the branches and joined her. 'Got a pair of uniforms giving your house a drive-by every couple of hours. They swept your car for fingerprints too; maybe we'll get lucky?'

'He was wearing gloves. I saw them.' The joys of living through a pandemic – every bugger had leftover PPE to commit crimes with.

'Oh.'

They scuffed their way past the roadblock patrol car.

Then the Dunk froze. Chin pulled in. Mouth pursed. A one-eyebrowed frown on his face as he blinked at her Bedford Rascal. 'Erm . . . Sarge?'

'Don't you start.' She unlocked it and climbed in behind the wheel. 'We've got a body to identify and sod all to go on.'

'Only, are those sausages doing what I think they're doing?'

'Dancing, Constable. Those sausages are *dancing*.'

'Because it looks like they're—'

'Well, they're not!'

He dug his hands deep into his jacket pockets, puffing away. 'Fair enough.'

'Do a missing-persons search: I need everyone added in the last' – going by the state of the body, the smell, and the unseasonably cold weather – 'month and a half? Male. Somewhere between five-nine and six-two. Thin. Brown hair, greying at the temples, side parting on the left.'

'Not a *great* deal of help.' The Dunk pulled out his notebook and scribbled that down. 'Eye colour?'

'Don't know, the rats got those.'

A full-body shudder curled him up for a moment. 'Fingerprints?'

'They got those too. We'll just have to do what we can, till the boss or Hairy Harry decide to tell us something useful.' She pointed off into the rain. 'Go. Work.'

'Sarge.' He tipped his leather bunnet, turned, and sauntered off into the rain.

There was nothing else she could do to ID their victim without more information, so might as well head back to DHQ and chase up a couple of things. Maybe it'd keep Tudor from sidelining her again?

Lucy parked the Bedford Rascal out of sight, on Guild Street, outside the boarded-up carpet warehouse, tucking it in between an overflowing skip and the rusting remains of a fifty-seater coach.

Bad enough she'd had to drive her dad's pink monstrosity to the crime scene this morning, without the added indignity of leaving it in the station car park for everyone to gawp and snigger at.

She worked her way around the van, locking each door individually – because why buy something with central locking, when you could make life difficult for yourself? – then froze, keys in the passenger door.

That feeling was back again. The pins and needles between her shoulder blades, as if someone was—

Lucy spun around, fists up . . .

But there was no one there. Just the road, curling away to the right, the tips of Camburn Woods just visible over the rooftops, lurking beneath the thick dove-grey lid of cloud as drizzle stole the colour from everything.

Could've *sworn* there was someone.

'Going a bit paranoid on me, are you, Lucy?' She pulled the key out and checked the doors were secure. 'Bad enough everyone thinking you're off your rocker without you confirming it.'

She stuck the keys in her pocket, pulled her hood up, and marched along the street, towards St Jasper's Lane.

'And while we're at it: stop talking to yourself. You sound like a crazy person.'

Yes, but it wasn't paranoia, was it? There definitely *was* someone following her. He'd even vandalized her car and hung around to take the credit. That wasn't paranoia, that was *fact*.

She sped up a bit, heels clacking on the concrete paving slabs.

What if he really *was* building up to something more serious? Starts with stalking her, moves on to slashing her tyres, and before you know it, he's . . .

Lucy pivoted on one foot, swinging around fast, ready to fight.

Stood there, breathing hard.

Rain dripped off the line of parked cars, their windscreens opaque in the drizzle. A small black cat, trotting across the tarmac, tail up. The grumble of passing traffic on the main road behind her.

Come on – it was broad daylight. Well, what passed for it at half eight on a miserable Thursday morning. No way he'd be arrogant enough to attack her here. Out in the open. So close to Divisional Headquarters.

She stood for a moment, watching the gaps between the cars, waiting for movement. But there was nothing.

Yeah.

Definitely going crazy.

Lucy strode up Peel Place, making for the ugly red-brick lump of DHQ.

No sign of the media yet. That'd change when they found out about the body in the woods. Then the hordes would descend with their cameras and microphones and shouted questions about how come O Division couldn't catch one little serial killer.

Someone had been at the war memorial opposite DHQ, and now each of the three soldiers, in their World War One kilts and bowl helmets, sported a rainbow-coloured knitted scarf around their cold bronze necks as they charged, bayonets fixed. It was weird, the things people did to—

'YOU, BITCH!' bellowed out from somewhere behind her.

Lucy stopped.

The sound of footsteps getting closer, faster, turning into a run.

She whirled around for the third time since locking the van, fists coming up. But not fast enough. A slab of pale flesh battered into her, hurling her off her feet and sending her booming into the side of a parked Transit. Lucy's head bounced off the liveried bodywork and the world filled with the sound of a church organ – all the keys and pedals being hammered down at once.

Hands grabbed at her raincoat's lapels, smashing her against the van again.

'YOU DIRTY, LYING, MURDERING BITCH!' It was a woman, mid-forties, greying brown hair pulled back in a vicious bun. Hard eyes, surrounded by creases, underlined with dark-purple bags. Skin pale, mottled, and lumpen – like spoiled milk. Little sharp teeth, bared in a snarl, spittle flying from wide lips. Sarah Black. 'YOU KILLED MY NEIL!'

Lucy pulled herself back against the Transit, away from the sprayzone. 'Get off me!'

A shout rang out from the other side of the road. *'HOY! WHATEVER YOU'RE DOING, CUT IT OUT!'* Followed by hurrying feet.

'YOU KILLED HIM, YOU MURDERING—'

Lucy jabbed her knee up, hard, thumping into something soft that brought a whoomping grunt with it. She stuck both hands in the air, as if surrendering, then slammed her arms in and down, across Black's fore-arms. Shoving them closer to Lucy's body, bending her knees to apply a bit more weight to it.

Sarah Black let loose a guttural howl and collapsed to her knees.

Which was when the cavalry appeared around the side of the van – a pair of uniforms in soggy high-vis jackets, the lights blinking on their Body-Worn Video units. One even had his extendable baton out and drawn back, ready to strike.

Sarah Black took one look at them and hauled in a deep breath. 'POLICE BRUTALITY! HELP! POLICE BRUTALITY!'

'Well, that was . . . unfortunate.' Chief Inspector Gilmore handed Lucy a glass of water. 'How's the head?'

She just shrugged, even though it was pounding. Took a sip. Cold and bland. Like the office.

Professional Standards had taken up residence on the fourth floor – presumably so they could look down on Plainclothes and Uniform alike – their offices decorated in magnolia and beige. Like a dentist's waiting room. Only without the sense of happy anticipation.

Gilmore settled his large backside on the edge of the desk. He was one of those officers who looked wholly out of place in a Police Scotland black T-shirt and black trousers. Both of which were stretched tight. The hair on his head hadn't managed to conquer the top bit; instead it'd retreated to a defensive circle from about ear-height downwards, leaving the crown of his head to shine pink in the room's single light. He pulled off his narrow glasses, huffed a breath onto the lenses, and cleaned them with a blood-red cloth. Voice soft and warm, like a concerned uncle. 'Mrs Black has made a formal complaint, alleging you attacked her on the street.'

Great.

Lucy opened her mouth, but Gilmore held a hand up before she could say anything.

'I know, it's nonsense, but if there's one thing we learned from the Fatal Accident Inquiry, it's that the Black family's version of reality is somewhat . . . *unique*?'

'Let me guess: there's nothing on the station CCTV?'

'Sadly, not. There would've been, if someone hadn't parked a dirty big Transit van in the way. Well, I say someone.' He popped his glasses back on, then peered over the top of them at his notebook. ' "Daren Black, Building and Landscaping Contractors". So I think we can be fairly sure the blind spot wasn't accidental.'

'I didn't touch her.'

'Yes. Well. As I said . . .' He picked an oversized iPhone off the desk next to his big fat backside, fiddled with the screen, then held it out. 'Unfortunate.'

It was a video, probably on YouTube, going by the controls along the bottom. The footage started just after Sarah Black battered Lucy off the van's side for the second time. That bounce making it look as if Lucy was lunging for her. Slamming her arms down across Black's and forcing the woman to her knees.

A cry of pain, then, *'POLICE BRUTALITY! HELP! POLICE BRUTALITY!'* as the two uniformed officers hurried into shot, one with his baton back, ready to attack the old bag. *'POLICE BRUTALITY!'*

Another scream as Lucy put her in an armlock.

'YOU'RE HURTING ME! HELP! SOMEBODY HELP ME!'

The pair of cops shuffled about, as if they had no idea how all this police stuff was supposed to work.

On-screen Lucy glowered up at them. *'Don't just stand there, you gorm-less pillocks, arrest her!'*

'POLICE BRUTALITY! POLICE BRUTALITY!'

Finally, Gormless Pillock Number One produced his cuffs and snapped them on Sarah Black's wrists. His mate launched into the official spiel as the pair of them dragged her to her feet. *'I am arresting you under section* one of the Criminal Justice, Scotland, Act 2016 for . . . ?' Pulling a face at Lucy. 'What am I arresting her for?'

'GET OFF ME! I HAVEN'T DONE ANYTHING!'

'Assault.'

'Okeydokey. I am arresting you under section one of the Criminal Justice, Scotland, Act 2016 for assault.' The pair of them frogmarched her towards Divisional Headquarters, with whoever was filming it puffing to keep up – the sound going all shonky as the footage wobbled about.

'YOU'RE BREAKING MY ARM!'

'The reason for your arrest is that I suspect that you have committed an offence and I believe that keeping you in custody—'

'HELP! POLICE BRUTALITY!'

'—is necessary and proportionate for the purposes of bringing you before a court—'

'I'LL SUE! I'LL SUE YOU FOR EVERY PENNY YOU'VE GOT!'

'—or otherwise dealing with you in accordance with the law. Do you understand?'

'HELP ME!'

Then the filmer's voice: a hard Kingsmeath accent, with flat vowels in all the wrong places. 'You bastards better get a good lawyer, cos you're going down!'

At that, one of the officers let go of Sarah Black and turned, holding a hand out, blocking the man's way. 'All right, sir, that's far enough. I need you to step back.'

'CALL THE PAPERS, DAREN! TELL THEM HOW THIS BITCH ATTACKED ME!'

A bit more camera wobble as Daren tried to get past the officer, and then the footage came to an end. A little grid of images suggesting what to watch next appeared, all of which seemed to be cookery shows.

'Sorry.' Chief Inspector Gilmore shut the app and put his phone back on the desk.

Lucy stared at the blank screen. 'Oh, for God's sake.'

'Posted by one Daren Black, along with a GoFundMe link to raise money so they can sue you, O Division, and Police Scotland.'

She covered her face with both hands and folded forwards, till her chest pressed against her knees. 'It wasn't my fault. I didn't want him to die, but I didn't have any choice!'

Gilmore's hand was warm against her shoulder. 'I know.' And the hand was withdrawn. 'We can charge her for assaulting you – and we will if that's what you want – but it might just add fuel to the fire.'

'That whole family is *insane*.'

'She's claiming you attacked her, for no reason, as she was walking past the station. Her son, Daren, is telling the same story. The attending officers backed up your statement, till it was pointed out that because they were on the other side of the van, there's no way they could've actually *seen* what happened. At which point they realized fibbing to Professional Standards probably wasn't the wisest move.' Gilmore huffed out a breath. 'But we've got no doubts that Sarah Black is lying. As such, I'm not going to recommend you be suspended pending investigations.'

That was something at least.

'Thank you.'

'I imagine we'll be putting out a statement about the incident, and the Black family will scream "cover-up" and "conspiracy" and "crisis actors" and "false flag" and "corruption", like they always do; then people will get bored and it'll all fade away till next time. So, maybe, given everything else that's going on, it might be better if you made yourself scarce for a while. Before the media descend on us like a rain of frogs?'

Lucy sat back in her chair. Stared up at the ceiling tiles. 'Urgh . . .'

'I know it's not your fault, Lucy, but it's for the best.'

'Fine.' Lurching to her feet. There were a couple of things she'd been meaning to chase up anyway. One of which was nowhere near DHQ, the media, or Sarah Bloody Black.

She stood, back straight, and marched out of the office. Closed the door behind her. Slouched against it, eyes closed, head doing a decent rendition of the finale to Tchaikovsky's '1812 Overture'.

Sarah Sodding Black.

The whole family needed locking up. Or shot. Either was good.

Lucy fumbled a crumpled packet of paracetamol from her pocket – only two tablets left. She popped both out of their blisters, swished a bit of saliva around her mouth, then swallowed them dry. Shuddering as they tried to stick halfway.

A man's voice: *'Detective Sergeant McVeigh?'*

Great.

She forced the pills down, then turned.

He was youngish – maybe mid-twenties? – with short dirty-blond hair that was a bit too spiky on top, high cheekbones, dark eyes, and a square jaw. Dark-grey suit, crisp shirt, neat tie, manila folder under one arm. Brown eyes narrowed in concern.

She waved him away. 'I'm fine.'

'I've been trying to get hold of you for the last couple of days. I left messages?'

'Good for you.' She marched towards the stairs.

He strode along beside her, not a hair out of place. 'Professional Standards aren't your enemy, DS McVeigh. We're not the scary Rubber Heelers of myth and legend, we're here to support and guide officers through—'

'Twenty seconds ago, *your boss*'s "guidance" was to make myself scarce, so that's what I'm doing.' Barging through the stairwell doors. 'Bye.'

'DS McVeigh, maybe we could stop and have a chat about Neil Black's family and some management strategies to avoid further—'

'I've just been assaulted and I'm busy with *actual* policework, so I'm going to say no.' Lucy's bootheels clattered back from the echoing walls.

He didn't follow her this time.

When she took the turn at the landing he was still standing there, staring down at her, folder under his arm, the concerned expression swapped for one of disappointment. 'I can make an appointment?'

Good luck with that.

12

PC Manson peered at Lucy over the top of his big square spectacles. 'The rest of it?' His skin had an unhealthy spoiled-milk tint, and the whites of his eyes were more of a yellowy-pink. Everything else was pinched and angular. As if he'd been supplied flat-packed and not assembled properly.

'The file, Constable. Where's the rest of it?'

Manson's lair, AKA: the Records-and-Productions Stores, was a gloomy warehouse with narrow frosted windows up at roof height, letting in a thin whispering light that only seemed to make everything look darker. Everything clarted in dust and misery.

The racks and racks of storage space were divided into two – one laden with boxes full of files, the other groaning under the weight of physical evidence. A special cage sat at the far end for contraband items like seized drugs, and weapons, and counterfeit cash, segregated from the rest of the warehouse by twelve-foot-high barriers of chain link, topped with dusty razor wire. Another chain-link barrier sat between her and PC Manson. Two small desks, one on either side of the wire, formed an almost-shared surface between their worlds, with a little hatch marking the boundary. Lit by a single harsh white spotlight.

Manson puffed out his narrow cheeks, opened the hatch and reached for the faded orange folder with 'BENEDICT STRACHAN' written in wobbly biro letters on the flap. 'He was the kid killer, right? Well, the kid who killed someone, not someone who killed kids. What's wrong with the file?' Opening it up to peer inside.

'Most of it's *missing*. Where's the interview transcripts, the door-to-doors, the actions, his sodding confession?'

'They're not here.' Whoever it was that assembled PC Manson, they seemed to have left him a few Allen keys short of a bedside cabinet.

Lucy made a big show of examining the chain-link barricade. 'Is this here to stop people hitting you?'

'Let me check.' He turned on his heel and stalked away into the gloom. Footsteps echoing on the concrete floor, fading into the distance . . . Then silence.

And more silence.

And a bit more, after that.

Should've got the Dunk to do this. Maybe he could've bored PC Manson into submission with a monologue on structural capitalism, political corruption, and the class system.

Speaking of which.

She pulled out her mobile, but before she'd got as far as scrolling through her contacts the phone *whirrrr-bing*ed in her hand.

Email.

And for once it wasn't spam, or some idiot memo from the top brass, it was a web link from one Gail McCarthy, with no message – just the subject line 'DI TUDOR SAID YOU NEEDED TO SEE THESE'.

That would be the crime-scene photos, then.

Lucy followed the link through to a secure server, where a single folder was waiting. 'FOR DS MCVEIGH'.

Deep breath.

Somehow, the pictures were worse than the real thing. All in blistering full colour, pin-sharp, and, to be honest, a bit too arty for what they were meant to be.

Gail had found a scar on their victim's right hip. Another line of scar tissue reaching almost the whole length of the left shin. But the kicker was a shot of his back.

Hairy Harry, AKA: Dr Harrison Jenkins, must've asked for the body to be rolled over before they bagged and tagged it, exposing a ragged hole in the grey-green skin. Something black and sticky clearly visible inside. The gash was nearly five centimetres wide by seven tall, according to the black-and-white scale held alongside it for comparison. Looked as if something had been driven in through his stomach and out through . . . well, the back.

But the interesting thing was what *surrounded* it.

Little twisted scraps of skin ran around the edge of the hole – an old tattoo, its colours faded to blues and oranges. Whatever the Bloodsmith had impaled his victim with, it had torn through the tattoo on the way out, fragmenting it.

Wonder if that was fixable . . . ?

Lucy parked her bum on the small desk and called up an image-editing app. Nothing as swish as Photoshop, but it would do. Hopefully. She loaded the last photo, zoomed in, and snipped out every bit of the tattoo that was still visible. Saved it to a new layer. Then played with the distorting tools – stretching and twisting the scraps until they were more or less back where they should've been.

There was a chunk missing from the centre of the image, where the skin was too fragmented to stitch together, but what she'd rescued was distinctive enough: a phoenix rising from the battlements of a burning castle, with a severed boar's head underneath. The shield had two bears as supporters and was topped by a knight's helmet with stag horns on it. 'SEMPER VIGILO' on a scroll across the bottom.

Sod.

She found 'DI TUDOR' in her contacts and hit the button.

It rang and rang and rang and—

'You've reached the voicemail of Detective Inspector Alasdair Tudor. I'm currently unavailable, but you can leave a message after the beep.'

Ah, of course – he was at the post-mortem, and the new Procurator Fiscal was maniacal about people switching off their phones.

Bleeeeeeeep.

'It's Lucy. Call me when you get this.' Then she hung up.

Had to tell somebody, though. Couldn't just sit on something like this. Not without ending up in a whole shedload of trouble. And Professional Standards were looming over her already, so there was no point giving their new boy any more ammunition. Which left only one option: follow the chain of command upwards.

He picked up on the sixth ring. *'DCI Ross.'*

'Boss? I think our victim's a police officer.'

Detective Chief Inspector Ross's mouth stretched outwards, lips thinning and turning down at the edges as he stared at the reconstructed image, Lucy's phone looking tiny in his ham-hock hands. 'Sodding hell.'

He stood, slightly stooped, in front of the small desk – dwarfing both it and her, bald head gleaming in the harsh glow of that single spotlight.

Any normal senior officer would've summoned her to their office so she could show them what she'd found, but DCI Ross had come to her, instead. Insisted on it. And unlike a lot of the other bosses, he wasn't done up in some fancy, expensive, never-going-out Armani number. He was wearing a fairly cheap-looking grey suit that probably came from Asda. The kind of suit you could chuck in the washing machine if a member of the public was sick on it at chucking out/up time. The kind of suit you could wrestle a coked-up druggie to the ground in. The kind of suit real plainclothes officers wore. A *fighting* suit.

'Well, that nails it, then.' Ross handed her phone back and frowned off into the gloomy depths of the Records-and-Productions Store. 'The victim's one of ours.'

Because, let's face it, not many civilians got the Oldcastle Police crest tattooed on their backs.

'Yes, Boss.'

'And it's the old crest, from before they made us all rebrand as Police Scotland with that stupid little logo, so we can eliminate anyone who joined after April 2013.' The creases on his forehead multiplied, then he pulled out his own phone and called someone. 'Bob? It's Andy. I need you to dig out the duty roster. Anyone gone AWOL in the last . . . ?' Raising his eyebrows at Lucy.

'Month, month and a half? Won't know for sure till they do the post-mortem.'

Back to the phone. 'Call it eight weeks, Bob, just to be safe . . . Uh-huh . . . Uh-huh . . . OK, let me know if you find anything.' DCI Ross hung up. Tapped the phone against his top lip as he embarked on another bout of frowning. 'We should check missing persons, too. Our boy might be retired, or off on the sick.'

She nodded. 'Got DC Fraser on it now, Boss.'

He stood there in silence for a couple of breaths. Then, 'I hear you had a run-in with Neil Black's mother this morning.'

Great. The O Division gossip tree had been at it again. 'Nothing I can't handle.'

'I'm sure you can.' Leaning back against the chain link, arms folded. 'It's not easy taking a man's life.' Looking away into the gloom. 'Willy

Thomson had a thing for knocking over Post Offices. He'd barge in there with his sawn-off and put a round in the ceiling, order everyone on the floor, then get the old woman behind the counter to fill a rucksack with all the cash, postal orders, and stamps in the place.'

Lucy raised an eyebrow at that. '*Stamps?*'

'Do you have any idea how much a book of twelve first-class stamps costs? Anyway, I was a PC on the Firearms Response Team when the call came in that Willy had put a round in a punter as well. Some have-a-go hero in his seventies, ex-traffic warden – blew his chest wide open. Then Willy panics and now he's got eight terrified hostages. I was given the green light and took the shot.' His voice softened. 'So I know what it's like.'

'Boss.' Heat flushed through her cheeks and ears.

'I understand they've lumbered you with an official therapist. Regular visits? Updates on your progress to the powers that be? "Tell me about your feelings"?'

A nod.

'I was the same. I know it seems like a load of rancid New Age hippy bullshit, Lucy, but do yourself a favour and play along. You might be surprised how much it could help. And at the very least it gets them off your back.' Then one of those massive hands thumped down on her shoulder and squeezed. 'You did good, today: with the tattoo. Now go find out who our victim was.'

The Dunk was perched on the edge of an office chair, pen sticking out the corner of his mouth, poking away at a creaky old Police-Scotland-issue laptop. He glanced up as Lucy placed a mug of coffee on the desk in front of him. 'Ooh, ta.'

The Operation Maypole office was empty except for the pair of them. Grey and lifeless, just the *hummm* of the fridge and the central heating's *ping-gurgle* to accompany the Dunk's two index fingers clicking away on the keyboard. That and the unwashed-feet smell of stale biscuits that seemed to ooze out of the carpet tiles.

'Any luck?'

He took the pen out of his mouth. 'Trouble with Oldcastle is loads of people go missing all the time. Do you want to know how many male—'

'Yes, Dunk, I'd *love* a wee lecture on missing-person statistics for O

Division. That would certainly be a lot more helpful than actually identifying our victim. Let me pull up a chair; I'm all ears.'

'I see.' He sniffed, then helped himself to a sip of coffee. 'I had about
two dozen possible IDs, then you said they'd be ex-Job, which brings us
down to three.' The Dunk poked one last key and the big printer in the
corner *whurrrrred* into life. *Chlack-whurr-chlack-whurr-chlack-whurr*. He
wandered over there, returning with three sheets of A4. Handed them
over.

They were still warm.

A trio of missing-person files, complete with full-colour photographs.
All men. Two looked youngish, the third was maybe DI Tudor's age –
complete with grey-flecked beard and silvered temples. Which ticked at
least one box.

The Dunk settled on the edge of the desk. 'PC Peter Barland, DI Christopher Gourley, and DC Malcolm Louden. Barland got signed off on the
sick, four years ago. Gourley took early retirement, after an unfortunate
incident involving a dawn raid, a Kingsmeath brothel, an Alsatian, and
a prozzie with a paring knife. And they fired Louden for helping himself
to little trinkets when he searched folks' houses. Drugs and cash mostly,
but the occasional bit of jewellery or electronics was fair game too.'

'What about distinguishing features – any tattoos?'

'Nothing on file, but let's see what Mr Facebook has to say.' He scooted
back into his office chair, those two fingers pecking at the laptop's keyboard again. 'Barland, Barland, Barland . . . Here we go. Things got a lot
easier when people started posting holiday pics on the internet.'

A photo stream filled the screen, featuring a thin man with a slight
paunch and receding hair. He was on a beach somewhere sunny, dressed
in nothing but orange Speedos, posing with a round freckly girl in a sar-
ong. Big smiles for the camera, holding hands, and toasting Lucy and
the Dunk with multicoloured cocktails. Barland had a big koi carp tattoo
covering most of his left thigh. Which wasn't in any of the crime-scene
photographs.

'Not our boy.'

'OK, next up . . .' The Dunk's fingers went to work again.

The older man appeared on screen, in a back garden somewhere,
kneeling behind an array of leeks. Grinning like a loon. Only he was
fully clothed – polo shirt, chinos, sandals.

'Hold on, here's some marked "Malaga" : . .'

He was fully clothed in those, too.

'Lossiemouth? Surely, you go there, you go for a swim, right?'

But when the Dunk brought the photos up, ex-DI Gourley was all wrapped up in a jacket, scarf, and welly boots.

'Kind of get the feeling he's not a "tattoo" kind of person. But we'll keep him as a maybe.' Lucy poked the last printout. 'Try Louden.'

'Ex-DC Louden, let's be 'avin' you . . .' *Clickity, click, click, click.* 'Not on Facebook. Weird. Thought it was, like, compulsory these days. Let's see if he's oot and aboot on Twitter . . .' The Dunk sat back in his chair. 'Half a dozen Malcolm Loudens. Or is it Malcolms Louden? Either way, none of them look anything like the pic we've got on file, and two of them are American.'

'So, it could be him *or* Gourley.' Assuming it wasn't someone else entirely, of course.

'Sorry, Sarge.' A shrug. 'On the plus side, as our victim was a cop, his DNA's going to be on file. Soon as they run it, we'll know.'

Lucy pulled in her chin and hissed a breath out through her nose.

It'd be nice to get back to DCI Ross with a result, instead of a maybe-maybe-not.

'Try a PNC search.'

The Dunk hunched over his laptop and did as he was told. 'OK. What's Mr Louden been up to?' Scrolling through a surprisingly long list of search results. 'Well, he did three years in Glenochil for that "thieving things while being a copper" malarkey, and I've got recent arrests for shoplifting, starting a fight in St Jasper's Cathedral, a fair few drunk and disorderlies, half a dozen urinating in publics . . . And a whole bunch of complaints from shop owners about him sleeping rough in the city centre.'

She checked her watch: twenty to ten. The post-mortem wouldn't be over before two, maybe three if Hairy Harry was feeling extra thorough, so if she was going to save the day, now was the time to do it. 'Get a car. We're going out.'

13

It was all really rather . . . *quaint*. A small village on Kings River, about five minutes outside Oldcastle. Corracholm had been a proper fishing port once, but the industry had picked up its nets and lobster creels long ago, leaving the small stone harbour to the guest houses, antique shops, artisanal cafés, and tourist four-by-fours. But before the fishermen went, they seemed to have painted every narrow house on the waterfront terrace a different shade of the rainbow. It looked unpleasantly cheery, even in the drizzle.

The Dunk parked in front of a bright-pink three-storey affair, between a baker's and a place advertising 'LOCALLY PRODUCED AND FAIR-TRADE *OBJETS D'ART*'. Pulled on his leather bunnet. 'Bet the houses here cost a fortune.'

Lucy climbed out into the rain. 'We're on the clock: in, establish the facts, and out, understand? Quick as we can.'

The Dunk followed her over to the house's front door – painted gloss black, giving the place a slightly liquorice-allsort vibe. 'THE PERCHES' was engraved into a wooden sign, mounted to the wall. 'Unless ex-DI Gourley is our victim, of course.'

'True.' She leaned on the bell. Then huddled into the doorway in an attempt to stay dry. Didn't work, though.

'Sarge?' The Dunk pulled his shoulders up, polo neck disappearing into the collar of his leather jacket like a beatnik turtle. 'Can you smell something *fishy*?'

'And try not to be too weird when we're in there, OK? No big anti-establishment rants.'

'It's like . . .' curling his top lip and sniffing, 'you know when fish fingers go all fusty?' He turned on the spot, nostrils flaring. 'Think it's seaweed? Or has a seagull been sick somewhere?'

'Dunk, I swear to God, your bunnet's on too tight and it's strangling your brain.'

'Bit harsh.'

Lucy was about to explain why it *really* wasn't, when the door opened and a small woman in leggings, trainers, and a 'FEEL THE BURN, BITCHES!' T-shirt peered out at them.

Her face was a shiny shade of pink, just a little too purple not to clash with her house. A bit on the chunky side. Grecian curls of grey hair sticking to her damp forehead. 'Can I help you? Only I'm doing an online aerobics class and—'

'Mrs Gourley?' Lucy flashed her warrant card. 'Can we come in, please? We need to ask a couple of questions about your husband.'

Her shoulders rounded, eyes rolling as both arms dangled at her sides like damp spaghetti. 'I suppose so. But make it quick – we're working on our glutes today and I need a nice arse for our Marion's wedding.'

'Sorry' – Mrs Gourley ushered them into a tiny family room at the back of the house – 'I'd put you in the lounge, but we've got Americans staying for a week, and you know what they're like.' She waved Lucy and the Dunk towards an overstuffed sofa, inflicted with animal-print scatter cushions.

'This is fine, thanks.' The Dunk parked his bum. 'Very cosy.'

'Mrs Gourley, we need to talk to you about—'

'Please, call me Daphne. Would you like some tea? It's no trouble, really.'

Lucy tried again. 'Daphne, we need to ask a few questions about your husband. Does he have any tattoos?' Taking care to stick to the present tense, there. 'Any distinguishing marks you could tell us about?'

'Ah . . .' Mrs Gourley wriggled back until the armchair enveloped her. The smile faded from her face. 'I never really believed it'd happen, you know. Always thought he'd stumble in through that door someday, reeking of booze, and I'd have to give everything up again.' She picked at the corner of a leopard-print cushion. 'Have you ever tried living with someone who's got proper depression? It's so *wearing*. The slightest thing sets him off and he'll be curled up in a darkened room, or screaming foul language, or storming around the house like an elephant with a hang-over.' Deep breath. 'He's dead, isn't he? Christopher's the man you found in the woods this morning.'

'In the . . . ?' Lucy sat up straighter. 'How did you—'

'It was on the news when I was doing the washing up.' She lowered her eyes. 'Christopher's dead.'

O Division strikes again. A string vest would leak less than Oldcastle's finest.

The Dunk elbowed Lucy in the ribs, jerking his head towards Mrs Gourley.

Yeah, he was probably right. Making comforting noises for the family was what you did when you were the senior officer.

'Mrs . . . Daphne. Constable Fraser and I are just checking up on a couple of missing persons. It isn't—'

'They said it was that Bloodsmith person.' Her head drooped, voice getting smaller. 'I read the papers. I know what that means. He cut out my Christopher's heart, didn't he?'

The only sound was a grey-muzzled Labrador, snoring gently in a bed by the radiator.

Lucy cleared her throat. 'I'm sorry. I know this must be horribly upset-ting, but there's nothing to say the man we found this morning is your husband.'

Not *yet*, anyway. Not until you answer the damn question.

'He was never the same after he left the police. Strange, isn't it? He complained about the job the whole time, but after he stopped, he missed it like you'd miss an ear. I thought Christopher getting stabbed would be a good thing for us. Let us spend some *proper* time together. Go travelling.' A small, sad smile; then her eyes glistened as the tears welled up. 'I always wanted to do a cruise on the Nile, or all round the Carib-bean. Hell, even the Isle of Wight ferry would've done at a push. Instead, I got to spend the last six years watching my Christopher die inside. Internal organs preserved in Tennent's Export and Bell's Whisky, like it was his own private formaldehyde.'

'Daphne, did Christopher have any tattoos?'

Mrs Gourley nodded.

Gotcha.

'His team broke up a people-smuggling ring – prostitution, drugs, modern slavery, *very* nasty – so they went out to celebrate. And when he sobered up, about two days later, there it was.' She wiped her eyes on the sleeve of her T-shirt, voice going tight and strangled. 'He moaned about the bloody job *so* much, then the silly sod goes and gets that stupid police logo thing permanently inked into his body?'

They had an ID.

Time to let her know the truth, then.

'Daphne, I'm sorry, but—'

'They'd all done it, of course. The whole team. Even the new boys. "Semper Vigilo".' A big soggy-nosed sniff. 'Must be Latin for "Easily Led".'

'Perhaps Constable Fraser could make you a nice cup of tea, and we can—'

'At least he didn't get it anywhere embarrassing.' Mrs Gourley tapped herself on the shoulder. 'Christopher's detective sergeant got it tattooed right on her bum!'

Sod. If it was on his shoulder, goodbye ID.

'She used to flash it at people when she was drunk. Anyone had a leaving do, or a birthday, or a funeral, and out would come DS Massie's tattoo for all the world to see.'

Lucy stood. 'I've got some good news for you, Daphne, the man in the woods definitely isn't your husband.'

'Oh . . .' It was as if someone had pulled the bung from an inflatable mattress, letting all the air hiss out of her. 'I see.' Sounding a little bit disappointed.

'Before we go, though: don't suppose you've got a photo of Christopher's old team knocking about?'

'Sure as I can be, Boss.' Lucy held the photograph up again, blocking her view through the windscreen as the Dunk took them left at the roundabout and onto Calderwell Bridge, making for the centre of town. In the photo, DI Gourley looked vaguely embarrassed as he stood in the midst of a team of twenty officers, all in plainclothes and all posing as if they were something off the television.

Some were pointing mimed guns, one doing that Bruce Forsyth thing, two blokes pretending to kiss, one woman showing off her muscles, another guy with his shirt unbuttoned, proudly displaying the Oldcastle Police crest tattooed on his chest . . .

And right at the back, doing his best tosser-from-the-Bullingdon-Club, DC Malcolm Louden. He wasn't as junkie-thin as the corpse, spreadeagled on the bloodstained floorboards – and his hair was a sort of bouffant Hugh Grant tribute act, without a hint of grey – but it was definitely him.

Or at least ninety-five percent definitely him.

Maybe eighty-five at a push.

DCI Ross gave a little grunt. *'I see. Hang on a minute . . .'* Then came the sound of some poor keyboard getting a spanking from those huge fingers. Then some muttering. Then silence.

The drizzle worked itself into a spitting rain, then something a lot heavier, as the bridge's lights flickered on in a miserable wave ahead of the pool car – their photoelectric sensors triggered by the growing gloom.

Half ten in the morning, on a wet September Thursday, and it was already dark enough to need artificial illumination. Welcome to sodding Oldcastle.

Yet more silence.

Maybe DI Ross had forgotten about her? Maybe he was—

'Lucy?'

'Still here, Boss.'

'Have you told Tudor yet?'

'He's attending the PM with that new Procurator Fiscal. Got his phone turned off.'

'Fair enough.' Another grunt. *'I see our ex-DC Louden has a somewhat . . . chequered past. The press will make a three-course meal out of that, which isn't going to help us any. Have you notified next of kin?'*

Did Malcolm Louden even *have* next of kin?

She looked at the Dunk. He just shrugged back at her.

'Actually, Boss, I wouldn't want to do that till we've got hundred-percent confirmation. Louden's DNA will still be on file, so once the PM's over we should know for certain. If someone leans on the labs, anyway.' Hint, hint.

'I'll get the Media Department working on a statement. Meantime, the only people who know are you, me, DC Fraser, and the Bloodsmith. Let's keep it that way. And I need you to put together his final movements. Last known associates: who did he speak to, did they see anything? You know the drill.'

'On our way now, Boss.' Because it never hurt to look efficient in front of the senior brass.

Another silence.

The Dunk sailed straight through the junction with Nelson Street – which would've been a much faster way back to the station, but then he'd have to cross the dual carriageway and they all knew what a wimp he was about that.

'Lucy, Malcolm Louden was a dirty cop, and no one hates a dirty cop more than me, but that doesn't mean we're not going to do everything we can to catch the bastard who killed him. Understand?'

'Yes, Boss.'

'Good work.' And that was it – this time the silence was final. DCI Ross had hung up.

She slipped her phone back in her pocket. 'Is it just me, or is Detective Chief Inspector Andrew Ross *not* a Teflon-shouldered, power-crazed, condescending, massive pain in the backside?'

A low whistle emanated from the driver's side. 'You've not got the hotties for him, have you, Sarge? Only he's old enough to be your . . .' The Dunk cleared his throat. 'He's far too old for you. And he's married.'

'Don't be a dick, Dunk.'

'No, Sarge. Sorry, Sarge.' Sideways glance. 'You know, we've been out and about for nearly an hour and you've *still* not said a word about what happened with Sarah Black this morning.'

'Is that right.' The gossip tree strikes again.

'She's a vindictive, scabby, fusty old shitebag, and you shouldn't be expected to—'

'Take the hint, Dunk, and drop it.'

He chewed on the inside of his cheek, lips pursed as if she'd just slapped him. But at least he kept his gob shut.

Good.

She pointed through the windscreen in the vague direction of Divisional Headquarters. 'We'll dump the car back at the shop, then hit the streets. See if we can find whoever reported Louden missing. Maybe they saw something and want to help?'

After all, there was always a first time.

*

'It's OK, take your time.' Lucy held up the photo they'd cranked out on the office printer: DC Malcolm Louden's last mugshot, taken after he'd been arrested for urinating in the doorway of CopyKwiK on Cupar Road. The Bullingdon bravado had long since disappeared, leaving behind someone who needed a shave, a bath, and a damn good going over with a hairbrush. One side of his face was swollen and red, from where the arresting officer had to wrestle him to the ground. 'He used to hang around the city centre, if that helps?'

Rain bounced off the dirty-grey pavement, gurgling in the downpipes, as the three of them huddled beneath the stripy awning outside Kelly's the Baker, wreathed in the crisp golden scent of fresh bread and pastry.

'Dunno.' The man in the tatty overcoat sniffed, then wiped his drippy nose on his sleeve. 'But I could probably, you know, think better if, you know, I had, like, maybe some cash in my hand?'

The Dunk shook his head. 'We're not giving out cash prizes the day, Bingo. It's soup and a sarnie from Lunchity Munchity, or nothing.' Holding up a voucher. 'Now, do you know the man in the photo?'

'Maybe.' Bingo had another sniff. 'Depends what he done, don't it?'

'You can't get him into any trouble.' Lucy put on her concerned face. 'No one can. Not any more.'

'Oh. Yeah, yeah, I get you. He's, like, you know, dead, isn't he? Right.' Then Bingo puffed out his cheeks. 'So it's a "definitely no" on the cash, yeah?'

A nod from the Dunk. 'Lunchity Munchity do a really nice cream of mushroom, if that helps?'

'Maybe he looks a bit like Malky. Used to hang about outside the King James, you know?' Stubby fingers reaching for the voucher.

'Thanks, Bingo.'

'Nah, never seen him.' Suspicious eyes squinted out from beneath the woman's ragged fringe. 'Why you got to keep hassling me?' Shoulders forward, hands rammed deep into her pockets. Dark-blonde curls escaping from underneath a mud-brown woolly hat. A toast-rack-thin greyhound shivering next to her on a tartan blanket as the rain thumped down. 'Haven't done nothing.'

There was a man outside the King James Theatre, whistling a jaunty freestyle-jazz version of 'God Save The Queen' as he pasted up an 'Extra

DATES ADDED!!!' banner on the poster for this year's panto. Completely ignoring the handful of people gathered in the alley, either side of the stage entrance, where a portico kept the worst of the rain off. A mini cardboard-and-bin-bag shanty town, sheltering against the theatre wall.

Lucy shrugged. 'It's OK if you don't know.'

The Dunk held out his voucher again. 'Soup *and* a sandwich, Mags.'

Mags cricked her neck from side to side. Then snatched it out of his hand. 'Don't know. Sod off. Or I'll set Ripper on you!' The greyhound whimpered.

He dipped into his pocket and came out with another couple of vouchers. 'Anyone else? Anyone seen this guy?'

Lucy showed them all the photo. 'We're not trying to get you into trouble. We're just trying to find out who killed him.'

Four pairs of eyes scowled back at her.

Rain hissed against the buildings.

The man kept whistling.

'Come on, don't you want us to catch whoever it was?' Jabbing DC Louden's picture at them. 'What if they come back for you? Or your friends? That what you want?'

A deep grunt rumbled out of a small man in an ancient parka jacket, then a groan as he levered himself to his feet. His thick beard stuck out in all directions, sprinkled with flecks of ash, the moustache stained yellow – a smouldering roll-up poking out between his teeth. Long grey-brown hair. A nose that had been broken at least two or three times. Broad Aberdonian accent. 'Aye, I kent him weil enough.'

About sodding time.

14

If it wasn't for Lucy, the Dunk, and their new friend, Dr Vincent Maurice Rayner – all squeezed around a table in the corner, furthest from the door – Lunchity Munchity would've been completely empty. It was one of those tiled-floor-and-pine-wainscotting places, the bright-white walls festooned with framed paintings from the local art college.

Dr Rayner slurped at his extra-large mug of milky builder's, leaving little beige droplets clinging to his stained moustache. 'Ah . . . Lovely.'

The Dunk had an espresso, with a glass of water on the side, as if this was some swanky trattoria in Bologna or Rome, rather than a greasy spoon with pretensions of grandeur in a slightly rundown bit of Castle Hill. Damp leather jacket draped over the back of his chair. 'Come on then, Doc, dish the dirt.'

Another slurp.

Lucy checked her watch. Nearly noon. Still got two, maybe three hours to make some sodding progress. 'No dirt, no soup, no sandwich.'

A sigh. Then Dr Rayner put his mug on the table, turning it until the handle was perfectly lined up with the rectangular metal cage of condiments. 'Yer mannie's cried Malky Louden, he wis a boabby afore he wis oan the streets, ken?'

'What?' The Dunk blinked across the table at her. 'Did you understand any of that?'

That got him a wrinkled scowl as Dr Rayner poked the table with a tar-yellowed finger, beard jutting. 'Are you mackin' fun o' the wie ah spik?'

She let some ice drip from her voice: 'You've got a doctorate in comparative literature, Vincent. You used to lecture at the university. So drop the hillbilly-teuchter act.'

There was a lopsided shrug, then Dr Rayner went back to his tea again. 'Can't blame a man for injecting a bit of fun into the daily grind, can you? Brightening up all our days?' Then he turned to the Dunk, placing a grubby hand on the sleeve of that perfect-black polo neck. 'I said, "The gentleman you are enquiring about is called Malcolm Louden, and he was a police officer before he became homeless."'

'Right.' The Dunk extracted his arm, lip curled as he examined it for smudges and dirt.

Wimp.

Lucy pointed across the table. 'And you're the one who reported Malcolm Louden missing?'

'Society seldom notices when people like us disappear, Detective Sergeant – if we don't watch out for each other, who will?' A sigh. 'It didn't help Malcolm any, though, did it?' Rayner picked a handful of sugar sachets from the bowl on the table and lined them up in a perfect grid. 'He liked to keep himself to himself. I think it was the ex-copper thing: sometimes people reacted badly when they found out he was once on the jackbooted side of the social divide.' He gave them a shrug and a hairy smile. 'No offence.'

A tall thin woman in a chequered pinny appeared with a bowl and a plate. 'Who's the soup?'

'That would be me. Thank you kindly . . .' peering at her nametag, 'Elizabeth, my darling. And I believe it comes with a freshly baked bread roll?'

She thunked the bowl and the plate down in front of him. 'I'll get your sandwich.' Then stomped off with all the grace of a tumble drier.

'Of course, we'd meet up from time to time, to pool our resources and expertise.' Dr Rayner tore off a chunk of bread, slathered it with a pat of butter, then dipped it in his sweetcorn-and-smoked-haddock chowder. 'Being ex-police, Malcolm was very good at distracting the security guards while my nimble fingers played amongst the wines and spirits.' The dripping chunk of bread got stuffed into that beard-rimmed maw. 'He was particularly fond of a good single malt, but you know what supermarkets are like these days. Anything better than own-brand blend and they just put an empty box on the shelf, so you have to ask at the checkout to get it filled. And they're not so keen on you saying, "I just shoplifted this, and you didn't catch me, so that means you have to hand over the actual bottle. Fair's only fair. I don't make the rules." '

Another chunk got dunked.

'When did you last see him?'

'That would be . . . oh . . . four and a bit weeks ago? It was a Monday, because that's the day we like to hit the Marks and Spencer on Cannard Street, opposite the train station? You can fill your pockets with little tins of pre-mixed G and T, quicker than a startled checkout assistant can say, "Someone's knocked over the display of Percy Pigs again!" '

So she hadn't been *too* far off about the body being in that crappy tumbledown cottage for a month and a half.

The last of the soggy roll disappeared. 'I remember he was sporting a rather swanky-looking new coat. Some child had given it to him, as a gift, just like that, out of the goodness of her little public-school heart. Doesn't that give you hope for the future, Detective Sergeant?'

'Ham, cheese, and pickle.' The waitress was back with another plate, this one garnished with crisps and a couple of green leaves.

'That would be me again, lovely Elizabeth. And please give my compliments to the chef: this chowder is simply divine.' Kissing his grubby fingertips.

She just grunted and stomped off again.

Lucy made a note. 'What kind of coat?' After all, it'd be a lot easier to pick Malcolm Louden up on CCTV if they actually knew what he'd been wearing.

'A lovely padded one, very stylish. And I'm sure, if Malky is sadly no longer with us' – making the sign of the cross: spectacles, testicles, wallet, and watch – 'then he would definitely want me to have it. Seeing as how we were so close?'

'Nice try. Colour?'

'It was what I like to call "Hemingway Burgundy". Did you ever read *The Old Man and the Sea*, Detective Sergeant?'

'Where did this altruistic gesture take place?'

Dr Rayner picked up half his sandwich and tore a big bite out of it, little curls of bright orange cheddar falling into his beard. 'No one ever seems to read the classics any more, do they? It's all romance and science fiction, and . . . crime novels.' Imbuing that last category with nostril-flaring disdain. 'I remember the days when—'

'Vincent!' She helped herself to one of his crisps. Cheese and onion. 'Where did the kid give him the coat?'

'All I'm saying is: what's wrong with broadening the mind with a little Virginia Woolf every now and then? Milton, Hardy, Tolstoy, Cervantes—'

'Where – did – she – give – him – the – coat?'

He chewed in silence for bit. Then sniffed. 'Fine, if you want to wallow in cultural ignorance, who am I to stop you? Malky was in his usual spot, outside the train station, by the main doors. Same as every morning, regular as clockwork.' Dr Rayner hunched his shoulders, curling over his soup and sandwich. 'Now, if you wouldn't mind, I'd like to eat my lunch, and philistines give me indigestion.'

'. . . departure of the twelve fifteen to Dundee, from platform six.'

The announcement echoed around Oldcastle train station, coming back in distorted waves from the huge domed ceiling – the glass dirty enough to bring the midday gloom down to late-evening levels. Only half the station's strip lights had come on, leaving the northbound platforms and most of the concourse swamped in darkness. The station's vaulted iron framework was blistered with rust and pale dripping stalactites. Conspiratorial murmurs coming from the pigeons roosting up there, in between the anti-bird spikes. Everything wreathed in that greasy smell of hot metal mixed with grey-blue diesel fumes and the scent of mouldering bin bags.

'Sodding freezing.' The Dunk had his shoulders up and both hands stuffed deep in his pockets.

'By the main entrance, you say?' Mr Cartwright ushered them through a door marked 'NO UNAUTHORIZED ADMITTANCE' and into a narrow corridor that stank of disinfectant.

Lucy nodded. 'Monday: four and a half weeks ago.'

'Pffff . . .' He led the way up a long flight of stairs, big round bottom wobbling in her face as he climbed. 'Dunno about that. Budget cutbacks mean we've only got about half the tapes we used to. Well, I say "tapes" . . . But we can see what we can see.'

At the end of the corridor lay another 'NO UNAUTHORIZED ADMITTANCE' door, this one with a pin-code security lock. Mr Cartwright blocked it with his body, so they couldn't spy as he clicked in the four digits, then turned the handle and waved them inside.

It was a cosy room with a row of monitors down one side and a filthy window overlooking the main concourse on the other. A portable heater sat on the end of an extension lead in the centre of the room, radiating lukewarmth at a pair of dented filing cabinets that looked as if they were given a stiff kicking on a regular basis. And, in the corner: a person-high rack of hard drives, little red and green lights winking away as they whirred.

Mr Cartwright lumbered over to a large cabinet and hauled up the roller door, revealing row after row of grey boxes about the size of a paperback book. 'Last week' – pointing at the top shelf. 'Week before' – next one down. 'Week before that' – down again. 'And that's four weeks.'

Get to the sodding point.

'This, though' – Mr Cartwright huffed his way down into a squat, both knees going off like starter pistols – 'is anything older.' He reached into the bottom shelf and scooped out an armful of grey boxes. Dumped them on the room's only desk, in front of the monitors. 'Don't know if they'll help, though. We had a stabbing here, round about then, and your lot confiscated a pile of our drives and never gave them back.'

Lucy picked one up. The grey plastic casing was littered with the tattered remains of dozens, if not hundreds, of white, lined stickers. Only one was still a hundred percent intact, with '09 AUG ➔ 11 AUG' printed on it in squint Sharpie letters, above 'CONCOURSE 3'. She put it down again. 'Constable Fraser?'

'Sarge.' The Dunk went for a rummage.

'This boy, your homeless man, he done something?' Mr Cartwright dipped into one of the filing cabinets and came out with a partially deflated two-litre bottle of Diet Coke. 'Only there's a bunch of them get off the train from Dundee every morning, you hear about that?' He took a long hard pull at the bottle, making the plastic creak and crunk.

'Got it, Sarge.' The Dunk held a box aloft. 'Main entrance, seventh to the ninth.'

Mr Cartwright took it from him, cracked open the box, and pulled out the black-and-silver rectangle inside. 'All done up in their "we're so cold and homeless" rags. But they can afford the day-return from Dundee? Some of them have *season* tickets.' He huffed a breath onto the connection strip at the end of the drive, then slotted it into a space on the rack, setting the built-in lights winking. 'And you can see them all round

town, you know, if you go out for lunch or you're picking up some messages? Our Denise is vegan, so everything has to be such a sodding
production at mealtimes. Kids, right?'

Lucy gave him the sincerest smile she could muster at short notice.
'Kids.'

'*Exactly*.' Another swig of Diet Coke, then he thumped himself into a
swivel chair that really didn't look up to his weight. 'What's wrong with
sausages all of a sudden? Used to love sausages, did our Denise.' Mr Cartwright pulled over a knackered beige computer keyboard and poked at
it with a single fat finger. 'Or McNuggets? It's not natural. Here we go.'

One of the screens stopped showing platform four and jumped to an
exterior shot instead – looking down, from a height of about twenty or
thirty feet, at the main entrance. The main doors were at the top of the
screen, the rest of the image taken up with a big swathe of pavement, all
the way to the anti-ramming bollards – installed in the wake of September the eleventh. Because apparently Al-Qaeda had a fatwa out against
those Great Satanic Bastions of Western Imperialism, AKA: the concourse branches of WHSmith, Costa, and the wee kiosk that cut keys and
sold lighters.

Still, at least the footage was in colour, which would help with identifying ex-DC Malcolm Louden.

Mr Cartwright's finger poked the keyboard again and the footage
lurched into fast forward, little people whizzing about their business. 'If
I'd told my mum and dad I was turning vegan, they'd've tanned my hide
with a belt. Now, all of a sudden, it's a "lifestyle choice", "everyone's
doing it", and you can't eat prawn cocktail crisps any more.'

The screen got darker, then the station lights came on and a sea of
humanity pulsed in and out of the station doors, every arrival or departure bringing a fresh wave with it. Until finally the last pulse broke on the
pavement, spreading out and evaporating as a dumpy woman in her
blue ScotRail uniform and yellow high-vis locked up. Then it was just
the occasional drunk staggering past.

'And don't get me started on bacon.'

The night flickered by.

It was still dark when another ScotRail high-vis unlocked the doors,
and a fresh wave of commuters broke against the station entrance.

Lucy pointed at the screen. 'Slow it down a bit. Don't want to miss him.'

'Anyway, yes, those guys coming up from Dundee.' Another swig of Diet Coke. 'We caught one of them selling drugs outside the gents. Can you believe that? Bold as brass, right there. Bet it's one of those county lines things you're always hearing about.'

During one low tide, between throngs, a lone figure appeared at the bottom left-hand corner of the screen. Hanging about for a loiter that only took a couple of seconds, but probably lasted fifteen minutes in real not-speeded-up time. He was pinched-in, thin, with shoulder-length greasy brown hair, a sharp face, grubby baseball cap, and a scabby jacket that had some sort of horrible brown stain all down the back. A bundle under one arm, a big wodge of cardboard under the other, a backpack over his shoulder. Then he glanced up at the camera.

'Can you pause it there?'

Mr Cartwright did. 'Someone's making a fortune, that's for certain. All those people, coming up here, selling *drugs* on our streets while we give them spare change for a cup of tea!'

The image was nice and sharp: that was definitely Malcolm Louden, looking pretty much identical to his final mugshot.

'OK, fast forward. We're looking for a little girl.'

The footage jumped to warp speed again – people whizzing by as Louden took up position just to one side of the entrance, laying out his cardboard and sleeping bag. He took off his hat, put it down for donations, and sat there, begging, until the timestamp hit 12:24:37.

'Freeze it!'

A child stood right in front of Malcolm Louden. Long red hair, held in a pair of Pippi Longstocking braids. Maybe ten or eleven years old. She was wearing a blue school uniform: not the normal red-and-grey ones that state-school kids wore, this was a blazer-and-tartan-skirt combo. There was even some sort of crest on the breast pocket.

The girl had a big brown-paper shopping bag with her, a smudge of turquoise on it that might have been writing. Maybe 'PRIMARK'?

'OK: play.'

Mr Cartwright poked the keyboard, and the footage started again.

The little girl said something to Louden, then gave him the bag. He reached in and pulled out a padded jacket, holding it up and staring as she put something in his baseball cap.

'Can we zoom in?'

'Let's see . . .' Mr Cartwright fiddled with the keyboard and the screen clunked into a partial close-up. Then again, and again, and again. The picture didn't start getting pixelated until the fifth or sixth go. 'That any good?'

The footage might've been in full colour, but it wasn't exactly great. There was a cold blue tinge to it, making the jacket look like old blood.

Lucy turned to the Dunk. 'Recognize the uniform?'

He squinted at the screen, moving in till his nose was less than a foot away. 'Oh, yeah. That's Bellside School for Girls, Castleview. Very swanky. Exclusive.' His bottom lip jutted out. 'Hang on: four and a bit weeks ago, wasn't that still school holidays?'

'Our Denise was on holidays.' Mr Cartwright glugged down some more room-temperature Diet Coke. 'But then she doesn't go to a posh girls' school.'

As if it mattered.

A nod from the Dunk. 'Bet this one wears it as a status symbol.' Putting on a posh accent for: ' "Look how precocious and special I am!", "I'm so much more important than you little people!", "My daddy drives a Bentley!" '

Lucy thumped him on the shoulder. 'All right, Leon Trotsky. Less social commentary, more policework.' She pointed at Mr Cartwright. 'Keep going.'

The footage whizzed forward till the shabby, hairy figure of Dr Rayner turned up to collect Louden for their shoplifting expedition, 13:09:23. And that was it; neither of them came back to the train station.

'OK. We need to see the same time period, every morning for the rest of the week.'

A confused look from the Dunk. 'Sarge?'

'You heard Dr Rayner: this was Malcolm Louden's morning spot, regular as clockwork. It took Rayner a week to notice Louden was missing, but soon as we can't find him on the footage . . . ?'

'We'll know when he really disappeared.' The Dunk nodded. 'Got you.'

They ran through the other two days on the hard drive, then moved on to: 'MAIN ENTRANCE, 10 AUG → 12 AUG', 'MAIN ENTRANCE, 13 AUG → 15 AUG', and 'MAIN ENTRANCE, 16 AUG → 18 AUG' just to be sure. But Malcolm Louden never appeared again.

Which meant the Bloodsmith probably abducted Louden on the

same day the little girl gave him his nice new coat, sometime after the shoplifting trip to M&S.

Now all they had to do was work out where and when. And, with any luck, that would be on CCTV as well, because if it *was*: the Bloodsmith was screwed.

Back at DHQ, the only member of Operation Maypole not out searching the woods was DC Stan Talladale – though, to be honest, what with the baggy bloodshot eyes, pale grey-green face, and trembling hands, it looked as if he would've been better off in the mortuary. Awaiting his turn on the cutting table.

Waves of Irn-Bru and extra-strong mint spilled out of him like chemical warfare, wafted on a gurgling burp. Clearly turning fifty didn't bring a whole heap of wisdom with it, if you couldn't tell you were too old to be getting wankered down the pub with your colleagues on a school night.

He blinked up at Lucy and burped again. Grimaced. Rubbed at his chest. 'Must've been something I ate.'

'Yes, Stan, I'm sure *that's* what it is. Nothing to do with several rounds of tequila, sambuca, Jägermeister, and whisky-Red-Bulls.' She perched on the edge of his desk. 'Should've taken today off.'

'Can't. Janet wants to spend a month in Australia with the grandkids. Going to max out my holiday allowance as it is.' He shuddered, then took another scoof from his tin. 'Now, would you mind sodding off, Sarge, so I can die in peace?'

'Before you expire, I've got a job for you.'

He groaned and slumped that bit further into himself.

Lucy pulled out Malcolm Louden's final mugshot and slapped it down on the desk. 'This is our body in the woods. He's one of ours: ex-detective constable.'

Stan hissed out an Irn-Bru-and-mint breath. 'Poor sod . . .'

'I need you to comb the city centre CCTV. Last seen on camera outside the train station: eighth of August, ten past one. That's PM, not AM. I need to know where he went and who he talked to.'

There was a wheezy silence.

Then, 'Please, Sarge, don't make me sit in front of whizzy security footage all day, I'll barf every—'

'He's one of *ours*, Stan.' She thumped the useless dick on the shoulder, and not gently either. 'Get a couple of support staff to help, but I want his movements on my desk by close of play.'

The door banged open, and there was the Dunk, with a folder tucked under his arm. 'Media's arrived.'

'Of course they have.'

'Setting up shop out front, getting ready for the lunchtime news. Superintendent Spence's doing a presser at one fifteen. You wanna hang around for it?'

'Of *course* I do, Dunk. Can't think of *anything* I'd enjoy more. Can *barely* contain myself with excitement.'

'Fair enough.' He held up his folder. 'Got the stills printed off.'

'Good boy. Give a couple to Stan the Man; he's kindly volunteered to find Malcolm Louden on the CCTV.'

'Ouch.' The Dunk produced a picture of Louden in his nice new coat, and one of the little girl who'd given it to him. 'Surprised you're in the day, Stanny. Monster Munch tells me you ate *two* deep-fried doners from Kebabarama, last night. Your innards must be like a Damien Hirst installation.'

'Oh God.' He tipped forward until he was half-prostrate on the desk. '*Told* you it was something I ate.'

Lucy thumped him again. 'CCTV footage, Stan. By the end of the day. Or you'll have more than dodgy guts to worry about.'

'Kill me now . . .'

Tempting. But they had other things to be getting on with.

She collected the Dunk and headed out into the corridor. Stopped dead.

'Sarge?' He blinked up at her.

That sod from Professional Standards, the one who'd been lurking outside DCI Gilmore's office, was lurking again, with his dark-grey suit and stupid spiky hair. A Police Scotland branded mug in one hand. 'Ah, Detective Sergeant McVeigh. Thought I might run into you here.'

'Dunk?'

'Yes, Sarge?'

'Get the car started. I'll be down in a minute.'

A shrug and the wee lump shuffled off down the corridor.

When he was out of earshot, Lucy made a show of checking her watch. 'I'm in the middle of trying to catch a serial killer.'

'I still need to talk to you, DS McVeigh, or can I call you "Lucy"?'

'No. And I don't have time for "guidance" and "support" right now.' Or ever. She marched off after the Dunk. 'Sorry.' Not meaning it.

The dick from Professional Standards appeared beside her, matching stride for stride. 'I can make a formal request, through the chain of command if you like, but it would be easier for us *both* if we could just sit down and—'

'Thanks for your concern, but I'm *busy*.' She barged into the stairwell, then took a hard right, shoving through the door to the ladies' toilets – letting it thump shut in his face.

His voice was muffled by the wood, but still audible as she made for the cubicles. *'You can avoid me all you like, DS McVeigh, but you're going to have to talk to me sooner or later. Might as well make it now.'*

No chance.

15

The Dunk hadn't been lying about the media. A handful of outside-broadcast vans sat by the kerb in front of DHQ, cameras and presenters braving the rain to do pre-records for the one o'clock news. Some of them already packing up to head in for Superintendent Spence's press briefing.

Lucy popped a couple of paracetamol from their blister pack and scowled out the passenger window at the assembled hordes. 'Sod . . .'

There was Sarah Black, elbowing her way in front of the ITV camera crew, holding a placard with 'LYING POLICE MURDERED MY SON!!!' on it in blood-red letters.

How could they let her out so quickly? Did they even give her a slap on the wrists? Or was it just, *'Here, you have a nice sit down, a cup of tea, and a biscuit, while we forget* all *about you assaulting that nasty police officer.'*

Didn't exactly make you feel valued.

'Ignore her, Sarge. Woman's a Dundee cake.' The Dunk sped the pool car up a bit, till the lard-pale lump of Sarah Black was nothing but a smear in the rear-view mirror.

Ignore her?

Easier said than done.

The Dunk turned their pool car off Keirbarrie Drive onto Bradley Avenue. 'I mean, how could anyone in their right mind eat even *one* of those things?'

Bellside School for Girls sat on the left, behind a chest-high stone wall topped with chain link. Presumably to stop a rogue hockey ball from flying out and beaning a passer-by. And to keep the precious, over-privileged little darlings safe from the dirty outside world, of course.

They'd added to the old Victorian building over the years: a swanky new glass-and-steel wing off to one side, a brutal concrete seventies block off to the other. Playing grounds – marked out for hockey, lacrosse, and football – that stretched nearly all the way down to the slate-grey river. The sky a solid lid of ash, raining hard enough to make the wind-screen wipers creak back and forth in grubby arcs.

The Dunk pulled up at the gated entrance. 'Because it's not just the doner meat they deep-fry, it's the *whole kebab*. Pita bread, salad, chilli-and-garlic sauce – it all gets battered and chucked in boiling oil.' He wound down his window and pressed the big red button on the inter-com fixed to the wall. 'You'd have to be absolutely *blootered*.'

A buzzing whine fizzed out into the rain, followed by a woman's dis-torted voice. *'Yes? Do you have an appointment?'*

He held his warrant card out at the camera. 'Police. We need to talk to someone about a student here.'

'And do you have an appointment?'

'You want us to come back with a warrant? Cos we can, if you like. Only that might not look too good when it gets in the papers: "Private school refuses to help police catch killer, shock!"'

'Hold on. I'll need to check school policy.'

Lucy glared at him. 'You're not supposed to tell people we're investi-gating a murder!'

'Oh, come on, Sarge: these posh twats need to learn a bit of—'

The intercom buzzed again and the gates swung open.

He grinned back at her. 'See?' The Dunk slid the car through onto school grounds, following the signs for 'VISITOR PARKING'. Nodding to himself, as if he was the wisest person in the whole soggy world. 'You've just got to know how to talk to these people. Show even a sliver of weakness and they'll walk all over you.'

'I see.' Mrs Pablo's office was in the new glass-and-steel bit of the school, with floor-to-ceiling windows offering a panoramic view south across the playing grounds as the rain hammered down. The headmistress her-self was a twinset-and-pearls type, her grey hair cut into a trendy layered bob, with discreet gold earrings and a shiny crucifix dangling from one of those expensive charm bracelets. She wielded the kind of voice that could probably slice across an entire hockey pitch to cut a kid in half. 'And you don't have a warrant.'

Not a question, a statement.

She hadn't offered them a seat, just sat there behind an 'executive' desk with her fingers steepled beneath the point of her sharp chin.

Lucy pulled out a printout of the little girl and placed it on the blotting pad. 'We're not looking to get anyone into trouble; no one's a suspect. We think this child might have seen something that could assist us, that's all.'

'I see.' Mrs Pablo pursed her lips and gave them both a cold hard stare.

The Dunk shifted his shoes on the polished floorboards, pink skin glowing above the collar of his black polo neck. Hadn't said a single word since they'd been shown into the headmistress's office. Stood there like a plank of wood instead. So much for his proletarian revolution and teaching 'these posh twats' a lesson.

'If you could take a *look*, that would be a great help.'

A sigh, then Mrs Pablo put on a pair of half-moon glasses and peered down her nose at the printout. She stiffened. 'Yes, I recognize this child.'

'And?'

'And nothing. She no longer attends Bellside School for Girls.' Mrs Pablo stood, doing up the buttons on her ugly cardigan. 'Now, if you'll excuse me, it's lunchtime and I have students to supervise.' Then she swept out of the room, leaving the pair of them standing there like a couple of prats.

So much for assisting the police with their inquiries . . .

Lucy marched after her into a small reception area. The kind of place where wayward girls would squirm on hard wooden seats, awaiting their summons to the dragon's lair. 'Is that it?'

The headmistress nodded at the room's small, and currently unmanned, desk. 'Mr Marlins will see you out.'

'You could at least tell us the kid's name.'

'We don't answer questions about pupils without their parents' permission. Present *or* former.' Opening the outer door and raising her voice. 'Mr Marlins! These officers are leaving.'

The reply came in a high-pitched obsequious Dundee accent. '*Yes, Mrs Pablo.*'

Then off she marched, head held high, back stiff, as if someone had jammed a flagpole up her backside.

The Dunk cleared his throat. 'See what I mean? Come the revolution . . .'

'Oh, *now* you're brave enough to speak, are you?' Lucy pointed at the open doorway. 'Where were all your proud class-struggle speeches when Madame Twin-Set was fobbing us off?'

'Excuse me?' The owner of the squeaky Dundonian accent appeared. His tweed suit, paisley-patterned waistcoat, polished brogues, and short white hair made him look like the illicit love child of the White Rabbit from *Alice in Wonderland* and Toad of Toad Hall. 'I believe Mrs Pablo would like me to escort you back to your vehicle, if that's all right? We don't like unaccompanied adults on school grounds, for obvious reasons.' He blanched, held up his hands. 'Not that I'm suggesting either of you would . . . with the girls, but rules have to be rules for everyone, or there's no point having rules at all, don't you think?' Then Mr Marlins ushered them out into the corridor. 'Horrible day, isn't it? Still, at least it's not snowing. Small mercies.'

They followed him downstairs to the ground floor.

Lucy stopped, made a big show of rolling her eyes and sighing, throwing in a slap on the forehead for good measure. 'What an idiot.' She dug the printout out of her pocket again. 'We came all this way and I forgot to ask Mrs Pablo if she knew who the girl in the picture is.' Holding it so close to Mr Marlins' face that he had to blink and back up a couple of paces to get it into focus. Put, literally, on the back foot.

'What, Allegra Dean-Edwards? Oh, she doesn't go here any more. Her parents got her into St Nick's. Which I know has a great reputation, but we pride ourselves at Bellside School for Girls on our top-notch curriculum and teaching excellence.'

St Nick's . . . Now there was a name she hadn't heard in a long, long time.

The Dunk pulled his chin up. 'What's St Nick's?'

'St Nicholas College, Auchterowan?' Mr Marlin's voice dropped to an awed whisper: 'Only one of *the* most exclusive boarding schools in the country.'

'Yeah, not really the kinda circles I move in.'

Mr Marlins peered at the printout again. 'Is she giving that homeless person a new coat? Well, I must say, that's very "on brand" for our Allegra. Don't think I've ever met a child quite as focused and sure of herself. Knew what she wanted to be from the start of primary one – the outreach stuff, the sandwiches and coats for the homeless, raising money for a hostel, that's Allegra working on her "brand". Thinks it'll give her the edge when it comes to getting into Oxford. I kept telling her: "They don't care about extra-curricular activities, Allegra. They only care about academic achievements." But once she gets an idea in her head?' He rolled his eyes. 'And she's only eleven.'

'Sounds like a nice kid.' Lucy took the picture back.

'Oh, *personality* like nails down a blackboard, but sharp as you wouldn't believe. And as I say: focused. She's going to end up ruling the world one day, you mark my words.'

'Penny for them.'

'Hmmm?' Lucy stayed where she was, staring out through the passenger window as the rain washed across the city in gritty-grey swathes, like smoke. Toning everything down. Leaching the life out of it.

'Let me guess' – the Dunk took the first exit at the roundabout, heading over Dundas Bridge, Castle Hill looming on the other side in all its twisted glory – 'Sarah Black.'

'Not everything is about Sarah Bloody Black.' A long breath hissed out between Lucy's pursed lips. 'Well, kind of.' A lopsided shrug. 'I was wondering: the guy who's been following me, what if he's not some random stalker pervert? What if the Blacks have bunged him a few quid to harass me?'

'Oooh . . . Yeah. Explains the slashed tyres, doesn't it? Sending you a message?'

Hard to tell if that made him more or less dangerous. The kind of man who'd happily menace a woman for money was probably the kind of man who'd think rape was a perk of the job. That she was his for the taking. And Lucy'd had more than enough experience of that kind of crap to last several lifetimes, thank you very much. God knew enough women got murdered every year by toxic, horny shitheads.

And what if he attacked her somewhere more secluded than right outside Divisional Headquarters? After all, he knew where she lived . . .

Lucy reached into her raincoat pocket. No sign of DI Tudor's rape alarm. It was back at the house, in her overcoat.

All that time, meandering about town this morning, did she take ten minutes to pop into Argos for that baseball bat? Of course she didn't. Still hadn't phoned anyone about getting the house fitted up with a security system, either.

Great. Well done, Lucy. Way to keep yourself safe.

The Dunk cleared his throat. 'Maybe you should, you know, crash at mine for a couple of nights? Zoe won't mind. Kind of. It's only a couch, but maybe better than being on your own, out in the middle of nowhere?'

So, the daft little sod was a mind reader now, was he?

'Thanks, Dunk, but—'

Her phone launched into its generic ringtone, and when she pulled it out, 'DI TUDOR' glowed in the middle of its screen. Think of the Devil. She hit the green button. 'Thought you were in the post-mortem.'

'Hairy Harry's declared a tea break. Our beloved Procurator Fiscal is off shouting at someone on her phone, so thought I'd give you a bell. See how it's going.'

'We've got an ID for the victim. He's—'

'I know, DCI Ross filled me in. He says you had a run-in with Sarah Black this morning. She's claiming you assaulted her.'

'I already had this conversation with Professional Standards and—'

'The woman's a bloody menace. Stay away from her, though, eh? Last thing we need is Sarah Cocking Black crapping in the swimming pool along with everyone else.'

'She attacked *me*, remember? It wasn't like I went looking for—'

'It's just, these last couple of months you've been . . . I don't want her setting you off, OK? I need you focused on the Bloodsmith, not fighting with Sarah Black and her idiot offspring.'

The Dunk was staring at her across the car, eyebrows raised as they trundled along behind a bus.

Lucy placed a hand across her eyes and squeezed, just hard enough to make little black dots, circled in yellow, appear. Forcing the words out between clenched teeth. 'Yes, Boss.'

'I mean it, Lucy.' A pause. *'So, where are you?'*

'Me and the Dunk went looking for the little girl who gave Malcolm Louden his new coat. Just in case she saw or remembered something.'

'Why am I hearing defeat?'

'Tracked her down to Bellside School for Girls, but she's left there. Goes to St Nick's now.'

A low whistle. *'Swanky.'*

'I've got DC Talladale digging through the city CCTV anyway, so we can probably do without traipsing all the way out to Auchterowan. Maybe talk to a few more of the homeless community instead? We could organize a—'

'After what happened this morning, you're better off staying as far away from DHQ as possible; Sarah Black's still out there with her bloody placard. Go see the swanky schoolkid. You never know: maybe she saw someone hanging around? Cover all the bases.'

'Wouldn't it be more productive to—'

'The top brass think ex-DC Louden's criminal record is going to spin round and sink its fangs in our arse. They're sending an assistant chief constable from Gartcosh to "liaise". Like I don't have enough arseholes breathing down my neck already! A hundred quid says he'll be one of those anal, misery-faced, everything-by-the-book types, and if he finds out we didn't follow up every – single – lead, no matter how crap or thin, it'll be me getting kicked in the nuts with a size twelve. So, you're definitely *going to see that schoolkid.'*

'But—'

'And how am I supposed to catch the Bloodsmith when I've got three million layers of management peering over my shoulder the whole time? It's not—'

Lucy pressed the phone against her chest as Tudor moaned and whinged. 'Change of plan, Dunk, we're going to St Nick's after all.'

'Not *more* posh twats?'

'Yes, more posh twats.'

'Gah . . .' He did a one-eighty at the next roundabout, heading back the way they'd just come. 'Any chance we can stop for food along the way? Starving.'

Back to the phone.

'—don't trust me to run an investigation, then why lumber me with it? It's like juggling handfuls of burning shite, Lucy, and I'm sick of it.'

'Look, Boss, about this Sarah Black thing—'

'Hold on, Spudzilla's on the warpath again. Think we're—' Then the line went dead.

Lovely.

Lucy put her phone away.

'So . . .' the Dunk tried his hopeful-puppy face, 'lunch?'

'Yeah, why not.'

The sticky-brown scent of fried onions slithered across the car park and in through the pool car's passenger window, courtesy of Bad Bill's Burger Bar – parked outside the Beaton Wood Sports Centre, in the heart of the Swinney, trees pressing in on every side. If this was California, or somewhere swanky, it would've been called a 'food truck', but here it was just a manky old converted Transit van: painted matt black, so Bad Bill could chalk up the day's specials on the sides. He had the serving-hatch flap raised, affording the Dunk a little protection from the slashing rain. But not much.

The soggy wee sod was at the counter, stretching his tiny frame and pointing at things on the menu board, like a small child at an ice-cream van. Not the most commanding of police presences.

Meanwhile, warmish and dry, Lucy sagged in her seat and frowned out at the dark mass of pine and birch that lined the business park. Raindrops crackled like fireworks against the Vauxhall's bonnet and, for a moment, they were loud enough to drown out the saccharine hold-music droning out of her phone, which was nice.

Who on earth thought a pan-pipes rendition of Ricky Martin's 'Livin' La Vida Loca' would be a good idea? And on a *loop*?

She had to listen to the tootling horror three more times before a woman's voice cut it off:

'*Miss McVeigh?*' About sodding time. '*Sorry: been checking the schedule. We can fit you in on Monday, if that helps? Can't do any sooner, I'm afraid – Kevin's away in Vegas for his daughter's wedding, and we're stappit foo. Everyone and their neighbour's dog want security systems fitted this month.*'

Sod.

Lucy suppressed a sigh. 'No, that's . . . Monday. OK.'

'*I can put you on the wait list, if we get a cancellation?*'

'Please.'

'*Righty ho. Stay safe!*' They hung up.

So much for that. *Definitely* have to get a baseball bat now.

16

The Dunk hurried around to the driver's side, hauled the door open, and scrambled in behind the wheel, bringing with him an extra-heavy waft of fried meat. A couple of Styrofoam containers balanced in one hand, a pair of wax-paper cups in the other. Dripping as he wriggled in his seat. 'Like a lake out there.' He gave himself a little shake, then held out one of the cartons.

'What is it?'

'You said, "Surprise me."'

Fair enough.

He put his own on the dashboard, then passed her one of the cups. 'Tea. Milk. No sugar.' Then went into a pocket for a handful of paper napkins. Gave three quarters of them to her, before tucking one into the collar of his soggy polo neck.

Lucy creaked her polystyrene container open and peered in at what was probably the dirtiest burger known to man. A couple of what looked like Bacon Frazzles had escaped from beneath the bun, turned slightly limp in a smear of pink sauce. 'OK: I'm surprised.'

'Double Bastard Bacon Murder Burger.' The Dunk opened his own container and dug at the brown-and-white sludge inside with a little wooden spork. Leaning forwards to take a delicate mouthful. Probably trying not to get anything sticky on his damp black ensemble. Chewing and swallowing before washing it down with a sip of tea. 'You know what I've been thinking about?'

'Is it me having a heart attack?' Because there was clearly enough saturated fat in this thing to clog an elephant's arteries. Didn't taste bad, though. Pickles, cheese, Bacon Frazzles, two burgers, lettuce, a sesame bun, and *all* the sauces: tomato, brown, Marie Rose, chilli, and mustard too. 'What've you got?'

'Stovies.' Another dainty bite.

'*I* like stovies.'

'Yeah, I know. But that wouldn't have been a surprise, would it?' More stovies were delicately nibbled. 'Anyway, what I've been thinking is: why did the Bloodsmith go back to the cottage in the woods? The first one, I mean, where he killed Abby Geddes. Why go back and write "help me" again?'

'Because we bleached the first one away.'

'Again: yeah, I know. But the words have to matter for him to do that, don't they? Otherwise, why bother?'

The Dunk had a point.

The Bloodsmith didn't—

Her phone rang, deep in her pocket.

'Sodding hell.' She placed the burger back in its Styrofoam coffin and sooked her fingers clean. Used one of the Dunk's napkins as a makeshift glove to haul her mobile out and answer it. 'McVeigh.'

A woman's voice, slurred and heavy, as if every word weighed a ton. '*I heard . . . it was . . . it was on the news juss . . . just now.*' Judith Thorburn. Again. Sounding even less sober than last time.

Don't swear.

The Dunk raised an eyebrow at her, spork poised with a glistening mound of stovies balanced on the end.

'Judith.'

He pulled a face and rolled his eyes.

'*They say . . . say you're not . . . and he's getting away with it! . . . He's . . .*' Silence.

'Judith, we're investigating as fast as we can, I promise you.'

'*My Craig . . .*' A sob. '*My little boy. I need his . . . his heart back! How am . . . how's he supposed to rest without . . . without his heart?*' Her tears howled down the phone. '*I want my baby's heart back!*'

'I know you do, Judith. I know you do. We're doing everything we can.'

'*I need his . . . heart.*' Then the line went dead.

Lucy sagged in her seat, head back, face screwed up.

'Sarge.' The Dunk hissed air in through his teeth. 'I don't mean to be insensitive or anything, but is it not a bit late for Judith Thorburn to play the doting mother? Last time I checked, she hadn't spoken to Craig for about six months before the Bloodsmith got him.'

'Does it matter?' Estranged or not, it was impossible to deny the pain in the poor cow's voice.

He didn't answer that right away, just sat there frowning. Then: 'No, I suppose not. You don't know what you've got, do you? Not till it's gone.' He munched on another sporkful of stovies. 'Anyway, yes: why does the Bloodsmith redo his "help me" messages?'

Lucy ate in silence for a bit, mulling it over. 'What if it's not a cry for help, what if it's . . . a *prayer*? A sort of votive offering.'

'Like, when you go to the Wailing Wall and fold up your prayer and stick it in the cracks?' He nodded. 'I can see that. And we bleached away his prayer at the cottage, so he had to write it again.' The nod turned to a frown. 'Didn't need to do that at Bruce Malloch's house, because it wasn't cleaned off in the first place.'

'But he wouldn't know that – the blinds were down, remember?'

'Oooh . . .' The Dunk's eyebrows went up. 'Unless he broke in.'

'Maybe he didn't need to? Not if he helped himself to a set of keys when he killed Malloch.' A dribble of Marie Rose escaped, snaking its way down Lucy's wrist. She caught it with her tongue. 'This thing is impossible to eat without it going everywhere.'

'Adam Holmes' flat must be driving the Bloodsmith up the wall. Whole place has been redecorated: his prayer's missing, and he can't paint it up again, because there's people living there. Shouty, horrible people.'

'We should check – see if the shouty, horrible people have had any weird notes pushed under their door lately. Or graffiti.' Lucy crammed the last chunk of meat and sauce and bun into her gob. 'Woosnrrrrr-noodnoo cheg mgnnno ooghnoow cwooemszheennn?'

'Not with your mouth full, Sarge!' The Dunk's next two sporkfuls were done with exaggerated care. 'God, it's like having lunch with a Labradoodle.'

She wiped her hands on a napkin. 'I said, "We still need to check the other crime scenes." You rude little sod.' Tossing the soggy, smeared napkin into the now empty Styrofoam container. Then had a tidy-up with a second one. And a third.

The Dunk went back to eating like a normal person. Munch, munch, munch. 'Want to do it on the way home from school? Jane Cooper's place is in Castleview, and Craig Thorburn's Blackwall Hill. Not that far out of our way.'

'Done.' Lucy opened her tea and took a sip. Lukewarm, slightly bitter from being over-brewed, the teabag floating in the beige milky liquid like a drowned man. 'Finish your stovies, then we'll go see a precocious little girl about an altruistic gesture.'

'Bloody hell . . .' The Dunk stared as the pool car drifted to a halt. Eyes wide, mouth hanging open. The windscreen wipers *thunk-squeak*ed back and forth, bringing the place into focus, before the rain blurred it all away again.

St Nicholas College, Auchterowan, sat just outside the little town, down a wide avenue of trees that shivered in the downpour. And. It. Was. *Huge*.

Looked pretty old, too: a vast Scottish baronial pile, complete with turrets, corbels, and steep-sloping roofs. Tall, narrow, mullioned windows. What looked like an old vampire's castle looming up behind one corner.

A gatehouse, complete with raised portcullis, sat about a third of the way down the drive, with what was either a drained moat, or a ha-ha stretching away into the distance on either side. As if they were expecting Visigoths to come charging over the hill at any moment.

And the Dunk just sat there, gawping. 'Can you imagine how much this place must be *worth*?'

'Yes. Now any chance you can actually drive us over there?'

'Sorry, Sarge.' The Vauxhall's gearbox made a horrible grinding noise as he struggled it into first. Then kangarooed forwards a couple of feet and stalled dead.

'Not making the best of impressions, here, Dunk.'

'No, Sarge, sorry, Sarge.' That familiar pink tinge was working its way up from the collar of his polo neck again. But he finally got the car going, taking them up to the gatehouse, where a striped barrier was lowered to block their way.

A middle-aged man in a bowler hat and black suit stepped out in front of them, hand up, face like an unhappy spud. One of his ears was all folded in and swollen, and his nose had been broken so often it was barely there. Broad shoulders, big hands. That, and his black suit, made him look like a boxer on his way to a funeral. 'Can I help you, sir? Madam?'

The Dunk shrank back in his seat, hands so tightly wrapped around the steering wheel his knuckles stood out like a row of white skulls. 'I . . .'

God's sake.

Lucy produced her warrant card and leaned across the car, holding it up so the porter could see. 'Police. We need to talk to someone about a pupil of yours.'

'Hmmmph . . .' The shattered nose came up. 'I shall have to contact the headmaster. Wait here.' Then he stomped away back into his lodge again.

'Hoy!' Lucy gave the Dunk a serious thump on the arm. 'What the hell is wrong with you?'

The blush deepened. 'It's not my fault, OK? I have . . . issues with—'

'Right.' And just like that, the porter was back. Didn't make a sound, just appeared at the driver's window, like a disapproving ninja. 'You're to go up to the main hall. Park out front.' He produced a pair of lanyards and thrust them in through the window. 'Wear these at all times.' Then he raised the barrier and scowled at them until the Dunk finally got his finger out and drove off.

Up close, St Nick's looked even bigger, towering over the pool car as the Dunk parked where he'd been told to.

A boy was waiting for them: mid-teens, tall and thin in a dark-grey suit, white shirt, and patterned burgundy tie. He was wearing a black academic gown over the top, reaching down to his knees, with a single gold epaulette on the left shoulder. Sheltering under a large black golf umbrella with the school crest on it: a mailed fist clutching a scroll and quills, with a Maltese cross on one side and three daggers on the other. The top half of a rampant lion roaring over the top of the shield, and 'FIDES ⫶ SILENTIUM ⫶ POTENTIA' on a scroll underneath.

As Lucy opened her door he stepped forward, shielding her from the rain with his brolly, before conjuring another one from behind his back and handing it to her.

His voice was stuffed with plums and cut crystal, the Scottish accent barely noticeable. 'Detective Sergeant McVeigh? The headmaster sends his regards and asks if you and your colleague would accompany me to the Archers' Gallery.'

'Of course.'

The Dunk scurried around from his side of the car, plipping the locks, and squeezing in under Lucy's borrowed umbrella. Mouth opening and closing, no sound coming out.

Not exactly his finest day.

Their escort turned and marched along the front of the building, taking a hard left through an open archway flanked by small turrets. It led through into a quadrangle that was probably big enough to hold a full-sized football pitch, enclosed on all four sides by more Scottish baronial buildings, tall windows looking out over the flagstone paths, grass, and an ancient oak tree. Its branches were heavy and twisted, the lower ones fluttering with black and red ribbons. That vampire's castle made up the far corner, jagged and dark against the lowering skies. Looming.

A group of four teenagers – two boys and two girls, dressed in identical dark-grey suits, white shirts, burgundy ties, and black gowns – swept out of a door to the side. Black golf umbrellas clacked up and the kids bustled along one of the paths, like a tiny murder of crows. Making for a door on the opposite side.

The Dunk kept his voice down. 'Jesus. Hogwarts, much?'

Lucy matched his whisper. 'Good grief: it speaks!'

He pointed at their escort as they followed him out into the quad. 'And what's with the outfit? Fancy-dress time?'

'The one gold epaulette means he's an under-prefect. Two gold makes you a prefect. Single red means you're a house leader. Blue: class monitor. And white's for new students.'

They passed the twisted oak, rain clattering down on the shared brolly.

'How come you know so much about St Nicholas College?'

Their escort cast a smile over his shoulder at them. 'Not far to go now.' Then took a right, onto an intersecting path, making for an older-looking, two-storey bit of the school – its sharp-pitched roof lined with gargoyles, water spewing out of their mouths. The windows here were little more than slits.

A heavy wooden door opened on a wide hallway with a sweeping stone staircase, the walls thick with coats of arms, each one picked out in carved wood or moulded plaster. They lined the staircase, too.

Their escort closed his brolly and slipped it into an elaborate brass holder by the door, then held his hand out. 'If I may . . . ?' He relieved Lucy of her umbrella and put it next to his. Then took the stairs up, pointing at a crest on the way. 'That was my great-grandfather's. We've been coming here for six generations.'

The Dunk's face went even pinker.

At the top of the stairs was a wide corridor with a vaulted ceiling. Big lancet windows sat at either end, vivid with stained glass. They glowed, casting multicoloured shapes across the flagstones, even though A: there was sod-all sign of any sunshine outside, and B: the buildings flanking this one were both a storey taller.

One side of the corridor had three ancient wooden doors leading off it, each bearing a small engraved nameplate: 'MR WINCHESTER ~ FINANCIAL STATISTICS', 'MRS WELLS ~ STOCK MARKET ANALYSIS', and 'MS PESTON ~ INTERNATIONAL TAX LAW'.

The other wall held more rows of family crests, broken up by those thin deep windows overlooking the quadrangle.

Their escort held up a hand. 'If you wouldn't mind waiting here.' Then he knocked lightly on the door to Ms Peston's class, slipping inside only when the word *'Enter!'* boomed out through the wood. A trio of children, each with two white epaulettes on their academic gowns, sat at individual, fancy-looking desks, behind swanky laptops with the school crest on them. They didn't look around, just kept their eyes on whatever the teacher had projected on the far wall.

Soon as the door closed behind their escort, the Dunk sagged. 'Bloody Norah. Did you *hear* him?' Putting on an exaggerated posh accent for: ' "We've been coming here for six generations." ' A snort, and the Dunk was back to his normal voice again. 'And where does he get off ordering us about?' Stomping over to the nearest window and glaring out at the rain.

'Yes, because you *definitely* put him in his place, didn't you? With your trademark not-saying-anything-and-blushing-like-a-nervous-teenage-girl.' Lucy gave him a slow round of applause. 'Made quite the impression. I had goosebumps.'

'That's what hereditary privilege gets you. Everyone in the whole sodding world only exists for your convenience, because you're *better* than them. You earned their obsequious kowtowing servitude just by dropping out of some stuck-up rich bint nine months after she shagged the footman. That's not an "accident of birth", no, that's *destiny*! Here, why not have a seat in the House of Lords while you're at it, you unqualified, unelected, toffee-nosed twat!'

'Are you finished?'

'Know what we should have? Hundred percent taxation on all inherited wealth over . . . a hundred grand. Then the buggers would have to spend it before they died – put it back into the economy, where it'll do a bit of good, instead of these Swiss-bank trust-fund wankers' pockets. They hoard money, they hoard power, they hoard privilege, and to hell with the rest of us!'

'Bravo.' It was a man's voice, right behind them: warm, round, and rich as a mahogany sideboard, with more than a hint of a chuckle to it. 'I see we have a maverick economic theorist in our midst.'

The Dunk's mouth shut so fast you could hear his teeth clatter together. Then his face paled a couple of shades, before the blush resurfaced again.

Lucy turned. 'Headmaster?'

The man beamed back at her. He was in the same dark-grey suit and burgundy tie as the pupils, but his academic robe was a deep shade of crimson, edged with gold. A wispy tuft of white hair clung on for dear life at the top of his head, while the rest was reduced to little more than fuzz. Piercing blue eyes, a hooked nose, and lots and lots of laughter lines. He stuck out a liver-spotted hand. 'Arnold Price-Hamilton, at your service, Detective Sergeant McVeigh.' He turned to the Dunk. 'I don't believe our head porter got your name, young man . . . ?'

Nope. You'd have more luck getting a reply out of a doorstop.

'This is Detective Constable Fraser. He's your basic strong, silent type.' As if. 'We need to talk to one of your students, an Allegra Dean-Edwards?'

'I see.' The headmaster's smile turned into a frown. 'May I ask *why* you need to talk to Ms Dean-Edwards?'

The door to the classroom opened again, and out slithered their escort. Clicking it shut almost silently behind him. Then stood there, not saying a word, hands clasped in front of his crotch.

'Allegra's not in any trouble, if that's what you're worrying about. She bought a new coat for a homeless man, about five weeks ago; we're hoping she might have seen something that could help with our inquiry. It's a long shot, but we have to be thorough about these things.'

'Hmmm . . .' Then a nod. 'Skye? Fetch Mr McCaskill for me, would you? We'll be in my office.'

'Yes, Headmaster.' And off the young man trotted. Six generations of wealth and privilege, and he was still stuck running errands.

Lucy raised an eyebrow. 'Sky? They named him after a TV station?'

' "Skye", with an "E". His family own large chunks of it.' The head-master turned on his heel, crimson robe swirling out behind him as he set off for the stairs at an impressive clip. 'Skye's got an older brother called Argyll, and a sister called Sutherland, for much the same reason. I guess you could say they're a family that finds a theme and sticks with it.'

The Dunk was already falling behind, but Lucy kept up fine.

'McVeigh, McVeigh, McVeigh.' The headmaster's eyes kept flicking in her direction. 'Excuse me if I seem nosy, but the name rings a bell.'

Of course it did, because after a year of Sarah Black banging on to any scumbag media outlet who'd listen, why wouldn't it?

She cleared her throat. 'There was an . . . incident last August; it was in all the—'

'No, I'm sure that's not it.' At the bottom of the stairs he marched straight for the door, snatching one of the brollies from the stand on his way past. Snapping it open like a magic trick. 'McVeigh. I'm sure we had a student here called McVeigh. Any relation?'

'Don't think so.' She grabbed the other umbrella, wrestling it up as she followed him out into the rain. 'I *almost* went here, when I finished primary school. Did the aptitude tests, interviews, and exams, then my dad . . .' *Had another breakdown* was probably oversharing a bit. Besides, that was no one's business but hers, now. 'Turned out we couldn't afford the fees after all. Never did the final assessment.'

The headmaster stopped. Put a hand on her arm. 'I'm *so* sorry to hear that. If it's any consolation, we now have a bursary scheme so children from less fortunate backgrounds can attend St Nicholas College.'

Which was both nice to know and insulting all at the same time. *Here's what you could've won.* If you hadn't had such a threadbare pauper basket-case for a father.

Then the headmaster was off again, taking one of the paths that branched towards the far back corner, where the vampire-castle bit reared up into the grey skies. Unlike the rest of the quad, the thick square tower had been Frankensteined together with random-shaped dark blocks, and was clearly a lot older than the neat sandstone buildings grafted onto either side of it.

At the end of the path, he shoved open the thick wooden door and held it for Lucy. 'I shall have to look out your records.' Throwing in a wink for good measure. 'See how you fared.'

Not sure she really wanted to find out . . .

17

The headmaster looked over Lucy's shoulder, out into the rain. 'Your friend, the financial revolutionary, he's not the fastest, is he?'

Difficult to tell if that was a dig at the Dunk's physical or intellectual speed. Didn't matter, though, because you didn't take the piss out of your fellow officers in front of civilians. Even civilians who were right on both counts.

When Lucy turned, the Dunk was still only halfway across the quad, one hand holding that stupid leather bunnet to his head, the other pinching his jacket's neck shut as he scurried through the rain on those short little legs of his. 'We probably better wait for him. Unaccompanied adult on school grounds and all that.'

A chuckle broke free, dark and patronizing. 'Oh, I wouldn't worry about it, Detective Sergeant. When we say our aim is to prepare our young academics for the world, we really mean it. Self-defence is one of the first classes anyone takes when they get here – it teaches discipline and self-control. Besides, you're police officers. If we can't trust you, whom *can* we trust?'

'You'd be surprised how seldom we hear that.' She stepped into a large open space, with a stone staircase on one side and a set of lift doors on the other. The whole scene promptly disappeared as her glasses misted up. Giving the lenses a polish revealed that the blurry wallpaper was really hundreds and hundreds of photographs, some black-and-white, some full colour, all head-and-shoulders portraits of middle-aged people wearing the familiar dark-grey suit and school tie. Most of the older photos were white men, but the more modern pics had a fairly even split of men and women from all ethnicities – the pictures squeezed in so tightly that there was barely an inch of wall on show. A big reception desk was manned by someone who seemed to have looked up 'spinster' in the dictionary and decided it'd be a good look for her. Poking away at a fancy new computer, mouth pursed, eyes narrowed behind her pointy glasses.

She looked up from the screen and smiled. 'Headmaster. Mr McCaskill wanted you to know he's on his way over now.'

'Thank you, Vanessa. If you've got a moment, could you be a star and whip up some . . .' He raised an eyebrow at Lucy. 'It's tea you police officers drink in all the crime novels, isn't it? That or whisky.' Back to Vanessa and her spinster cosplay. 'Better find some doughnuts too; if we're going for the cliché we might as well do it properly.'

'It's a kind offer, but Detective Constable Fraser and I will be fine.'

'Well, if you're sure.' Striding off towards the stairs.

Lucy followed him. Jerking a thumb at the photos on the way. 'Ex-teachers?'

'Oh goodness me, no.' The headmaster paused, one foot on the bottom step. 'These are our alumni. As we only accept thirteen new students every year, I think it's nice to celebrate each and every one of them, don't you?'

She leaned in and peered over the top of her glasses at the nearest one, so the nameplate was in focus. 'JEREMY OLDHAM CBE ~ SCOTIA PETROLEUM PRODUCTS, CFO'. Your average puffed-up white bloke with squint teeth and an expensive haircut. Then a proud woman with hard eyes and skin the colour of burnt umber: 'ADAKU IGWE CFR ~ GOVERNOR OF BAUCHI STATE'. Followed by, 'PORSCHE FITZROY-SMYTHE OBE ~ BROADCASTER & COLUMNIST', 'ZHŌU XIÙYĪNG ~ SHENZHEN FÈNGHUÁNG DĀO TRADING CO. LTD., CHAIRWOMAN', 'BARONESS PHILLIPA MCKEEVER QC' . . .

Lucy straightened up again. 'Never heard of any of them.'

The headmaster looked slightly pained at that. 'My dear Detective Sergeant, you are surrounded by captains of industry, political movers-and-shakers, innovators, and leading academics from all across the globe.' Sweeping an arm out to indicate the vast array of faces beaming out of their individual frames. 'Entrepreneurs, philanthropists, influential thinkers, the very pinnacle of humanity. We take only the best, we mould them, we equip them for the world and they, in turn, mould the *future*.'

Bit up himself.

'If it's any consolation, I recognize this one.' She pointed at the portrait of a man who clearly loved himself more than he'd ever love anyone else. Sharp features; hair swept back, greying at the temples; a smug smirk pulling one side of his face up; cold eyes. 'PAUL RHYNIE ~ H.M. GOVERNMENT, BUSINESS SECRETARY'. Not exactly a success story, given all the scandals getting aired on the news right now. Probably best not to mention that, though.

'Some of the most powerful people in the country have emerged through our doors.' A sigh. 'Which is why it's such a shame you couldn't join us. Still, onwards ever upwards.' Taking the stairs two at a time, all the way to the next floor.

Thanks for rubbing it in.

Lucy took her time, following him at a slow climb. Frowning at all the double-barrelled posh people in their school robes. Industrialists; doctors; lawyers; members of parliament, both Scottish and Westminster; overseas politicians; foreign royalty; editors of right-wing newspapers; editors of left-wing newspapers; the people who *owned* those newspapers; the heads of massive media corporations . . .

The headmaster wasn't kidding when he said they were powerful.

'Gah . . .' The Dunk squelched through the main door and stood there, dripping on the flagstones in all his short-and-squishy glory.

'Serves you right for being a slowcoach.' She went back to full speed, leaving him struggling to catch up, yet again.

The first floor was less impressive than the ground. Still lined with photos, but it was little more than a wood-panelled corridor with four or five doors leading off from it.

The headmaster's feet pounded ever upwards.

Second floor had a small landing with a single door: 'RECORDS R–Z ~ STAFF ONLY'.

Third floor was M to Q; fourth: G to L; and fifth: A to F.

The sound of the Dunk puffing and wheezing echoed up the stone staircase. Sounded as if he'd swallowed a set of leaky bagpipes.

The sixth floor had a much grander landing than the ones below, complete with pot plants and a trio of padded leather armchairs arranged around a coffee table. On a sideboard in the corner, a pair of crystal decanters and matching set of glasses glittered on their silver tray. More photos.

Four doors this time: the lift, one marked 'BURSAR', one 'ASSISTANT HEADMASTER', and one lying wide open. That would be the headmaster's, then. Lucy stuck her hands in her pockets and wandered through it, doing her best nonchalant, not-impressed-by-this-in-the-slightest act.

His office wasn't quite as big as the one Operation Maypole had been given, but it wasn't that far off it. Only instead of cubicles, whiteboards, and filing cabinets, this one was like a *very* rich family's sitting room. It stretched the whole width of the tower: dark, wooden panelling, hung with oil paintings; display cabinets laden with school trophies; matching leather couches and armchairs; spectacular antique Persian carpets in rich tones of gold and burgundy; shelves upon shelves of books; and a huge, ornate wooden desk. The windows weren't large, but the views out over the surrounding countryside were quite something, even in the drowning rain.

'Sure I can't tempt you?' The headmaster poured himself something from a small crystal decanter.

'I don't. But thank you.'

'Very wise. It's a terrible habit.' Then he took a sip, smiled, and lowered himself onto the edge of the desk. 'But *so* good for the soul, don't you think?'

She wandered over to the north-facing windows. Between here and Holburn Forest lay an array of playing fields that put Bellside School for Girls' to shame, complete with tennis courts, a walled garden, and what looked like a covered swimming pool. Another quadrangle sat behind the main one, separated from the school buildings by a small orchard. That would be the dormitories. Though, going by the rest of the place, you could bet the kids weren't sleeping in big draughty rooms on rows of hard metal-framed beds. With only thirteen new students a year, the overprivileged little sods probably had their own luxury suites. They must be rattling about in a school this size.

'Do you think I would've liked it here?'

'Of *course* you would. We don't believe in the sackcloth-and-ashes approach to boarding school; we keep numbers low so we can really look after our students. No crowded classrooms and underfunded, under-resourced teaching here: every single young person *matters*.' Another sip, followed by a faux-modest tilt of the head. 'That might be why our alumni are so very generous to us when they find success in their chosen careers.'

Here's what you could've won . . .

A knock on the doorframe. *'Headmaster?'*

Lucy turned.

The newcomer was mid-thirties – maybe early forties? – with a strong jaw and big brown eyes. One of those floppy haircuts only posh blokes could carry off. Wearing the standard-issue dark-grey suit and burgundy tie, but his academic robe was midnight-blue edged with silver. He strode into the room and cranked his boyish smile up to full beam, bringing with him the antiquated musty scent of sandalwood aftershave. Sticking out his hand. 'Hello, you must be the Detective Sergeant that Skye was so excited about.'

She ignored the proffered hand. 'You didn't see a detective constable on your way up, did you? Only I've lost one.'

'Ah, the sweaty, wheezing chap in the 1950s counter-culture getup? We *may* have to send a St Bernard to revive him with a tot of brandy.' The assistant head must've realized he was still proffering his hand, because he cleared his throat and used it to brush that floppy fringe out of his eyes instead. *Smooth.* Then turned to the headmaster. 'I've taken the liberty of collecting Allegra from Organisational Politics; she's outside.'

'Excellent, thank you, Argyll. Can you keep DS McVeigh company while she talks to Allegra? Not that we suspect you of ulterior motives, Detective Sergeant, but there are policies and procedures for these sorts of things.'

'That's fine. I wasn't expecting to interview her without a responsible adult present. Policies and procedures.'

'Policies and procedures.' He toasted her with his glass, drank, then placed it on a coaster. 'Now, if you'll excuse me, I'm off to have a rummage on the third floor. See what I can dig up.' Rubbing his hands together. 'Do check in when you're finished, Detective Sergeant; I'd feel very guilty if you left before I could say goodbye.' And he was off.

Lucy tilted her head to one side. 'Argyll. You're Skye's older brother.'

'Much, *much* older, for my sins. Now, why don't you get settled in' – pointing at one of the couches – 'and I'll fetch Allegra?'

A huffing, wheezing, sweaty lump lurched into the office. The Dunk. He'd unzipped his soggy leather jacket, bunnet clutched in one hand as he bent double. Back heaving. Face the colour of strawberry ice cream. '. . . stairs . . . God . . . stitch . . .'

Lucy settled into the leather sofa – much more comfortable than the ones at home – pulled out the two printouts they'd been showing round town that morning and placed them on the coffee table.

The Dunk staggered over, collapsing into an armchair, arms dangling, head hanging over the back of the chair, peching and heeching. '. . . dying . . .'

She placed her phone on the coffee table too, bringing up the voice memo recorder, because given his current state, there was no way the Dunk would be much use on the note-taking front. 'How did you ever pass the bleep test this year?'

'. . . why so . . . why so many . . . bleeding . . . stairs?'

'Allegra, this is Detective Sergeant McVeigh.' The assistant headmaster was back, bringing a young girl with him. 'She needs to ask you a few questions.'

Allegra was dressed in the same school uniform, but her academic gown had the two white epaulettes marking her out as a new girl. Long red hair, pulled back in a shiny ponytail. Freckles standing out against her pale skin. Blue eyes. Pretty, in a conventional kind of way.

Lucy nodded in the direction of the panting sweaty lump in the armchair – which probably wasn't the best of looks when it came to interviewing little girls. 'This is my colleague, Detective Constable Fraser.' Just in case she thought he was as sketchy as he looked.

Allegra skipped over there, as if the Dunk was a lovely puppy, instead of the kind of man Mummy and Daddy wouldn't let within a hundred feet of their delicate princess. Her voice was soft and saccharine. 'It's *lovely* to meet you.' She did a cute kind of curtsey and shook his hand. Sneakily wiping it on the back of her academic robe when he wasn't looking.

Then she stuck the same hand out to Lucy. Firm grip. Direct eye contact. No curtsey.

Interesting . . .

Allegra pulled her chin up. 'It's simple neuro-linguistic programming.' Sounding less saccharine and more strychnine. 'Your colleague now feels that he holds a degree of patriarchal power, which means he'll underestimate me in any business dealings. While you know that we are equals and will afford me due respect, during our interactions.'

Mr Marlins, back at Bellside School, had been right about her personality, anyway.

Lucy pressed the button that set her phone's voice memo recording. 'Allegra, we're here because you bought a coat for a homeless man, four and a bit weeks ago.'

'Did I?'

Lucy pointed at printout number one: the security camera shot of Allegra handing the bag over.

'I'm not trying to be arch, Detective Sergeant McVeigh, it's just that my charitable works all tend to bleed into each other. I've lost track of the number of coats I've been able to supply for poor, unfortunate, *cold* souls like that.'

Since when did eleven-year-olds talk like that? As if they were mini-grown-up people with mortgages and stock portfolios and dinner parties, instead of pre-hormonal monsters about to be unleashed upon the world . . .

'Do you recognize this man?' Lucy poked the close-up of Malcolm Louden.

'I think it's important to give back to the community, don't you, Detective Sergeant McVeigh? Those of us born with a certain degree of . . . let's call it "privilege", have a responsibility to help out members of society less fortunate than ourselves.'

'I notice you're not answering my question, Allegra.'

A little girl shouldn't have a smile as cold as that. 'Am I in trouble for helping a homeless man stay warm and dry?'

'You're not in any trouble. We're trying to piece together this man's movements and we think you can help.'

'So is *he* in trouble?'

'No, he's dead.'

The smile got even colder. 'That sounds like a great deal of trouble to me.' She picked up Malcolm Louden's picture, little creases forming between her pale eyebrows. 'I'm sorry to hear that he died, but I don't see how I can possibly help you. I bought him a coat, because he looked cold. My allowance is generous enough that I can do good deeds like that on a fairly regular basis. I also volunteer at a soup kitchen once a month, help with fundraising for an outreach programme, and support my local art gallery.'

Lucy matched the arctic smile. 'This isn't a competition, Allegra.'

'*Everything* is a competition, Detective Sergeant McVeigh. Everything is a test. And I intend to pass with flying colours.'

Argyll raised his eyebrows, rocking on the balls of his feet – setting his academic robes swaying.

OK . . .

'Let me give you some unsolicited advice, Allegra. Something that'll stand you in good stead for the rest of your life.' Lucy sat forward and gave her a good dose of the evil eye. 'When you evade a police officer's questions like that, it doesn't make us think, "Gosh, isn't this little girl smart and self-assured!" It makes us think, "This one's got something to hide. I'd better keep an eye on her. Maybe take a *much* closer look and see what I can find out."'

Those creases between Allegra's eyebrows deepened. 'I see.'

'It doesn't make you clever, it makes you a person of interest.'

The only sound was the Dunk's wheezing breath.

Then Allegra nodded, and the frown was gone. 'Thank you for the advice, Detective Sergeant McVeigh.' The smile defrosted too. 'I always value the opportunity to learn new things, and grow as an individual.'

Because that didn't sound *at all* creepy.

'Good. Now, tell me about—' Lucy's phone *buzzzzzzz-ding*ed at her – incoming text message. The preview appeared on the screen, hiding the recorder.

DI TUDOR:
> I was wondering
> Maybe it would be a good idea if you spoke to your
> therapist about what happened this morning with S
> Black?!?

Oh shut up, you condescending—
Buzzzzzzz-ding.

DI TUDOR:
> I'm worried about her upsetting you Lucy

I'm trying to help
We're all here to support you
If you need to take some time off for your mental health
that's OK!!!

God's sake, could the bloody man not leave her alone for five minutes?

DISMISS.

Shame there wasn't a button for SOD OFF.

'Sorry: work.' Lucy made sure the app was still recording. 'Tell me about Malcolm Louden.' A short pause. 'Please.'

Allegra swished her academic gown out of the way and perched on the edge of the sofa opposite. 'I'd seen him outside the train station a number of times, wearing this grubby thin jacket, covered in stains. He looked colder than usual that day, so I bought him a new coat.'

'Just like that?'

'I'm planning on going to Oxford to study Philosophy, Politics, and Economics. Then a DPhil in either Politics or International Relations. It's not like it was in the old days, when you could simply waltz into Oxbridge with a good family name and a crate of Dom Pérignon; now you need top marks in every subject. Except *everyone* applying to Oxbridge has top marks, or they wouldn't *be* applying.'

'Your old teacher, Mr Marlins, says Oxford and Cambridge don't care about extra-curricular activities.'

'If you have two identical candidates, with the same academic scores, who are you going to pick: the one who's done nothing, or the one who's done everything?'

Suppose she had a point. 'OK.'

'It's a war, Detective Sergeant McVeigh, and whatever gives you an edge against the enemy is a weapon to be wielded.' Allegra shrugged. She probably meant it to come across as self-deprecating, but it looked artificial. Forced. As if she'd practised it in front of the mirror. 'I think a summer job helping underprivileged children in Africa, or South America, for UNICEF or Oxfam will seal the deal.'

'So, you don't actually care about the homeless, you're just using them to climb the ladder.'

'Does the starving man care *why* you feed him, or does he only care that he's got enough food in his belly to live another day?'

Oh yeah, this one was definitely destined for a job in politics.

'And you thought buying Malcolm Louden a jacket would help get you into Oxford?'

'Helping him helps me, what's wrong with that?' She placed the photo back on the coffee table. 'I bought him the coat: he was very grateful. He was happy because unlike everyone else who'd marched past that morning, not looking at him, pretending he wasn't there, I actually stopped and helped.'

Suppose she had a point.

'Did Malcolm Louden say anything about what he was going to do later? Was he planning to meet someone, or go somewhere?'

'No. To be honest, I got the impression he was mostly trying not to cry. Some people do that when no one's been kind to them for a long, long time.'

'And did you see anyone hanging around when you gave him the coat? Anyone suspicious? Anyone paying a bit too much attention to him?'

'Hmmm . . .' The frown was back. She chewed on her bottom lip for a bit. Then shook her head. 'No one that comes to mind. But I was a little preoccupied with preparing for my final assessment for St Nicholas College.' Allegra shared a bright smile with the assistant headmaster. 'Wanted to do my best.'

Argyll doffed an imaginary cap. 'Flying colours.'

Back to Lucy. 'And it's *so* much better here than at my last school. Bellside spend all their money on flashy new buildings, management consultants, and PR campaigns; here it's invested in the curriculum and equipment and facilities. You should *see* our science lab, it's like something out of a Bond film!'

Difficult to tell if she was aiming for more Brownie points from the assistant headmaster, or just genuinely excited. Didn't really matter in the end.

Allegra sighed. Shook her head. 'I'm sorry I can't be more help, Detective Sergeant McVeigh. I truly am.'

'So am I.' Lucy stood. Passed over a Police Scotland business card. 'If you remember anything, doesn't matter how small, get in touch.' She snapped her fingers. 'DC Fraser: we're going.'

The Dunk groaned, sagged, then struggled to his feet. 'OK, OK, but can we *please* take the lift this time?'

'No.'

18

The Dunk stomped down the stairs, grumbling away under his breath like a sulky child.

Lucy paused every time she recognized one of the portraits that packed the walls on either side of the stairwell. Mostly because it wound the Dunk up to see her peering at another 'posh twat'.

Served him right for being a useless unfit sod.

By the time they'd got to the fourth floor she'd spotted two controversial journalists, three business types that were always getting interviewed on the *Today* programme, two former cabinet ministers, and a whole heap of—

Her phone blared out its ringtone.

'Unknown Number'.

She pressed the button. 'DS McVeigh.'

A banjo-country accent grated its way out of the earpiece. *'Aye, aye, it's Mike Scobie. Hiv you seen the boy, the day?'*

'What boy? Who is this?'

'I telt ye: it's Mike Scobie. Lucas Weir's Criminal Justice social worker? Lucas Weir? Wink, wink, maybe no' his real name, cos he got his heid kicked in when "They" found out far he lived?'

'Benedict Strachan.'

'The very loon. Far is he?'

'How am I supposed to—'

'He's meant to report in every morning, like the court telt him to. But there's nae sign. And yon halfway hoose I got him intil havnae seen him, the day, either. If we canna find him, he's back ahin bars by dinnertime.'

Bit difficult to lock him up if they couldn't find him, but fair enough.
She started walking again. 'So, what do you want *me* to do about it?'

'There's only you and me gives a badger's fart about the boy. I mak it official and he's screwed. And if he doesnae turn up soon, I'm gonna have til.'

Maybe being sent back to prison would be the best thing for Benedict? He clearly wasn't coping on the outside. The drink, the drugs, the paranoia. All that stuff about 'Them' knowing everything and being after him . . .

At least inside he'd get the help he needed.

Hopefully.

Not counting another round of budget cuts.

And there were *always* budget cuts.

And prison services were an easy target.

And—

'You remembering I'm still on the phone, here?'

'What? Yes. OK: look, I'm investigating a murder, I don't have time to go chasing after people right now.'

'Aye, weil, I'm heading oot and aboot to see if I can find him, because I actually give a toss. You think it's OK for him to get hauled in and banged up again? That's on you. Dinna come crying to me when he gets his throat slit in the prison showers.'

Then silence. Scobie had hung up.

'Yes, because I can just *wave* my magic wand and make all the bad things go away.' Cramming the phone back in her pocket.

The Dunk clumped down the stairs beside her. 'Let me guess: bad news?'

'Benedict Strachan's done a bunk.'

'Ooooh . . . Not good. Want me to start the paperwork? "Have you seen this man?" posters, media briefing, lookout request, etc.?'

She stopped. Stood there, staring up at the sloped ceiling. 'If we make it official, that's it for Benedict. He gets hauled in, done for violating his release conditions, and it's right back to HMP Oldcastle for the next three or four years.'

'Should've thought of that before he murdered a homeless guy.'

'He was *eleven*, Dunk.'

'Tell that to the victim's family.'

They stomped down to the next landing in silence. Then the one after that.

The Dunk let out a big hissing breath, cheeks puffed out like a trumpet player. 'OK, so you want to make it "off the books", then? Could put out some feelers; ask Uniform to keep their eyes peeled, but don't tell them why; maybe pay his parents a visit?'

That wasn't a bad idea.

Lucy nodded. 'We can pop past his halfway house, too. See if they know anything. After all, it's not as if we can do a whole lot more till the post-mortem on Malcolm Louden is . . .' She turned the final corner, and there, at the bottom of the stairs, was the headmaster. Waiting for them.

He held up a slim brown file. 'Thought I'd catch you, if I was fast enough.'

Lucy nodded. 'Mr Price-Hamilton. We're finished with Allegra. Thank you for the use of your office.'

'No, my pleasure, my pleasure. Civic duty's a keystone of our curriculum, so it's important to practise what we preach. Was she able to help?'

'Didn't see anything.'

'Oh, I *am* sorry to hear that. Anyway'– holding up the folder again – 'look what I found.'

The Dunk had gone all pink and silent again, so Lucy shoved him towards the exit. 'Go: get started on those feelers.'

His only reply was a deepening blush, then the Dunk zipped his jacket up, slapped that stupid leather bunnet on his head, and hurried out into the rain. Ridiculous little spud that he was.

The headmaster opened the folder and squinted at the contents. 'I have to say that I'm impressed with your test results. *Very* impressed. Academic, psychological, physical . . . They're some of the highest scores I've seen in years.' He put a hand on her arm again, the grip warm and firm through her jacket. 'I'm sorry we couldn't welcome you to our family, Lucy. I was right: you would have been perfectly at home here.' A squeeze. 'Imagine what you could have achieved if we'd had the chance to mould those raw talents of yours.'

Patronizing dick.

As if St Nicholas College was the centre of the sodding universe and no one could succeed if it hadn't sprinkled its overprivileged, overpriced, overbollocksed pixie dust on them.

Chin up. 'I've got an MSc in criminal psychology, first class honours;

I own a three-bedroom house, in a lovely rural setting, with no mort-gage; and I'm on the fast-track programme with Police Scotland. I'll make DI before I'm thirty. Maybe superintendent by forty. I'll be run-ning the whole division by forty-five.' A brittle smile. 'So, yeah, I did OK, thanks.'

'Lucy, Lucy, Lucy.' He sighed and shook his head. 'O Division? You could've been running the whole *country*.'

Here's what you could've won . . .

'Yes. Well. Thanks again for the loan of your office.' Then, with her back ramrod straight, Lucy marched out into the rain.

The whole country.

And somehow she got the feeling he wasn't just talking about Police Scotland.

Which really didn't sodding help.

What was she supposed to do with information like that? Oh, yes, Lucy, you could've been First Minister, or Prime Minister, if only your poor father had been able to afford the fees.

Well, he couldn't, so there was no point—

'Leaving so soon?' A large figure appeared at her shoulder, bringing with him that familiar musty aroma of sandalwood. Just like Dad used to wear. The blue academic robe, trimmed in silver, was the clincher, though.

'Mr McCaskill.'

'It's Argyll, please. Oh, and here.' There was a *click*, then a *whoooom* as a school brolly popped open above them both. The downpour thrummed against the tight black fabric. 'Can't have you getting wet on the way back to your car.'

'What happened to Allegra?'

'Ah.' His smile turned into a one-shouldered shrug. 'Yes, she can be a bit . . .' He pantomimed a shudder. 'Don't get me wrong, a lot of the first years have . . . challenging personalities when they get here, but I have to admit there's something decidedly *unsettling* about Miss Dean-Edwards. Like she's, I don't know, playing chess in her head every time she talks to you?'

'More like something out of a Brothers Grimm story, emerging from the deep dark woods, wearing the skin of a little girl, trying to pass for human.'

They stepped out into the quad.

'Thanks, I'm probably going to have nightmares about that now.' Argyll moved closer, making sure they both stayed dry. 'Mind you, having met her parents, I'm not surprised she's a little monster.' That boyish smile was back. 'But luckily I like a challenge: keeps life interesting. We'll get those sharp corners polished off her in no time. After all, she's only eleven.'

The same excuse she'd given the Dunk for Benedict Strachan's behaviour.

'The kids are always a little rough around the edges when we get them. They're used to being top of the class in their primary schools, spoiled at home, feted by their friends. It usually takes a while to realize that the whole world *doesn't* actually revolve around them.'

They marched past the twisted oak in the middle of the quadrangle, Argyll slowing his pace to an amble, so she had to either slow down too, or march out into the rain.

Lucy matched his pace. 'A whole school full of creepy wee egomaniacs.'

'By the time she hits the second term, you won't recognize her. Promise.' He cleared his throat, looking out straight ahead as he and Lucy strolled down the path. 'You gave Allegra your card. I wondered, you know, if it's not being too forward or anything, if you'd like to give me one too?'

She raised an eyebrow at that, and pink rushed up his cheeks.

'I mean, a *card*. If you'd like to give me a *card* too.' Going redder by the moment. 'Or not. It's understandable. I didn't mean to . . . Yes.' Picking up the pace again. 'Anyway, right now, Allegra has been assigned her academic brother, so it's all about establishing peer-to-peer support networks, and next term she'll get an academic father and mother from the senior years. That's when the pupils really get into their stride.'

'And learn they're not the centre of the universe.'

He licked his lips. 'You may not have noticed, but I might be babbling somewhat.'

Really?

They'd reached the archway back out into the real world, where the Dunk was sitting in the pool car, engine running.

She pointed. 'This is me.'

'Yes. I'm sorry. About the babbling.' Getting all flushed again. 'Here.' Holding out the brolly and stepping back, so she was the only one underneath its swollen black wings.

'My car's just over there.'

'I know, but . . . you might get wet later. And it's good advertising for the school, of course. With my compliments.'

'Fair enough.' She took the proffered umbrella.

He stood there in the downpour, smiling and blushing at her. Like something from the closing scenes of a particularly cheesy romcom.

To be painfully honest, he wasn't actually that bad-looking. Maybe even attractive, in an upper-class cry-havoc-for-Harry-and-St-George kind of way. Or however that quote went. The point being: he was a nice guy, and not a complete arse-faced minger, so would it kill her to throw him a *small* bone?

Pfff . . . Lucy rolled her eyes, pulled a face, then dug a hand into her inside pocket. 'Fine.' She handed him one of her Police Scotland business cards. 'My mobile number's on the back, in case Allegra remembers anything.'

'Definitely.' He tucked the thing away, inside his jacket. 'I'll be in touch. I mean, if she remembers anything. Definitely.'

And with that, Lucy turned and marched off towards the pool car, leaving him in the rain. 'Bye, Mr McCaskill.' Not bothering to hide her smile, now that he couldn't see it.

His voice boomed out behind her. *'It's been lovely meeting you!'*

'You OK, Sarge? Only you look a bit . . . you know.' The Dunk took a right at the junction, into the sprawling nest of housing estates that formed the northernmost edge of the Wynd, windscreen wipers making slow-motion, groaning arcs through the drizzle. 'It was those snotty posh twats, wasn't it? Tell you, they give me the willies.'

'Yeah, I noticed, what with all the terrified looks and awkward silences.'

'It's not my fault! I have . . . issues.'

'You certainly do.' Lucy frowned down at the phone in her hand and the text sitting at the top of the list. Rereading DI Tudor's message for about the fifth time since leaving St Nicholas College.

I'm worried about her upsetting you Lucy
I'm trying to help
We're all here to support you
If you need to take some time off for your mental health
that's OK!!!

Now *why* did that read as if he was covering his backside, in case she tried suing the force for constructive dismissal? *Here is written evidence that I have done my best to ensure that DS McVeigh got the help she needed, but she would not cooperate, m'lord. Therefore, she can't sue us, because we did everything right and she's just an obstinate, bloody-minded, thrawn, scrawny bitch.*

Or maybe they were going to sign her off on the sick? When they started talking about 'taking some time off for your mental health' you knew you were in trouble. Wouldn't be long before they stuck you out to pasture, like ex-DI Christopher Gourley, drinking yourself into oblivion, till one day you just upped and disappeared . . . And it wasn't as if anyone would even bother to report Lucy missing. There was no one to miss her.

So much for her good mood.

Why could no bugger ever let her be?

Fine, she'd make *yet* another sodding appointment to see Dr McNaughton. Play along, like everyone wanted. Maybe then they'd all sod off.

'And dear God, was that Allegra kid *creepy* enough?' The Dunk turned left, into a wide, curving cul-de-sac. 'With her "neuro-linguistic programming" and her "Oh, my allowance is so huge I can hand out new jackets, willy-nilly, to the oiks and tramps, for I am Lady Muck from the Manor!"'

'That's it, up there.' Lucy pointed through the windscreen at a large fifties bungalow, set back from the road, like all the other large fifties bungalows on this street. Every drive boasted at least one four-by-four, every lawn a couple of large trees and a collection of well-tended flowerbeds. The kind of place where it'd be safe to raise a kid.

Only it hadn't really turned out that way. Not for Benedict Strachan.

The Dunk pulled up at the kerb. 'Anything I need to know before we go in?'

'Give us a minute, would you? I need to make a call.'

'Fair enough.' He reached into the back for his leather bunnet, then climbed out into the dreich afternoon. 'Don't be long, though, eh? We've still got those two Bloodsmith crime scenes to go visit.'

She waited till he was *at least* six feet away, before bringing up Dr McNaughton's number.

Might as well get it over with . . .

The bungalow was much bigger than it'd looked from the outside. Grander, too. Mr and Mrs Strachan were clearly worth a bob or five and wanted everyone to know it: from the big BMW tank and sporty-looking bright-red Audi TT on the driveway, to all those photos of the happy couple on fancy foreign holidays adorning the walls. Oh, and the whole place had been hoovered and dusted till it shone. Which just wasn't natural.

The floral-print couch creaked as Lucy sat forward and curled her stockinged feet into the oatmeal-coloured carpet. Deep and rich and luxurious.

The Dunk had his feet tucked beneath his chair, trying to hide the holes in the toes of both stripy socks. At least the Strachans weren't posh enough to bring on his class-induced muteness. And he had his note-book out – ready to be useful, for a change.

Mr Strachan took up centre stage on the other couch: flannels and an open-necked linen shirt; pale hair swept back from his widow's peak; a wide, tanned face with a squishy nose; short, salt-and-ginger beard rippling across both of his chins. A voice that was clearly used to telling people what to do. 'Of course we haven't seen him.' Strachan turned and scowled at a cougary woman in a tight knitted sweater and blue jeans, chest-length blonde hair betrayed by a thin stripe of grey at the roots. 'Have we, Nikki?'

'Definitely not.' She worried at a string of pearls with her long Barbie-pink nails. 'We haven't seen him. Why would we have seen him?'

Lucy leaned forwards. 'Because he's your son?'

'He's no son of mine!' Her top lip curled, but the rest of her face was held rigid in a Botox fist. 'No child of mine would *ever* kill a homeless person.'

A snort from Benedict's father. 'And no son of mine would be stupid enough to get caught!' He narrowed his eyes. 'Wait a minute, I recognize you. You were that student who came round asking all those questions about . . . him. Years ago.'

'Mr Strachan, it's important we find Benedict. If we don't, they'll send him back to prison.'

A carriage clock on the mantelpiece *tick, tick, tick*ed.

Mrs Strachan fiddled with her pearls.

The Dunk shifted in his seat, pen poised.

'Good.' Mr Strachan poked a finger at them. 'He ruined *everything*. Have you any idea what we did for him? What we sacrificed? The strings I had to pull?'

Nikki placed a hand on his arm. 'Ian was on the council. The Labour Party selected him to run as MP for Oldcastle South.'

'And then that stupid little . . .' Ian Strachan looked away. 'Of course, I had to resign from the council. Then I got *un*selected and they found some chinless moron to stand in the general election. And he lost, by the way. I would've won.'

She gazed at him, like an adoring puppy. 'You would've been a great MP, Ian.'

'The scandal was just . . . It took years to get my business off the ground after that. No one wanted to be tainted by association. He ruined *everything*.'

Wow. With a loving family like that, how on earth did Benedict turn out the way he did?

His mother sat up straight. 'We only visited him in prison once, and that was to disown him. Whatever he did, whoever he's hurt, it's nothing to do with us.'

'And Benedict hasn't been in touch since he got out?'

Ian went back to poking again, getting redder and redder with each word. 'We spent every penny we had on that boy. Remortgaged the house. Made sure he had the brightest future money could buy, and how does he repay us? Goes out and stabs some . . . *tramp* to death. And when they catch him, he doesn't even have the brains to say "no comment", he gives them a full bloody confession!'

'Has he been in touch?'

'OF COURSE HE HASN'T BEEN IN BLOODY TOUCH!' Trembling, spittle flying, eyes bugging.

'Shhhhh . . .' Nikki stroked her husband's arm. 'Shhhhh . . . It's OK. It's OK, Ian.' A kiss on his flushed cheek. 'Why don't I go make everyone a nice cup of tea? Maybe the police officers will help me?'

Now why did that sound like an invitation to talk about Benedict behind Ian Strachan's back?

Lucy stood. 'We'd love to.'

19

Nice kitchen. Big. Retro. With windows looking out over a large garden and tidy patio.

Nikki Strachan stood at the open back door, vaping a cloud of marzipan-scented steam out into the drizzle. Keeping her voice down. 'Sorry, he's . . . It's not been easy for us. Took Ian years and years to get over what happened with . . . with what happened. Then he built his business up from scratch and it was all going so well and we'd finally managed to pay off all the loans, and the debts, and actually have a nice holiday for once, then Covid-sodding-Nineteen comes along and bang: we go from employing two hundred and sixty staff to losing everything.' A bitter-almond laugh. 'So we're back to square one. Up to our ears in debt, house remortgaged, and no one'll take our calls because they let . . . they let *him* out of prison and suddenly our name's all over the papers again.'

Lucy took a sip of lukewarm tea. 'It must've been very difficult.'

'Don't get me wrong, Detective Sergeant, I loved my little boy. I loved him so, so much. And then he went and did *that*.' She wiped the heel of her hand across one eye. 'And you ask yourself, "Where did I go wrong? How did my sweet little baby turn into this monster?"'

Out in the garden, the Dunk emerged from a large wooden shed, wiping cobwebs off the front of his leather jacket with nitrile-gloved hands. He waved at the kitchen window and shook his head.

Ah well, it'd been worth a try.

Then the Dunk squelched off through the wet grass towards the garage. Probably should've loaned him her new brolly, but it'd only get in the way of the searching.

'My baby was such a *perfect* little soul. Do you know he could name all the constellations and recite the periodic table by the time he was six? Clever and kind and artistic and musical . . .' Nikki stared out into the rain. 'Then five weeks after he leaves primary school, bang. The whole world falls apart.'

'And he never tried to keep in touch?' Lucy jerked her head in the general direction of the living room. 'Maybe without your husband knowing?'

Nikki was silent for a moment, not turning around, barely moving at all.

'Mrs Strachan, I wouldn't ask if it wasn't—'

'He writes to me every week, has done for the last sixteen years. Ian doesn't know. They all get delivered to a PO box in Blackwall Hill.' Now she turned, eyes shiny and blinking. 'Please, you *can't* tell him. It would break . . . You've seen how he gets.'

Sixteen years' worth of correspondence. Who knew what little nuggets Benedict let slip? Maybe even something that would identify his accomplice.

OK, Lucy, deep breath.

Don't sound too keen.

Lucy had another sip of tea. Pitched her voice a little on the bored side. 'Do you still have the letters?'

Please, please, please, please.

'I burn them.' Mrs Strachan curled her shoulders in, vape cupped against her jumper. 'What if Ian found one and then he'd know I've been speaking to . . . to *him*. I can't do that to Ian. Not after everything he's been through.'

Bastard.

Couldn't catch a break today.

Lucy put her mug down. 'Did Benedict ever talk about the boy who helped him kill Liam Hay? Or why they did it?'

'We never talk about . . . what happened. It's too upsetting. Besides, you never know who reads your letters when you send them, do you? People at the prison.'

'What about since he got out?'

This time the silence stretched on for a long, long while.

'Mrs Strachan? He's been in touch, hasn't he?'

She stared down at the kitchen floor, pulling her top lip in.

'Did he come to the house?'

Nikki wiped at her eyes again. 'You don't understand how *hard* it is.'

'They're going to catch him sooner or later. And when they do, he's going to be in a lot of trouble.'

'It's not fair. It wasn't his fault!'

'If we find Benedict now, today, no one else needs to know. We slip him back into the system, so he doesn't get arrested for violating his release conditions. He doesn't get stuck back in HMP Oldcastle till his thirty-first birthday.'

Nikki didn't raise her eyes from the kitchen floor. 'I can't. He trusts me.'

'Help me to help him, then! If we can keep him from getting locked up, Benedict can focus on getting better.'

'I promised . . .'

'He needs you, Nikki. He needs his mother to help him do the right thing.'

'Oh God.' Her free hand came up and covered her eyes, shoulders quivering; then her back hunched as she heaved out a huge, jagged sob. Followed by another one. And another. Knees bending till she was slumped forwards against the doorframe.

The summer house was tucked away behind a trellis festooned with honeysuckle – the blooms wilting and grey, battered into submission by the week's rain. But their sickly-sweet perfume still scented the air, leaves glistening in the cold drizzle.

Nikki stood in the middle of the wooden floor, beneath the peaked roof, eyes screwed shut, one hand pressing the vape against her forehead as if she was trying to trepan herself with it. The other held her phone. 'I know, sweetie, I know, but it's— . . . Yes . . . No, I know that, but— . . . It's—' Her shoulders drooped even further. 'You have to understand it from your father's— . . . Please. We have to— . . . No.'

Lucy sat on the edge of a folding chair, frowning up at the remains of a wasps' nest. It hung from one of the joists that held the summer house's roof up. Not a big nest, just a little ash-coloured circle the size of a golf ball, with a hole in the bottom.

'Sweetie, we need to— . . . I understand that, but it's *important.*'

That was a queen's nest. Where the future mother of all wasps would hibernate her way through the winter.

'I know you do, but I *need* to see you. In person . . . Uh-huh.' She opened one eye and glanced at Lucy. Then closed it again. 'No, just you and me. I'll . . . I'll bring you some sandwiches. Egg and onion. Your favourites . . . Yes . . . I know, I know.'

Surprised the nest was still there. Maybe the queen emerged too early and just starved to death? Even so, you'd think the Strachans would've got rid of it by now. Must've been there since last winter.

A silent empty home for dead little monsters.

'Good. Yes . . . I'll see you there . . . No, I promise, sweetie, I promise.' Nikki nodded. 'OK. OK, bye. Bye. Bye . . . Bye.' She hung up. Hissed out a long breath. Then hauled in another one through her vape. Puffed a thick plume of marzipan steam at the summer-house roof, enveloping the wasps' nest.

Lucy stood. 'He'll be there?'

She pinched her lips together, fixed her gaze on the garden outside. 'You *swear* you won't hurt him?'

'Of course I won't.' Well, not unless he kicked off. Or tried to get away. Which he probably would. But Nikki didn't need to know that. 'I swear.'

'Then he'll be there.'

The Dunk clumped his way down the drive, past the swanky BMW four-by-four and the sporty Audi, over to the manky pool car. Hauled open the driver's door and thumped in behind the wheel. 'Urgh . . . For someone who keeps such a clean house, her shed, garage, and attic are a *disgrace.*' He took off his soggy dust-streaked bunnet and tossed it into the back of the car. 'And what are you looking so damned cheerful about? Is it because you didn't have to go rummaging about in the filth, looking for Benedict Buggering Strachan?'

Lucy gifted him the most annoying smile she could muster. 'Blackwall Hill: there's a coffee shop on Brindle Road, opposite the train station.'

The Dunk unzipped his grubby leather jacket. 'If that's supposed to get my Y-fronts in a swirl, it's not working. Unless you're buying?'

'Benedict Strachan's going to be there at half seven tonight.'

'Oooh . . .' Eyes widening. Then, 'Sod.' The Dunk checked his phone.

'I'm going to the theatre with Zoe tonight. Had the tickets booked for months.'

Lucy pulled her seatbelt on. 'It's not as if I can't handle Benedict Strachan.'

'I'd cancel, but her sister and brother-in-law are in it.'

'Isn't even an official operation. You go, enjoy your show.'

'Yeah.' He grimaced, then started the car. 'An am-dram musical version of *Silence of the Lambs*. No way *that's* going to be a festering sack of old garbage.' The Dunk hauled the wheel round in a three-point turn, till they were heading out of the cul-de-sac again. 'Where next? You wanna hit Jane Cooper's flat in Castleview first, or Craig Thorburn's place in Blackwall Hill?'

Victims number four and five.

'Jane Cooper. Then I need you to drop me back at the station. DI Tudor wants me to talk to someone.' Whether she liked it or not.

Jane Cooper's flat was one of the swanky new ones on St Bartholomew's Road, down by the river. Eight storeys of 'luxury apartments', most of which were still sitting empty – either not sold yet, or snapped up as an investment by people with more money than brain cells.

Jane's was near the top, with floor-to-ceiling glass, looking out across gunmetal water to the long, thin stretch of Dalrymple Park, then on to the bit where Cowskillin merged into Castle Hill. A balcony of wooden decking sat outside, complete with a patio set – the rattan furniture tainted green where patches of moss and algae had taken hold. Damp and soggy in the permanent drizzle.

The Dunk let loose a long, low whistle, standing there with his nose pressed against the living-room window. 'She must've been absolutely minted.'

Not that it had helped her any. The Bloodsmith had killed Jane Cooper just as dead as the others.

Lucy furled up her brand-new umbrella and leaned it against the oversized fireplace, then slapped the case file down on the dining table – a big chrome-and-beech thing with matching chairs, sitting beneath a complicated chandelier festooned with LED lights. 'Read.'

'Man, I would *love* to live somewhere like this.'

'Case file, Dunk, read. Out loud.'

A sigh and he wandered over, running his fingertips along an expensive-looking sideboard punctuated with tasteful ornaments. Leaving parallel tracks in the dust and fingerprint powder. 'Imagine the dinner parties you could have . . .'

Lucy did a slow tour of the living room while he opened the folder and dug out the paperwork.

It was all very nice, and the furniture and artworks had clearly cost a small fortune, but the place was somehow devoid of personality. As if Jane Cooper had handed the whole thing over to an interior designer and asked them to make it look as if someone rich lived here.

'Right, off we go.' The Dunk performed a theatrical clearing of his throat. 'Jane Izabella Cooper; twenty-four; shoulder-length curly brown hair; heart-shaped face with a fairly uncomfortable smile. The features look a bit too small for it, too. You know, like she's one of those spooky porcelain dolls little girls used to play with in the Victorian times?' A sigh. 'She looks sad.'

Lucy wandered out of the lounge and into a long corridor lined with doors and original artworks.

He followed, nose in the file. 'Pretty enough, I suppose, if you're into that sort of thing.'

The kitchen wasn't quite as big as Lucy's dad's, but it had a lot more gadgets in it. Their gleaming metal surfaces dulled by time and the SOC team's powders.

The Dunk thumped his bum against the work surface and pouted. 'Oh . . .'

Lucy opened a cupboard at random, exposing three shelves full of pots and pans that still had the paper price tags dangling from the handles. '"Oh", what?'

'She worked in that bookshop on Castlewall Terrace. I *like* that place; they do great coffee.'

The next cupboard held a pasta machine, fancy blender, and some sort of vacuum packer. None of which looked as if they'd ever been used.

Lucy closed the cupboard door and moved on to the fridge. 'She bought this place by working in a *bookshop*?'

'Nah: inherited a massive chunk of cash when her parents died in a scuba-diving accident off Mauritius. Dad was some sort of investment banker; Mum was a corporate lawyer.'

The fridge was still fully stocked: mostly Marks & Spencer ready meals, all now eight months past their sell-by date, their plastic films swollen and stretched taut. The milk carton had blown up like a rugby ball, its contents separated into dirty liquid and a thick layer of yellowy sludge.

She shut the fridge before anything in there went off with a bang. 'Who reported her missing?'

'Erm . . .' He followed Lucy across the hall, into a spacious bathroom with a freestanding bath and fancy shower. 'Ah, OK. It was a Russell Fowler, of Robinson, Fenton, and Fowler Limited. They're solicitors. Been working for her family since before the accident.' The Dunk sniffed. 'Now that's just depressing.'

Next up was a cosy study. The views weren't as good on this side of the flat – looking out across a building site to the unconverted warehouses and ratty little alleyways that used to cover this whole area.

The search team must've had a field day in here: all the drawers were open, the contents heaped up in wobbly piles on an antique desk. They'd even emptied out the wastepaper basket. Looking for clues. Finding sod all.

'Says here she was meant to attend a "financial management and planning consultation", which is sketchy lawyer talk for squirrelling cash away in the Cayman Islands where the taxman can't get his hands on it. Because, you know, why should rich people pay their fair share?' A snort. 'Anyway, when they couldn't raise her over the next couple of days, Fowler called the local station.'

'Why didn't the bookshop call it in?'

'She was only part-time.'

No family. No friends. Not even colleagues who gave a toss. It had been down to the lawyers to report her missing.

The Dunk was right, that really *was* depressing.

He looked up from the file. 'You want PM results next, or crime-scene photos?'

Neither.

But she held her hand out anyway. 'Photos.' Took them out into the corridor again without looking at the bloody things. Down to the master bedroom at the end.

Another long, low whistle. 'Wow.' The Dunk scuffed into the middle of the space. 'I mean, waking up to *that* every morning.' Standing there, with his hands on his hips, looking out through the patio doors, across the balcony, and off towards the castle – balanced on top of its granite blade – fading in and out of focus as the rain drifted by.

Didn't seem to bother him that the rest of the room was a disaster area.

The crime-scene cleaners had been in, hacking big random chunks out of both carpet and underlay, exposing the mottled chipboard floor-ing below. They'd sprayed the wall behind the bed with their industrial-strength bleach, replacing the Bloodsmith's prayer with a large patch of urine-yellow blotches, but clearly the mattress, sheets, and pillows had been too contaminated to rescue. Now only a purple furry throw lay draped across the naked bedframe.

Like the study, all the bedside-cabinet drawers were open, their con-tents rummaged through. Same with the make-up stand. Only the built-in wardrobes looked as if they hadn't been ransacked. Or at least someone had bothered to hang Jane's clothes up again, afterwards.

'How much do you think a place like this would set you back?' The Dunk unlocked the patio doors, sliding them open to let in the muffled roar of the city beyond. Dampened by that thick blanket of drizzle. 'I should start buying lottery tickets.'

Lucy risked a glance at the crime-scene photographs.

Jane Cooper lay spreadeagled on her bed, stripped naked, eyes and mouth hanging open. Chest and stomach, too. He'd draped Jane's innards across her thighs, hiding her crotch. Pale skin smeared with dark scarlet. The bedding saturated with it. 'HELP ME!' on the wall above what was left of her.

The next pic was a close-up of her face, frozen forever in an expression of horrified surprise. The Dunk had been right about that too – she really *did* look like a porcelain doll. One some angry child had taken its rage out on.

After that was a shot of her left arm, where a faded circular mark sur-rounded a small dark dot.

'You want PM results now?'

'Might as well.' Lucy lowered herself onto the end of the bedframe.

'OK. Back of her skull was partially caved in. Must've hit her a bit too hard this time. Organs were removed after death, again, and instead of slitting her wrist, the Bloodsmith drained her with a large-bore needle.

Pathologist estimates eighteen to twenty gauge, but doesn't think he would've got much before her heart stopped, because of the head wound.'

'Why do it in here?' Pointing at the room.

'Says it's *probably* the same kind of needle they use for blood donations. The larger gauge means you don't damage the red blood cells as they go through the needle on their way to whatever tubing and bags you're using to collect it. Something to do with fluid dynamics and shearing forces?'

She turned, setting the frame creaking. 'He knows it's going to be messy, but he doesn't take her into the bathroom like Adam Holmes or Craig Thorburn. He does it here.'

'Cause of death was the brain trauma. Like I said: hit her too hard.'

'Maybe they were romantically involved? Maybe that's why they were in the bedroom?'

'Took her heart, a big chunk of liver, and a kidney.'

'What about the profile? They speculate about why here?'

The Dunk juggled his paperwork. 'OK, right. Blah, blah, blah, "I don't know how to use punctuation properly, and everything is one big run-on sentence." Blah, blah . . . "Given that the readily accessible and sizeable bathroom was ignored in favour of exsanguinating Jane in the bedroom we can conclude that either the Bloodsmith was less concerned with making a mess, given that the flat below remains unoccupied, was confident that his new methodology for extracting blood through a big needle wouldn't cause as much mess, or there was a sexual element to this encounter that wasn't present with the previous victims," deep breath, "though it's unlikely that this was planned, given his modus operandi to date, if it occurred organically during his encounter with Jane it is likely to have taken him by surprise and his sudden arousal may well have startled and revolted him in equal measure, which could explain the excessive use of force when attempting to render her unconscious with a hammer." So, maybe you were *half* right about the romance. "This may also explain why the Bloodsmith placed Jane's intestines where he did, covering her genitalia, because he was ashamed of becoming sexually stimulated by her physical presence," then it just sort of rambles on for a bit, about platonic love versus spiritual love versus just wanting to jump someone's bones.' Turning the page. 'On and on and on . . .' The Dunk curled his top lip. 'People shouldn't get to be Police-Scotland-approved forensic psychologists if they can't write in proper sentences.'

'No sign of sexual activity, though.'

'Not according to the PM report.'

Lucy stood. 'Right, let's check the other rooms. See if he snuck back in here and rewrote his prayer.'

20

Twenty minutes later, they were back in the master bedroom.

The Dunk had returned to his spot in front of the patio doors, being all starry-eyed about the balcony and the view, doing far too much wistful sighing for a grown man. His already dirty beatnik outfit had picked up an extra layer of dust and fingerprint powder, fading everything to a mottled grey.

Lucy stared at the stained patch of wall above the hollow bedframe.

If the words 'HELP ME!' really were important to the Bloodsmith, why wouldn't he come back and rewrite them here? He must've known that the crime-scene cleaners had scrubbed it away with industrial-strength bleach. Didn't even have to visit the sites to know that – soon as the police guard had been removed from the cottage where Abby Geddes was killed, the press swooped in with their cameras and Dictaphones. That empty, rat-gnawed room had featured on the front page of every newspaper in the country. His prayer was gone, but it mattered enough to make him rewrite it in that manky attic bedroom.

So why not here?

Three bedrooms, one bathroom, two en-suite wet rooms, a kitchen, study, and lounge. No sign of 'HELP ME!' in any of them.

Maybe he couldn't get in?

Yes, but he would've taken keys to the apartment, wouldn't he?

Lucy flicked through the file, but there was nothing in it about missing keys. Then again, how would the search team know how many spare sets Jane Cooper had?

'Pfff . . .' She placed the folder on the bed.

'You know what I think?' The Dunk still had his nose pressed to the glass, like an urchin outside a sweetshop. 'I think we, the people, should be allowed to occupy places like these. You can't sell your overpriced flat? It's sitting empty? Good, honest, working people should be able to move in.'

'Then why would anyone ever build flats like these again?'

'Maybe they shouldn't. Maybe they should build places that normal folk can afford, instead of pandering to super-rich tax-dodging bastards.'

Lucy peered into the bedside cabinet.

One drawer for socks. One for pants. One for bras. All spilling out over the sides like their owner's innards.

'Seriously, Sarge, there's so much income inequality in the country, and they're building places like this to sit empty, because some hedge-fund tosser has decided it's a quick way to make a buck when property prices go up? Makes you sick.'

Wonder why the search team put her clothes back in the wardrobes? They didn't bother with Jane's underwear, so why her clothes?

Lucy stood.

Knowing O Division, there would be some bras and pants missing. Bet any sex toys Jane had hidden in her bottom drawer were long gone, too. That kind of thing probably went for a *lot* of money on the Dark Web, to sickos who collected serial-killer memorabilia.

The Dunk waved his arms about. 'We've got people dying, homeless, on the streets, and what, three-quarters of this building has never been occupied?'

She crossed to the nearest wardrobe. It wasn't a cheap mirror-doored job, it was a bespoke wooden one, crafted to fit the space perfectly, with drawers and racks and rails. Jane's shoes were in a pile on the floor, and so were her jeans and jumpers, but the stuff on the coat hangers was all where it should've been. Maybe not hung up in any sort of logical order – more crammed back in at random. No system to it. As if it was OK to mix up colours, basics, formal, and casual all in one disorganized lump.

'We're *never* going to have equitable distribution of opportunity, till we have equitable distribution of wealth.'

Some nice stuff in here. She checked the labels on a couple of cocktail dresses: one from Dolce & Gabbana, the other Prada. Gucci leather trousers that probably cost more than Lucy made in a month. Eminently nickable, but somehow they and everything else had escaped the long sticky fingers of the law.

Which made it all the more suspicious that they'd been hung back up after the search team had gone through everything else like a threshing machine.

'And we'll never have equitable distribution of wealth as long as we've got overprivileged posh twats running the country.'

Lucy bent down and shoved her hands in between a cashmere dress and a silk jacket. Like the pans in the kitchen, both still had the price labels attached. She pushed them apart.

'They don't give a toss, Sarge, because inequality works in their favour. The whole sodding system's corrupt and it's the poor that get beaten about the head with the shitty end of the stick every single time.'

'Dunk?'

'The whole class system only exists to keep the poor in their place. These posh—'

'Dunk!' Lucy unhooked the jacket and hurled it onto the skeletal bedframe. Did the same with the dress.

'Sarge?'

'Get the SEB over here, now.'

'You mean the Forensic Services Scene Examination Resources, right? They're—'

'Now, Constable!'

Shirts, blouses, slacks, skirts: they all went flying, till she'd made a gap in the wardrobe three feet wide. And there, right at the back, still partially hidden by the remaining clothes, were two words, written in big, dark-brown, dripping letters: 'HELP ME!'

The Dunk stood in front of the living-room window, one finger in his ear as he curled over his phone. 'Uh-huh . . . Yeah, OK.'

Lucy left him to it, heading out into the hall instead.

In a normal house, there would be a coatrack by the front door, but Jane Cooper's place had a cupboard instead. Hiding away any potential messiness. Inside was a collection of remarkably cheap-looking coats and jackets – compared to the stuff hanging in her wardrobe.

A thin cabinet was mounted on the cupboard wall closest to the front door. It opened to reveal rows of hooks, about a third of which held various keys, all with labelled fobs. A big bunch marked 'SHOP'. Two sets of Aston Martin keys marked 'CAR'. A small bunch marked 'HOLIDAY COTTAGE (CORNWALL)' and another marked 'HOLIDAY COTTAGE (SPAIN)'. And two identical single keys marked 'HOUSE'.

Not 'HOME', 'HOUSE'.

They were those fancy-pants security keys – the ones that didn't have serrations on the blade, just little dimples that matched up with whatever fancy-pants locks they had in a fancy-pants apartment like this one.

A row of empty hooks sat beneath the last row of keys. One would be for the set the Dunk had unlocked the door with, three-quarters of an hour ago. One for the keys the Bloodsmith used when he came back to rewrite his votive prayer in the back of Jane's wardrobe.

Her solicitors probably had a set, too. Maybe that was worth chasing up? Maybe the Bloodsmith was—

Lucy's phone warbled into life and, when she dug the thing out, 'DC TALLADALE' glowed in the middle of the screen. Their very own deep-fried-kebab-eating, hungover birthday boy. 'Stan.'

'*Please, please,* please *can I go home now?*'

'Depends. How did you get on with the CCTV?'

'*Louden's on a couple of cameras, hot-footing it from Markies in the afternoon, being chased by a security guard. Then we've got him getting pished on the steps of the cathedral from half three till five. After that it gets a bit ropey. Couple of sightings around the city centre – begging outside John Lewis, eating a burger on Harvest Lane, and that's pretty much it. Last seen disappearing down Parditch Road at half eleven.*'

'Anyone with him? Anyone who looks as if they shouldn't be there? Anything unusual happen?'

'*He throws his empties at some pigeons, if that helps? Now I'm begging you: my head's killing me, my stomach's like a tumble drier full of gravel, and I just want to go home and die.*' Sounded a bit like a sob at the end, there.

'OK. But let this be a lesson to you: old people can't get blootered on a school night.' She hung up.

'Sarge?' The Dunk appeared through from the living room. 'FSSER are on their way over. So's the boss. He sounds . . . stressed.'

She checked her watch: 17:17.

Two hours thirteen minutes till she had to go pick up Benedict Strachan.

'When's your show start?'

'Curtain's up at seven.' He looked down at his dirty polo neck. 'Could do with a shower. Maybe slope off home at half five? Six at the latest.'

'Yeah.' She closed the cabinet, then did the same with the cupboard, hiding the cheap coats away again. 'Well, we probably don't have to worry. It's not as if we get to follow things up any more.'

DI Tudor marched over the threshold, face even more creased than usual. Mouth pinched. A curl of hair had broken free of his gelled quiff, wafting about as he turned to survey the living room. 'Where is it?'

Lucy pointed down the hall. 'Master bedroom. In the wardrobe.'

A grunt and he was off.

You're welcome. A pleasure to be of sodding service.

The Dunk pulled a face.

Then a new figure appeared in the apartment doorway. Black Police Scotland fleece on over the standard-issue clingy T-shirt. The fleece had *much* fancier epaulettes than normal – which could only mean one thing: Big Boss. He had a thin military moustache perched beneath a Roman nose, narrow eyes, thinning brown hair cut short. He pulled off a pair of black gloves and tucked them into his fleece pockets. Posh-as-you-like Inverness accent. 'And *we* are?'

The Dunk actually snapped to attention. 'Detective Constable Duncan Fraser, sir.'

'DS McVeigh.' Lucy gave him a small wave. 'We found the message.'

'I see.' He stared off down the corridor, in the direction Tudor had disappeared. Then marched into the living room instead. Stood there, surveying the contents. 'What do we know about the victim?'

Lucy followed him in. 'Inherited a fortune from her parents, no siblings, no living relatives, no friends. Murdered eight months ago. Her family lawyers reported her missing.'

'Hmmm . . .' He strode over to the fireplace, forehead creasing as he stared at the rolled-up umbrella. A rippled version of the school crest was visible amongst the damp folds of black fabric. 'And I see she went to St Nicholas College.'

'Actually no, Boss, that's mine.'

'Is it now?' A smile flickered at the corners of his mouth. 'Assistant Chief Constable Findlay Cormac-Fordyce, Major Investigations and Operational Engagement.' Out went his hand. 'How nice to meet an alumna from my old alma mater.'

'DC Fraser and I were there this afternoon, talking to one of their pupils. They gave me an umbrella, because it was raining.'

'Ah.' The hand was lowered and the smile disappeared. 'Well, it's good to know St Nicholas College hasn't lost its sense of civic engagement.' One last look around the room. 'Now, where's this message from the Bloodsmith?'

The Dunk huffed out a lungful of smoke, crossed his arms, uncrossed them again. Had another puff on his cigarette. 'I'm only saying.'

Out here, on the decking, their view of the city faded in and out of focus as drizzle swayed across it in thick sheets, smothering all colour from the river and Castle Hill beyond. Lucy's new brolly kept the worst of it off, but that didn't stop the chill from leaching into her bones. 'Well, don't.'

'When he found out you didn't go to the same school, he dropped you like a sock full of warm diarrhoea.'

'Dunk, this isn't helping.'

'Double-barrelled dickhead.'

The patio doors cracked open behind them, and there was DI Tudor, looking as if it was his sock. He grimaced as he stepped out onto the balcony and slid the doors shut behind him. Then slouched back against the glass, eyeing the Dunk's cigarette. 'Wish I still smoked . . .'

She didn't offer to share the umbrella. 'We met your friend.'

'Urgh . . .' Burying his face in his hands.

'Yeah' – the Dunk nodded – 'he seemed *really* nice.'

Tudor shuddered, shoulders coming in as he curled up into a semi-standing ball. 'DC Fraser, could you give DS McVeigh and me a minute?'

'Boss.' The Dunk took one last sook on his fag, pinged the butt out over the handrail, then let himself back into the living room.

Once the doors were safely closed, Tudor hauled himself upright, head doinking off the double glazing. 'I swear to God, Lucy . . . It's like being a ring-piece at the World's Roughest Prostate Exam Competition. I get one more "motivational" speech from a senior officer, I'm going postal with a claw hammer.'

Maybe not the most tactful of metaphors, given what had happened to Jane Cooper's skull.

Down on the river, a dilapidated trawler chuntered by, pulling a thick cloud of pale-blue diesel fumes behind it. Herring gulls screamed and swirled in its wake, angular white-and-black shapes against the stainless-steel water.

Tudor snuck a sideways glance at her. 'Good work finding the message.'

'He's revisiting every crime scene he can. Probably stops off to masturbate on the way home, assuming he doesn't do it while he's here. Reliving the memories, phone in one hand, cock in the other.'

'Phone?'

'You never wonder if he films the bodies while he works on them?'

Tudor buried his face again. 'Thank you for that image.' Another sideways glance. Then he fixed his gaze on the rain. 'We're going to reseal the crime scene. Get the FSSER in to do another sweep. Which means—'

'You want me and the Dunk to sod off.'

A sigh. 'Lucy, it's not—'

'No, I get it. We're surplus to requirements.'

'You're not surplus to . . . Look, you found the message out in the woods, you found it here. That *matters*. It gives us another chance to catch him.'

Be still her beating heart.

Tudor cleared his throat. 'You know I've had patrol cars swing past your house all day, right? Well, I got a couple of uniforms to door-to-door your neighbours, too. All three houses' worth. Nobody's seen anything.'

Shock horror.

'Mind you' – he tried on his charming smile, the one that never worked – 'according to PC Sullivan, everyone in Ballrochie looks like they could give first-hand accounts of the Boer War, so it's not surprising.'

She nodded. 'Thanks for trying.'

'The Dunk tells me you think the guy following you might be some sort of heavy, hired by Sarah Black? Maybe you should stay somewhere else, tonight. Just in case?'

'Got my hundred-and-fifty-decibel rape alarm, remember?'

'Yes, you do.' He chewed on the inside of his cheek for a bit. Frowned out at the rain again. 'Anyway, one more crime scene to go and then we can talk about where best to deploy your and the Dunk's talents.'

'Can't.' Lucy hooked a thumb at the living-room window. 'The Dunk's got a prior appointment and I've got to go see a man about a couch.'

'But—'

'Hey, it was your idea, remember? "You need to talk to your therapist, Lucy", "I'll get you signed off on the sick if you don't, Lucy." Unless you want me to cancel?' She pulled out her phone. 'Not a problem, believe me.' Scrolling, one-handed, through the contacts till she got to 'DR JOHN MCNAUGHTON'. Thumb ready to pounce. 'Honestly, it'll be my pleasure.'

'That's not fair: I *never* threatened to get you signed off!' Tudor stepped out to the edge of the balcony, leaning on the railing in what was probably meant to be a casual and manly way. 'When you came back after . . . Neil Black, I was amazed at how well you seemed to be coping, but these last couple of months?' A huffed sigh, then a shake of the head. 'You're spiky and abrupt and sarcastic. OK, you've always been sarcastic, but you weren't usually cruel with it.'

'I am *not* cruel!'

'Maybe it's all this crap with Sarah Black? Or maybe you came back to work too soon? And maybe going off on the sick would be good for you. Help you figure out how to be the real *you* again.'

Bastard.

Her jaw tightened, teeth making squeaking noises in her head as the pressure grew. 'You – just – said – I was – doing – good – work.'

He stared out at the miserable rain-soaked view. 'When's your appointment?'

'Earliest I could get was six.'

Tudor checked his watch. 'Better get a shift on, then.'

Lucy popped her brolly up and marched out the front of Jane Cooper's building onto a wide area laid with paving slabs. They'd planted a handful of trees in amongst the stones, their wilting branches already losing swathes of yellowed leaves in the rain. Because that's what life was: disappointment and death.

The Dunk hurried out after her, face pink, air wheezing out of him in shallow panting breaths. 'Hold up, hold up . . .'

A couple of patrol cars sat by the kerb, an SOC Transit parked behind them – the driver had his head buried in a tabloid, while the passenger foostered about on her phone.

Lazy sods.

Lucy banged on the driver's door.

He looked up from his paper – face like a ruptured beanbag – then buzzed the window down a couple of inches. 'What?'

'Should you not be up there *doing* things?'

He curled his lip, setting both chins quivering. 'Nah. His Holiness the ACC says we gotta wait here till he gives the all-clear.'

The passenger leaned over the gearstick. 'I'm saying nothing.' Then went back to playing with her phone again.

Yeah.

Lucy looked up at the seventh floor, where Jane Cooper's flat was. Forced the burning wedge of bile out of her voice: 'Do me a favour and sweep for body fluids. Could be our boy gave himself "a little treat", before heading home.'

The driver closed his eyes and said something under his breath. Then, 'Why do I *always* have to get the wankers? Why can't I get a nice whole-some murder-suicide for a change?'

'Perks of the job.'

The Dunk dropped her off on Guild Street, back where she'd parked the Bedford Rascal in all its embarrassing pink glory. He grimaced at the jolly meat characters painted on the sides. 'I still say those sausages look like they're shagging.'

Lucy watched him drive off, then checked her phone. Ten to six. Should be *just* enough time to make her appointment with Dr John Tosspot McNaughton.

Because who wouldn't relish the opportunity to drag something hor-rible like Neil Black out into the open all over again?

'God . . .' She sagged her way into the driver's seat and cranked the rattling engine into life.

Next stop: the thing Lucy swore she'd never talk about.

21

A long pause from Dr McNaughton, then: *'And how does that make you feel?'* He'd positioned his chair in its usual place, just outside the circle of light, lurking in the shadows of his industrial-chic office. Rattling his jewellery every time he moved. Asking stupid questions. Being a pain in the arse.

'How the hell do you *think* it makes me feel?' Lucy scowled up at the ceiling with its stupid exposed ducting and pipes. 'They're basically threatening to sign me off on the sick, and I'm the only bastard making progress on this damn case! How is that fair?'

Silence.

Always with the bloody silence.

Ask the same 'how do you feel' question, then sit there, not saying anything, like a pot plant, as the world slowly dies.

Well, two could play at that game.

She folded her arms and thumped further back into the couch's seat cushions. It sent a little flurry of dust motes out to dance in the spotlight's glow.

And wasn't he supposed to be on *her* side? Little sod should be defending her, sticking up for her, telling her that DI Tudor was a dick and that she was completely right to feel hacked-off and betrayed.

Tosser.

'AARRRRRRRRRRRRRRRRGH!' Going rigid as a crowbar. *'That's* how it makes me feel.' Then sagging into the cushions again.

McNaughton might have been all hidden away, but his reflection wasn't – caught in the brushed-stainless-steel surface of a decorative chunk of faux machinery that some idiot designer had probably been paid a fortune to come up with. If anything, the dimpled metal reflected back the *real* Dr McNaughton. Not the face he presented to his friends and family, or his employers, or his patients, or his students: the real him. Twisted and distorted, greedy and devouring, hazy and monstrous. Like the minotaur, lurking in the gloom at the centre of its labyrinth, waiting to rip Theseus apart and feast on his bones . . .

Yeah.

Thinking in metaphors based in Greek mythology, now. Clearly going back to St Nicholas College after all this time hadn't stirred anything up *at all*.

'And why do you think Detective Inspector Tudor wants you to talk about what happened with Sarah Black?'

Urgh.

She let the silence stretch for a while, but there wasn't a lot of point, was there? McNaughton would win in the end, because people like him always did. One word to Tudor, or DCI Gilmore, would be all it took to get her thrown off the job.

'Because he thinks I'm going to obsess about what happened with . . .' A small, unfunny laugh hiccupped out of her. 'Even after all this time, I can't say his name out loud. How stupid is that?'

Oh God, Tudor was right, wasn't he?

Wonderful.

She draped an arm across her eyes.

Groaned.

What was DCI Ross's advice again? Something like, *Do yourself a favour and play along. You might be surprised how much it could help. And at the very least it gets them off your back.*

Or just give up and let them sign you off on the sick.

OK then.

Deep breath.

After all, what did she have to lose?

'It all started on a Friday night, at the Fisher King, on Smithchris Road . . .'

Five past nine and Gillian's already hammered. That's what happens when you adopt *eatin' cheatin'* as a religious belief. Still, at least she's not been sick yet, so that's something.

Might be a good idea to not sit opposite her, though. Just in case.

Lucy shifts one chair to the left and knocks back the last mouthful of Pinot Grigio. 'How's our birthday girl doing?'

That gets her a blurry two-thumbs-up, a broad grin, and a burp. Gillian's got her long, curly red hair pulled back in what had started life as a ponytail, but turned into a frizzy pompom somewhere between the Bart and the Postman's Head.

'Budge up, losers.' Mandy – back from the bar with both hands clamped around an unfeasibly large collection of glasses. Wine glasses, beer glasses, and most worrying of all: shot. They click-rattle onto the sticky tabletop. 'Tequila!' She probably thinks her new asymmetric bob makes her look chic and stylish, but it just makes her face look fat.

Not that Lucy would ever tell her that, of course. After the divorce, Mandy needs all the self-esteem she can get.

All three of them, done up to the nines in their best party frocks, like civilized human beings for a change. Instead of a lawyer, a cardiothoracic specialist, and a detective sergeant.

Gillian wobbles forwards, one eye screwed half-shut as she peers at the drinks. 'Thought . . . thought we were . . . flaming Drambuies?'

'You set fire to your fringe last time, remember?' Lucy helps herself to the glass of white. 'Flaming Drambuies are banned, and so's flaming sambuca, and anything else that poses a risk of tonsorial ignition. It's in the Most Excellent Girls' Night Out Constitution.'

'Oh . . .' Then the grin is back as she picks up one of the shot glasses, accidentally slopping a little onto the back of her hand. 'Slippery.'

Mandy raises the toast, 'Happy birthday, Gills!' Pronouncing it 'Gills' as in 'like a fish' rather than 'Jills', and hurls back her shot of tequila. Shudders. 'Ghaaaa . . .'

'Happy birthday, Gillian.' Lucy raises her new glass of Pinot Grigio, leaving the tequila the hell alone.

'Yeah, happy birthday.'

Mandy and Lucy turn in their seats to look at the newcomer.

It's a man: early twenties, thin, pointed face, one of those chav haircuts – almost shaved at the sides with a short, greasy, combed-forward fringe. Rugby shirt with the collar popped. Combat trousers. Sovereign rings on most of his fingers, thick gold chain around his neck. Little diamond stud earring. One of those boys whose default expression is a leer.

He's got a pint of something lagery in one hand – uses it to salute the table. 'Gillian, isn't it? You're very pretty, Gillian.'

'Not . . . not interested.'

'Double negative, that. Means you *are* interested.'

Mandy rolls her eyes. '*Men*. Don't take a hint, do you? Go bother someone else.'

'Hey!' He pulls his chin in, shoulders flexing. Making himself look bigger. 'Just being nice to the pretty lady, aren't I? Nothing wrong with buying a girl a drink for her birthday.'

There's always one on every night out. Some bloke who's seen too many romcoms where all you need to do to get the girl is keep pestering her. Because in the movies it's 'romantic'. In real life it's called 'stalking'.

'Hoy, cockwomble' – Mandy's half out of her seat now, jerking a thumb towards the door – 'sod off.'

'Hey, don't be so rude, *fatty*. Wasn't talking to you, was talking to the birthday girl.' And there it is, the threat hidden just below the skin of every arsehole like this: the aggression. Women aren't fawning all over you? Just throw your weight around a bit and they'll be gagging for it. 'Wasn't I, Gillian?'

Probably been watching those 'how to pick up women' videos on YouTube, posted by even bigger arseholes than he is.

Lucy puts her wine down. 'She's got a boyfriend, OK? And he's a police officer, so . . . ?'

He doesn't move. Just stands there, radiating his menace.

'Is this dickhead bothering you?' Another man, but this one's in a decent suit and open-necked shirt. He's a good three inches taller than the arsehole. Broader, too. Wide shoulders and serious eyes. Nice haircut. Voice like a newsreader. Stepping between the table and the arsehole. Putting himself in the way. 'Lady said she's got a boyfriend.'

'Fuck's it got to do with you?' Puffing out his chest.

The newcomer rolls his shoulders and clenches his fists. Cricks his neck from side to side in complete silence.

'You want some of this? Do you?' More puffing. 'Do you?' But the arsehole's backing away all the same, mouth pinched before it gets punched.

Still no reaction.

'Yeah.' The arsehole takes a gulp of lager. 'Didn't think so.' He jerks his chin at the three of them. 'Later, bitches.' Then slopes off, back to whatever rock he crawled out from under.

The man in the suit shakes his head. Turns. 'Sorry about that. I know it's not the done thing to say "not all men", but genuinely: we're not all misogynistic wankers.'

Mandy toasts him with her empty tequila. 'Thanks.'

'Nah, my pleasure.' Then he checks his watch. Frowns. 'Anyway, I'll get out of your hair.' Nods at Gillian. 'Hope you enjoy your birthday.' And slips away towards the crowded bar.

Lucy smiles. 'Did I imagine that, or did a man just stop another man from being a dick, and leave without expecting to be patted on the back?'

'Oh yes.' Mandy reaches for Lucy's untouched tequila. 'And I would so shag the living hell out of him for it.'

Then Gillian bangs on the table. 'The birthday . . . birthday girl . . . demands more drink!'

Of course she does.

'Oh, Jesus, Gills!' Mandy holds Gillian's hair out of the way as her back heaves and a torrent of yuck spatters into the alley behind the Falling Down, next to the big council wheelie bins full of empty bottles, lit from above by a sickly yellow streetlamp. Mandy dances her feet out of the way as Gillian retches again and again and again.

Lucy grimaces at the spreading puddle of vomit. 'OK, new amendment to the MEGNO Constitution: no snakebites. And maybe: *eat* something first.'

'Are you all done? OK.' Mandy pats Gillian on the back, top lip curled as the stench of an evening's alcohol and bile wafts up from the tarmac. 'There you go, that wasn't so bad.'

'On second thoughts: definitely eat something first. Eatin's cheatin' is hereby banned. All in favour?'

A nod from Mandy. 'Seconded.'

Gillian raises a thumb, then is sick again.

'Nah. No way. Not going to happen.' The taxi driver shakes his head, setting his dreadlocks rattling. Not a great look on an overweight lump of gristle with skin the colour of cold porridge. 'She's gonna puke all over the car.'

'Come on!' Mandy throws her arms wide. 'She needs to get home!'

'Not in my taxi she doesn't.' Then he buzzes up the window and pulls away from the kerb, leaving the three of them standing there.

Well, two of them standing. Gillian's slumped sideways against the lamp post, hair all anyhow. Reeking of booze and puke.

'BASTARD!' Mandy steps into the road and gives the departing car the finger.

Lucy sighs. Then shrugs. 'On foot it is, then.'

'Urgh . . . I've got a breakfast meeting with new clients, like at *seven thirty*. And it's Saturday! What kind of monsters schedule a breakfast meeting at half seven on a Saturday morning?'

'It's OK. I'm off tomorrow, I'll take her.' She hooks an arm under Gillian's, hauling her upright. 'We're off to see the wizard. You ready?'

'Mmmmnnnt. Everything . . . tastes . . . tastes funny . . .'

'And whose fault is that?'

Mandy leans in and kisses Lucy on the cheek. 'Thanks, babe, I owe you, OK?'

'Yeah, yeah.'

She stays there, watching as Mandy hails another taxi, clambers in the back, and drives off into the night.

'Right, you drunken monkey, let's get you home.'

You'd think, at this time on a Friday night, there would be more people going about. Instead the street is deserted, just a black-and-white cat prowling its way between the parked cars. Trees line the road, casting rippling shadows as their leaves block out the streetlight one moment only to let it through the next, like scrambled Morse code signals from the great beyond.

Gillian has her head on Lucy's shoulder, leaning on her as they walk-stagger down Newman's Lee. 'I love you, I really do. You're my best . . . best friend.'

'You're only saying that so I don't abandon you.'

'No! No, you're my *best* friend.'

The junction with Camburn Walk looms up ahead in the undulating darkness.

'Remember . . . remember when . . . when *Steve* left?' Pronouncing his name as if it was a venereal disease. 'And . . . and he took everything. He took . . . took everything, Lucy! Even Mr Rumples! What . . . what kind of . . . sick . . . sick bastard takes a . . . takes a person's dog?'

'He was a dick.'

'He *was* a dick.' A little whimpering sound makes its way out of her, escaping into the night. 'I loved him *so* . . . so much, and he . . . he took my doggie.'

'Come on, we're nearly home.'

'And you . . . and you found out where . . . where he was staying.' Gillian swings out her spare arm, hand curled into a claw. 'And . . . and you went over . . . over there . . . and you got . . . you got Mr Rumples back.' She pulls her claw down hard, as if she's ripping the testicles off a very tall gentleman. 'And kicked him in the nuts!'

'I didn't kick him in the nuts, Gillian. He fell down and injured himself.' Honest, officer.

'Pow!' Pausing to lash her foot out. 'Right in the nuts!'

'No: because that would be assault, and I didn't . . .' Lucy freezes. Is that footsteps? Behind them? But when she whips her head around to check, there's no one there.

So why is that familiar feeling back? The one that crops up every time she walks down a street at night. The one that came free with being born female. Like pins and needles, prickling out across the base of her neck.

Like she's being watched.

Dark street, late at night, not too far from Castle Hill Infirmary – the sort of place a certain kind of man would think is a good hunting ground for nurses. Where you can sneak up on them and do what you like.

'Come on, Gillian, let's get a shift on, eh? Could murder a cup of tea.'

'Sod . . . sod tea.' But she starts moving again. 'I've got . . . nice bottle of . . . bottle of vodka from . . . from a very grateful-to-be-alive . . . patient. We'll put . . . put on some music . . . and . . . and dance all night!' A rattling burp. 'And . . . and we don't have to shhhhh . . .' – finger to her lips – ''cos no one's bought . . . bought poor old Mr Rayburn's house yet.'

'Great. Let's do that.' Lucy picks up the pace, works her spare hand into her jacket pocket and grabs hold of her keys. Fiddling with them until one pokes out between each finger in her clenched fist.

There's the sound of footsteps again. Speeding up now. Getting closer.

She swings around onto Gillian's street. Twin terraces of sandstone townhouses face each other across the wide stretch of tarmac, big pavements, small front gardens, expensive cars. More trees. Not just on either side – the looming mass of Camburn Woods lurks at the end of the road. About as inviting as a fairy-tale wolf.

She keeps her voice low. 'Come on, Gillian, faster. We're almost there.'

Number six is just up ahead, a little light glowing above the door. The houses on both sides are empty – the one on the right crawling with scaffolding, a skip sitting outside, full of rubble where the contractors have ripped the building's guts out. The one on the left lies in darkness, just a drooping for-sale sign to mark the death of its owner. All the other homes have their curtains shut, blinds drawn, letting light and life leach out. Which means no witnesses. No one to help.

Almost there.

The footsteps are so close now, she can almost feel the rasp of his breath on the back of her neck.

'Up the stairs, quick, quick!' Hauling Gillian up the six steps to the front door. 'Keys. Keys!'

'I can't find them!' She fumbles through her pockets, dropping things to ping and clatter on the stone.

A footstep on the stairs behind them.

Lucy spins around, shoving Gillian behind her. Drops into the fighting stance they taught her at Officer Safety Training.

It's the man from the Fisher King. Not the arsehole – the one in the suit.

He stops where he is, hands up, eyes wide as he clocks the makeshift knuckleduster in her raised fist. 'Whoa, whoa, whoa!' Backing away a couple of paces. 'Your friend dropped this at the pub.' Holding up a bulging tatty purse. 'I'm . . .' He cleared his throat. 'Look, I know this isn't the best way to make a good impression, and normally I wouldn't chase after women on dark streets, but her address was inside and her keys, and I thought if I caught you then you wouldn't have to break in . . .' He licks his lips. 'I did shout, but you didn't seem to hear me.' His cheeks darken in the jaundiced streetlight. 'I've kind of made an arse of this, haven't I? Sorry.' Clears his throat. 'Didn't mean to make you think . . . Yes.' He offers Gillian the purse. 'Sorry.'

Lucy lowers her key-studded fist as Gillian unlocks the door. 'It's just, we thought you were—'

'I know, I'm an idiot. And kicking myself right now.'

The door swings open and Gillian staggers inside. 'It's my birthday. Vodka, vodka, vodka, vodka . . .'

He tries for a smile. 'Think your friend's going to have a *very* sore head in the morning.'

'Oh, like a complete beartrap.' Lucy smiles back. 'Thank you.'

'It's Neil, by the way. Neil Black.'

'It was nice of you to return her purse, Neil, we—'

His fist smashes into Lucy's cheek, sending her stumbling back over the threshold to crash down onto the tiled hallway floor as the world screams and jagged shapes writhe in the darkness.

'Yeah.' He steps in after her. Closes the door behind him. Locks it. 'Let's see if we can find a way for you both to thank me.'

22

Silence reigned supreme. Not so much as a breath to break the weight bearing down on Lucy's chest as she lay on Dr McNaughton's dusty old sofa.

Then a rattle of jewellery as he shifted in his seat.

Then more silence.

Lucy cleared her throat. 'If you say, "And how did that make you feel?" I'm going to come over there and break your knees.'

She shifted on the couch, setting free another plume of dancing dust motes. 'How does that make me *feel*.'

Thumped her head back against the cushion a couple of times.

Jaw clenched, fists too.

'He was a *rapist*.' Sitting up. Snarling it out: 'Neil Black was a violent, drug-taking, rapist arsehole. For two days, three nights. No food, no drink, not even bathroom breaks. You *happy* now?'

A sigh rattled out from the gloom. *'I'm sorry, I truly am.'*

'He'd looked so *normal*.' She collapsed onto the couch again, glaring up at the fake ducts and pipes. 'But then the worst ones always do, don't you? Men.'

Nothing back from the good doctor – not rising to the bait.

'His rape kit was right there, waiting in the living room. When he stole Gillian's purse, he must've seen the address and the keys and thought, "Why not let myself in and case the joint?" Maybe he was going to lie in wait for her? But that wouldn't have been as much *fun*, would it? He'd have missed the thrill of the chase.'

The quiet stretched again.

Stretched and stretched and stretched.

God's sake . . .

McNaughton really wanted his pound of flesh, didn't he?

'The hospital got worried when Gillian didn't turn up for a surgical consultation on the Monday morning. We could hear them leaving messages on the answerphone.'

'Hi, Dr Harper? This is Sophie, from the surgical team, again? We were supposed to be meeting at ten, and it's quarter past, and I'm just calling to make sure everything's OK. Can you call me back to reschedule? I'll try you on your mobile.'

The answer machine gives a long sharp *beeeeeeeeep*, then the only sound is Gillian's muffled crying.

It stinks in here. The sharp-yellow stench of stale urine, mingled with dried vomit, smeared shit, and the warm-iron tang of blood. All of it oozing out of the sodden, stinking carpet.

Neil Black stretches his arms along the back of the couch, a huge joint smouldering away between his lips, nostrils swollen and dark pink as if he's got a heavy cold. But it's what he's been putting up there that's caused the problem.

A mirror sits on the coffee table in front of him, still bearing the tell-tale dusting where two powdery white lines had been less than five minutes ago. What's left of a six-pack of Stella sits next to it, the empties rattling about beneath the table.

Cocaine to rev you up, cannabis to level you out, lager to keep you good and angry.

The bastard's pulled on a pair of boxers, indulging in a bit of post-rape modesty.

Through in the hallway, Gillian's mobile phone launches into its ring-tone: 'Shiny Happy People'. It jangles away to itself for thirty seconds, as if it's never heard of irony, then falls silent as the call's transferred to voicemail. That'll be Sophie from the surgical team again, still wondering why Gillian hasn't turned up . . .

But Gillian's in no state to do a cardiothoracic consultation. Her face is a swollen mess of purples, blues, and greens. Both eyes puffed up like blood oranges. Dark-scarlet flakes crusting her battered lips and broken jaw. A mashed-up nose that'll never be straight again.

The rest of her is a map of bruises.

He's tied her hands behind her back, leaving both legs free. Not that Gillian can actually go anywhere: not with her left leg all twisted and misshapen from when the bastard stamped and stamped and stamped on her knee. Blood smeared on the inside of her thighs.

Through all of it, he hasn't forced himself on Lucy. Not yet, anyway. Not since she woke up, stripped naked and tied to the living-room radiator – thick knots around both wrists, the rope in the middle looped behind the radiator pipe, so she can't go anywhere as he attacks Gillian over, and over, and over again.

And while he does, he doesn't look at the woman he's *raping*, he stares at Lucy. And if she doesn't stare back, if she dares to look away, if she doesn't watch what he's doing to her friend, he hurts Gillian even more.

He's forced them both to swallow pills, but they don't stop the horror, they just make everything fuzzy and heavy. The bastard still gets the screams that seem to turn him on so much. And with the buildings on either side being empty, there's no one else to hear them. No one to call the police. No one but Gillian and Lucy and Neil Black.

Lucy peers at him, head hanging forwards so her hair hides her eyes. He only likes to be watched while he's rutting away, not when he's limp and flaccid.

Neil Black doesn't know she's watching him; he's too wrapped up in whatever bastards like him think about when they're not hurting women. Assuming he can think at all, because he's pretty stoned right now. Eyes half closed and bloodshot, ash from his spliff crumbling onto his naked chest. Those grey flakes sticking to the suntanned sweaty skin.

'Mmpphhh . . .' He wipes the ash into curling smears. 'You bitches don't know you're born. You know that, don't you? Nah, course you don't.' A long draw on his joint sets the tip glowing angry orange. 'But doesn't matter really, does it? Nearly done here.' Pointing at the answering machine. 'I reckon they're going to send someone round, sooner or later. Don't worry, though: I'll be long gone by then.'

He sits forwards and selects a tin of Stella. Clicks back the ring-pull and takes a deep swig. 'I'm thinking a fire. That'll do you, won't it? Get rid of all that DNA and fingerprint nonsense. Just be two charred bodies, lying under a whole heap of burning rubble.' Another swig. 'You got any cash knocking about the place, Gillian? Course you do, you're a big-shot doctor, right? Bet there's all sorts of valuables in a swanky house like this, stashed away somewhere safe. You're not going to need them, only fair that you share.'

Tears roll down Gillian's battered face.

'So where's the safe, then?' Levering himself out of the couch. 'Well? Where – is – it?'

But all she can do is mumble.

'ANSWER ME, BITCH!' He hurls the tin at her head. It bounces off the side of her face, falling to the floor where it glugs out its piss-yellow froth into the carpet. Adding to the stench. 'WHERE'S THE BLOODY SAFE?'

Lucy glares back. 'You broke her jaw, you moron. She can't!'

'What did you say to me?' Neil Black's eyes bulge. 'WHAT DID YOU SAY?'

'I said . . . you broke her jaw.' Walking it back *fast*. 'She . . . she can't answer you.'

'Nah, you called me a moron.' He lunges forwards, grabs Lucy's face in one of his rough hands, fingers digging into her bruised cheeks. Bringing his nose so close to hers that the smell of second-hand cannabis overpowers even the stink rising up from the carpet. 'Who's the moron now, bitch?' Shoving her down. 'You sluts are all the same. That cow at the depot thinks she can fire me and get away with it? Oh *hell* no she can't.' Banging Lucy's head off the drenched carpet, setting her ears ringing. 'Said I'm not a team player.' *Bang*. 'Said I've got "attitude problems".' *Bang*. 'What even is that?' *Bang*. ' "Attitude problems", my thick throbbing cock.' Straddling her now. Leaning in close again. 'Your mate's turned a bit too . . . saggy for me. All used up. But I bet you're ripe and ready, aren't you? I've seen you watching me; getting all riled up and horny. Desperate for your turn.'

'GET OFF ME!'

He slams a hand down on Lucy's face, shoving her cheek into the damp carpet, digging his thumb into the bridge of her broken nose, making sharp-edged fireworks explode through her head. 'Play nice and I might be kind: put you out of your misery *before* I torch the place.' Neil Black sits back on his haunches. 'But first I'm off for a slash.'

He saunters out of the living room, humming 'Shiny Happy People' as he goes.

When he's out of sight, Gillian mumbles something, but it's impossible to know what.

'I'm sorry.' Lucy blinks hard to shift the tears that make the room swim. 'I should've . . .' What? 'I'm a *police* officer, I should've been able to stop him.'

Gillian's hair is drenched where it touches the carpet, hanging limp, darkening as the lager soaks into it. The tin of Stella is lying there, on its side, like they are, mouth open and hollow. Silently screaming.

Maybe . . . ?

Lucy glances over her shoulder at the door. He's going to be, what, five minutes? Slightly longer if he bothers to wash his hands?

They could make a run for it.

Lucy lowers her voice to a hissing whisper. 'Get up! We need to get out of here!'

'Gnnnnn fnnnnnt . . .' Gillian shakes her head, good leg shoving at the carpet, the other one flopping uselessly with its distended ruined knee.

OK. So they can't *both* make a run for it. But if Lucy gets out, she can raise the alarm. Call the police. Get someone to burst in here, kick the shit out of Neil Black, and rush Gillian to hospital.

All she has to do is get free from this bloody radiator.

No sign of a knife, or scissors: nothing to cut the rope.

But there's that empty tin of Stella.

Lucy shuffles her way down as far as she can go, stretching out her whole body, reaching for the tin with her toes. Straining towards it until every muscle in her body screams . . .

Her toes brush the edge of the cold metal, turning it slightly, then a little further, pulling it closer, till it's near enough to cup with the arch of her foot. Bending her knee and dragging the thing towards her. Twisting and contorting herself till the can's up at her head. Pushing it towards her hands.

Got it.

One tin of lager.

This has to work. Because they're both dead if it doesn't.

Lucy crumples the tin in half, then *clacks* it back again, scrunching it back and forth, twisting until the metal separates with a squealing creak. Unravelling it, so she's left with a long curl of razor-sharp metal with a rounded lump – the base and the lid – at each end.

She presses her makeshift blade against the rope between her bruised wrists and saws.

'Come on, come on, come on . . .' Pressing harder, gritting her teeth as the tin slips with every other shove, slicing thin bloody ribbons into her forearm.

COME ON, YOU BASTARD!

It's working: hacking away, slowly, through the unravelling rope.

Warm red dribbles run down her lacerated skin and drip into the filthy carpet.

She saws and saws and saws—

From the bathroom overhead comes the sound of a toilet flushing.

—and saws and saws and saws.

Then finally the last strands give way and she's *free*.

It worked.

Jesus Christ, it *worked*.

Lucy scrambles to her knees.

Gillian gazes up at her, tears streaming down her battered face. 'Plllsssss, dnnnt leeeeee mmmmm!'

'I'll get help. I promise!' Scrambling for the open living-room door.

'*Dnnnt leeeeee mmmmm!*'

Out into the hall.

Footsteps thump on the landing upstairs.

RUN.

Lucy grits her teeth and runs for the front door. No key, no key, no key . . .

There – Gillian's purse on the little table.

The contents spill and clatter out onto the tiled floor. WHERE'S THE SODDING KEY?

She drops to her hands and knees, bloody fingers skittering through the bits and bobs till she finds a little bunch of keys. Lucy snatches them up. One has a red fob with the word 'HOME' on it.

'*WHERE THE HELL DO YOU THINK YOU'RE GOING?*' Those footsteps are hammering down the stairs, now.

Lucy jams the key in the lock, turns it, hauls the door open, and lunges out into the morning rain. 'SOMEBODY HELP ME! HELP!'

'No you don't!'

Her head yanks backwards, razors slashing across her scalp as Neil

Black grabs a handful of her hair, his other arm wrapping around Lucy's throat. Hauling her back inside and kicking the door shut.

'You stupid BITCH!' Letting go of her hair to slam a fist into her kidneys. 'YOU STUPID FUCKING BITCH!' Flinging her against the wall hard enough to send framed photos crashing to the ground.

Lucy's legs give way, and she falls, landing on the cold tiles, amongst the debris.

'Oh, you are *so* dead.'

'NO!' She snatches a shard of glass from its broken frame, big as a carving knife. 'GET AWAY FROM ME!' Swinging it at him.

'What, you think someone's coming to help?' He kicks her, right in the ribs. He's not wearing shoes, but it's still enough to smash her back into the wall again. Sending the glass blade flying to shatter against the skirting board. 'Think the cavalry's going to break down the door and rescue you?' He curls a fist into her hair and drags her back to the living room. 'No one cares. I could strangle you right out there, in the middle of the street, and the most anyone would do is film it on their sodding phone.'

'GET OFF ME, YOU BASTARD!' Legs kicking out, both hands wrapped around his wrist, trying to stop him ripping out a chunk of scalp.

He dumps her next to Gillian. 'But I'm going to strangle you right here, instead.' Shoving Lucy over onto her back. 'You can die knowing your mate's going to *burn*, because of you. She'll still be alive when the flames get her.' He straddles Lucy, pinning her to the ground, both hands wrapping around her throat. 'Bye, bitch.'

She pulls at his wrists, jerks her hips up, doing everything they taught her about 'how to escape being strangled, from a prone position' at Officer Safety Training . . . but he's too big, too heavy, and too into it.

Claws. She rakes at his face with her nails, but he's just out of reach.

'You having fun, yet?' Grinning as he leans his full weight on her throat.

Blood *whooooosh-whump*s in Lucy's ears. The pressure growing behind her eyes. No breath. No breath . . .

That ripped-open can of Stella – it's lying right there.

The living room dims, as if there's an eclipse outside, getting darker and darker . . .

Lucy's fingers scrabble for the tin, snatching it up, and slashing it across his forearms. The thin metal tugs in her fingers, but nothing seems to happen. Damn thing isn't as sharp as it—

'AAAARGH!' Blood wells up across both of Neil Black's arms, in a bright-red straight line, left to right, as the skin opens wide. His hands leave her throat, and he stares in horror at the damage, thick waves of scarlet pulsing out of his wounds.

Air screeches back into Lucy's lungs; throat burning, head pounding.

'WHAT HAVE YOU DONE? YOU BITCH!' Fingers curled and useless.

Maybe she's severed a couple of tendons? Can't strangle someone if your hands don't work.

She gasps in another breath and swings her makeshift blade again – only he's leaning forwards now, unable to support his weight on his arms, so the tin carves its way across his right cheek, then on through his nose and out the other side.

His scream gets higher pitched as he rears backwards, blood raining down. 'AAAAAAAAAAAAAAAAAAAAAAAAAAAARGH!'

Another slash across his arms and he tumbles off her, trying to get out of the blade's reach. Crawling towards the door.

Lucy gets to her knees, staring around her: magazines, a couple of romance novels with the spines all creased, an empty wine rack, wilting flowers in a vase. Geode. It's heavy in her hand, about the size of a large baked potato, cut through to expose the blues and purples sparkling away inside. It'll do.

Two strides and she's standing over Neil Black, breath wheezing in her tortured throat.

Her whole arm shudders as she smashes the geode down on the back of his head. There's a muffled *thunk* and he jerks.

Then pushes himself over onto his back, one eye partially shut, the other glaring at her as if she's out of focus. 'Bitch . . .'

Lucy raises the geode and cracks it down again, right into his bloody face. Then again. And again. And again. And again. Hitting, battering, and hammering away, until there's nothing left but dark-red mush and Neil Black is never going to hurt anyone ever again.

23

This time, the silence was so thick you could choke on it.

Dr McNaughton's jewellery rattled.

The blood sang in Lucy's veins. Fingers trembling. Breath coming in shallow panting gasps. As if the bastard's hands were still wrapped around her throat.

'And you still feel responsible?'

'I killed him.'

'Lucy' – Dr McNaughton's voice softened – *'you were traumatized and drugged. He tortured your friend and made you watch. He subjected you both to unimaginable horrors.'*

'They couldn't even identify him from dental records.'

'His actions were what led to his death. All you did was defend yourself.'

She blinked up at the ceiling, trying to keep the knots in her throat from tightening. All those stupid pipes and cables up there, going nowhere, doing nothing. Just gathering dust.

Like her.

'We wanted to keep it as quiet as possible, not tell anyone what actually happened, but Neil Black's family . . .' A deep shuddering breath. 'We were liars; it never happened; we faked the PM tox report so we could ruin his reputation by saying he was a junkie; we planted drugs in his flat, too; Gillian was a crisis actor; the whole thing was staged, a false-flag event to cover up Neil's murder.'

McNaughton had gone back to being a pot plant again. Giving her enough quiet to hang herself. As usual.

'Dad had a stroke when he heard about what happened. Took an hour for the ambulance to arrive, and by then there wasn't much left of him. Died in hospital six weeks later, a hollowed-out figurine of a little old man. Never said another word.'

All those stupid pipes and cables and ducts.

'Gillian tried to get over it; she really did. Took a leave of absence. Put the house on the market – because you wouldn't want to live there, would you? Not after everything *he*'d done. Only no one wanted to buy the "Horror Rape House".'

What was the point of them?

'We found her three days after Christmas. She'd been dead for nearly a week, full of pills, in the bath, with her wrists slashed all the way to the elbow.'

What was the point of any of it?

'And the *pain* Neil Black caused, just goes on and on and on . . .'

What was the point of *anything*?

'*Lucy, it's no surprise that you've been having these episodes. The things you've been through would've broken anyone. You need to not blame yourself; you need to give yourself time to get better.*'

As if that was ever going to happen . . .

Lucy blinked at the Bedford Rascal's dashboard. Seven twenty-five, according to the dusty clock.

Where the hell . . . ?

It had actually stopped raining. Sunlight brushed the top of the buildings in front of her with a sliver of gold, making the pantiles glow.

She leaned over, staring into the wing mirror. Down the valley, across houses and rooftops, to the river, then on to Castle Hill and Logansferry. The twin red lights on CHI's incinerator chimneys glowing away in the twilight.

How did . . . ?

She had her phone in her hand; had she been calling someone? But when she unlocked it, the screen showed an unsent text message.

> Mandy, I know we haven't spoken since the funeral, and
> I know you blame yourself for not getting that taxi to take
> Gillian home, but

But what?

Lucy swallowed. Let loose a trembling breath.

Why should it be *her* job to make contact first? If Mandy didn't want to talk to her, she could go screw herself. Not like Mandy was the victim here, was it? Not like she'd been trapped in that bloody living room with the bastard. Had to watch what he did to Gillian.

So what if they'd been friends since university? That was just something else Neil Black had taken away.

Lucy deleted the text, opened the van door, and stepped out onto tarmac.

It was a parking lot, outside a small line of shops.

A man's voice – bored, crackling, and echoey – boomed out through a tannoy, somewhere behind her: *'Passengers are advised to take care, as the platform may be slippery due to weather conditions.'*

She turned.

That small, branch-line train station in Blackwall Hill sat on the other side of the road. The one that was meant to be the start of an integrated transport project, twenty years ago, that hadn't integrated anything and got cancelled in the next round of budget cuts.

Nearly half seven, and here she was, at the wee shopping centre where Benedict Strachan was due to meet his mum. Must've driven over here on autopilot.

That was Dr Sodding McNaughton's fault. Same thing happened last time she saw him – stirring up things that should be left alone. Making her go through all . . . *that* again. As if it wasn't bad enough at the Fatal Accident Inquiry, or the internal investigation, or when all the bloody press were shouting questions through her letterbox. No wonder she'd been sending Mandy a text – he'd torn the wound open again and filled it full of salt.

Why could no bastard ever leave anything alone? Why did they have to pick, pick, pick at the scab, and then act all surprised when the bleeding started? Why did . . .

Lucy froze.

That feeling was back again – the one where all the hairs on the back of her neck rippled, as if waves of electricity pulsed through them. But when she spun around, there was no one there. Just the fading evening sky, the spreading web of streetlights glittering away down the valley and up the other side, the glowing lump of the tiny train station, and the little row of shops.

Still, hard to shake the notion that someone was out there, watching her. Someone who *definitely* wasn't friendly.

God's sake.

Bet that was Dr McNaughton's fault as well: getting her all wound up and jumping at shadows.

OK. Deep breath.

The coffee shop was second from the end, sandwiched between a dry cleaner's and a place that did shoe repairs and key cutting. The other shops' shutters were down, but 'MOLLY'S BEAN MISSING YOU' had a big 'OPEN TILL NINE, EVERY NIGHT!' sign in the window. All lights blazing.

The only other vehicle in the car park was a big BMW four-by-four. The one that'd been parked outside Mr and Mrs Strachan's house earlier. No one in it now, though. Mrs Strachan would be inside.

Lucy wandered over to the coffee shop, doing her best to look casual, as if she was out for an early-evening stroll and fancied an overpriced hot beverage. Not a police officer looking to pick up an idiot before he fatally violated his release conditions and needed carting back to the nick.

No sign of him through the window, but his mum was sitting all alone at a table near the counter, facing the door. Fidgeting with a napkin while a large mug steamed away in front of her.

The door bleeped as Lucy entered into the earthy fug of freshly ground coffee.

Benedict's mum, Nikki, stood, mouth pursed.

Lucy ignored her, walked up to the counter instead and made a big show of examining the menu chalked up on the back wall. Kept her voice low. 'It's probably best if you pretend I'm not here. Don't want to scare Benedict off, before we can help him.'

'Yes. Of course.' She flushed pink, then sat down again. Went back to fiddling with her napkin. 'Sorry.'

'It's OK.'

A young man appeared behind the counter, all spots and jutting chin, bumfluff clinging to his jaw, but nothing on his top lip. 'Help you?'

'Latte: hazelnut syrup, chocolate sprinkles, and a raspberry muffin, please.' Then she helped herself to a copy of that morning's *Daily Standard* from the small selection of papers on the rack. After all, if she was going undercover, she might as well look the part.

Dear Lord, but the *Daily Standard* was an awful right-wing rag. If it wasn't ranting on about migrants, or travellers, or the EU, or lefties, or 'woke' celebrities, it was praising the idiots in government, or bowing and scraping to the royal family, while having a pop at anyone daring to be brown-skinned in public life. Not in a *racist* way, of course. No, no, no, it was simply reflecting the thoughts and fears of its loyal readership. 'Will of the people', and all that rancid . . . Lucy scowled. The bloody Dunk was rubbing off on her, wasn't he? If she wasn't careful, next thing you knew she'd be dressed head-to-toe in black, shouting, 'Smash the system!' and 'Groovy, daddio!'

'Hello?'

When she looked up from the paper, there was Benedict's mum, Nikki, holding her coffee mug as if it were a security blanket. 'Mrs Strachan.'

'I'm really sorry, but I don't think he's coming.'

Quick glance at the clock above the counter: ten to eight. Benedict was twenty minutes late.

Nikki pulled out the chair opposite and sank into it, shoulders slumped. 'He used to love coming here. I mean, this was when it was one of those places that did sweet and savoury pancakes? He'd have a Nutella-and-banana stack and watch the trains going to and from the distilleries for hours.' She stared into the half-drunk depths of her mug. 'Before it all went wrong.'

Might as well face it, Lucy was going to have to call Benedict's CJ social worker and tell him to get the paperwork started. Their good deed for the day was a complete failure.

'Ian used to work as a management consultant at Glendorchadas, you know, when he was on the council. People said it was a conflict of interest – city councillor working for a distillery – but he always maintained it was good for Oldcastle. That if local businesses didn't thrive, neither could the city.'

Still, it wasn't as if she hadn't tried. In the end, Benedict only had himself to blame. Again.

'We used to be such a happy little family . . .'

Lucy folded the paper and placed it on the table. 'Did he fall in with a new crowd? Or maybe there was a girl he was trying to impress?'

Frown. 'What, Ian?'

'Benedict.'

'Oh . . .' The creases between her eyebrows deepened. 'No. Not really. Benny . . .' She cleared her throat. '*He* was always very young for his age. Romance hadn't even registered on the horizon: too busy with astronomy and palaeontology. It's hard for a girl to compete with quasars and dinosaurs.'

'What about new friends?'

'He was working hard, gearing up for the first term at a new school, looking forward to getting his hands on some fancy science kit. Then . . .' Nikki shook her head. 'He wasn't *like* that. He was such a sweet little boy. He was my angel.'

Not exactly helpful.

Maybe try another tack? 'When I spoke to him, yesterday, he kept saying "They" were after him.'

Nikki shuddered. 'Please, just the word's enough to . . .' Her mouth hung open, eyes fixed over Lucy's shoulder at the coffee-shop window. 'Oh my God.' She stood. 'My little boy . . .' Then she was out of her seat and hurrying through the door.

By the time Lucy caught up, she was wrapping her son in a hug, kissing his forehead, tears glistening on her cheeks.

'Oh my baby, what have they *done* to you?'

Benedict's arms hung limp at his sides, the cast on his left arm a lot filthier than before, face turned to one side, those bruises looking dark and heavy in the streetlights' glow. 'Mum, I need some money.'

'I've missed you so much.'

That bored voice buzzed out from the tannoy system again: '*Passengers are advised to take care, as the platform may be slippery due to weather conditions.*'

'There's things I need to do. Things . . . You and Dad aren't safe, because of me, but I've figured it out!'

'Shhh . . . Shhh . . .' Stroking his lank hair. 'It'll be OK, I promise.'

'I need to *fix* things. I need to . . .' And that was when he looked at Lucy. His swollen mouth clacked shut.

'Hi, Benedict.' Lucy stepped forward. 'I'm here to help you.'

'What's she *doing* here, Mum?' Wriggling his way free and backing off a couple of paces. 'You were supposed to come alone!'

'Shhh . . . Baby, shhh . . . It's—'

'You didn't report to your Criminal Justice social worker today, Benedict. I need you to come with me and speak to him, or they'll find you in breach of your release conditions.'

He turned on Nikki. 'You lied to me!' Shoving her away from him.

'Oh my poor baby, I didn't—'

'They're going to throw you back in prison if you don't come with me, Benedict.' Advancing slowly, being as unthreatening as possible. 'It's not too late.'

'Baby, we can—'

'YOU WERE SUPPOSED TO COME ALONE!' The fingers on his good hand curled into a fist.

OK, this was going downhill fast.

Lucy inched closer. 'It's all right, Benedict, everything's going to be fine. You're not in any trouble.'

His unswollen eye went wide. 'They got to you, didn't They? You're working for *Them* now!' Paranoid and stoned, all over again.

'Come with me, Benedict, and we'll sort things out with your social worker.'

'You're going to kill me because I got caught!' Lurching backwards, as if the tarmac shook beneath his feet. 'I never told anyone! I didn't! I kept the secret!'

Should've brought her collapsible baton with her, or at least some pepper spray. 'You're safe now. No one's trying to kill—'

'I KEPT THE SECRET!' He turned and ran.

Damn it.

Lucy chased after him, as that same bored voice tried something new for a change: *'Please stand behind the yellow line. The next train at Platform One will not stop.'*

Why did everyone have to run?

Though, to be fair, he wasn't running very fast.

He hurpled out of the car park and across the road, Lucy closing the gap at an easy jog. Whoever had beaten him, they'd done a thorough job and now his top speed wasn't anything to worry about.

'Come on, Benedict, I'm trying to help you here.'

No answer, just huffing and panting as he lumbered up the steps to the train station.

'They're going to send you back to prison if you don't come with me.'

It'd been a manned station at one point, but now the ticket office and the waiting room were all boarded up, the walls clarted with bills advertising local bands and car boot sales. A ticket machine sat inside a bus-shelter affair, and a footbridge connected this side to the other platform – though, from the looks of things, no one had used that one for years.

'Please stand behind the yellow line. The next train at Platform One will not stop.'

He lumbered down the platform, making for the bridge.

'Benedict, don't be stupid: there's nowhere to go.' An eight-foot-high chain-link fence ran the length of Platform Two, blocking off both ends, the mesh woven through with drooping purple stalks of rosebay willowherb and the grasping claws of coiled brambles.

The train tracks pinged and sang, sounding like far-off laser blasters.

She followed him up the stairs. 'All you're doing is making things more difficult for yourself.'

Onto the bridge. Metal bars lined both sides, arching above their heads to join together, like a bird cage. A broken gate halfway along, hanging open.

'Come on, Benedict, don't be a dick.' No point rushing now: he was barely limping along. A proper low-speed chase. 'It's over.'

'Please stand behind the yellow line. The next train at Platform One will not stop.'

'Mr Scobie's happy to turn a blind eye, this time. We can get it sorted and you can stay out of prison.'

Benedict hobbled down the stairs on the other side, lurching out onto Platform Two, which would've been cloaked in darkness if not for the leftover, greasy yellow glow from the station across the tracks. Weeds snaked their way out through cracks in the concrete surface; small heaps of crisp packets, crumpled beer tins, empty Buckfast bottles, and used condoms sprawled against the metal control box.

The laser blasters got louder.

'I never told anyone!' He stumbled to a halt, halfway down the abandoned platform. Trapped.

Reason wasn't working, maybe she'd get on better humouring him, instead?

So Lucy nodded, walking out after Benedict. 'I know. You did well. They're very pleased with you.'

'They are?'

'Definitely.' The low grumbling roar of a big diesel engine joined the *twangs* and *peeeeoows*. 'In fact, They're so pleased with you They want you to come with me, so you can get your reward.'

A smile blossomed on his bruised face, then faded. 'You're lying, aren't you? They want you to kill me because I *failed*. We killed Liam Hay, but I got caught. I wasn't supposed to get caught! I can do better this time, I promise!'

'No, honestly, Benedict, it's OK. They don't care about that, because you didn't tell anyone. You passed the test!'

His head snapped to the side and back again.

The front end of a huge shed-like engine rumbled into view – flat-faced, with a slightly peaked roof, painted in grubby shades of red and rust-brown, 'WHISKYFREIGHT' stencilled in yellow down the louvred side. Hauling the first of what was probably a long line of unmarked wagons behind it.

He tensed, shuffling closer to the platform edge.

The train might not have been going full pelt, but it was still moving at a fair click – thirty, maybe forty miles an hour?

Lucy raised her hands. 'Come on, Benedict: you *passed*. That's great, right?'

He moved again. Licking his split and swollen lips. Knees bent.

The engine passed the signals a hundred yards from the end of the platform, bearing down on them fast.

'Don't!' She closed the gap, blocking his way with an outstretched arm. 'You can't jump the gap; you won't make it. This isn't the movies, you can't—'

'I'm not.' And he shoved her. Hard. Sending her sailing over the edge to crash down on the gravel below: tumbling backwards, limbs flailing, then sprawling to a halt with a sickening jolt, stretched across the two sets of tracks, right in front of the train.

24

Lucy's head bounced off the metal rail with a ringing clatter, hard enough to make her teeth throb. One arm stretched out above her head, draped over the vibrating metal as the train growled towards her like a huge angry animal. 'AAAAAAARGH!'

She jerked sideways, rolling onto the filthy gravel, arms and legs curled up against her chest as the stench of hot diesel washed over her. The air greasy and acrid in her mouth, burning its way into her lungs as the train wheels yelled their song into the rail, inches from her head, the warm foetid wind tugging at her hair.

'AAAAAAAAAAAAAAAAAAAAAARGH!'

She rolled again, flinching away as the freight trucks lumbered past.

Then thump: her back hit the other set of tracks. Finally, out of harm's way.

Lucy scrambled across them to the platform and pulled herself upright. Stood there, staring, as the train rumbled by, breath heaving in her lungs, head pounding, full of burning glass. Then turned. 'WHAT THE BLOODY HELL DO YOU THINK YOU . . .' But there was no sign of Benedict Strachan on the platform. 'WHERE THE HELL ARE YOU?'

He wasn't on the footbridge.

'YOU SON OF A BITCH, YOU COULD'VE KILLED ME!'

Truck after truck after truck after truck rattled past.

'I HOPE THEY SEND YOUR ARSE BACK TO PRISON WHERE IT BELONGS!'

*

By the time Lucy had limped her way across the road – one hand clutching the back of her head – her bright-pink Bedford Rascal was the only vehicle in the car park. Benedict Strachan's mum had disappeared, too. Maybe she'd given him a lift? Or maybe she'd just sodded off. Either way, Nichola Strachan was in for a not-so-friendly visit.

To hell with playing nice and doing Benedict favours, it was time to get the bastard picked up and thrown in jail. No more Miss Nice Girl.

Lucy pulled out her phone.

Blinked at it.

Perfect. That was just . . . 'BASTARD!'

The screen looked as if someone had taken a hammer to it, a spider's web of cracks radiating out from a big round impact crater. Wouldn't turn on, either, just sat there in her hand like a sodding paperweight.

A voice, right behind her: *'Detective Sergeant McVeigh?'*

Lucy dropped her phone and whirled around.

Man. Dark-grey suit. Short dark-blond hair. The dick from Professional Standards, getting out of one of O Division's manky pool cars.

Perfect.

Because that just rounded off the whole day, didn't it?

She stormed towards him, flinging a finger at the train station. 'WHERE THE HELL WERE YOU? I COULD'VE DIED!'

'Are you all right, DS McVeigh, only you seem a little . . . stressed.'

'STRESSED?' Her whole face felt as if someone was crushing it in a vice, jaw clenched, eyes bulging. 'Why didn't you stop him?'

'Stop who? I only just got here.' Holding his hand out for shaking. 'It's Charlie, by the way. Hope you don't mind me popping past, but your DC told me where to find you. Thought we could have that chat you've been avoiding. And, as we're both off duty, it won't interfere with you catching your serial killer.' Big bland smile. 'Everyone wins.'

She slapped his hand away. 'Give me your phone.'

'My phone?' He frowned, leaning sideways to peer at her head. 'Are you *sure* you're OK? Only I think you're bleeding.'

Idiot.

Lucy grabbed her shattered mobile off the tarmac. 'Mine's broken; I need to call this in.'

'Ah, my *phone*.' He dipped into his pocket. 'Won't do you any good, though. Battery's flat.'

Wonderful. Better and better.

'Thanks.' She unlocked the driver's door. 'You've been a *great* help.'

'You're definitely bleeding.' Charlie pointed as she climbed in behind the wheel. 'Are you sure you're safe to drive, DS McVeigh?'

She slammed her door and cranked the Bedford Rascal's awful engine into life. Threw it into gear and screeched out of the car park.

If she couldn't call it in, she'd just have to do this the old-fashioned way.

The police station on Forbes Drive looked more like a high-security prison, with its high boundary wall topped with razor wire and punctuated with CCTV cameras. But that was Kingsmeath for you.

On the plus side: it was a damn sight closer than driving all the way back to DHQ.

It wasn't a huge station: just big enough for half a dozen officers, all of whom must've done something pretty terrible to end up here. In any normal city it would've been part of the Great Police-Estate Selloff, but that would leave Kingsmeath without a visible police presence, and *that* was just asking for trouble.

Lucy waited in the tiny canteen – barely big enough for two kitchen cabinets, a microwave, kettle, sink, fridge, and a small round table – checking her watch every two minutes and sighing. How long did it take to get a sodding lookout request under way?

She pulled another green paper hand towel from the dispenser and ran it under the cold tap, dabbing it against the huge throbbing lump growing out of the back of her skull. Wincing at every touch. The first lot of paracetamol hadn't even put a dent in her blistering headache, and the second dose wasn't helping much either.

Bloody Benedict Bloody Strachan . . .

When she checked the paper towel it was still spotted with soggy scarlet patches, but at least they were getting smaller. Lucy dumped the sodden stained wodge in the bin, with the others, and dug out another fresh towel.

A knock on the door.

About sodding time.

But it wasn't the Duty Sergeant who slipped into the room, it was the Charlie from Professional Standards. 'There you are.' Jerking his chin up. 'How's the noggin?'

'Are you *following* me?'

'Given how upset you were, back outside the train station? Yes.' He leaned against the room's tiny table. 'Besides, when you drive a bright-pink Bedford Rascal, covered with copulating sausages, you're not as hard to track down as you might think.'

Lucy pressed the dry towel against her lump. 'I'm *fine*.'

'I see.' He picked at his nails, not looking at her. 'Your colleagues are worried about you, DS McVeigh.'

'Are they now.' She made herself a cuppa, filching one of the day shift's teabags, and helping herself to a slug of semi-skimmed from a carton marked, 'DUNCAN'S MILK ~ HANDS OFF, YOU THIEVING BASTARDS!!!'

Didn't bother making Charlie one, because sod him.

He kept his mouth shut while she was doing it, though, so that was something.

Lucy leaned back against the work surface and took a sip, scowling at him over the rim of her mug. 'Why are you here?'

'Have you considered going to Accident and Emergency? You must've hit your head pretty hard.' Glancing at the bin with its collection of bloodstained paper towels.

Did they go out of their way to recruit only the most annoying of bastards for Professional Standards?

'I'm not your enemy, DS McVeigh, I'm really not.'

'Then why – are – you – here?'

'DCI Gilmore thinks I should keep an eye on you, help out where needed. Said you were under a lot of pressure, what with the case and Sarah Black and this guy who's been harassing you and everything. Said it would be a shame to lose you.'

There was no mistaking the threat in that last sentence: play the game, or else.

Lucy cleared her throat.

Antagonizing the little git wasn't helping, was it? If anything, it was making things worse.

'Is that right.'

'Have you seen the size of the bump on the back of your head? It's like a hard-boiled egg.' He pointed at the notice pinned up above a shabby old piggy bank. 'And you should *really* put money in the kitty for that cuppa.' He wandered over to the canteen's narrow window, peering out through the grime, across the barbed wire to the grubby terraces and council flats. 'If I'm honest, what concerns me the most is that someone's been following you. Slashing your tyres. Knows where you live. I mean, what if they're working for Neil Black's family?'

Hark at Captain Sherlock.

Lucy bit back the sarcastic reply, opting for something more neutral instead: 'I *had* already thought of that.'

He stood on his tiptoes to get a better look. 'Even worse: what if it's the Bloodsmith? Your visit to the cottage where Abby Geddes died was all over the news yesterday. Today it's all about our finding DC Malcolm Louden's body in the woods. He knows you're getting closer.'

She sipped her tea.

DI McNaughton wasn't the only one who could do the silent treatment.

Charlie looked over his shoulder at her. 'It's worth considering, isn't it? Apart from anything else, you saw him, which means you've got a physical description. You can circulate it around the Division, see if he's come up in the investigation.' Staring out the window again. 'Someone has to know who this guy is.'

She let him have a little more silence.

Charlie gave up on the view, turned, and rested his bum on the windowsill instead. 'Look, we appear to have got off on the wrong foot. So, how about we get you over to A & E, have you checked over for a concussion, then I can buy you a collegial drink.' One hand against his chest. 'As an *official* representative of Professional Standards. Show you we're not all horrors.'

'I don't drink.' Not any more, anyway. Not after what happened last time. She forced a smile. 'But thank you for your kind—'

Another knock on the door, but this time it *was* the Kingsmeath Duty Sergeant who stuck his big bald head in. 'You McVeigh?'

She hid the illicit tea behind her back. 'Any news?'

'Lookout request's active, citywide. Got a patrol car popping past the halfway house on Stirk Road every now and then, but they lock the doors at nine, so . . . ?' A shrug. 'Got someone watching the train station, too.'

'What about his mother?'

'Officers on their way now. And I got the Automatic Number Plate Recognition team to put a flag on her BMW, just in case she does a runner to Aberdeen or Dundee with the boy hiding in her boot.' He nodded, setting his chins rippling. 'Now you *are* going to remember it's fifty pence in the kitty for that tea you pilfered, right? We might not chuck scallywags in the cells here any more, but wayward police officers are another matter entirely.'

Lucy clomped out into the car park, round the back of the station, bathed in the wan yellow glow of a security spotlight that didn't seem able to get properly going.

Charlie followed her over to the Bedford Rascal.

'So, Benedict Strachan gets picked up, night in the cells, then back to prison tomorrow. You OK with that?' Climbing inside and fastening his seatbelt.

Lucy stared at him. 'What do you think you're doing?'

'Coming with you to A & E. I can pick up my car tomorrow.'

She tightened her hands around the steering wheel. 'I'm not *going* to A & E.'

'Ah . . . You're not thinking of going after Benedict Strachan again, are you?' A sigh. 'Do you never worry that you're a little . . . obsessed with him?'

'I dobbed him in, didn't I? Just now – you saw me!'

'Yes, but you like him. And I don't mean *like*, like, I mean you identify with him.'

Lucy started the engine and crawled the van over to the exit gate. 'He killed a homeless man.'

'I know.'

The gate buzzed open and Lucy accelerated out onto Forbes Drive.

'*But* . . .' Charlie held up a finger. 'A: Benedict's a former child prodigy.' Another finger. 'B: he was prevented from reaching his full potential.' Finger number three. 'C: he has a difficult relationship with his father.'

'I do *not* have a . . .' She cleared her throat. 'I didn't have a difficult relationship with my father. My father loved and supported me.'

'You do realize that your therapist submits formal reports to O Division, don't you?'

Lucy took her foot off the accelerator, letting the Bedford Rascal drift to a halt outside a dimly lit kebab shop. Then turned and stared at him. 'You're reading my *therapy* reports?'

'Of course we are. How else are we supposed to know if you're OK to be at work, or what support you need? Do you really think we don't care if you're going off the rails or not?' He pointed at her head. 'No pun intended.'

'My *therapy* reports?'

'Oh, don't worry, it's not some sort of blow-by-blow recording of your sessions, just a high-level summary: Dr McNaughton's impressions, how he thinks you're getting on, that sort of thing. It's all on a strictly need-to-know basis.'

'*You* don't need to know!'

'Anyway, where were we?' A frown, then one last finger joined the others. 'D. Benedict Strachan killed someone, too.'

Lucy's jaw clenched. 'Don't you *dare*!'

'I know, I know – the situations were completely different. He had a *choice* about that, he *chose* to go out and murder Liam Hay; you didn't have any option. While Neil Black deserved everything he had coming.' Charlie brought one shoulder up, palms facing the van roof. 'I'm just saying: maybe that's why you're spending all this time chasing about after Benedict Strachan when you're supposed to be out catching the Bloodsmith instead?'

'My shift ended nearly four hours ago! What I do in my spare time isn't anyone's—'

'Is it just your spare time, though, DS McVeigh? Again, I'd remind you: your – therapist – sends – in – reports.'

That did it: she was going to bloody well kill Dr John Dickhead McNaughton.

Lucy hauled on the handbrake. 'Get out.'

'I'm on your side, Lucy.'

'Are you deaf? Get – out.'

'Come on.' Charlie tried a chummy smile. 'You wouldn't leave a fellow police officer stranded out here in the middle of Kingsmeath, would you?'

'GET OUT OF THE VAN, BEFORE I THROW YOU OUT!'

'Jesus. All right, all right, I'm going.' He climbed down onto the pavement. 'You know, I really *am* on your side, Lucy. Take a deep breath, OK, and—'

She put her foot down, letting the van's forward motion slam the passenger door shut.

He could bloody well walk home.

The van's headlights swept across the front of her house as she pulled the thing into the driveway, gravel scrunching under the wheels.

'Oh, for God's sake.'

No sign of her Kia Picanto, just an empty oil-spotted stretch of chuckies where it should've been.

'You were supposed to bring the damn thing back with new tyres!' Hauling out her phone and . . . swearing, because it was still broken. Funnily enough.

Bloody garage.

Lucy clambered out and slammed the driver's door. Sod the neighbours. Then grumbled her way around the van, making sure everything was locked, and slumped her way into the house.

She dumped her keys in the bowl, hung up her raincoat, stuck her new brolly in the umbrella stand with all of Dad's old walking sticks, then opened the sideboard's drawers. Rummaging through the contents for her old phone. The charger was in there too, which was about the only bit of luck she'd had today.

She took both through to the kitchen, swapped over the SIM card from her broken phone, and put the old handset on to recharge: one red bar, glowing away on the battery icon.

Next: another two paracetamol and a pair of aspirin, washed down with a big glass of cold water. And finally: a bag of peas from the freezer, pressed against the back of her head. 'Urgh . . .'

Lucy stood there for a while, eyes closed, till the throbbing headache eased a bit.

Bloody Benedict Bloody Strachan.

And she did *not* identify with him, thank you very much.

The phone still displayed that single red stripe, so Lucy left it charging. Plucked the Blairrachan Garage business card from the corkboard by the fridge, made a cup of tea and took both through to the living room. Gave the useless gits a call from the landline, scowling while it rang and rang and rang.

'Aye, aye, you've got through to Blairrachan Garage, we're a' awa' the noo, but you can leave a messagey oan the thingie aifter the beep.'

Beeeep.

Well, of course there was no one in, it was after nine on a Thursday night.

'This is Lucy McVeigh. Where's my car, Fergus? You promised me it'd be back today!' Then hung up with as much venom as she could muster with a thumb and a button, and stood there, seething for a while.

When her jaw unclenched, she had a sip of tea and went over to stare at her murder board in all its frustrating and ineffable glory. And, of course, she had a new victim to add to the wall.

Lucy nipped out to the hall and dug a chunk of paperwork from her raincoat pocket. AKA: everything she'd managed to nick from Operation Maypole about ex-DC Malcolm Louden. She stood there, frowning at the pocket. There was something else in there. Something heavy.

'Sod.'

It was the little bunch of keys she'd found yesterday, down near that meat-packing place. Supposed to have handed those in at the Lost and Found.

Ah well, they'd just have to wait till tomorrow. They went in the bowl with her house, car, and van keys, then Lucy took the printouts through to the living room and pinned them up with the others. No crime-scene photos yet – just the one of Louden's back, with the broken tattoo – but she could print those out tomorrow, when she was back in the office, along with anything else the teams had found out about him.

Right: so now they had a software engineer; a molecular biologist/call-centre worker; an unemployed project manager; a debutante/part-time bookseller; a philosophy student; and an ex-detective constable/home-less person. They didn't look alike, they weren't all the same age, they weren't even all the same gender, but *something* had to connect them.

A long breath hissed out of her.

Not getting anywhere tonight at all.

A little light winked away on Dad's old answering machine. Probably a marketing call, or a scammer, or something. It wasn't as if she'd given the landline number out to anyone. But she pressed the button anyway.

A loud *bleeeeeep* sounded, followed by:

'*Did you know the Scottish Government has put aside money to help you buy a new boiler? Well—*'

Delete.

'*Miss McVeigh? It's Mr Unwin, from Unwin and McNulty. I just wanted to remind you that your father's ashes are here and ready for collection whenever you feel ready. There's no rush.*'

Delete.

'*Congratulations! You may already have won—*'

Delete.

So much for that.

She sagged. Grimaced. Rubbed a hand across her face.

God, what a day.

Should really go have another crack at her wall of suspects. Try to achieve something. As if that was going to happen by sheer force of will.

Yeah . . .

Back in the Before Times, pre-Neil-Sodding-Black, it would've been bottle-of-Pinot-Grigio o'clock. But now? Just have to make do with a nice hot bath instead. Because, while that wouldn't *fix* anything, it would make life feel a hell of a lot better.

The Bloodsmith and the dead would just have to wait.

25

The ten o'clock news burbled away in the background as Lucy scuffed through to the kitchen; dressing gown, slippers, damp hair wrapped in a towel.

Clunking open the fridge revealed the usual depressing array of not-very-much. Some milk. A bag of salad that'd turned to dark-green mush. Carton of eggs. Pat of butter. Jar of pickled onions. Chunk of mousetrap cheddar, wrapped up in clingfilm. Half-empty jar of blackcurrant jam with white mould furring its dark-purple surface. Not like Jane Cooper, with her stacks of swanky ready meals.

Wonder what a search team would make of the contents here. What it'd say about the body lying upstairs in the bath. Or maybe they'd find her at the bottom of the stairs? Or out in the garden. Or right here in the kitchen. On her own. All alone.

Here lie the mortal remains of Detective Sergeant Lucy McVeigh, unloved, unknown, and unmourned . . .

Cheese on toast with pickled onions it was.

She stuck the grill on and checked her old phone. *Still* only one red bar, and that was, what, an hour it'd been charging?

Lucy picked it up, leaving the power cord plugged in, and turned it on.

Took a moment, but the screen finally flickered into life as the system booted up. That was something, at least. She unlocked it and the thing buzzed and dinged in her hand. Three text messages – one from the Dunk, the other two from unknown numbers – and a couple of voicemails – both unknowns as well.

THE DUNK:

> You OK Sarge? Got a message from the Boss saying you
> got clattered a nasty one? Need me to do anything?

'I'm not a weak and feeble woman, Dunk.'

DELETE.

Don't know why physicists got so excited by the speed of light – it travelled at a snail's pace compared to gossip through O Division.

UNKNOWN NUMBER:

> Dear DS McVeigh,
> I hope you are well. It was very nice meeting you today
> (at St Nicholas College) and I hope you are making good
> use of the school umbrella.
> If you would ever like a tour of the facilities here, I would
> be delighted to show you around.
> Yours sincerely,
> Assistant Headmaster, Argyll McCaskill

Apparently, Argyll didn't send a lot of text messages. Probably got all confused about where to put the stamp, or why he didn't have to tie it to a pigeon's leg any more.

UNKNOWN NUMBER:

> Hope you're pleased with yourself! The BULLY BOYZ
> just been round & they'll be jackbooting Benedict back
> to prison soon as they find him.
> YOU WERE MEANT TO HELP!!!!

Presumably that would be Mr Scobie, Benedict's CJ social worker.

'Didn't see *you* getting chucked in front of a moving sodding train.'

DELETE.

And last, but probably least – voicemails.

YOU HAVE – TWO – *NEW MESSAGES AND* – NO – *SAVED MESSAGES.*
MESSAGE ONE:

A plummy posh-boy voice bounced out of the phone. *'Hello, DS McVeigh, erm . . . well, Lucy, if I may. Yes. I, erm . . . Whoooo, this is a bit more . . . than I thought. Look, I'll cut to the chase. I know we, erm . . . you know,* chaps, *we're supposed to play it all cool, but I thought I'd . . . break with tradition and say I was rather taken by you and I'd like to get to know you better?'* You could almost hear him fiddling with his floppy fringe. *'Oh, it's Argyll, by the way. Argyll McCaskill? I'm the assistant headmaster at St Nicholas College? Anyway, erm . . . yes, so I wanted to say . . . that . . . and ask if you'd, perhaps, like to . . . erm . . . you know, we could go to the pictures, or a play, or concert, or something. If you'd like to? Or for dinner, or even just a coffee?'* There was a pause, then a long, huffing sigh. *'You can probably tell I don't do this very often . . . call women up out of the blue, I mean.'* The words getting faster and faster. *'But you've got my number now, and if you want to get back in touch that's great, and if not, erm . . . I'm sorry to bother you. Bye.'*

Well, that was *slick*.

Bleeeep.

With patter like that, bet Argyll McCaskill was a *massive* hit with the ladies. Like Casanova on steroids. Ahem . . .

MESSAGE TWO:

The next voice wasn't anywhere near as posh, but still had that Castleview-upper-crust edge to it, along with a sibilant, missing-teeth smushiness, accentuated by the speaker being obviously drunk and/or stoned. *'I'm sorry. I hope . . . hope you're . . . all right. I don't know if you're . . . all right, but . . . but I hope you're all right.'* Benedict Strachan. *'If you . . . if you are all right, if . . . if you're listening to this . . . I want you to know . . . know I didn't mean to hurt you. It's just . . .'* A couple of wheezing breaths and a whine. *'I cocked it up! I wasn't . . . wasn't meant to get caught, but . . . but I got caught and I . . . I kept the secret, but I cocked it up and the only way . . . the only way I can . . . can make it right . . .'* Silence.

Lucy made sure the power cable was still plugged in.

Maybe he'd hung up?

'I have to . . . to do it properly. Do it properly and not get caught . . . like last . . . last time . . . If you're . . . if you really are working for . . . for Them, tell Them I'm . . . Don't hurt my mum and dad. I'm going . . . going to get it right this time. Promise.'

Bleeeep.

She sagged back against the kitchen table.

Well, that was just . . . Yeah.

Do it properly and not get caught.

He was going to find himself another homeless person to kill.

She marched through to the living room, grabbed the landline handset, dialled, and took it back into the kitchen, listening to it ring on the way.

'*O Division Control Room, how can I—*'

'DS McVeigh. I need you to put me through to DCI Ross. And I know it's late, and I know he's off duty, but just do it. Please.'

'*Can I ask what it's—*'

'Possible attempted murder.'

A keyboard clattered in the background. '*Putting you through now.*'

The O Division hold music was utterly terrible, but finally a gruff voice cut it off. '*DS McVeigh. I assume this is—*'

'Benedict Strachan's breached his release conditions and he's planning on killing someone, possibly tonight. He's doped up, delusional, paranoid, and dangerous.'

'*I see.*'

'I'm telling you, because he left me a message on my phone, which means I've got the mobile number he was calling from, which means—'

'*We can trace his whereabouts.*' Some muffled crumps and banging. '*I'll get a warrant.*' The sound of breathing, then, '*You're sure he's going to hurt someone?*'

'Can play you the message, if you like.' Lucy held her mobile up to the phone and hit the button.

The geode's heavy in her hand – so heavy she can barely raise the thing high enough to smash it down on—

Lucy scrambled out of bed, pyjamas sticking to her back, face: cold and clammy. Chest heaving as she dragged in urgent wheezing gasps. Trembling. The bedside rug cool beneath her bare feet. The only thing that broke the darkness was the alarm clock, glowing '03:02' at her in blurry red digits.

Jesus.

She slumped forward and grabbed her knees, closed both eyes, and tried to calm her breathing down. Going through the exercises they'd given her. In and out. In and out. In and out.

Hadn't had a nightmare like that for months and months.

Thank you, Dr Sodding McNaughton, for stirring everything up again.

Eventually, her breathing slowed to something more like normal and Lucy straightened up. Wiped a hand across her damp face.

Why did psychologists always have to make things worse? Surely the whole point of therapy was to . . .

What was that?

She padded her way to the bedroom door and eased it open.

The landing was shrouded in gloom; what little light there was seeped in through the window at the end. Cold grey slivers of moonlight traced the top of the trees opposite.

Maybe she'd imagined it? Still jittery after the dream. It wasn't as if—

A noise downstairs: scratching, scraping.

She *absolutely* didn't imagine that.

Lucy inched out to the balustrade and peered down into the dark.

Why was it that the first thing anyone did in books and films, when they heard some weird noise in the night, was shout, 'Hello?' Instantly letting the axe-murdering psychopath know exactly where they were. Presumably because all fictional people were idiots.

She crept along the landing to the stairs.

Maybe it was mice? Old house like this, middle of nowhere, bound to get the odd mouse or six. Gnawing on the wiring, breeding in the gaps . . .

The top step creaked beneath her bare foot. Not loud enough to stop the scrabbling noise, though. She eased her way down the stairs, slow and steady.

It was even darker down here, the air scented with tendrils of mildew and dust.

That sound was coming from the front door. A shadow covered the stained-glass panel set into the wood. There was someone outside.

Lucy stayed close to the wall as she snuck forward. Eyes on the door handle. Did that just move? Because she'd made sure all the doors and windows were locked before going to bed. Hadn't she?

It did. It definitely moved.

This was it. The bastard in the corduroy jacket had finally come to finish the job. Following her, slashing her tyres: it had all been building up to this moment.

Should've bought that bloody baseball bat.

Well, just have to improvise, wouldn't she?

Lucy slipped one of Dad's old walking sticks from the umbrella stand. A nice hefty metal stick with a Bakelite handle, the rubber tip long since crumbled to dust. Old, but perfect for caving someone's head in.

The door handle twisted.

Time to give them a helping hand.

She reached for the handle, but it snapped back into place before her fingers touched it. Then the whole door rattled as a fist slammed against it on the other side, the booming sound nearly deafening in the silence.

Boom, boom, boom, boom.

She flinched back.

Boom, boom, boom, boom.

OK.

Didn't matter.

She had the walking stick.

Yes, but what if they had a knife? Or a shotgun?

Boom, boom, boom, boom.

Her hands tightened on the cold metal.

What if there were two of them?

Yeah . . .

Wouldn't hurt to have some backup.

Lucy grabbed her keys from the bowl on the sideboard – jammed the front-door one in the lock and twisted it all the way over. Leaving it in there, so they couldn't pick it from the outside, before sprinting into the living room.

She snatched up the house phone and pressed the green button. Nothing. No dialling tone. It was dead. They'd done something to the line.

Boom, boom, boom, boom.

Lucy edged over to the bay window and eased one side of the curtains open an inch. Just enough to see out.

A red-and-white Mini sat on the drive, next to Dad's old van, engine idling a curl of exhaust into the night, running lights glowing blood-scarlet. He'd reverse parked, ready for a quick getaway, which gave her a blurred view of the number plate. Squinting didn't make it any clearer, nor did rubbing her eyes. Should've put on her glasses, but the stupid things were still lying on the bedside cabinet, upstairs.

Boom, boom, boom, boom.

She shifted around another couple of inches, till the front door came into view. It was her stalker – the bastard who'd slashed her tyres. And he *was* alone. Didn't look as if he had a shotgun, either. Hammering on the door with both gloved fists.

Right.

Lucy marched back into the hall, raising the walking stick on the way, ready to batter it down. Grabbed the key, unlocked the front door and threw it open. 'AAAAAAAAAAAAARGH!' Swinging as she lunged over the threshold.

But he wasn't there – he was scrambling in behind the Mini's wheel. Engine roaring as he put his foot down.

Got to put it in gear first, idiot.

She leaped after him – gravel cold and sharp beneath her feet – swinging the heavy metal walking stick in a slashing arc. It smashed down into the Mini's roof, making a long puckered dent in the bodywork, sending a network of jagged cracks curling across the rear windscreen.

Sharp little stones flew from beneath the wheels and the car shot forward, accelerating out onto the road before she could get another swing in.

'YEAH, THAT'S RIGHT: RUN AWAY!' Lucy staggered after the Mini, across the painful gravel, waving her dad's walking stick like a sword at the disappearing tail-lights. 'AGAIN!'

She stood there, in the middle of the road, feet frozen and aching. Breath whoomping out in thick grey lungfuls.

Turning up here, in the dead of night, to hammer on her door like something out of a horror film. Well, if the plan had been to terrify and intimidate her, it hadn't sodding worked. All it did was make her even more pissed off. And if Sarah Black thought she was winning this one, she was in for a nasty surprise.

Lucy limped back into the house. She had some calls to make.

— a song of blood and darkness —

26

Lucy finished up her tea and toast, then yawned her way towards the living room. One eye screwed shut against the headache pounding away behind it. Waiting for the pills to kick in.

She shambled across the hall and unlocked the living-room door. Hadn't been easy, keeping everyone out of there last night, but if she hadn't it'd be halfway around O Division by now: *Detective Sergeant McVeigh's been nicking case files from Operation Maypole! Her walls are plastered with them!* DI Tudor would've had her suspended, signed off on the sick, and probably fired as well.

She dumped the key back in the bowl on the sideboard as the doorbell chimed out its two miserable notes.

Urgh . . .

Probably one of the OAPs from the farm cottages across the road, wanting to know what all the excitement had been about last night, with the patrol cars and SEB Transit van. Normally, the old buggers only communicated via passive-aggressive notes, pushed through her letterbox. 'YOUR FATHER ALWAYS PUT HIS BINS OUT ON THE MONDAY MORNING'; 'YOUR FATHER ALWAYS KEPT THE FRONT LAWN SO TIDY'; 'YOUR FATHER ALWAYS CLEARED UP THE GRASS VERGE OUTSIDE HIS HOUSE . . .'

The Grim Reaper couldn't come fast enough for the lot of them.

She hauled on an artificial smile, then unlocked the front door and threw it open.

Only it wasn't a boot-faced pensioner standing on her top step, it was Charlie, the dick from Professional Standards, waving at a patrol car as it drove off down the road. He turned to face her. 'Detective Sergeant McVeigh. I understand you had an unwelcome guest?'

Tempting to give him the same treatment she'd given the Mini last night, and cave his skull in with that walking stick. But it wouldn't exactly help, would it?

No, she had to be a good little girl and play the game.

She fixed her fake smile in place. 'Colin, wasn't it?'

'Close. It's Charlie.' If getting his name wrong annoyed him, he didn't let it show. Instead, he peered up at the front of the house. 'And whoever it was, they cut the phone line, too? That's the trouble with these old houses – it's all external boxes, isn't it? Easy to sabotage with a pair of wire cutters.'

'Was there something *specific* you wanted?'

He pulled out a sheet of paper from his jacket pocket. 'Says here they dusted the front door for prints and swabbed for DNA. Think they'll get a match on the database? Be great if they did, wouldn't it? Especially if he really *was* the Bloodsmith.'

'Well, thanks for popping by.' Moving to close the front door again.

'And shouldn't you have been in the office . . .' Charlie checked his watch, 'nearly an hour and a half ago?'

She threw the door wide again. 'For your information, *Sergeant*, Forensics didn't finish here till after five. Tudor doesn't want me in till noon.'

'That's very kind of him.'

Lucy folded her arms.

He smiled his bland little smile at her.

Blackbirds pop-hopped across the tufted lawn.

Wind rustled in the trees opposite, as Auld Dawson's Wood stirred.

Lucy sagged. 'You're not going to go away, are you.'

'Why thank you, DS McVeigh, I *would* love a cup of tea.'

Of course he would.

She retreated down the hall, making sure the living-room door was still shut before pointing at the kitchen. 'In there.'

He gave her a small nod, then followed her finger through into Dad's kitchen. 'Nice house you have here. Must be worth a fair bit?'

'If you're asking, "How can I possibly afford somewhere like this?", it was my father's.' Which probably made her a low-rent version of Jane

Cooper. No holiday homes in Spain and Cornwall, though, just a static caravan somewhere outside Portsoy.

'I'm sorry for your loss.' He leaned back against the work surface as she refilled the kettle. 'I suppose that's the only consolation of not having any living relatives: no one fighting over the will.'

Mug. Teabag. Milk.

The kettle rumbled to a boil.

Lucy sloshed the hot water in.

'Are you always this . . . taciturn, DS McVeigh?'

She handed him the mug. 'Yes.'

The kettle clicked and ticked as it cooled.

The fridge hummed.

Charlie smiled his bland smile.

Then the ancient mobile, still plugged in and displaying a single red bar, burst into life. Its screen lit up as the handset buzzed and dinged with a new text message.

Fergus – Garage:
> Got your message. Tried phoning back. No answer.
> Car needs new brake discs & pads. Not legal to drive.
> Front suspension is shagged.
> Can't get parts till Tuesday.

Lucy pulled off her glasses, screwed up her eyes, and pressed her fingertips into the sockets till little yellow-black bubbles popped across her vision. *Tuesday*. That's what she got for trusting a doddery old fart who did jobs for cash, instead of a proper bloody garage: four more days stuck driving that stupid pink Bedford Rascal.

By the time she'd pulled on her police officer face, straightened up, and turned, Charlie from Professional Standards was nowhere to be seen.

Sod.

She hurried out of the kitchen, into the hall, and froze.

The lounge door was wide open, and there was Charlie, standing in the middle of the room, gob hanging open as he stared at her completely unauthorized and possibly illegal murder board.

He pursed his lips. 'It's all a bit . . . Please tell me you have permission from DI Tudor to take sensitive case material home with you?'

'You're not supposed to be in here.'

'Detective Sergeant McVeigh, you do realize how this looks, don't you?' Turning to point at her walls of victims, crime scenes, notes, and potential killers. 'It's like something out of a movie. The lone-wolf detective retreats to their lair and obsesses over the case they couldn't crack.'

There was that word again: *obsess*.

'I'm just trying to catch the Bloodsmith.' She pulled her shoulders back, chin up. 'At least I'm *doing* something.'

Charlie puffed out his cheeks and settled onto her green leather sofa, blinking at the wall of suspects. 'I mean, does Dr McNaughton know? You'd think he would've mentioned something like *this* in his reports. As a warning bell . . .' There was a pause, then he took a sip of tea, not taking his eyes off the array of faces. 'It's . . . Why are these seven separate from the rest?'

Heat pulsed in her cheeks. 'The profile says he's probably had a string of one-night stands.'

'Ah, I get it.' Charlie leaned forward. 'So you've isolated the suspects who women would probably find attractive.' His eyebrows went up. 'It's certainly *one* way to whittle down the field.'

'Look, it's been *seventeen* months; we need to do something different or we'll never—'

'I take it someone's checked that they've all got alibis for when Malcolm Louden was murdered?'

She opened her mouth, then closed it again. Maybe, maybe not. You never could tell with DI Tudor – depended on how martyred he felt at any given moment. 'Of course someone's checked. Not sure what the result is, though.' Because no way she was ratting Tudor out to Professional Standards.

Charlie peeled himself off the couch and plucked the framed photo from the mantelpiece – the one nestled in amongst her possible Bloodsmiths: a man and a woman, standing together in a back garden, arms around each other as they smiled for the camera. 'How come these two don't have names and details?'

'Because they're not suspects, they're my parents.'

'Ah.' A nod. 'Your mum's really pretty; is she . . . ?'

The silence stretched.

God's sake.

As if it wasn't all in Dr McNaughton's sodding reports.

Lucy sighed. 'Fine: she died. Cancer. I was five. Happy now?' The heat was building in her cheeks again. 'I'm surprised there isn't a whole *volume* dedicated to it: "Lucy McVeigh and Her Terrible Childhood".' Getting louder with every word as she flung her arms out. 'Roll up, roll up: see the little girl whose mother hated her! Laugh at her pain and trauma! Cheer as her dad has a breakdown and she's sent off to live in a home run by sadists!' Glaring at him as she lowered her arms again. Blood fizzing behind her eyes. Ready for a fight.

'Sorry to hear that. Must've been tough.' He wandered over to the wall dedicated to the Bloodsmith's victims. 'Have you noticed how none of them are smiling?'

Jesus, talk about a sudden change of topic.

'What?'

'They all look so sad.'

Same thing the Dunk had said about Jane Cooper.

'How happy would *you* be?'

Charlie paused for a moment, head on one side. 'Yes, but when these photos were taken, they'd no idea they would end up slit open with their hearts ripped out. It's almost like they know they're going to have a horrible death.'

'Don't be such a . . .' She swallowed it down. Not helping, remember?

Besides, had to admit: he had a point. Normally, when it came to getting photos of the deceased from their families, everyone produced pictures taken at birthdays, anniversaries, barbecues, parties, graduations. Happy times. Something that showed the victim was a real person who was loved. But everyone on Lucy's wall really *did* look sad, if not borderline miserable.

But then that wasn't surprising, was it?

There was Abby Geddes, with her tired eyes and drooping mouth – she'd dreamed of being a molecular biologist, and ended up working in a call centre. Barely known by the people she worked with. And Bruce Malloch, with his brow puckered in a partial frown – who still had his ex-fiancée down as next of kin, even though she'd dumped him months before. Adam Holmes, with his serious face, mouth pinched – laid off from work a year and a half ago. Jane Cooper, with her gloomy

Victorian-doll's face – an orphan devoid of friends. Craig Thorburn, with a forced smile that didn't go anywhere near his eyes – lying dead in his one-bedroom flat for three weeks before anyone bothered to report him missing. Malcolm Louden, with the bruises and haunted look – sleeping rough, while the closest thing he had to a friend was the old man he saw once a week to go shoplifting with.

Charlie rested his bum against the back of the couch, arms folded. 'I know the profiles say the Bloodsmith doesn't really have a type, but it doesn't take a genius to see he likes them lonely and miserable.'

Lonely . . .

Lucy unpinned Bruce Malloch's missing-person report from the wall and scanned down to the section saying who'd reported him missing: 'ARTHUR POPE [MISPER'S LINE MANAGER]'. And Jane Cooper was reported missing by her family solicitor. Craig Thorburn was only reported missing by Oldcastle Dundas University because they finally noticed he hadn't turned up to class for nearly a month. Ex-DC Malcolm Louden didn't get reported missing until well over a week after the fact, when he failed to turn up for the planned raid on M&S's booze aisle. There wasn't even a missing-person report for Adam Holmes: he'd been found when his landlord went round to check on complaints about the smell coming from his flat.

'Are you all right, DS McVeigh? You've gone even quieter than normal.'

'The only victim reported missing by their family was Abby Geddes.' Lucy unpinned the report. Even then, according to this, it'd taken her mother nearly a week to do it. How did it take a *week* to report your daughter missing, when she lived at home with you? What kind of crap parent did you have to be? 'They weren't just lonely, they were *alone*. Every single one of them.'

'Suppose.' Charlie looked over his shoulder at the wall of potential killers. 'Doesn't really help us any, does it?'

'Maybe.' Lucy cracked open her laptop and powered the thing up. Logged in . . . And swore.

'What?'

'No wireless.' But then there wouldn't be, would there? The bastard cut the phone lines last night.

'Lucy?'

She clunked it shut again. 'Grab your coat, we're going.'

He followed her out into the hall. 'Thought you said DI Tudor didn't want you in till noon?'

'Change of plan.' Pulling on her raincoat and hauling the door open. 'We'll take your car.' She stepped outside into the crisp morning drizzle. The sky was a blanket of gunmetal grey, so low it skimmed the top of Auld Dawson's Wood, hiding the tips of the trees. Lucy stopped on the wet gravel. 'Where's your car?'

The only vehicle in sight was her dad's old van, its pink paintwork glistening in the rain.

Charlie emerged out onto the driveway, pulling the house door shut behind him. 'Got dropped off by a patrol car, remember?'

Oh, that was just . . . great.

'Hmmm . . .' Charlie ran a finger through the dust coating the van's dashboard. 'It's a little unfair, isn't it? Inspector Morse gets a classic Jag to swan about in, and you're stuck with a prolapse-pink Bedford Rascal?'

The van's windscreen wipers moaned and groaned, the drizzle building up in their wake, frosting over the view of muddy-green fields, before being swept away again. Miserable-looking sheep glared back at her, their coats flattened and darkened by the rain.

He wiped his finger clean on his trouser leg. 'So, are you going to tell me what your earth-shattering epiphany is?'

Nope.

Less than a minute later she was pulling into the car park outside Sainsbury's, perched on the northernmost edge of the Wynd, its flattened boxy warehouse not exactly fitting in with the general Edwardian gentility of the place. The locals had probably wanted a Waitrose.

She parked her horrible van as close to the entrance as possible.

'Wait here.'

'DS McVeigh, I'm Professional Standards, remember? I promise not to steal the credit for your insight, idea, or revelation.'

Might as well throw him a scrap to whet his appetite.

She hopped out onto the tarmac and pulled the school umbrella from the back. Snapped it up. 'The shortest time the Bloodsmith's gone without killing someone is three months.'

'Yes, but Malcolm Louden was four and a bit weeks ago.'

'Exactly.' And with that, she turned around and marched for the supermarket's entrance.

The savoury fug of sausage butties coiled its way through Divisional Headquarters, even though it was far too early for tenses. Half nine, and the place was nearly deserted – everyone off trying to keep Oldcastle from slitting its own throat.

Lucy marched up to the counter. 'Morning, Bob.'

The Duty Sergeant didn't look up as she signed in, just raised his pen from the sudoku book he was fiddling with and used it to point at a big bouquet of flowers sitting on a desk behind the counter. 'Those came for you.'

It was clearly a cut above anything you'd get on a garage forecourt, or even in your more medium-sized supermarkets: a riot of pinks and yellows and reds and whites, framed with assorted greenery, all presented in a cellophane-wrapped vase of some kind.

'Oh. Yeah . . .' Lucy pulled her chin in. 'Did you check that for razor blades, dirty needles and the like?' Just in case they were another message from Sarah Black and her family of horrors.

'Like I care enough?' But he turned and plucked a small white envelope from the red ribbon holding the whole ridiculous package together. 'Came with this.' He tossed it onto the counter.

She took a deep breath and tore it open, keeping her fingertips clear of anything that might be sharp or contaminated. A small card fell out onto the scarred wooden surface, the words churned out on the florist's printer:

> Dear Lucy,
> I hope this note finds you well and that these flowers will in some way help convince you to have dinner with me tonight. As an added incentive, I know the owner of La Poule Française?
> All the best, and with warmest wishes,
> Argyll McCaskill

At least he'd stopped adding his job title; maybe he was loosening up a bit? 'Warmest wishes', though . . .

Charlie sooked a breath in through his teeth. 'I hope that's not some sort of *bribe*, Detective Sergeant. Or have you landed yourself a boyfriend?'

'Oh, bugger off.'

The Duty Sergeant went back to his sudoku. 'Charmed, I'm sure.'

Charlie leaned against the filing cabinet, arms folded, watching as Lucy swallowed a couple of paracetamol and unpacked her new phone. Not the cheapest model in the shop, but nothing too fancy either. It was SIM-free, so she fiddled the one out of her old mobile and slid that into the vacant slot. Clicked the back into place again.

She'd grabbed an abandoned office on the second floor, its usual occupant off on the sick and probably never coming back. They hadn't made much of an effort to personalize the place, before they'd left – just a couple of wilting pot plants and a framed photo of the Queen shaking hands with some auld wifie in an ugly hat.

It was a bit of a fight, getting all the phone's bits and bobs out of their plastic tombs, but eventually she had her new handset plugged in and charging.

'There.' Lucy powered up the office's ancient creaky desktop and logged in. Left it chugging while she smiled at Charlie in what was hopefully a very annoying manner. 'Figured it out yet?'

A shrug. 'I'm in no rush.'

Lucy called up the missing-persons database and sent a search scurrying off through its rows and columns.

A knock on the door and the Dunk appeared, bringing a couple of coffees with him and what looked like a packet of fancy biscuits. 'How's the head?' He gave her one of the mugs, then held the biscuits up like a captured flag. 'Wagon Wheels! But don't tell Backshift, OK? They'll think it was Smith's team of shiftless thieving bastards.'

'Oh dear . . .'

Lucy glanced at Charlie, then back to the Dunk. 'Constable Fraser, while I appreciate the joke, I'm sure you *actually* brought these in from home, or bought them on your way to work, as you would never steal biscuits from another shift. Especially not when there are members of Professional Standards' – jerking her eyes in Charlie's direction – 'knocking about.'

'Ah. Yes.' The Dunk nodded. 'In that case, I absolutely didn't pinch them.'

Charlie shook his head. 'It's all right, I'll overlook the petty Wagon-Wheel-flavoured larceny this time. I'm only supposed to be observing, so why don't you both just pretend I'm not here? Won't say another word.'

'Good.' Lucy poked at the keyboard again, but nothing was coming back.

'Oh, before I forget, Stan's looking for you, and . . .' The Dunk reached into his pocket and came out with a jewel case. '. . . PC Manson dropped this off. Said he's been rummaging through the files and found that. It's a DVD of Benedict Strachan's interviews and there *might* be some CCTV on there, too.'

She took the case, turning it over to frown at the hand-printed evidence label. 'Where's the rest of it? The transcripts, door-to-doors, impact assessments, shift rosters, reports, actions?'

A shrug. 'Maybe the mice ate it?' The Dunk sidled his way around the desk till he could see the screen. 'What you doing?'

'Trying to get the misper database to work.' Poking at the keyboard again.

The Dunk cricked his head from side to side. 'Budge over and let the search-meister have a crack.' He settled into her vacated seat, hands poised like a two-fingered concert pianist. 'What am I looking for?'

'All missing-persons reports in the last five months where a relative or loved one didn't report them missing.'

'Hmmmm . . .' His fingers stayed where they were. 'Not as easy as you'd think. I mean, imagine you work in Burger King and your shift manager reports you missing: how are we to know if you're boinking them in the walk-in fridge, on the boxes of wee individual tomato-sauce sachets?'

Charlie raised a hand. 'Those wouldn't be in the fridge. They're pasteurized so you can store them at room temperature. The mayonnaise and mustard, too.'

Lucy stared at him.

'What? Oh, right: not saying another word.' Miming padlocking his lips.

'Tell you what' – the Dunk's two fingers clattered across the keys – 'how about we start by eliminating everyone who's got the same last name as the person they've reported missing, or who's listed as next of kin?' He sat back and nodded at the screen. 'Since April, that leaves us with ninety-two.'

'What about boyfriends, girlfriends, that kind of thing?'

'There's a box you can put "relationship to the missing person" in, but half the buggers never bother.' More clattering. 'OK, that takes us down to forty-one.'

'They've got to say where they live when they report it, right? Abby Geddes is the only victim who lived at home, so get rid of anyone living at the same address as their misper.'

'Dinky-doo . . . There we go: we're down to nine.'

'Bring them up.'

'Mr Printer, do your thing.' The Dunk hit a button, then sat back and gulped down half his coffee as the machine in the corner clanked and whirred. 'I take it you want a pool car, to go a-visiting?'

'Ring round first: see if anyone's turned up back home, but they haven't bothered to tell us yet.'

'Sarge.' He took his coffee, the printouts, and the packet of Wagon Wheels with him.

Charlie gave Lucy a slow round of applause. 'Have to admit I'm impressed. Let me guess: you said the shortest time the Bloodsmith's gone without killing anyone is three months – Jane Cooper in January, Craig Thorburn in April – but he's been getting quicker, hasn't he? Six months between Abby Geddes and Bruce Malloch, five between him and Adam Holmes, four between *him* and Jane Cooper, three between her and Craig Thorburn, but *four* between Thorburn and Malcolm Louden.' A nod. 'Everyone assumed the Bloodsmith took a break, but you think he's killed someone else, don't you? Between Craig and Malcolm. And as he likes them lonely, you went looking for someone whose friends and family didn't care enough to report them missing.'

Damn straight.

'Assuming they've been reported missing at all.' Lucy logged out and powered the computer down. 'We've probably got about fifteen minutes, so if you want to go stretch your legs, now's the time to do it.'

'You know it's a long shot, don't you?'

'Better than nothing.' Making for the door. 'Out front: fifteen minutes. And if you're not there, we're going without you.' She slipped into the corridor, shutting the office door behind her, leaving him inside. Shame she couldn't lock him in there, too.

Instead, Lucy hurried along the corridor and into the stairwell.

Footsteps echoed up from the floor below, getting further away with every step.

'Dunk?' She rushed down the first flight, wheeched around the corner onto the next.

The Dunk was on the landing below, printouts tucked under his arm, looking up as she clattered towards him. 'Sarge?'

She didn't stop. 'Change of plan – we'll call from the car.'

'But I was going for a—'

'Arse in gear, Constable!'

'Urgh . . . Yes, Sarge.'

And with any luck, they'd be long gone before that right and proper Charlie from Professional Standards even noticed they were missing.

27

Lucy hunkered down in the passenger seat, watching as Divisional Headquarters shrank in the rear-view mirror.

'You OK, Sarge, only you're acting all . . . squirrelly. I mean, more than usual.'

No sign of Charlie waiting for them out front. He was probably off having a wee, or a fag. Or perhaps he was reporting to his superior officers? Didn't really matter as long as he was somewhere else.

Yesterday's media circus had moved on from outside Divisional Head-quarters. Ex-DC Malcolm Louden was already yesterday's news, because who cared about one more dead copper? The only remnants were Sarah Black and her placard: 'LYING POLICE MURDERED MY SON!!!' All dressed up with no one to protest in front of.

Poor thing.

Lucy glared at Sarah Black's reflection. The rotten cow attacks her in the street, gets someone to slash her tyres, gets them to follow her, gets them to hammer on her door at three in the morning, and what happens? Nothing. No prosecution, no arrest, no caution, not even a warning. Because why should O Division stand behind its officers when they could be busy worrying about the 'optics' instead?

'Sarge?'

They turned the corner onto St Jasper's Lane and Lucy sat up again. 'Just making sure that dick from Professional Standards isn't following us.'

'Professional Standards . . .' The Dunk's mouth stretched out and down. 'Have we done something we shouldn't have? Only I've never been in trouble with Professional Standards before.' A small shudder. 'Professional Standards.'

'Don't be such a baby.' She reached into the back for Dunk's collection of printouts: misper reports for their nine possible victims. Each one came with a photo, supplied by whoever reported them missing. They didn't *all* look lonely and miserable – a couple were actually smiling – but if the Bloodsmith got his hands on them, that wouldn't have lasted long.

First form on the pile: 'Tristan Solomon, twenty-five, receptionist at a dental practice in Blackwall Hill. Reported missing by his boss when he didn't turn up for work six weeks ago.'

A nod from the Dunk. 'Sounds promising.'

'Give me your mobile.'

'Sarge?' Not sounding too keen.

'I had to buy a new phone this morning, OK? To replace the one that got knackered when Benedict Strachan tried to kill me? It has to fully charge, or the battery'll be ruined.'

He groaned, then dug his mobile out, one-handed, as he slowed for a zebra crossing. Passed it over. 'Well, *I* can't afford a new one, so don't break it. Passcode's six, zero, one, nine. And don't use up all my minutes!'

There were three phone numbers listed on the first form: Tristan's mobile, his boss's mobile, and the dentist's main number. Lucy tried Tristan first – straight to voicemail. She hung up and tried his boss instead – it rang and rang and rang.

The Dunk took them around the roundabout and onto Harvest Lane. 'You see DI Tudor this morning? Looks like someone forgot to take him out of the washing machine.'

And rang and rang and rang.

'He was out at my house last night, with the SEB.'

'Don't know if he got any sleep after leaving yours, but he's got bags under his eyes you could hide a frozen turkey in.'

And rang and rang and— She hung up and tried the dentist's instead.

'Hello, Danbroch Dental Practice? It's the perfect day to feel great *about your smile! How can I help you, today?'*

'I'm calling about Tristan Solomon; is Dr Rutherford free?'

'Speaking. Well, it's not Dr Rutherford speaking, it's me. Tristan. Is this Chloe's mum? Tell her I'm really sorry, I really want to make this work, and I really, really love her very—'

Lucy hung up. 'It's not him.' She shifted Tristan's form to the bottom of the pile. Next up: 'Joan McTavish – now there's a name to wrangle haggises with. Thirty-one, missing for eight weeks, reported by one Derek Garland, doesn't say what his relationship is with her.'

This time it was picked up on the second ring, and a man's voice, brash and cheerful, boomed out of the earpiece, *'Hello?'*

'Is this Derek Garland? I'm calling about Joan.'

'Hold on a minute, she's hanging the washing out.' There was a muffled clunk, then, *'JOAN! JOAN, PHONE!'*

Lucy poked the red button and gave Joan's form the bottom-of-the-pile treatment. Number three: 'Errol McIntire, seventy-one – so a lot older than any of the other victims. Urgh . . .' She held the printout away from herself. 'Retired *priest*. Reported missing by his next-door neighbour three months ago.' It went against her principles, but Lucy dialled anyway.

'Who is this?' A woman's voice: wobbly, but hard with it. *'I don't want to take part in your bloody survey.'*

'Mrs Hawthorne? I'm calling about your neighbour, Errol McIntire. Is he—'

'That thieving Fenian shite was meant to paint my hallway salmon pink in June. June! He took money, up front, for paint, and just buggered off! Never trust a Catholic. A hundred pounds, I'm down. When am I going to get that back?'

Well, she sounded . . . nice.

'Is he still missing?'

'No, he's in my living room right now, celebrating Holy sodding Communion. Of course he's still missing! And if I ever get my hands on him, I'll wring his papist neck. Where's my money?'

'OK, well, sorry to bother you.' Lucy hit the red button again. This time, the form went on her lap. 'Errol McIntire's a possible.'

Three down, six to go . . .

Lucy checked the form again. 'This is it.' The bungalows had that soulless seventies look: pantiles and salt-and-pepper harling, with small rectangular gardens – mostly given over to gravel and planters – and a short driveway for off-road parking. Move two cul-de-sacs over and you'd be looking at Shortstaine's swankiest four-bedroom new builds, but here it was all crumbling pavements and potholed tarmac.

The Dunk climbed out after her and locked the pool car. 'I hear this was like a little village before they built the bypass. Must've had a pretty good view, till the developers moved in.'

Net curtains twitched in the bungalow next door. That would be the neck-wringing, bigoted OAP harpy: Mrs Hawthorne. Lucy gave her a cheery wave.

An old Saab sat on the driveway beside Errol McIntire's house, the windscreen nearly opaque with a tacky grey film that was flecked with leaves and seedpods. Probably courtesy of the sycamore tree, drooping in the gravelled-over garden.

'What do we think?' The Dunk scrunched his way past it to the house. 'I hope he's *not* dead. I mean, can you imagine a seventy-one-year-old man, lying there, stripped naked, everything on show? Enough to make you lose your Shreddies.'

She handed him the form. 'Apparently none of our lot really bothered looking.'

'There's a surprise.' He skimmed the paperwork, then stuck it in a pocket. 'And they wonder why some people have no confidence in the police.' The Dunk stood on his tiptoes, cupping his hands either side of his face to peer in through the nearest window. 'No sign of "help me" in the kitchen.' He tried the next one along. 'Curtains are closed . . . so maybe?'

'Go see if the neighbour's got spare keys.'

'Why do *you* think he strips them naked, Sarge? What if Jane Cooper wasn't the *only* sexual encounter, and our forensic psychologist hasn't got a clue what she's talking about? And what's he doing with all the blood: drinking it?'

'Anything else?'

A frown. 'Not that I can think of.'

'Good. Now go see about those keys.'

His shoulders slumped. 'Yes, Sarge.'

While the Dunk scrunched off, Lucy snapped on a pair of purple nitrile gloves and tried the Saab's door handles – definitely sticky, but locked.

The front door was tucked away down the side, behind the Saab. Crap-brown paint, peeling off the wooden door. Fliers for double glazing and stairlifts sticking out of the letterbox. A shabby catflap that looked about ready to collapse. She leaned on the bell and some sort of jazz standard started up inside, then faded away. Took all sorts. She gave it ten seconds before setting the thing playing again. Knocking didn't produce any results, so she tried the handle. Also locked.

A small garage sat at the end of the drive, welded to the house on one side and Mrs Hawthorne's garage on the other. Up-and-over door. Probably too much to hope for, but she tried the handle anyway.

Not locked.

Wow.

She hauled and the door rattled up on its springs, revealing an array of dusty shelves, covered in boxes and jars and things. A chest freezer humming away to itself against the far wall. You'd've thought, by now, someone would've been in and nicked the lot, but no.

There wasn't a door through to the house, but there was one into the back garden – an overgrown jungle of knee-high grass and weeds landmined with cat shit, a pair of apple trees bent under the weight of blood-red fruit. Three gnomes leering at her from the undergrowth. They weren't alone – eight fat furry felines prowled through the long grass, each one staring up at Lucy and licking its lips. OK . . .

A small area had been laid out with paving stones, grass sprouting up between the slabs. The planters were choked with it, too – green blades doing their best to choke out whatever was meant to be growing there.

'Sarge?'

'Round the back!' She waded her way to the rear of the house, where a pair of patio doors gave a dusty view of the living room. Bigger than you'd think, from the kerb out front, with an ugly patterned carpet and heavy anaglypta walls. A grey suite — its sides all scratched and fraying.

Two times lucky?

Lucy gave the patio-door handle an experimental tug, but it didn't shift.

The Dunk appeared from the garage. 'You know what I think? I think he's taking their clothes as trophies.'

'Keys?'

'Nope. But I did get an earful about how good, honest, God-fearing Protestants shouldn't have to live next door to thieving papist scum. Didn't think we had that kind of sectarian bollocks in Oldcastle, thought it was more of a Weegie thing. Who *cares* what imaginary man-in-the-sky you worship? I'm with Karl Marx on that one.'

Shock horror.

'Hey puss-cat.' He stooped to pet one of the tabbies, then stood and squinted in through the patio doors. 'Lots of serial killers do that, though, don't they? Take things from their victims, so they can have a little fantasy wank over them.'

'Or maybe he's just forensically aware?' She pushed into the weeds again, making her way to the first window: a small room with a desk and shelves of old books. The last window showed a miserable dining room, with an ugly mahogany table and even uglier chairs. Thin, mangy, gingery moggy washing its backside on the tablecloth. 'Wears gloves, so no fingerprints; probably wears a facemask, so he's not exhaling his DNA over everything; taking their clothes is pragmatic – leaves us with less to examine for trace evidence.'

'Suppose. Doesn't explain the blood, though, does it?'

She pointed. 'Check the patio; maybe he's hidden a spare key under one of those planters?'

He hadn't. It was in the lamp belonging to the ugliest of the three gnomes.

The Dunk turned the key in the lock and hauled the patio door open. Flinched back. 'God, cat pee, much?' Deep breath. 'MR MCINTIRE?' Stepping onto the nasty carpet and lowering his voice. 'Or is it "Father McIntire"? Do you stop being called "Father" after you retire? I got excused RE at school, on account of my mum and dad being socialists.' A pause. 'Maybe he makes black pudding out of it?'

A sharp, ammonia reek stampeded out through the open door, burning eyes and throat and lungs. 'What?'

'The Bloodsmith. Maybe he collects all their blood and makes black pudding out of it, so he can eat it.'

'Don't be revolting.' Lucy followed the Dunk inside, trying not to gag. The smell was even worse in here, making every breath scald on the way down. And it wasn't just cat pee, there was a heavy undertone of shit, too. Jesus, you could actually *taste* it. She slapped a hand over her nose and mouth. 'Better try the bathroom first. After the mess he made at Jane Cooper's place, maybe the Bloodsmith's learned his lesson.'

'Well, you'd have to be a moron to drink it raw, wouldn't you? No idea what kind of diseases someone has. Cooking it would kill any pathogens, hence the black pudding.' The Dunk peered at the grey-screened TV. 'What about you, Sarge?'

'Never been a fan of black pudding.'

'No: Religious Education, did you get to skive off, or did they make you go?'

'Can we get on with some actual policework , before we're gassed to death?' She pointed. 'Bathroom.'

'Only asking. When you said Father McIntire was a priest, you were all . . .' Contorting his face into a weird grimace. 'Didn't peg you for a Mrs Hawthorne.' The living-room door was ajar, so the Dunk gave it a shove. Then froze. 'Sarge?'

'I'm *not* a sectarian bigot, thank you very much, Constable. I just don't like priests, or ministers, or nuns, or any of that—'

'No, Sarge: look!'

'You found something?' She squeezed past him into the hall. 'Ah.'

'I think we can rule out "Bloodsmith" as cause of death.'

A hatch in the ceiling hung open like the tongue from a gaping mouth, and the body – or what was left of it – lay entwined with a tipped-over stainless-steel stepladder, directly underneath. There was still some skin there, but mostly it was just dark patches clinging onto the filthy bones that stuck out of his clothes. That scraggy, ginger moggy sauntered through from the dining room, glaring at them on the way past, before clacking its way out through the catflap, leaving Lucy and the Dunk alone with the chewed remains. Scattered brushes and rollers surrounded the body, along with crumpled lumps of tarpaulin and tins of paint. 'SALMON PINK', according to the labels, so at least Mrs Hawthorne would get something for her hundred quid.

Seven down, two to go.

'Oh, in the name of . . .' DI Tudor sighed down the phone at her. *'Do I not have enough to deal with, without you turning up even more dead bodies?'*

Lucy unlocked the front door and stepped out onto the driveway, drawing in a blissful lungful of clean air. 'Look on the bright side, Boss: it's definitely not one of ours, and it's not suspicious, so it's the GED's problem.' And the General Enquiry Division were welcome to it. 'Soon as they turn up, we'll hand over the keys and Foxtrot Oscar.' Let them deal with the rotting, half-eaten corpse and cannibal cats.

'What were you doing there, anyway?'

The Dunk was leaning back against the pool car, arms folded, scowling at her as she used up all his minutes.

'Chasing a dead end.' Literally. 'Do you know if the SEB got anything from the DNA or fingerprints they took at my house this—'

'Lucy, you're supposed to be checking the victims' houses for the Blood-smith's messages, not running around chasing useless hunches!'

'I thought we had a good shot at identifying—'

'Are you trying to give me an aneurism? I've got DCI Ross clambering halfway up my rectum, it feels like I'm wearing the Chief Super as a bloody backpack, the Assistant Chief Constable won't leave me alone, and half the country's media are hacking away at my knees. I don't need you going off the sodding script!'

'But, Boss, we—'

'I have cut you a hell of a lot of slack, Detective Sergeant, and I expect a bit of loyalty in return!'

The Dunk raised his eyebrows and tapped a finger against his watch.

What was the point of arguing? DI Tudor wasn't listening anyway. 'Yes, Boss.'

'I should bloody well think so!' Then he was gone.

The moment she lowered the phone, the Dunk scurried over, hand out to take it back. 'Sounds like he read you the Riot Act.' A huff of breath, then he polished the mobile's screen on his black polo neck. 'So, I guess we're off to Blackwall Hill and Craig Thorburn's place?'

After all, it's what DI Tudor wanted.

'Of course we are, Dunk, because I'm a good little girl who *always* does what she's told.'

He groaned and sagged. 'We're going to get in a massive shedload of trouble, aren't we?'

'Probably.'

28

'You sure we should be doing this?' The Dunk took the next right, onto a winding country road, lined with drystane dykes on both sides.

'Nope.'

The sky had darkened, its low clouds like ink dropped onto wet paper. Drizzle turned to rain, dampening the windscreen wipers' lament.

This far south of the city, the fields were rough and stubbled with reeds. Lots of gorse and broom tumbling along the crumbling walls. Hills and clumps of dark-green forest lurking in the background.

He gave a little shudder. 'Because DI Tudor sounded pretty pissed, and I wasn't even on the phone with him. That's from standing, like, twenty feet away.'

'Don't, OK?'

'I'm just saying, with Professional Standards sniffing around, maybe now's not the best time to ignore orders?'

No doubt the idiot Charlie would have something to say about that when they finally got back to DHQ. After he'd finished sulking about being left behind, of course.

Urgh . . .

She sagged in her seat. Watched the fields go by. Then watched the Dunk for a bit.

How could he think she was a bigoted, sour-faced bag-of-pus like Mrs Hawthorne? And why did she care *what* he thought? He was a beatnik tribute act, a junior officer with delusions of socialism, not her best buddy. But, somehow, it still mattered.

'I'm not, by the way.'

'Sarge?'

'I don't give a toss what religion anyone is. I just . . .' Get it out. Get it over with. 'After my mum died, I ended up in this care home run by a minister and his wife.' A snort. '"Care" home. Oh, they'd walk around the village like they were God's gift, and everyone would bow and scrape – tell them what a lovely couple they were, and what a *kind* thing they were doing taking in all those waifs and strays.'

More fields. More miserable sheep.

The Dunk kept his hands on the wheel, eyes on the road. Mouth shut.

The rain fell.

The windscreen wipers sang a song of pain and loneliness.

Lucy chewed on the inside of her cheek.

Seemed to be a week for confessions.

'Mrs Nesbit kept a diary, marking down every "sin" we committed during the week, and then, every Sunday, after church, the Reverend Jason Nesbit would get staggering drunk and beat those sins right out of us.'

The Dunk bit his top lip.

'You were late down to dinner: that's a sin. Don't like broccoli? Sin. Didn't make your bed properly? Sin. Answered back? Sin. Caught crying after lights out? Sin.' She frowned out the passenger window. 'So, no: I don't like priests much.'

The Dunk cleared his throat. 'Did the police—'

'He fell down the stairs and broke his neck. She got breast cancer and drank herself to death. Couldn't have happened to a nicer couple.'

'Jesus, Sarge.' Looking at her as if she was an injured puppy.

'Just don't, OK? Was a long time ago. I didn't want you thinking I was anything like that old bag back there. And if you tell *anyone*, I'll break your knees.' She unlocked the Dunk's phone and checked the map. 'Should be round about here, somewhere.'

He pointed off to the left. 'Is that it?' Slowing the car.

A tiny whitewashed house sat at the end of a rutted driveway, the straight rods of Forestry Commission pines crowding in on three sides. The wooden sign at this end of the road had 'BARRADOON CROFT' painted on it, along with what was probably supposed to be a horse, but looked more like a goat. No sign of any horses in the two weedy paddocks out front, though.

Lucy checked the paperwork. 'That's it.'

'Right.' The Dunk hauled their pool car onto the lumpy track, clearly forcing a bit of levity into his voice. 'But if the Boss does his nut, I'm going to say you kidnapped me.'

'"Abducted" you. It's only kidnap if someone makes ransom demands.' Back to the form. 'Olive Hopkins, thirty-three, worked as an adult literacy tutor till the pandemic hit. Now she stacks shelves at that big Winslow's in Logansferry. Didn't turn up for three shifts in a row, so their HR department tried to get in touch, and when they *couldn't*, reported her missing.'

'They didn't just fire her?'

'Maybe they were angling for some sort of HR-department-of-the-year award?'

The pool car lurched onto a flat area of grass in front of the house. Up close, the whitewashed walls were tainted with brown and green streaks, the guttering drooping at one end. Couple of slates missing. One window sat on either side of the front door, two more above them in what must've been an attic conversion. A rust-flecked pea-green Mitsubishi Mirage was parked outside, nettles snaking out of the wheel arches.

The Dunk pulled up next to it. 'What do you want to bet Uniform didn't even bother coming out here?'

Lucy flipped the hood up on her raincoat. 'Come on, then.'

He grimaced out at the long, wet grass. 'Going to get soaked, aren't we?'

'Yup.'

They squelched their way around the house, peering in through every window. A frosted, rippled one at the back of the house was probably the bathroom. No patio this time, and no gnomes either, just a small rectangular outbuilding with a sagging corrugated roof. Rain hissed in the trees surrounding the property, making the bushes shiver.

The Dunk stretched up to his full height and ran his fingertips along the frame above the back door. Then slumped back to his full shortness and sparked up a cigarette, puffing smoke out into the rain. 'Ah well, it was worth a try.'

No spare key.

He peered through the narrow window into the kitchen again. 'What do you want to do now?'

Only one thing for it.

Lucy pointed. 'You better try the front of the house again. And maybe sing yourself a little song while you're there.'

'Oh, Sarge . . . you're not going to—'

'Make it something nice and loud. Go on, off you squelch.'

He shook his head as off he squelched. 'Going to get in *so* much trouble.'

She gave him a count of ten, then pulled on a fresh pair of nitrile gloves, marched out into the back garden, and selected a good fist-sized rock from the wall. Marched back and—

'*You know, you* really *shouldn't do that.*'

Didn't need to turn around to see who'd just sneaked up on her; the voice was familiar enough.

'Charlie.'

He waded through the wet grass, wearing a high-vis waterproof over his dark-grey suit. He'd borrowed a police cap from somewhere and wrapped it in one of those ridiculous clear-plastic shower-cap things. 'Only that's definitely breaking and entering.'

'Not if the occupant's dead.'

'Doesn't matter, you should still get a warrant and a locksmith. Not a rock.'

The sound of the Dunk murdering 'Bohemian Rhapsody' wafted around from the front of the house.

Charlie pulled his chin up. 'Suppose you thought that was clever: telling me you'd be fifteen minutes, then running for it? Why? Because you didn't want me to find out you were disobeying DI Tudor's orders?'

'Because I don't *need* a babysitter.' She weighed the rock in her hand. Heavy enough to do some serious damage . . . 'How did you find me?'

'Wasn't difficult. Your sidekick, DC Fraser, forgot to clear the printer's memory before he left. I just reran the print job.' He reached into his high-vis and pulled out a folded clump of paper. 'Simple process of elimination and here I am.' Hooking a thumb over his shoulder. 'Parked in a lay-by and walked over, just in time to stop you doing something stupid.'

A dark-blue Vauxhall sat in the entrance to a field, just up the road from Olive Hopkins' house. Should've noticed it when they got here.

But then Lucy hadn't been looking out for devious Professional Standards scumbags.

She glanced down at the rock, then up at Charlie, then round at the house. A frown on her face. Head cocked on one side. 'Did you hear that?'

'Oh please, DS McVeigh, don't be stupid. This is wrong, OK? It's—'

'Shhhh . . .! I'm sure I heard someone crying for help.'

'That's just DC Fraser doing the "let me go" bits!'

'It's my duty, as a police officer, to assist members of the public in distress.' And the Dunk's singing certainly sounded as if someone was in terrible pain.

'You're not thinking straight. We need to—'

She swung the rock, cracking it into the glazed panel on the back door, aiming for the bottom corner of the glass, just up and in from the handle. It wasn't even double glazed, so the whole thing just collapsed in a loud shattering clatter. 'Oops.'

'God's sake: I'm *Professional Standards*! Do you *want* to be suspended?'

'You do what you need to.' The handle was cold against her palm as she reached in through the empty frame. 'I'm going to make sure the householder is all right.'

She twisted the handle, but it didn't budge. Key was still in the lock, though, and once she'd turned it the back door swung open on a galley kitchen that probably hadn't been decorated since Harold Wilson was in power.

It led onto a small gloomy lounge with a brown corduroy sofa and a wonky coffee table. 'Can you smell that?' Rich and rancid, a sort of brown *sticky* scent, like the one lurking beneath all the disinfectant at the mortuary.

'DS McVeigh, you shouldn't be . . .'

But she'd already moved on to the hallway. No point trying the small bedroom, or the tiny study – they'd looked in through all those windows. The only room they hadn't seen was the bathroom. And given that the mortuary odour got stronger and stronger the closer she got, there were no prizes for guessing what lay behind the door.

Charlie scurried after her. 'Have you got *any* idea how much trouble you're in right now?'

'Will you shut up and be a police officer for once?' She took hold of the handle and pushed. The door swung open and a tsunami of stench burst over them.

'Oh Christ . . .' Charlie covered his nose and mouth with one hand, backing away, blinking.

The floor was thick with little dead black bodies, the white walls smeared with dark brown. Olive Hopkins was in the bath. Or at least, what was left of her. And above the body, on the tiles, in three-foot-tall letters, the words 'HELP ME!' screamed.

There was a selection of keys hanging on hooks in the hall: a couple of Yales, two sets for the Mitsubishi Mirage parked outside, a couple that looked as if they probably belonged to the tiny outbuilding in the garden, and a pair of stubby brass numbers with heads like anvils. Lucy went through them till she found one that unlocked the front door, and stepped out into the blessedly clean air.

Turned her face up to the rain.

Maybe she'd get lucky and it'd wash away some of the stench?

The Dunk sidled over, fag poking out the corner of his mouth, eyes narrowed against the smoke. Then they widened and he flinched backwards, snatching the leather bunnet from his head and wafting it in front of his face. 'Wow . . .' Coughing a couple of times. 'Did we find what I think we found?'

She turned, but there was no sign of Charlie behind her. Probably out spewing his ring in the back garden.

'Call it in: DI Tudor, Procurator Fiscal, Pathologist, SEB, the whole circus.'

At least, this time, Tudor couldn't complain about them not obeying orders.

Hopefully . . .

She left the Dunk pulling out his phone and headed through the house into the back garden again. Charlie was over by the outbuilding, bent double, spitting into an overgrown flowerbed.

'You OK?'

'No.' His shoulders curled in, but nothing came out but a dry heave. Another gobbet hit the weeds and long grass. 'Before you say anything, I . . . It must've been something I ate.'

'Course it was.' She leaned back against the outbuilding, as far away from the bitter stench of partially digested yuck as possible. 'Olive Hopkins was reported missing about ten weeks ago. She hadn't turned up for work in three days.'

He straightened up, one hand wiping the yellow-green strands from his lips, face pale and shiny in the rain. 'And no one bothered popping over to see if she was OK?'

'Even if they did, what would they see? Bathroom's got a privacy window.' Lucy stuck her hands deep in her pockets. 'Given the Bloodsmith's been at this for nearly two years – that we *know* of – might be an idea to get a team going through all the missing-person reports for the last . . . five? Maybe Abby Geddes wasn't his first, after all?'

'What are you telling me for?'

Good question.

'Oh, I'm *sorry*' – she stiffened – 'I thought we were all on the same side, trying to catch a *serial killer*.'

Charlie huffed out a sour breath and sagged a bit more. 'I just mean . . . I can't authorize stuff. Being Professional Standards doesn't give me superpowers; I'm the same rank as you.'

The only sound was the rain pattering against the hood of her raincoat.

'Look, because you were right about Olive Hopkins, I won't tell anyone you broke into the house. How's that? Far as they know, you entered the place legally – there won't be any trouble. But . . .' He shook his head. Spat into the long grass again. Wiped his mouth with the back of his hand. 'You need to think about what you're doing, DS McVeigh. Where you're going to end up with all of . . .' He waved his other arm at the broken kitchen door. 'Is this really the kind of cop you want to be?'

Whatever.

Still, at least he wasn't going to land her in it with his bosses.

She aimed a kick at a small thistle, popping the head right off it. Keeping her voice neutral. 'And are you hanging around?'

He looked at the bathroom window and shuddered. 'Think I might leave you and DC Fraser to it. Otherwise we'll have to explain what I was doing here in the first place, and do you really want DI Tudor—'

'Fine with me.' She patted him on the shoulder – all colleagues together, being supportive. 'Thank you.'

She stood there and watched as he climbed over the garden wall and disappeared into the pine trees. Maybe he wasn't so bad after all?

'Sarge?' The Dunk had gone the long way around, rather than through the house. Either avoiding the stench or following proper crime-scene-management practices. Which she really should've done, too. 'The Boss is on his way.'

'How'd he sound?'

'Ha. Yes.' The Dunk winced. '*Not* happy.'

The Dunk leaned forward and rubbed a clear porthole in the fogged-up windscreen. Sat back with a pointed sigh. Peered at Lucy with his mouth pursed.

She turned as far sideways in the passenger seat as possible and transferred the Dunk's phone to her other ear. 'Emma?'

'*Sorry, I missed that last bit.*' The wail of a siren dopplered past in the background. '*What?*'

'I said: when you're double-checking everyone's alibis, are you making sure they've got one for when Malcolm Louden went missing?'

What sounded like cars and buses grumbled by.

Someone shouted.

More vehicle noises.

'Emma, you still there?'

'*Sodding, buggering, fuck-fingered wank!*' That would be a no, then. '*You have any idea how much of a pain in the hoop this is already? Going through every sodding sighting of every sodding victim to make sure we know for sodding sure when they sodding disappeared, then going through every sodding witness for every sodding alibi for every sodding suspect?*'

'It's just: Professional Standards are taking an interest, so . . . ?'

'*Arrrrrgh!*' Then a groan, followed by more background shouting. '*OK, OK, I'll check.*'

'And if anyone asks, you were doing it all along.'

'*All right, thanks. Got to go. I've suddenly got a cock-tonne more work to do.*' She hung up.

Lucy handed the Dunk's phone back. 'See? I didn't use all your minutes.'

'Hmmmph.' He polished the screen again, as if she'd got girl-cooties all over it.

Through the porthole, a constant shuffle of figures wearing white oversuits stomped in and out of Olive Hopkins' house, taking empty blue plastic crates in, full ones out. In, out. In, out. Like ants.

Lucy stretched in her seat. 'How long we been here for?'

'Since we arrived, or since we called it in? Cos either way it's ages.' The Dunk hid his phone away. Sagged. 'You know what gets me? There was only one cat bowl in the kitchen. Father McIntire only had the one cat. But you see how fat the neighbourhood moggies were?'

She let her head fall back. 'At least he was good for something.'

'They ate his *face*, Sarge.' A shudder. 'James Herbert missed a trick there.'

Rain drummed on the car roof, battered the bushes and long grass.

The porthole started to mist over again – those white figures getting fuzzier with every breath.

He reached for the dashboard. 'I could put the radio on, if you like?'

'You'd think he'd have been all, "Hey, great work IDing a victim we never knew was out there, Lucy and Dunk! Maybe this time we'll find the clue that cracks the case. Here's a commendation for using your initiative." Wouldn't you?'

'No point dwelling on it, though, Sarge. Think about something else, like . . . remember you said Benedict Strachan told you he was going to kill another homeless person and get away with it this time, so They don't beam messages into his brain via his fillings, or whatever?'

'But no, it was, "Go wait in the car, I'll deal with you later!" '

'Well, what if we only *think* Malcolm Louden was killed by the Bloodsmith? What if it was really Benedict Strachan? That'd be a way to do it, wouldn't it? To get away with killing Louden by pinning it on a serial killer. Even if we *can* catch the Bloodsmith, if he says he didn't kill Louden we're not going to believe him, are we?' A nod. 'That's your perfect crime, that is.'

'You're right, Dunk. Absolutely perfect. Except for two things.' She closed her eyes. 'One: no one knows the Bloodsmith writes "help me!" on the wall in his victims' blood, because that's just about the only part of Operation Maypole we've managed to keep secret. And two: Benedict Strachan was still in prison when Malcolm Louden was killed. So, unless he's some sort of deadly ninja version of Uri Geller, I think we're *probably* safe to assume Benedict's not our guy.'

'Sarcasm again. Great. Thanks.' Big huffy sigh. 'You notice his parents couldn't even say his name? Imagine having a kid and you can't bring yourself to say its name. That's . . .' The Dunk poked her on the arm. 'Incoming.'

Lucy sat up straight again, peering out through the cloudy porthole at a white-clad figure advancing on their pool car. Tall and broad-shouldered. He threw back the hood of his SOC suit, revealing a *Peaky Blinders* short back and sides.

DI Tudor hauled open the Dunk's door, voice a hard flat line. 'DC Fraser, time for you to take a walk.'

'Boss.' The Dunk grabbed his leather bunnet and scrambled out of the manky Vauxhall as if it was about to explode, scurrying away into the rain.

Tudor thumped himself down into the vacated seat and pulled off his facemask. His cheeks were a trembling shade of puce. Staring straight at the windscreen, not looking at her. 'What, *exactly*, the hell were you thinking?' Almost shouting now, little flecks of foamy white spittle land-ing on the dashboard. 'You gave me your word!'

'I figured it out, OK?' Jabbing a finger at the house. 'If I'd just gone trotting off like a good little girl, we'd never have found Olive Hopkins! We'd—'

'Not *that*!' He turned to face her now, eyes bulging, mouth pinched. 'You promised me you'd go see your therapist! I kept you on this inves-tigation when I could've had you signed off on the sick, like that.' Snapping his nitrile-gloved fingers. 'I trusted you and you *lied* to me.'

'What?' She stared back. 'I was there yesterday! *And* the day before.'

'Don't, Lucy. OK? Don't.'

'I'll prove it.' She went to haul out her phone . . . but, of course, it was sitting back at DHQ, charging up for the first time. 'Son of a bitch.' Deep breath. 'Look, I don't know what he told you, but I've been *going*. He's playing some sort of . . . mind game, with us.'

'Lucy, you—'

'Bad enough I had to go through the whole Neil Black thing with the bastard yesterday, but to pretend I hadn't even *been* there?' She slammed her palm down on the dashboard. 'I'll kill him!'

'Lucy, it's—'

'Fine: I'll make a formal complaint.'

And *then* she'd kill him.

29

The one o'clock news burbled out of the car radio as they sat, parked on the forecourt of an abandoned petrol station, eating sandwiches in the rain. Which was pretty much a metaphor for her whole life, right there.

'. . . *Bloodsmith, as police discovered a second body in two days . . .*'

A sniff from the Dunk. 'Got to be a record, that.' He had another napkin tucked into his polo neck, sleeves pushed halfway up his forearms, leaning forwards as he delicately nibbled at a sub-of-the-day from the Happy Haggis. 'We only discovered Olive Hopkins, what, hour and a half ago? And some sod's already leaked it to the press.' Pausing to realign a wayward cucumber slice. 'You'd think we could keep something like that secret till at least teatime.'

'. . . *Police Scotland declined to comment, but neighbours believe the victim to be Miss Olive Hopkins . . .*'

Lucy chewed a mouthful of coronation-chicken-salad roll, not really tasting much other than bitterness and disappointment. Gazing out at the rusting pumps and boarded-up kiosk. The weeds forcing their way up through the cracked concrete forecourt.

With the Bloodsmith all over the news again, it wouldn't be long before Craig Thorburn's mother was on the phone, slurring with gin and crying about her son's missing heart.

Yeah, way to go, Lucy: the poor cow was grieving for her child. Didn't matter if he was in his thirties when the Bloodsmith ripped him open and drained his blood, he'd always be Judith Thorburn's little boy.

'. . . *that the victim lay undiscovered for two and a half months.*'

Lucy sagged just that little bit further.

When did she get to be so *cynical*? So callous? So devoid of any—

'Sarge, you still with us?'

'Hmm? Yeah.' She took a sip of Irn-Bru, suppressed an orange burp. 'Just wondering who keeps tipping the media off.'

'. . . calls for a judicial inquiry as the hunt for the Bloodsmith enters its seventeenth month.'

'Maybe somebody in the control room? You'd have access to all sorts of info up there.'

They'd swung past DHQ to pick up Lucy's new phone, and now it sat on the dashboard in front of her. Waiting.

'. . . embattled Business Secretary, Paul Rhynie, has hit back at his critics, claiming the attacks against him are "politically motivated" and "fake news" . . .'

Yes, there was instant gratification to be had by calling Dr McNaughton up right now and telling him precisely what she thought of him and his unethical lying-bastard practices, in a VERY LOUD VOICE. But then he could always hang up. *However*, if she stomped around there and yelled at him in person, he'd have no choice but to sit and take it.

And McNaughton deserved everything he had coming to him – if he hadn't *lied* about her not attending therapy sessions, DI Tudor wouldn't have torn a strip off her. He would've been singing her praises for finding Olive Hopkins.

'. . . as new photographs emerged, which appear to show the Business Secretary being intimate with Russian embassy staff . . .'

'Or maybe it's one of the senior officers?' The Dunk had another dainty bite of his sandwich. 'It's always us plebs that get blamed, but no one looks at the upper classes, do they?'

She'd have to ditch the Dunk first, though, and he was being more than a little clingy right now. That's what she got for telling him about growing up with the Nesbits. And she'd given him the sanitized version: Christ knew what he'd be like if she'd told him about the *darker* stuff.

'. . . Prime Minister's complete support.'

A familiar blustering voice brayed through the car's speakers. '*Look, I think we all know the public aren't interested in tittle-tattle like this; everyone wants to see us getting on with the job . . .*'

The Dunk wiped up an errant blob of mayonnaise with his thumb, before it could drip on his beatnik-black outfit. 'I read somewhere that loads of High Heidyins on company boards, or in politics, or pretty much any hierarchical thing, score off the charts on tests for psychopathy. Makes sense, when you think about it – to get to the top you have to be more ruthless and underhand than any other bugger in the organization, and manipulative enough to get away with it.'

'. . . *hunt continues for missing teenager Sophia McKellar. Sophia was last seen at the Camburn Woods Outdoor Adventure Centre on Wednesday . . .*'

Should probably send the Dunk on some sort of Bloodsmith-related errand. How about digging through the missing-persons database again, going back three or four years, like she'd suggested to Charlie? That would work.

Right now he was nibbling away like a gerbil. 'Probably better get Craig Thorburn done after lunch. See if we can't crawl our way back into the Boss's good books.' A little shudder. '*Sure* you don't want to talk about why DI Tudor had a traffic cone up his arse at the crime scene?'

'Positive.'

'. . . *with any information. Entertainment news, and Donny "Sick Dawg" McRoberts has announced three dates at City Stadium in January . . .*'

'I heard Tudor's wife's . . . well, what's the best way to put this . . . shut up shop in the bedroom department?' A raised eyebrow. 'Mind you, it was Monster Munch who told me, and you know what she's like. Woman could gossip for Scotland and you still couldn't believe half of it.'

Lucy gave up on the roll, stuffed it back in its paper bag, and dumped it in the rear footwell. Wiped her curried fingers on a napkin. 'Any noise about Benedict Strachan?'

'. . . *after his reality TV show was cancelled. Tickets are on sale now and going fast . . .*'

'Murdered homeless people, you mean? Nah. Not last night, anyway.' The Dunk frowned. 'At least not that we *know* of. Maybe he's lying low, working on a plan? Or he might've just been pulling your metaphorical plonker, so we'd keep our eyes on Oldcastle while he sodded off up to Aberdeen, or pastures south?'

It was difficult imagining Benedict being that cunning. He'd have to sober up first. But perhaps he didn't have to do his own thinking this time? Perhaps he had help. 'We should go see his mum again: Nikki. Have to get her away from the husband first, though.'

'. . . *rain forecast to continue for the next few days, as yet more cold air moves in from the Arctic . . .*'

The Dunk froze, mid bite, eyes widening as he pulled back from his sandwich. 'You *are* kidding, right? You saw DI Tudor this morning: he went berserk at us after we'd just made the biggest break Operation May-pole's seen in seventeen months! What's he going to say if we—'

'I'm talking about a ten-minute diversion, Dunk. It's practically on our way.'

'Noooo . . .'

She offered him the half-drunk tin of Irn-Bru. 'Consider this a bribe.'

The Dunk suppressed a belch, grimaced, then rubbed a fist against his breastbone. 'Ow . . .'

Served him right.

'Told you – you shouldn't have shotgunned it.' Lucy leaned on the doorbell again.

That huge BMW four-by-four sat all alone on the driveway outside the Strachans' bungalow. No sign of the Audi. Which, hopefully, meant Benedict's dad was off doing something else.

The Dunk checked his watch. 'Ten minutes.' Shuffling his feet in a little nervous dance.

'Will you cut it out? Looks as if you're bursting for a wee.' Still no response from the bell, so she tried a policeman's knock instead. Putting a bit of weight into each of the three loud raps.

He groaned. 'Did you have to say that? I didn't need to go, till you put the idea in my head.'

'Your bladder: your responsibility.' She raised her fist for another knock, but there was a rattling sound on the other side of the door, fol-lowed by a clunk, and the door creaked open a couple of inches till the chain pulled tight – making just enough space for a bloodshot eye to peer out.

Mrs Strachan's words were all mushy and wobbly, bringing with them the acetone wash of stale booze. 'Now's not . . . not a good time.'

Lucy didn't move. Stood there staring back, instead.

The Dunk's feet scuffed on the paving slabs.

A car drove by on the road behind them.

Finally, Mrs Strachan sagged, groaned, and closed the door. The chain rattled once more; then the door swung open, revealing a Nichola Strachan who didn't look quite so cougary any more. Her other eye was ringed with red, the skin beneath it a rich aubergine colour. It was only visible for a moment, before she flipped a curtain of blonde hair over it, hiding the damage. 'Suppose you'd better come in, then.' Turning on her heel and limping away down the corridor and in through the open kitchen door.

'So, Sarge' – the Dunk raised his eyebrows – 'you thinking what I'm thinking?'

Of course she sodding was.

Lucy followed Benedict's mum through into the fancy kitchen. Two packets of painkillers sat on the worktop, next to a large cut-crystal tumbler. 'Where's your husband, Mrs Strachan?'

A small bitter laugh as she plucked the tumbler from the countertop and stuck it under the ice dispenser on the big American fridge. Setting cubes clatter-rattling into the glass. 'What you mean is: did he hit me?'

'Did he?'

The ice got drowned in a serious quantity of Tanqueray. 'Why do you think I'm limping?' A splash of tonic joined the party, then she took a long, slow drink. 'Kicked the bastard so hard in the nuts, think I might've broken my foot. Raise his fist to me?' Another swig. 'Won't be doing that again.'

Lucy leaned back against the worktop, arms crossed. 'You should still report him.'

The Dunk took up position on the other side, notebook out, pen poised, shifting from foot to foot with an uncomfortable look on his face.

'Ian wasn't happy when I came home with . . .' Deep breath. 'You know what? To hell with Ian's rules: Benedict.' Raising her voice. 'MY SON'S NAME IS BENEDICT!' The last of the gin got thrown back and another huge measure glugged into the glass, not bothering with tonic this time. She limped to the kitchen door and flung it open, letting the sibilant whisper of the rain slither in.

'Where is he? Where's Benedict?'

'You should've *seen* Ian: ranting and swearing and throwing things – the lounge is an absolute tip now, but I'm the one supposed to tidy it up, aren't I? – then he hit Benny. Punched him to the ground. Kicked him.

And all the time Ian's crying and swearing and going on about how my beautiful Benny ruined his life . . .' She pulled out her vape and huffed a marzipan cloud into the downpour. 'But it was all *his* fault, wasn't it? Ian's. *He* was the one insisted Benny go to that stupid school. *He* was the one said we should mortgage the house to pay the first year's fees – in advance! That it was an investment in the future.' A mouthful of neat gin disappeared. 'Have you *any* idea how much St Nicholas College costs? Of course you don't. Well, it's a bloody fortune.'

St Nicholas College. Interesting. Maybe—

'Oh God . . .' The Dunk's dancing reached fever pitch. 'Excuse me, Mrs Strachan, I really, really need to use your toilet?'

Lucy glowered at him. 'Tie a knot in it. We're in the middle of—'

'It's not my fault!' Hobble-running out of the kitchen.

Mrs Strachan watched him go. 'First door on the right. DON'T USE THE GOOD TOWELS!'

Useless little *sod*.

'Sorry about that.' Lucy dug out her new phone and set it recording. 'Where's Benedict now?'

'If it wasn't for that bloody school and its stupid tests and exams and everything . . . Benny was under *so* much stress, and he was such a sensitive little boy, and he's running around doing all these evaluations and Ian's telling him we'll forfeit the fees if he doesn't get in, and we'll have to sell the house, and it'll all be Benny's fault for being stupid and lazy.' She sucked her cheeks hollow on the vape, let the steam trickle out through her nose like an angry mother dragon. 'He was *eleven*. How could you put that on an eleven-year-old?'

Yeah, Councillor Ian Strachan sounded like real father-of-the-year material.

'Do you know where he is now, Nikki? It's important.'

Mrs Strachan took another swig of tonic-free gin. 'Benny didn't mean to hurt you. He was going to jump. Going to . . . kill himself. But you got in the way and he panicked.' She toasted Lucy with the glass. 'So, I guess I have to thank you for saving my baby's life.'

'Nikki, we need to know where he is. What if he tries to hurt himself again? Or if he hurts someone else?'

That bitter little laugh was back. 'It's not been much of a life, though, has it? Most of it spent in that horrible prison.'

The sound of a toilet flushing came from somewhere down the hall.

Lucy stepped closer. 'Benedict's not well, Nikki. He thinks if he can kill another homeless person, and get away with it this time, then "They" won't hurt him, or you.'

She didn't look up. 'He's my baby. I'd do anything for him.'

'You saw what happened when they printed his picture in the paper: you saw the bruises, the broken arm. You have to help us find him, before he gets attacked again.'

A dog barked in one of the neighbours' gardens.

The rain hissed.

A distant stereo pumped out old-fashioned pipe-band music.

'Ian never loved him, you know. It's meant to be mothers who get postnatal depression, but for Ian it was like I'd given birth to this . . . *rival*. Someone he had to compete against.' The last of the gin disappeared. 'His own son.'

Down the corridor, a door opened and closed again.

'Where's Benedict, Nikki?'

Then another door opened.

'I don't know.' She stuck her nose in the air, eyes hard and cold. 'I gave him the keys to Ian's car and told him to run as far away from this horrible city as possible.'

'And your husband was OK with that? After everything that happened? Loaning his Audi TT to a boy who doesn't even have a provisional licence, because he's been inside since he was *eleven*?' Because that sounded incredibly sodding unlikely.

'*JESUS!*' The Dunk's voice boomed out from down the hall. '*SARGE? SARGE, CALL AN AMBULANCE!*'

Mrs Strachan nodded. 'Benny's my baby. I'd do anything for him.'

'DI Tudor's going to kill us.' The Dunk stood on the top step, grimacing as the paramedics loaded Ian Strachan into the back of an ambulance. The rain hadn't let up any, bouncing off its white roof, sparkling in the slow spin of its blue-and-white lights. A patrol car sat on the other side of the road, the two uniform officers out in their high-vis jackets, going door to door.

Lucy pointed. 'Go: see what the medics are saying.' She went back to her phone. 'Number plate's for a red Audi TT, last seen driving away from

Torridon Avenue, the Wynd, sometime between ten past eight last night and . . . call it half an hour ago.'

The man on the other end hummed for a while, accompanied by the clicking of a keyboard. *'Now then, let's see what we can see . . .'*

'And I need a flag on that vehicle. It pops up anywhere, I need to know about it, ASAP.'

The Dunk had made it as far as the ambulance, waylaying one of the paramedics on their way to the driver's door.

'This is going to take a while. There's a massive *amount of footage to search through. And there's no guarantee I'll find anything.'*

The Dunk lumbered back up the drive, rain drumming on his shiny, black leather bunnet.

Lucy put her other hand over the phone's microphone. 'How is he?'

'Not great. As in: might not even make it as far as A & E.' The Dunk peeked over Lucy's shoulder, back into the house. 'Looks like she battered the living crap out of him with a *sledgehammer*. Well, you know, assuming it wasn't Benedict. Or maybe they took turns?'

Great. That was all they needed.

A high-pitched, electronic wail tore through the downpour, then the ambulance pulled away from the kerb, the engine getting louder as the driver floored it, lights and siren going full pelt.

'Sarge?' The Dunk's forehead wrinkled. 'What if we got the uniforms to say it was *them* who turned up and found Ian Strachan? Maybe we were never here? They take the credit, and DI Tudor doesn't shout at us again?'

Lucy nodded. 'That's a great idea, Dunk. I'm sure Mrs Strachan will be happy to play along. You know, while she's confessing to her husband's attempted murder. After all, why wouldn't she lie to protect us? We're only the ones who caught her.'

'OK, OK. But for the record, I said we should've gone straight to Craig Thorburn's place.'

'I know.'

But right now? They were both screwed.

30

'Come on, Trev, finger out!'

One of Sergeant Trevor Weir's spartan eyebrows made the long climb up his narrow forehead as he stared at Lucy from behind the custody desk. He was so thin he could've been fashioned from pipe cleaners. God knew who he thought he was fooling with the straw-coloured hair, but if that mop was any less convincing it would've come with a chinstrap. 'These things take as long as they take, DS McVeigh.'

'Trev, I'm begging you here. We need to be gone before DI Tudor gets finished at Olive Hopkins' house. And I mean *long* gone.' And given they'd been buggering about here for nearly an hour, time was running out fast.

A sigh, then Weir went back to his paperwork. Making slow methodical notes with a pen as he worked his way down the form.

The clock ticked.

Someone in the cell block started singing a slow, sad Scottish ballad.

Someone else screamed at them to shut up.

Weir turned his form over and went to work on the other side.

The singing and screaming continued in discordant harmony.

'Trev!'

Finally, he pulled the sheet of paper from its clipboard and slipped it into a pigeonhole. 'Done. I'll let you know when the duty solicitor turns up.'

'Thanks, you're a star.' Lucy turned and hightailed it out of the custody suite, into the corridor, and—

'Well, that wasn't unedifying at all.'

She jerked to a halt. Swore. Turned.

Charlie from Professional Standards was leaning against the breeze-block wall. Face like stone, voice flat with disappointment. 'Tell me, DS McVeigh, when I cut you a bit of slack, back at the cottage, did you not think to yourself, "Maybe I should use this opportunity to take a good long hard look at what's been going wrong in my professional life and mend my ways"?'

'Sorry, can't stay and chat, I've got—'

'To make yourself scarce before DI Tudor gets back? Because when he finds out you've been spending your time looking for an ex-con who's violated his release conditions, instead of revisiting the Bloodsmith's crime scenes like he's told you to, *multiple times*, he's going to be less than impressed?'

She licked her lips. 'Something like that.'

'So, you're what: rushing off to Craig Thorburn's in the vain hope you'll find something there to crack the case, and Tudor will forget all about you ignoring yet another direct order?'

'Nichola Strachan battered the living crap out of her husband. If we hadn't turned up when we did, he'd be dead by now.'

Charlie pushed himself off the wall. 'You're playing a very dangerous game here, DS McVeigh. The margin for error is *vanishingly* small.'

'You're going to dob me in?'

'It's not me you have to worry about, it's DI Tudor. Think I've done about as much as I can.'

'Good.' She turned on her heel, marched down the corridor and out the back doors.

The Dunk was waiting for her, sheltering under the narrow concrete canopy just outside, on the phone, kicking his heels on the painted concrete floor.

She flipped her raincoat's hood up and swept past him into the downpour. 'Quick as you like, Constable.'

'Yeah, OK. Thanks, Mr Myers . . . No, I know . . . Yup, terrible. Got to go. Bye.' He hung up and rolled his eyes. 'God, that man can *moan*.'

' "Quick as you like" means get a shift on.'

He lumbered after her. 'That was the guy who moved into Adam Holmes' old flat, in Ruthkopf House? Says he *did* get little notes through the letterbox with "help me!" on them, but they stopped a couple of months ago. And he thought it was the guy in Two G screwing with him, so he threw the lot out.'

'You tell him, if he gets another one, he has to keep it?'

'In a sandwich bag and everything.'

Who knew, maybe they'd get DNA or fingerprints off the thing? Probably not, though.

They scrambled into their pool car, the Dunk gunning the engine, down the ramp and out onto Peel Place. 'Blackwall Hill?'

'Blackwall Hill.'

And one last chance for redemption . . .

Cardon House was a six-storey block, mouldering away at the end of a short street lined with tired terraced housing. It had probably looked pretty stylish when it was put up sometime in the late sixties, but its sleek curves and bold lines had greyed and streaked over the years. Some of its cladding had been replaced with cheaper brown panels where the original white had crumbled. Now the building looked more like a brutalist sculpture of a decaying tooth than somewhere anyone would want to live.

Thankfully, the rain had stopped for the first time today, leaving the air crisp and clear – a lone shaft of sunlight piercing the coal-coloured clouds, as if the Rapture was struggling to find anyone in Oldcastle worth saving.

The Dunk locked the pool car and held up a manila folder. 'You want to be the reading person this time or shall—' He flinched as his phone launched into something punk-rocky. He pulled it out and grimaced at the screen. 'It's DI Tudor.'

Damn.

'Let it go to voicemail.' Lucy dug her mobile from her pocket and put it into sleep mode.

'Oh dear . . .' The Dunk held his phone as far away as his little arms would reach, till it fell silent.

'Now switch it off.'

'He must've heard about Mrs Strachan.'

Yup. Tudor would be pacing up and down the Operation Maypole office right now, wearing a groove in the carpet tiles, face all pink and trembly, looking for someone to shout at.

Still, it was too late to worry about that now.

Lucy made for the block of flats' entrance. There would've been an intercom system at one point, but all that remained was a rectangle of plywood with people's names written on white stickers, partially covered by a big green, yellow, and black graffiti tag. More graffiti in the stairwell.

To be honest, some of it was quite good, but every three or four steps someone had drawn a squirting knob or some boobs or just scrawled a fistful of obscenities.

'Sarge?' The Dunk trotted along behind her, already breathing hard as they hit the second landing. 'DI Tudor, do . . . do you think he . . . think he . . . pfff . . .' Puff, pant. 'Can we slow down a bit?'

'We're on a deadline, Constable.' Around the corner, onto the third floor.

'Yeah, but . . . do you think . . . the Boss . . . is going to blame . . . blame me?' Sounding like a broken steam train now, falling further and further behind. 'Cos it's not . . . not really my . . . fault . . .'

By the time she'd reached the fifth floor there was no sign of him, just the sound of peching and heeching echoing up the stairwell, accompanied by the slow scuff of shoes.

Lucy leaned over the handrail. 'COME ON, SLOWCOACH!'

'Arrgh . . . Stitch. Stitch . . .'

Four doors led off the landing, but only one of them, 5C, still had fragments of blue-and-white 'POLICE' tape attached to the frame. Someone had removed the little plastic plaque that had once sat above the letterbox. Maybe a souvenir for sickos to buy on eBay. God knew, if you were into serial-killer memorabilia, Oldcastle was like a cash-and-bloody-carry.

The door to flat 5D creaked open and an old lady squinted out from a shadowy hallway, bringing with her the scents of lavender and shortbread. A black cat wound itself around her legs like a small hairy tentacle. 'You kids aren't allowed to play in the stairwell!'

Lucy dug out her warrant card. 'Police. We're here about Craig Thorburn.'

'Oh, you're back, are you?' She pulled out a pair of smudged glasses and gave Lucy's warrant card a good looking at. 'It was *terrible* what happened to poor Craig. Terrible.'

'Has anyone else visited his flat? You know, recently?'

'Lying in there, dead as a dog, for three weeks. They said the smell was quite something, but I lost mine in the second wave. Covid.' Tapping her wrinkly button-mushroom nose. 'So I never noticed. It comes in handy when you live with lots of students, I suppose. Being all sweaty and smoking weed and whatnot.'

'A man, or a woman. They might have had keys to Craig's flat?'

'Oh God . . . Argh . . . Dying . . .'

'Don't get me wrong, students are fine, really.' The old lady smiled, face creasing like a shammy leather. 'I mean, I enjoy a good spliff as much as the next person, but the music they play is awful. Whatever happened to Led Zeppelin, or Rainbow, or the Sex Pistols? Why does it all have to be so *bland* these days?'

Ah well, it'd been worth a try.

'OK, sorry to bother you.'

A sweaty heaving lump staggered up the last flight of stairs onto the landing, then stood there, one hand against the wall, holding himself up as he coughed and wheezed.

'I think your friend could do with a decent burial, dear.'

Lucy gave the Dunk a poke. 'Keys?'

'In . . . in . . . in here . . .' He doubled over, one hand still clutching the wall, the other holding the folder out.

She dug into it, finding a Yale key in a clear-plastic evidence bag.

The old lady shuffled forwards, voice cranked up in volume, as if the Dunk was deaf instead of hideously unfit. 'DO YOU WANT A GLASS OF WATER?'

Lucy pulled on a fresh pair of nitriles, unlocked the door, and stepped into a small hallway.

Gloomy in here, and stale-smelling, that lingering odour of industrial bleach seeping through from when the cleaning crew must've got rid of the blood.

A pile of mail sat on the bare floorboards. She stuck the folder under her arm and scooped it up, flicking through envelopes and fliers. Junk, mostly: leaflets for takeaways, affordable funeral solutions, double glazing, please vote for me, have you seen my cat? Three official-looking envelopes turned out to be threatening letters from the Royal Caledonian Building Society, demanding to know why Craig Thorburn wasn't keeping up with his mortgage payments. They were a bit late for that.

Halfway down the hall, a coatrack bulged under the mass of about a dozen jackets, all piled up, three or four on each hook. Two pairs of muddy trainers on the floor beneath them. The search team would've been through all the pockets, but Lucy had another trawl, just in case, coming up with the usual collection of pens and scraps of paper and receipts and fliers for the Samaritans.

Three doors led off the small corridor, all closed.

The first opened on a room barely big enough for the double bed that'd been squeezed in there. Clothes lay strewn across it, the built-in wardrobes – much cheaper-looking ones than Jane Cooper had in her swanky Castleview flat – hollowed out and empty. No hidden messages in there.

Door number two revealed the bathroom where Craig Thorburn had breathed his last. The stench of bleach was strongest in here, a large clean patch on the tiles above the bath showing where they'd got rid of the Bloodsmith's message, plea, prayer . . . Taking the grout from a mould-darkened grey to dirty ivory instead.

Lucy stuffed the fliers and letters into her jacket pocket, pulled the folder out from under her arm and rummaged for the crime-scene photographs. Held up the wide shot, so it more or less lined up with the room.

Craig Thorburn lay on his back in the bathtub, head and right arm hanging over the side. His hand was open, the palm facing towards the camera, a small purple bruise visible in the crook of his arm. That would be where the eighteen-gauge needle had gone in. But it faded into insignificance compared to what had happened to Craig's torso. Chest split open, the contents sagging into his gaping stomach.

Urgh . . .

She stuffed the photo back in the folder and sank down onto the closed toilet lid. Shut her eyes and breathed for a moment, till the stench of bleach and pain made her stomach clench.

Nope. Sod this.

Lurching out into the hall and through the final door.

It was the largest room in the place, with a living area on one side and a galley kitchen on the other. The search team had left all the kitchen cabinet doors open, their contents stuffed in willy-nilly, without any apparent thought or order.

A tatty old couch sat side-on to the room's only window – a view out over a rectangle of dying grass, featuring four sagging whirligigs, and off towards another bland beige housing scheme. Lucy lowered herself into the couch, setting the frame and springs creaking.

She sat there, not moving, till her churning innards stopped threatening to spatter the threadbare rug with a mixture of bile and coronation chicken.

Wonder what Dr McNaughton would make of that? Never been sick at a crime scene before – not since she was a probationer, anyway. And a lot of what she'd seen over the years was just as bad as anything the Bloodsmith did to his victims. But now, somehow, even the *photographs* were enough to set her off. Definitely had to ask McNaughton, after she'd finished beating him to death with his own severed genitals.

The Dunk slumped into the room, all pink-faced and shiny. 'The lovely Mrs Pearce is making us a nice cup of tea.' He collapsed onto the sofa next to Lucy with a dying-beanbag *whoomph*. 'Why does everywhere have to be up so many stairs?'

She slapped the folder against his chest. 'Read.'

'Let me get my breath back!' Wheezing for effect. 'Nearly had a heart attack, coming up here.'

Lucy abandoned him on the sofa and wandered around the living area instead. In addition to the half-dead couch, there was a smallish TV, a decrepit sound system with an ancient MP3 player plugged into it, a wooden stool with half the paint flaked off, and a sideboard squatting on four fat little legs. There was more junk mail piled up on top of it, along with a couple of opened letters. That would be the search team again. At least they'd done a tidier job than they had in the bedroom.

Lucy had a quick nosey through the mail. Mostly takeaways, but there were a couple of leaflets for the local church's outreach coffee mornings and a handful of fliers from the university about various psychological studies you could take part in for extra credit and a bit of cash in hand. The money wasn't great, but looking at the state of this place, Craig probably needed all the help he could get.

She opened the sideboard's doors: a DVD player lurked inside, along with a collection of unmarked jewel cases – all of which contained plain disks with film names printed on them in blue Sharpie. Craig hadn't even pirated the latest blockbusters; this lot were at least two years old. Oh, and there was some pretty nasty porn in there too, going by the titles. God knew what *Shitty Titty Gangbang* was like, but Lucy had *no* intention of finding out. And no intention of *ever* sitting on that couch again, given what he must've been doing while watching it.

The heavy breathing coming from that direction settled down to sub-pervert levels, then the Dunk cleared his throat. 'Right. OK. Craig Thorburn, thirty-one, studying philosophy. So a mature student. Had a part-time porter's job at Straik Infirmary. Used to work as a mechanic down by MacKinnon Quay.'

Which explained how a philosophy student could afford his own place. Even if it was tiny. And crappy. She put the DVD back with the others. 'But the hospital didn't report him missing?'

'Nah. No one gives a toss about part-timers. Next of kin's down as his mum, but we all know how that worked out.'

The joy of families.

The Dunk turned to the next stapled lump of paperwork, lips moving silently as he traced a finger down the page. 'Post-mortem says he died from blood loss. Then his heart, both kidneys, and about a third of his liver got hacked out. Looks like our boy's worked on his blood-extraction technique, but hasn't really bothered improving his knife skills.'

'Why would he, if it works?' Lucy shut the sideboard doors and stood. To be honest, given the porn collection, it was probably best not to touch anything else in here. Even *with* gloves on. But when she went to put her hands in her pockets, the left one scrunched into all those fliers, leaflets, and the three mortgage demands.

No point taking them with her.

'True.' The Dunk nodded. 'But it probably means we can rule out any-one who knows what they're doing: butchers, surgeons, anatomists, vets, or anything like that.'

She dumped the lot on the sideboard, where the pile promptly slith-ered apart, half of it falling straight onto the floor. 'Sodding hell.'

'You want the Behavioural Evidence Analysis, too, or shall we take the babbling run-on sentences and lack of proper punctuation as read?'

'Go for it.' Lucy scooped the junk mail up and deposited it back on the sideboard. Frowned.

'Gluttons for punishment, we.' He dragged out another stapled-together wodge of paper. 'So . . . Rambling introduction. Blah, blah. Meandering summary of previous profiles, et cetera . . .'

There were only two letters from the building society now. She dug in her pocket, but it was empty.

'Warning that this is all supposition and not to be taken as gospel . . .'

Perhaps the third letter had fallen down the back of the sideboard and got stuck?

'Here we go: "The Bloodsmith demonstrates further learning in his exsanguination methodology," because why use normal words when you can sound like you've just had a thesaurus suppository, "suggesting he has either started giving blood recently, or has befriended someone who works for the Scottish National Blood Transfusion Service and a possible line of inquiry will be to examine records appertaining to those—"'

'Did we?' Lucy hunkered down and peered underneath the sideboard. 'Look into the blood-donor angle?'

'Yeah, Angus got a team on it. No prizes for guessing what *that* turned up.'

There were a couple of bits of paper poking out between the wall and the bottom edge, but the sideboard's legs were too short to get her arm in there and pull them out.

'Where was I? OK: ". . . to those activities, it may also be beneficial to see if official blood-transfusion clinics have experienced any thefts of equipment, especially needles and blood bags, as it is unlikely that having become more proficient and professional in his extraction of the blood"' – the Dunk hauled in a big pantomime breath – '"he is still using old jam and pickle jars to store it." Ladies and gentlemen, we have a full stop!'

Scuff marks scarred the floorboards where the sideboard had clearly been moved many, many times. Which meant that losing stuff down the back of it must've been a regular occurrence for Craig.

Only one thing for it, then: Lucy went round to the end of the sideboard, grabbed it with both hands and half lifted, half dragged that side away from the wall. An avalanche of trapped papers tumbled to the floorboards.

' "Given the increase in the volume of tissue removed from his victims after death, it is tempting to say that the Bloodsmith's possible earlier experimentation with cannibalism has proven fruitful for him, and now that he has a taste for it is looking to take away as much comestible material from the bodies as can practically be consumed while fresh"' – another exaggerated breath – '"however it is also possible that the Bloodsmith is removing these organs for another, more ritualistic purpose, or doing it as a diversionary tactic in order to purposefully mislead the investigation into following avenues not applicable to the series of crimes at hand . . ."' Silence. 'Did that make *any* sense to you at all?'

She picked up the papers.

The missing building-society letter had been joined by a flier for a kebab shop, one for an exhibition at Oldcastle Art Gallery, a hand-written shopping list, another leaflet about taking part in a psychological study – into loneliness this time – and a birthday card from the old lady next door.

Not much to show for a life, was it? Some scraps of paper and a mutilated corpse.

Lucy placed the lot back on the sideboard.

'New sentence: "Clearly we can't ignore the fact that Operation Maypole has been widely reported on in the media, therefore the Bloodsmith may well be monitoring the coverage and adapting his behaviour in order to mislead or even discredit the investigation, as such, all evidence, in addition to being taken at face value, must also be evaluated as if it has been purposefully staged by the offender."'

She wandered over to the window, looking down at the miserable whirligigs. Little blue bags dangled from the sagging washing lines, where dog walkers had decided a bit of festive faecal decoration was needed. Imagine standing here, every day, looking out at that depressing vista. Estranged from your family, no friends, no one to even notice you've been dead for three weeks.

A horrible death, in a horrible little flat.

'You know, Sarge, I'm thinking of retraining as a forensic psychologist. Apparently you can spend your days churning out nonsensical rubbish and Police Scotland will pay you a fortune for the privilege. You don't even have to get anything right: load your reports up with enough weaselly caveats, and you can get away with murder.' A snort. 'It's like being a weather forecaster, only with more dead bodies.'

Lucy narrowed her eyes and moved closer to the glass.

There was a figure down there, a man in a corduroy jacket, high forehead surrounded by curly brown hair. Staring right back up at her.

Her back tightened. Jaw, too.

No point charging down there: he'd be long gone by the time she'd even reached the third floor, and they both knew it. He was mocking her.

He stayed where he was, not moving, just staring. Face slack as a corpse.

Then he reached into his pocket and pulled something out. Something the size and shape of a whiteboard marker, only brown. Was he lighting a *cigar*?

He was. The cheeky bastard was having a Hamlet moment . . .

A half-dozen thick clouds of smoke got puffed out into the damp afternoon, then he turned and sauntered off, no hurry, not a care in the world.

'Sarge? Sarge! You OK?'

What was the point? Wasn't as if the Dunk could actually *do* anything about it.

She huffed out a breath and turned her back on the window. Rubbed the palms of her hands into her closed eyes till little fireworks bloomed in the darkness. Wait a minute . . .

Lucy lowered her hands and frowned at the sideboard.

'Sarge?'

Two steps and she was there, scooping up the bits of paper, rummaging through them till she got to the one about that psychological study into loneliness. Skimming the text.

Then a smile spread across her face.

'Tell the nice lady we won't be staying for tea, Dunk. We've got places to be.'

31

The Psychology Department reception room was far too hot and sticky, lined with framed journal articles and awards, a nice big window at the far end looking out over Oldcastle Dundas University's sodden playing fields, trapped beneath a coal-scuttle sky.

'Sarge?' The Dunk shifted in his seat, setting its vinyl upholstery squeaking, face pulled into a droopy frown as he stared at the blank screen of his phone. 'Are we still—'

'Do you *want* DI Tudor to shout at you?'

His seat squeaked some more. 'No.'

'Then leave your phone switched off till we've got something positive to tell him.'

'Yeah, but—'

'Oh, of course, how *silly* of me! My trying to protect you from a bollocking is getting in the way of valuable Candy-Crush-playing time, isn't it? You go ahead and switch your phone on, Dunk, and to hell with the consequences.'

He sagged, then put his phone away. 'Fine.'

They sat there, in silence, as the room's clock *tick-tick-tick*ed, and the radiator grumbled, and the rain hurled itself against the windowpane. Until, at long last, the door behind the reception desk opened and a woman in a Breton top loped out, all long hair, long limbs, and toothy smile.

'Sorry to keep you waiting, it's been absolutely mad here for ages.' Settling herself down behind the desk. 'It's all go; I honestly don't know how we cope.'

Yes, because working in academia was so much more challenging than, ooh, let's think, catching murderers?

She shuffled the papers on her desk. 'How can I help you today?'

Lucy checked the Dunk had his notebook and pen out, then pulled the leaflet from her pocket – now safely ensconced in a clear-plastic evidence bag. 'Craig Thorburn. He was a student here.'

'Was he?' Clearly not trying to be evasive, just a bit dim.

'We believe he was taking part in some psychological studies for money.' Placing the leaflet on the desk.

'Lots of students do. It's a bit of a drain on the departmental budget, but it helps us meet our quarterly research targets. You know what it's like these days: league tables, this; performance indicators, that.' A shrug.

'I need to know who ran this study' – poking the evidence bag – 'and if Craig was on it.'

'Ah . . .' She bared her teeth again, but not in a smile. 'General Data Protection Regulations mean we can't simply—'

'He's dead. Craig Thorburn was murdered, five months ago.'

The clock went *tick-tick-tick*.

The Dunk's seat squeaked.

The rain rattled the window.

Lucy stared across the desk at her.

Finally, the receptionist's shoulders drooped and a pained expression crawled across her thin face. 'Well . . . let me talk to the head of department and see what I can dig up.'

Professor Rattray led them down the corridor, past office after office, none of which seemed to have anyone working in them. She was a short woman with long grey hair pulled back in a ponytail. Purple denim jacket on over a white T-shirt, black jeans, and well-worn cowboy boots. A voice marinated in single malt and tobacco. 'I know, I know: it's five to five on a Friday, and the place is like a morgue.'

The Dunk had to semi-jog to keep up. 'Actually, we don't have morgues in the UK, it's mortuaries. Morgues are a US thing.'

She flashed him the kind of smile that probably had male undergraduates going all sweaty in their dirty little dreams. 'Well, how about that? I learned something new today.'

Pink rushed up his cheeks.

'Strictly speaking, I should insist on a warrant to see anything, but given what you say happened to this young man, my department wants to make sure it does everything it can to help.' The professor stopped dead, and the Dunk nearly crashed into her back. 'We could even look at some of the evidence, if you like? Crime scenes, post-mortem reports, that kind of thing? We run a Forensic Psychology course here, and a little practical—'

'Actually' – Lucy made a show of checking her watch – 'I don't mean to rush you, but we've got a load more interviews to do before we finish today, so if we can . . . ?'

'Yes, of course.' And they were off again. 'I checked the roster for who was doing what research, and that flier is for one of Dr Christianson's studies. His office is just down here.' Pointing at a door near the end of the corridor. 'I'm afraid he won't be able to help, though.'

'Let me guess, GDPR again?'

'Oh, no. He took a leave of absence, a couple of months ago? Bethany will have the details. Something about his mother going in for chemotherapy so he has to look after his dad. Dementia. Terribly sad.' Professor Rattray stopped in front of the door marked 'DR JOHN CHRISTIANSON', opened it, and ushered the pair of them through into a fairly large office with high corniced ceilings.

Two walls were lined with shelves, packed full of textbooks. Twin ranks of filing cabinets either side of the door. The desk was of the big mahogany variety, with a pair of stylish chairs arranged in front of it, a big leather status-symbol sitting behind it like a throne. There was even a Le Corbusier chaise longue, just to make sure all the cliché boxes were ticked. A trio of lancet windows gave a view down the hill, across the woods, to the River Wynd, then up the other side where fields and trees slowly faded into the rain.

The place smelled of lemon furniture polish, but there was something familiar lurking underneath that. Desperation? Or maybe it was mildew? Old buildings like this must be full of both.

Lucy turned and pointed at the filing cabinets. 'I assume he kept records of who was on his studies?'

'Of course. We have an A-star reputation for psychological research.' Lines deepened on the professor's forehead. 'I suppose it's got something to do with Oldcastle being fertile ground for the kind of work we do. Never short of something to look into here; opportunities abound! Especially when it comes to abnormal psychology. But then I don't have to tell *you* that, do I? As a police officer.'

At least someone saw an upside to living in the serial-killer capital of Europe.

'So . . . ?' Still pointing at those filing cabinets.

'Yes.' Professor Rattray pulled on a pair of glasses and ran a finger down the first cabinet, lips moving as she read the labels to herself. Then did the same with the second, third, and fourth cabinet. 'Loneliness, loneliness, loneliness . . .' Fifth. Sixth. 'Ah, here we go.' Rattling one of the drawers out and flicking through the tabs. 'Just have to find the current academic year . . .'

While the professor was flicking, Lucy had a quick look around the office.

Dr Christianson had the usual framed diplomas behind his desk – because what was the point of having a PhD if you couldn't rub people's noses in it – along with a handful of photographs, and an ancient map of Oldcastle. Back before Blackwall Hill, Castleview, Shortstaine, Cowskillin, or even Kingsmeath existed.

'Aha! And *voilà*.' Professor Rattray pulled out a thick suspension file and carried it over to the desk. Opened it up. 'Now, what was the name you were looking for again?'

'Thorburn. Craig Thorburn.'

More flicking.

Lucy turned from the map to the photographs. And froze.

'Simpson, Summerville, Tarbert, Templeton, Thorburn. Here we go.' Rattray pulled out two or three sheets of paper, stapled together. 'Craig Thorburn was definitely part of the study.' Professor Rattray held them out to Lucy. 'Is there anything else we can help you with?'

God damn right there was.

'Who's this?' Lucy took the proffered sheets and tapped them against one of the smaller photos – an intimate shot of a couple on a restaurant balcony, somewhere warm going by the clothes and tans. She was bright and blonde, hair in a spiky pixie cut, wearing a floaty top with bare arms, glass of something fizzy in one hand, her other arm wrapped around a man who appeared in most of the other pictures. High forehead, round glasses, beard, curly brown hair. He'd swapped the corduroy jacket for a Hawaiian shirt, but it was definitely him. 'The man, who is he?'

Professor Rattray pursed her lips, eyebrows pulled in as if she was trying to work out how best to explain something really obvious to someone really stupid. 'You're standing in his office. It's Dr John Christianson.'

Of course it was.

Lucy pointed at the filing cabinets again. 'I need you to check six other names for me.'

'. . . *buggering about with your phone switched off when I* specifically *told you—*'

'WILL YOU JUST SHUT UP FOR TWO MINUTES AND LISTEN?' Lucy braced herself against the dashboard as the Dunk rallied the pool car around the roundabout, siren wailing. They shot across the dual carriageway and onto Burns Road. 'WE KNOW WHO HE IS: THE BLOODSMITH!'

'*You know who . . . ?*'

'DR JOHN CHRISTIANSON. HE'S A LECTURER AT O.D.U. HE'S THE GUY WHO SLASHED MY TYRES. THE ONE WHO'S BEEN FOLLOWING ME!'

'*Where . . . ? How . . . ?*'

Houses flashed by the car windows, a church whizzing past – what looked like a funeral in full swing.

'WE'VE GOT AN ADDRESS; WE'RE ON OUR WAY THERE NOW. MIGHT BE NICE IF YOU GOT SOME BACKUP ORGANIZED!'

'*Jesus . . .*' There was something else, but it was lost beneath the siren's cry. '*OK, give me the address.*'

'EIGHTEEN BIRREL CRESCENT, CASTLEVIEW.'

Quarter past five and rush hour was in full crawl, but most of it was going the other way, heading up towards the Parkway, and the stuff that wasn't had the sense to get the hell out of the way.

'*Done.*' DI Tudor must have turned away from the phone, his voice echoing off the office walls, '*STAN: GET A CAR! ANGUS: ROUND UP EVERYONE YOU CAN GET YOUR PAWS ON AND FOLLOW US OUT TO CASTLEVIEW!*' Then he was back again. '*I'll get an OSU sorted, maybe some dogs. You and the Dunk are* not *to go in until we get there, am I clear?*'

'WE'RE GOING TO BE—'

'*Am I sodding clear, Detective Sergeant?*'

Great.

Kingsview Hospital wheeched by, its ancient Victorian frontage partially concealed with scaffolding. Like a cage.

'*Lucy? I mean it.*'

'Yes, Boss.'

'*What? Can't hear you over the . . . That better be a yes!*'

'I SAID, "YES, BOSS"!'

The Dunk slowed down for the T-junction at the end of Burns Road, waiting for the idiots to slam on their brakes before he roared out onto Langburn Drive, foot hard down, the back end slithering on the rain-slicked tarmac as he wrenched the steering wheel to the right.

Not long now . . .

They both had their seats reclined nearly all the way back, keeping a low profile as rain drummed on the pool car's roof.

Lucy sat up a little – just far enough to see through the passenger window.

Birrel Crescent was a nice residential cul-de-sac on the westernmost edge of Castleview, backing onto a swathe of scabby fields – thick with reeds and bordered in gorse. A handful of miserable sheep squelched around in the rain behind the houses, looking as if they'd never be dry or happy again.

The curving road was lined with large bungalows on both sides, set back behind big front gardens. Twee names on cast-iron gates. Garages at the end of lock-block driveways. Nearly every home had an attic conversion, but a couple had decided to annoy the neighbours and added on an extra storey. Dr Christianson's was one of those: surprise, surprise. As if being a serial killer wasn't bad enough, he had to ruin people's view of the countryside, too.

She scooted down again and checked her watch. 'What the hell's taking them so long?'

On the other side of the car, the Dunk cracked a big yawn, rounding it off with a stretch and a shudder. '*Surely*, this has to wipe out all debts, right? I mean, we've broken the case: we've *ID*ed the Bloodsmith; it should be party time for Lucy and Duncan. Maybe even a promotion?'

Lucy scowled over the lip of her door for about the sixth time in two minutes. 'Fiver says he's not in.'

A dark-red Skoda estate sat outside number eighteen, its metallic paintwork turned matt with dirt. Windscreen, too.

'Who do you think they'll get to play us when they make a Hollywood blockbuster out of this?'

'One: that car hasn't moved in ages. And two: there's no sign of the Mini he's been driving.' The one with the cracked rear window and dented roof. 'Unless he's parked it in the garage, of course . . .'

'I see myself as a Brad Pitt, or a Chris Hemsworth. You want to be Charlize Theron, or Scarlett Johansson? Charlize has the range, but Scarlett's got the box office.'

Lucy checked her watch yet again: quarter to six. 'How long does it take to get over here from Peel Place, for God's sake?'

'Mind you, I bet if they *do* make a film, we'll see sod all out of it. Police Scotland will claim the rights, won't they? We do all the work, they take all the profits.' A pout. 'Maybe we should write a book? I know a journalist who could help – she did that one about the Coffinmaker, last year.'

'Pass.'

Lucy's phone rang, deep in her pocket, and when she dug it out 'WITHHELD NUMBER' glowed at her from the screen. 'McVeigh?'

'Very good. Now, are we planning on heading back to DHQ at some point?'

'Who *is* this?'

'You abandoned one Nichola Strachan in my cells this afternoon. Her duty solicitor's been in with her for an hour, and they're ready to talk. So . . . ?'

She pinched the bridge of her nose. 'Sergeant Weir, I'm sitting outside the Bloodsmith's house, waiting for the cavalry to arrive. I don't have time to sod about with a domestic.'

'Attempted murder.'

'Don't care. Give it to Stan, or Emma. I'm *busy*.'

A long, disappointed sigh huffed out of the phone. *'Very well. But don't come crying to me if they get a conviction and take all the credit.'*

'Sarge?' The Dunk sat up and poked her. Then pointed back towards the main road as the growl of multiple engines raced up Birrel Crescent. 'We're on.'

'Got to go.' She hung up.

A police van was in the lead, riot grille up, lights off, followed by two unmarked Vauxhalls and a couple of patrol cars.

The van put on one final burst of speed, mounting the kerb outside Dr Christianson's house and slamming on the brakes – the side door flew open and four very large officers hammered out into the rain. They were dressed in the full Method-of-Entry kit: crash helmets; shin guards, kneepads, forearm protectors, and elbow pads; thick gloves; dirty big boots. Shoulders up, backs hunched as they charged along the garden path. The officer at the rear wielded the big red door key, and as her colleagues flattened out on either side of the front door, she smashed it in with a single blow of her tactical battering ram.

Lucy was out of the car, running across the road through the downpour, the Dunk bringing up the rear, hitting the opposite pavement as the Operational Support Unit swarmed in through the broken doorway.

Their voices boomed out from inside. *'POLICE, EVERYONE STAY WHERE YOU ARE!'*

'NOBODY MOVE!'

'POLICE!'

DI Tudor and DC Talladale clambered out of their Vauxhall, joining Lucy and the Dunk in Dr Christianson's front garden.

Bangs and crashes. The occasional *'CLEAR!'*

Then silence.

Tudor shifted his feet, scuffing up the long grass. Not looking at Lucy. 'We're *sure* this is our guy?' Sounding a lot less thrilled than he should've been, given they'd just IDed the Bloodsmith.

'Well, I suppose it *could* be a massive coincidence, what with him harassing me, slashing my tyres, and every single victim being part of his loneliness study at ODU? Yeah, you know what, maybe it's not him.'

The Dunk cleared his throat. 'Well, not *every* single victim. Ex-DC Malcolm Louden wasn't.' He held up his hands as Lucy scowled at him. 'But everyone else was!'

Tudor nodded. 'OK. You two did good.' Huffing out a breath. 'Just have to hope this Dr Christianson is . . .' He stared at the hole where the front door used to be, as one of the massive officers in MOE gear lumbered out into the rain again.

The officer raised her helmet's visor. 'No one home. Hasn't been for a while.'

'Sod.' Tudor sagged, head in his hands.

'You think that's bad, wait till you see what we found in the garage.'

32

The faint glow of a rainy evening seeped in beneath the garage door, but other than that, the place was wreathed in darkness – the only strip light hung lifeless and littered with the ancient corpses of long-dead moths. But the harsh white circles of half a dozen police torches were focused on the contents of a large chest freezer.

Lucy stared.

Someone cleared their throat.

Someone else let out a long, hard sigh.

'Wow.' The Dunk fidgeted, his SOC suit rustling like a scrunched-up crisp packet.

It was easily big enough in here for Christianson's Mini, or even the estate car parked outside, but instead there was a row of modular shelving, mounted to the garage wall, full of cardboard boxes and other household junk. A couple of bicycles. A lawnmower.

And the chest freezer.

Light glittered back from the dozens of glass jars, neatly stacked inside it, their surfaces beginning to fur with frost. Some were pot-of-jam sized, others big enough to have taken a hefty amount of pickles or sauerkraut, before they were repurposed to contain something a deep purple-scarlet colour. Next to them was a stack of plastic pouches – the kind they used when you donated blood. One of the Forensic team lifted a bag free from the pile. It was half filled and frozen solid, sparkling with a thin fur of ice crystals.

The SEB tech whistled. 'He's even put the names on them. See? This one's Olive Hopkins.'

Their rambling forensic psychologist had got that bit right at least – Christianson had upgraded more than just his exsanguination method.

'Jesus . . .' DI Tudor pulled one of the smaller jars from the stack, turning it in his gloved hands till a white label appeared. 'Bruce Malloch.'

Lucy backed away from the freezer and had a squint at the shelves instead. Some of the cardboard boxes had labels on them, too. She pulled out the one marked 'JANE COOPER'. Blew the dust off. Opened it. A neatly folded blouse sat on top of a pile of other clothes. All of them stained with dark spatters of what had to be blood.

She moved onto the next one. 'CRAIG THORBURN'. It contained a pair of jeans, trainers, and a 'WOLFRABBIT WORLD TOUR 2004' T-shirt covered in little dark-brown spots. There were four more marked boxes: 'ADAM HOLMES', 'BRUCE MALLOCH', 'ABBY GEDDES', and 'OLIVE HOPKINS', each one full of folded bloodstained clothes. It didn't take long to rummage through the unmarked boxes, but they were full of random crap – old wedding presents, broken toasters, dusty crockery, and a fondue set. No sign of a large dark-red padded jacket. 'Is it just me, or is anyone else wondering what happened to Malcolm Louden's stuff?'

There was a pause, then Tudor clapped his gloved hands. 'All right, everyone who *isn't* a Forensic Services Scene Examination Resource: out. Those of you who *are*, I want this lot catalogued, fingerprinted, and every container of blood matched with a victim. Maybe our boy mixed and matched, or maybe DS McVeigh is right and Malcolm Louden is missing. Either way, we need to know what goes with who.' Another clap of the hands. 'Come on, move it, people, daylight's wasting!'

The Dunk peeled off his SOC suit in the small Identification Bureau marquee, set up in Dr Christianson's front garden – bridging the gap between the house's front door and the outside world. The blue tarpaulin gave everything a sickly hue, shrouding them in gloom as rain thrummed against the marquee's roof. He wodged up the crinkly white Tyvek and stuffed it into a black bin bag marked 'CROSS-CONTAMINATION DISPOSAL', followed by booties, facemask and gloves. Then stood there, waiting for Lucy to do the same. 'Well, that's been quite a day.'

Bit of an understatement.

She'd only got as far as unzipping her suit when Tudor appeared in the house doorway, still done up in the full SOC kit. Arms crossed. Voice

hard and flat, muffled by the facemask. 'DS McVeigh: with me. Now.'
Then he turned and disappeared back inside.

God's sake, what had they done wrong *this* time?

The Dunk grimaced at her. 'You want me to get the pool car warmed
up, in case we have to make a quick getaway?'

She zipped her suit up again and scuffed into the house.

Tudor was in the kitchen, arms still folded, glowering at her through
his safety goggles. 'Close the door.'

Lucy did what she was told. 'Is there a problem, Boss?'

The room was large enough for a small dining table at one end, the
rest of it done up in country-farmhouse style, with patterned tiles on the
splashback, pictures of sheep and cows on the walls, and over-elaborate
cabinet doors. A knitted chicken-shaped cosy brooded over a basket of
eggs that would be well past their sell-by date. Dust everywhere.

Tudor turned his back on her and frowned out the kitchen window.
Never a good sign when a senior officer wouldn't look you in the eye.
'What do we know about this Dr John Christianson?'

OK . . .

She'd just cracked the whole sodding case, so why was Tudor acting
like someone had jammed a jagged stick up his backside?

'He's a psychology lecturer at Oldcastle Dundas University, runs three
or four studies a term, using students and members of the public as sub-
jects. They get paid a small fee; he uses their data to apply for research
grants and publish papers. Took a leave of absence nine weeks ago to
look after his dad while his mother's having chemo.'

A nod.

'Only, when I checked: his mum's been dead six years, and his dad's
in a home down south. Bristol, to be exact. They say Christianson hasn't
visited since before the pandemic. So best guess is—'

'He thought we were getting close, and he did a runner.' Tudor
unfolded his arms, leaning both fists on the worktop. Still staring out at
the rain. 'Bet he hasn't been back here in nearly two months. He's found
himself another lair; could be anywhere by now.'

'Only we know he's still local. He's been following me. Saw him this
afternoon outside Craig Thorburn's flat.'

Tudor groaned, back hunched as if she'd just dumped a huge load on
those broad shoulders. 'You *saw* him?'

'Well, I didn't know he was the Bloodsmith at that point, did I? Thought he was some thug Sarah Black hired. Didn't find out who he really was till we went to the university.' Lucy stiffened her back, chin up. 'You want to tell me why you're acting like I just poisoned your dog?'

'I spoke to your therapist. *Again*.' A proper growl worked its way into Tudor's voice. 'Dr Abernathy says you've never even—'

'Abernathy? Who the hell is Dr Abernathy?'

'YOUR THERAPIST!' At that, Tudor did turn around, fists trembling. '*Jesus*, Lucy, how am I supposed to trust you, when you—'

'Oh for . . . I was assigned to *Dr McNaughton*! And I know he sends in reports every week, because Professional Standards have been reading the damn things. You've been chasing up the wrong bloody psychologist!'

He froze. Cleared his throat. 'McNaughton?'

'Typical!' Lucy stormed out of the room, down the hall, and out into the SEB marquee again.

The Dunk was loitering by the front flap, staring at her like a lost little boy. 'Sarge? Are you . . .'

You know what? Screw him: Tudor didn't deserve to get off that easily.

'Sarge?'

Lucy turned around and marched back into the kitchen. Right up to DI Tudor. Poking him in the chest hard enough to make him flinch. 'How *dare* you!'

'I . . . They told me Dr Abernathy—'

'How can you "*trust* me"?' Jabbing her poking finger towards the garage this time. 'I JUST FOUND YOU THE FUCKING BLOODSMITH!'

'Lucy, I'm sorry, I didn't mean to—'

'If it wasn't for me and the Dunk, they'd be using this case to *bury* you. And you *know* that's the only reason they put you in sole charge. You're here as a scapegoat for when this whole operation dissolves into a festering pile of shite!'

He put his hands up. 'You're right, I'm sorry, it's—'

'But we just *saved* your arse.'

Rain hissed against the kitchen window.

Through in the garage, one of the SEB launched into a muted a cappella version of an old Coldplay song.

The miserable sheep bleated in the field behind the house.

Tudor stared at his blue plastic booties, Tyvek suit rustling as he brought his shoulders up. 'I'm sorry.'

Should bloody well think so too.

He huffed out a breath. 'Look, it's . . .' He stared at the closed kitchen door, as the Dunk's voice rattled down the corridor, unnaturally loud.

'*Assistant Chief Constable Cormac-Fordyce, how nice to see you again, sir.*'

Their very own canary in the coal mine.

'Sodding hell.' Tudor curled forwards for a moment, hands twisting into blue-nitrile claws – then straightened up. Stared at the ceiling for a couple of breaths. 'Why me?' A heavy sigh and he was back again. 'Look, the scene examiners are going to be a while before they come up with anything. Hours. Why don't you check up on the lookout requests and call it a day?'

She narrowed her eyes. 'So now you're trying to get rid of me.'

'I'm trying to say, "Well done." I'm trying to say, "Thank you," and, "I'm sorry."' He sagged. 'You did a damn good job today – you and DC Fraser. They'll probably bump you up to DI for this, and you'll deserve it.' A sigh. 'Now go have some time off. Rest. Back in tomorrow, seven sharp, and we'll see if we can't finally catch this bastard. OK?'

She gave him a one-shoulder shrug. 'Yeah.'

'Good. Now we need to—'

The kitchen door thumped open and there was the man himself, ACC Cormac-Fordyce. The full SOC get-up might have rendered him anonymous, but it couldn't conceal the posh Invernesian accent. 'DI Tudor.' A pause. '*Alasdair.* I understand congratulations are in order: you've identified the Bloodsmith!'

'Actually, it was DS McVeigh and DC Fraser.' Pointing at Lucy.

'Good man. A successful general always gives his troops the credit.' The ACC turned and graced Lucy with a small nod. 'Well, well, well, if it isn't my *almost* fellow pupil. So, you managed to crack the case with the aid of this DC . . . ?'

'Fraser.' She hooked a thumb towards the front of the house. 'That was him outside.'

'Of course it was. Excellent work, the pair of you.'

'Right, well, if you'll excuse me.' Tudor headed for the garage. 'I'd better go see how the team's getting on.'

'Yes, of course.' The ACC stayed where he was. 'I'll join you in a minute. Just want to have a quick word with the Detective Sergeant here.'

Soon as Tudor was out of the room, Assistant Chief Constable Cormac-Fordyce leaned back against the worktop. 'Alone at last.'

Why did that sound like a bad thing?

'Sir?'

'I have to say that I'm impressed, DS McVeigh, or can I call you Lucy?' He didn't wait for permission, but then some men never did. 'Seventeen months this investigation's been spinning its wheels, but here we are, standing in the Bloodsmith's kitchen. All because *you* figured it out.' He tilted his head to one side, looking her up and down. 'I understand you're on the graduate fast-track programme, Lucy. How would you like to accelerate that even more? I'm always looking for high-fliers – or more accurately, high-*achievers* – to join my team at Gartcosh.' The ACC made a little see-saw motion with one gloved hand. 'It's clear that DI Tudor, though he means well, is perhaps . . . a little less suited to the rigours of command than someone with your talents. Perhaps you'd flourish in a more constructive environment? Out from his shadow.'

'And into yours?'

'Only in that you'd be under my wing, Lucy. It would mean promotion, of course. "Inspector McVeigh" has a nice ring to it, doesn't it?'

Had to admit that it did. And a good few years ahead of plan, too. Just a shame that she'd have to work for this slimy tit.

'My team has a . . . let's call it a "roving brief". It allows us to get involved in all sorts of *interesting* things and I think someone of your unique abilities would fit in very well indeed.' He turned to look out the window, at the soggy sheep, his voice light and nonchalant. 'Tell me, yesterday, when you said you'd been out to St Nicholas College, why was that?'

The offhand tone only made him sound more shifty.

Lucy pulled her chin in. 'Why: shouldn't I have?'

'Just interested how St Nick's connects with the Bloodsmith. I like to have all the pieces – that's why I'll be the next Chief Constable when the current one retires.' His voice changed slightly, as if twisted around a smug smile. 'You said you were talking to a pupil?'

Difficult to tell if that 'Chief Constable' comment was a boast: look how great I am; an enticement: look what I'll be able to do for you; or a threat: look how screwed you'll be if you cross me. Or maybe it was a combination of all three?

'Allegra Dean-Edwards. She gave ex-DC Malcolm Louden a new jacket the day the Bloodsmith gutted him. We wanted to know if she'd seen anyone hanging around looking suspicious when she handed the coat over.'

'And had she?' Back to sounding all casual and unconcerned again.

'No. Apparently she hands out a lot of coats to homeless people. Says, after a while, they all kind of bleed into one.'

'Hmmmm . . .' A nod. 'It's nice to know that you're thorough, Lucy. I value that in my team, almost as much as I value loyalty.' The ACC rubbed his hands together, setting the nitrile squeaking. 'I think we should talk, once this Bloodsmith investigation is out of the way, don't you?'

Promotion to Gartcosh, a roving brief, and the ear of the next Chief Constable. He was promising a *lot* more than she'd ever get here with DI Tudor and O Division. And maybe Assistant Chief Constable Findlay Cormac-Fordyce wasn't so bad, once you got to know him? Possibly . . .

Anyway, it wouldn't hurt to play along, would it?

'I'd like that, sir.'

'Excellent.' Then he marched out of the room, without another word.

Question was: had she just sold her soul to the Devil, or only rented it . . .

The Dunk was waiting for her, out in the marquee, watching as she clambered out of her SOC kit. 'Everything OK, Sarge?'

'We're done for the day, Dunk.'

'Right. Good. Time to celebrate!' He fell into place behind her as she pushed out through the front flaps into the rain. 'What do you think: hit the Bart first, or work our way over there one pub at a time? Ooh, how about cocktails at Wobbly Bob's?'

Lucy marched down the path. 'Maybe.'

'What's up, Sarge?' Scurrying along at her side now.

'It's just . . . Nah, it's nothing. Someone asked if I'd have dinner with them tonight, but I can blow him off. It's not as if—'

'Oh my God: do you have a *date*?' Eyes wide.

'It's not a date.' Well, maybe. Argyll McCaskill definitely thought it was. But that didn't mean she had to.

They hurried across the road, the Dunk plipping the locks on their pool car and scrambling in behind the wheel, out of the downpour. Grinning at Lucy as she sank into the passenger seat. 'Where's he taking you? Better not be somewhere lame like Pizzageddon, or Big Tam's All-You-Can-Eat Chinese Buffet.'

'French place. La Poule something-or-other.'

'Shut *up*! La Poule Française? *The* La Poule Française, with a Michelin star?' Both his eyebrows came close to achieving escape velocity. 'Wow. He must be seriously minted: that place costs a fortune.'

She fastened her seatbelt. 'His family own big chunks of Skye and Argyll.' Frown. 'And I think Sutherland, too. Anyway, I haven't said yes yet.'

'Oh, *Sarge* . . .' The Dunk's whole face fell. 'He's that posh twat from St Nick's, isn't he? The assistant head. Tosser was making goo-goo eyes at you the whole time. Sarge, how *could* you?'

'Haven't said I would, have I? Besides, thought I could talk him into slipping us a copy of Benedict Strachan's file.'

'Bet that's not all he wants to slip you.' The Dunk must've felt her stiffen from the other side of the car, because he held up his hands in surrender. 'Sorry. That was . . . sorry.' He started the engine. 'So, you're basically using the posh twat so he'll give you information. That's cool. Clever.'

'Good save.'

He hauled the car into a three-point turn, heading back towards town. 'You're going to wear something nice, though, yeah? Not your usual jeans and a top. Cos, no offence, Sarge, you might get more out of the guy if you flash a bit of leg.'

She tightened her jaw. 'I'm not flashing *anything*.'

'OK, but don't come crying to me if he doesn't put out at the end of the date.'

33

Lucy stomped along the pavement in the rain, heat flushing her cheeks. 'You don't have to walk me to my car, *Constable*.'

'Nah, I do, Sarge.' He bustled along beside her as they made their way down Guild Street, stupid leather bunnet bobbing at Lucy's shoulder. 'If this Dr Christianson's been following you, it's not safe. Besides, if he murders you, that's yet another body we've got to find and clear up and investigate and that bloody forensic psychologist will write one of her horrible rambling reports without any punctuation and I'll have to read it out to whoever they get to replace you.' A smile. 'So, letting me walk you to your car is really *you* doing *me* a favour, when you think about it.' Like he was some sort of chivalrous short-arsed suitor.

Didn't help that she was carrying the massive bunch of flowers Argyll had sent to the station that morning.

The Dunk stood there, waving, as she climbed in behind the wheel of her ridiculous pink Bedford Rascal, dumped the bouquet in the passenger footwell, and cranked the van's engine into spluttering life.

She pulled out her phone and thumbed a text to Argyll.

> OK, you've convinced me. Dinner tonight. What time?

SEND.

Maybe he wouldn't be able to get a table? After all, it was Friday night and if the restaurant was as fancy as the Dunk seemed to think, a place like that probably got booked up months in—

Buzzzzzzz-ding.

UNKNOWN NUMBER:

> Thank you for accepting my offer, Lucy.
> Would 2030 be an acceptable time to eat?
> I'm afraid I have a PTA meeting to attend beforehand, or
> I would make it earlier.

That gave her just under two hours to get home, run a swift bath, scrub up, and get back into town.

Doable.

> See you there at half eight.

SEND.

When she looked up from her phone, the Dunk was still standing there, waving like an idiot.

Right, time to go home.

Lucy finished drying her hair and frowned at the scrawny pale lump in the saggy grey bathrobe, looking back at her from the full-length mirror. It was all very well the Dunk banging on about flashing a bit of leg: his probably didn't look like knotted pipe cleaners that'd never seen the sun. And she wasn't shaving them either.

Surprisingly enough, the blusher, eye shadow, and lipstick in her dresser hadn't solidified after sitting there, unused, for over a year. They felt strange against her skin, though. Like a mask. Maybe that was a good thing? Might help her pretend to be someone she wasn't any more.

She hauled on a sensible bra and a pair of hefty pants – after all, it wasn't as if Argyll McCaskill would ever get to see them – then tried on her best suit. The one for weddings and funerals. Didn't really scream 'first date', though, did it? Nor did her second-best suit. Or *any* of her fighting suits, come to that. A stripy top and black slacks made her look as if she hadn't bothered to change after work. Blouse and jeans?

Bit casual for a Michelin-starred restaurant. They might not let her in. Urgh . . .

Bet *men* didn't have to go through this nonsense. No: their one smart suit did for everything, didn't it? Because the world was inherently sexist.

She sagged in front of the mirror.

Well, that's what you got for burning all your dresses, isn't it? And your skirts. And anything else that made you look in the least bit feminine. After Neil Black . . .

She hauled her shoulders back. Chin up. 'Do you want information on Benedict Strachan, or don't you?'

There was *one* other option, after all.

Lucy scuffed her Crocs through to Dad's bedroom and over to The Forbidden Wardrobe. When she opened it the scent of lavender and mothballs collapsed out into the room like a corpse. Her mother's things, hanging in here for years. And years. And years.

Strange, but now Dad was gone, the fact he'd held onto all this stuff didn't bother her any more. No idea why it ever did, to be honest.

Maybe it was because she couldn't really remember anything about Mum? Well, other than the screaming and throwing things. Even looking at photos of her didn't spark any good memories. You'd think, if you lost your mother when you were almost six, there would be *something* nice worth remembering.

She selected a few dresses and laid them on the dusty bedspread – it was the first time she'd touched anything in The Forbidden Wardrobe since Dad caught her playing dressing-up in one of Mum's old skirts and blouses, many, many times too big for her. Not long after the funeral. They probably heard the shouting and the swearing and the threats all the way to Fiddersmuir. Certainly gave her first-ever therapist something to talk about for months.

Wonder what happened to him . . . ? Probably dead by now. Let's face it, he wasn't far off retirement age when he started treating her. Shame, though. He was nice.

Lucy tried the pink dress: far, *far* too short. The brown-with-orange-spots was hideous on. But the dark-blue wraparound maxi, with the floral pattern, wasn't all that awful. It covered a multitude of unshaven sins, and wasn't too revealing on the cleavage front. Wouldn't be as warm as jeans and a top, but at least she looked the part, now.

Rummaging about in the bottom of The Forbidden Wardrobe produced a pair of strappy leather wedges that were exactly the right size. She wasn't what you'd call stable on them, though – probably be a while till the muscle memory for how-to-walk-in-heels kicked in after all this time.

A pair of dangly jade earrings and a thin, silver necklace from Mum's jewellery box finished the outfit off.

She stood in front of the mirror, frowning at herself. There was . . . just a vague hint – little more than a flash, really – of Mum screaming about whatever it was Lucy had done wrong this time. Then it was gone.

She shuddered. Teetered her way over to the window and pulled back one side of the curtains, just far enough to peer out.

The unmarked car sat across the road and down a bit. One of the two officers DI Tudor had assigned to watch her clambered out into the rain, jacket pulled up over his head in a makeshift hood, shoulders hunched as he lit a fly cigarette. Shuffling his feet on the soggy grass verge.

Silly sod.

Still, at least if Dr Christianson decided to come back and hammer on her door again, at three in the morning, he was in for a shock.

Lucy clomped back through to her own bedroom and stuffed her new phone, her wallet, a hankie, and a packet of Polos into one of her mother's small leather handbags, with—

A voice echoed up from downstairs. '*Hello?*'

She whipped around, teeth bared. Grabbed the hair straighteners like an unextendable baton and crept out onto the landing.

But when she peered between the balusters, it wasn't the familiar corduroy-jacketed stalker standing in her hallway, it was Charlie from Professional Standards frowning up at her. 'DS McVeigh? Are you all right?'

'WHAT THE BLOODY HELL ARE . . . HOW DID YOU GET IN?'

He backed away a couple of steps, hands up. 'The kitchen door was open; I was worried about you.'

'GET OUT OF MY BLOODY HOUSE!'

'Given the Bloodsmith's been following you around town and knows – where – you – live, I think you're being a bit unreasonable, don't you? I'm *trying* to help.'

She stared at him. 'You're in my house!'

He folded his arms and leaned against the sideboard. 'You should get a security system fitted. And make sure you check all the doors and windows are locked. Imagine what would happen if the Bloodsmith decides it's time to harvest your heart, and the kitchen door's lying wide open.'

'Aaaaaaargh . . .' Lucy dumped the straighteners on the chest of drawers again, picked up Mum's bag, and stomped downstairs, scowling at him all the way. 'There's an unmarked car sitting outside!'

'All the more reason for Dr Christianson to sneak in round the back.' Charlie rested his bum against the sideboard and smiled that bland smile. 'You've had quite the day, DS McVeigh. First you find a missing Bloodsmith victim, then you make *another* massive breakthrough and ID our killer. Then there's the big bunch of flowers and dinner date with a handsome and very wealthy young man.' Tilting his head towards the bouquet sitting on the sideboard. 'I hear you've had a job offer, too: working for Assistant Chief Constable Findlay Cormac-Fordyce.'

'God: you really *have* been spying on me, haven't you?'

'Going to take the job?'

'None of your damned business.' She stepped closer, towering over him in her mother's wedges. Spitting the words out. 'You think, just because you're Professional Standards, you can get away with anything, don't you?'

'What about the Dunk: planning on taking him with you to Gartcosh?'

Hadn't thought about that.

'We're not joined at the hip.'

Charlie's face pinched in. 'I'm not entirely sure how to put this, but as we're going to be stuck with each other for a bit – which means, you know, we're basically colleagues – and I genuinely *do* want to see you succeed, I sort of feel I have to. Understand?'

Not even vaguely.

He squirmed a little. 'You see, while I can't speak in any *professional* capacity, because it would be unethical for someone from Professional Standards to talk about individual cases, or investigations, I . . .' Charlie bit his bottom lip, brow furrowed like a battered accordion. 'Let's just say it might not be a great idea to hitch your star to Assistant Chief Constable Cormac-Fordyce.'

'You're saying he's dodgy?'

'Nope. Didn't say that at all. Didn't say anything of the kind. Because that would be unethical, remember?'

Interesting . . .

Lucy nodded. 'I'll think about it.'

'See?' The wrinkles faded as Charlie's bland smile reappeared. 'I'm not kidding when I say I'm here to help and support you, Detective Sergeant. Consider me your very own Jiminy Cricket.'

She pulled her raincoat on, zipping it up. 'You ever read the original book: *The Adventures of Pinocchio*, Carlo Collodi, 1883?'

'No. But I saw the film.'

'Pinocchio batters Jiminy Cricket to death with a hammer.' She grabbed her new St Nick's umbrella from the stand.

'Just watch out, OK? Not everyone has your best interests at heart.'

So Professional Standards were sniffing about the ACC? Did that mean he'd been up to something? Mind you, the top brass were always up to something; it's how they became the top brass in the first place.

Still, had to admit Cormac-Fordyce hadn't exactly sounded squeaky clean when he'd offered her the job.

And what was it he'd said about her being his '*almost* fellow pupil'? She'd told him St Nicholas College only gave her that brolly because it was raining – '*almost* fellow pupil' made it sound as if he knew she'd been a prospective student at St Nick's. Which meant he must've been speaking to someone at the school. Probably the headmaster. Or maybe even her date for tonight? And *that* meant the 'why were you there' question was a test. The ACC already knew why.

Didn't matter, though: she'd told the truth. Passed the test.

Lucy pointed at the front door. 'Now, if you don't mind, I'm going to dinner.'

'Of course. And it's OK, I locked the kitchen door when I came in.' Charlie levered himself off the sideboard, pointing at the bowl next to the flowers as he sauntered past. 'Don't forget your keys.'

Patronizing dick.

She snatched her house keys and the van keys from the bowl. Then swore. Those sodding keys she'd found – the ones she should've handed in to Lost and Found – they were *still* sitting there.

He stepped outside into the rain. 'And you'd better take some comfy shoes with you, in case you get sore feet.'

'Don't push your luck.' She killed the lights, popped up her brolly, and marched out the front door – shutting it behind her and making a big show of checking it was locked.

By the time she turned around again, a drenched Charlie was climbing into the back of the unmarked pool car.

With any luck, he'd catch pneumonia and die.

Lucy clambered into the Bedford Rascal, cranked the engine, and stuck her foot down hard enough to make some gravel fly.

Why did men have to be such complete arseholes?

Lucy parked her motorized embarrassment a good distance from the restaurant, popped open her new umbrella, then tottered her way along Motte Row – already regretting wearing strappy leather wedges when wellington boots would have been more practical – clomping from one patch of jaundiced streetlight to the next. Wind snatched at the hem of her mum's maxi dress. Rain rattled against the St Nick's brolly, filling the gutters and spilling out across the corbels. The Old Castle's crumbling remains were all lit up on the other side of the road, glowing red and blue and green, like something out of a nightmare. Behind it, the land fell away – straight down a jagged granite cliff, the lights of Castleview and the Wynd glittering in the storm-soaked darkness beyond.

Had to hand it to Argyll, the setting was impressive enough.

La Poule Française sat halfway along a curling terrace of huge sandstone townhouses. Doubt you'd get much change from two million around here. The restaurant's mullioned windows glowed with dim candlelight – discreet enough to hide the diners' identities from the vulgar gaze of any passer-by.

A man in a kilt opened the door for Lucy, ushering her into the warmth. Small round tables, booths, and crisp white linen. Sparkling glasses and silverware. The place was busy, but not crowded, bathing the room in a muted hum of candlelit conversation.

Definitely *far* too fancy in here for jeans and a top.

The kilted man didn't ask who she was, or if she had a reservation, just took her umbrella and raincoat, then escorted her straight to a booth in the corner, where Argyll was nursing a gin and tonic.

Argyll struggled as upright as he could get, trapped between the seating and the table, and smiled. 'DS McVeigh! I mean, Lucy, I'm so glad you came.' He'd ditched the school uniform for a tan suit. 'Please, sit, sit. You look lovely, by the way.' Then his forehead puckered. 'I hope that's OK for me to say. I know there are times when it's inappropriate to compliment a woman on her appearance, but—'

'It's OK.'

The kilted man gave her a nod and headed back to his station.

'So . . .' Argyll rubbed his hands. Puffed out his cheeks. Looked down at his cutlery. 'Have you been before? The turbot is spectacular, and so's the *soufflé au fromage*, or the sweetbreads, or . . .' It was hard to tell in the dim lighting, but that definitely looked like a blush. 'Sorry.' A glug of gin and tonic. 'Babbling my way through the menu, like an idiot.'

A woman in a crisp black suit appeared at Lucy's elbow, her French accent soft and musical. 'Compliments of Mr Garvie.' Setting two glasses of something fizzy down on the table.

Lucy didn't move. 'I don't drink.'

'My apologies, madam,' and one of the glasses disappeared, 'may I suggest a sparkling elderberry and rhubarb pressé instead? It is – how you say – *quite* delicious. *Oui? Bien.* My colleague, Marguerite, will be along *momentanément* with your *amuse-bouche* and menus. If you need anything, please do not hesitate to let me know.' Then she swept off, just as silently as she'd arrived.

Argyll fiddled with his complimentary glass of fizz. 'You don't drink?'

'Not since . . . Not for a while, no.' Lucy forced a bit of jollity into her voice. 'Besides, I'm driving. And a police officer. Not that police officers don't drink, but not when they're driving, because it wouldn't look good, would it, for public confidence, if we behave like the law doesn't apply to us.' Smooth, Lucy. Very good. Now the *pair* of them were babbling away like spotty teenagers at their first school dance.

'Yes, I see, definitely. I . . .' Still fiddling with his glass. 'Is it OK if *I* do, though, because I'm just a little bit more nervous than I thought I'd be, because I think I mentioned I really don't do this very often, because . . . yes.' He downed the rest of his gin and tonic in one. 'Sorry.'

Then they both cleared their throats and stared at the tablecloth for a while.

Oh God. It was going to be one of those nights . . .

Had to admit, Argyll had been right – the turbot was lovely.

He was tucking into veal short ribs, telling stories about how great St Nicholas College and its staff and pupils and facilities were. To be honest, it should have bored the large sensible pants off her, but there was something endearing about the man's passion. He'd put away the nervous teenager along with half a bottle of Sancerre, then two large glasses of shiraz. The rosy glow in his cheeks coming from something other than embarrassment for a change.

Lucy scooped a new potato through a glob of wobbling hollandaise. 'I spoke to one of your alumni today, Findlay Cormac-Fordyce?'

A beaming smile. 'Freaky Findlay? How's the old bugger doing?'

'Assistant Chief Constable.'

'Of course he is. We were Raxton House boys. There was us, Spoony Simpson, Matchbox Morrison, and Rhino Rhynie.' Argyll must've seen the look on Lucy's face, because he shrugged. 'What can I say: alliterative nicknames were all the rage. The five of us were inseparable in our never-ending battle to get one over on Glenogil House. And yes, I know that makes me sound like a character out of *Billy Bunter*, but when you're twelve and you're away from home ten months of the year, this kind of nonsense seems like the most important thing in the world.'

She kept her voice neutral, hopefully doing a much better job of it than ACC Cormac-Fordyce had done. 'You still keep in touch?'

'Spoony's Senator for North Carolina; Matchbox is some sort of UN bigwig; Rhino ended up as Business Secretary; and Freaky you know about. We try to have a reunion every five years or so, if we can carve a slot in everyone's diaries.'

'Would've thought "Freaky" might have popped in for a visit, seeing as he's in town?'

'Hope so. Be good to catch up.' Argyll eased another chunk of meat off his short rib. 'Are you sure you don't want to try this? It's like butter.'

So much for getting him to rat out 'Freaky' Findlay for checking up on her. Unless Argyll didn't know, of course. Could be that the ACC went straight to the headmaster. Or that she'd read too much into that '*almost fellow pupil*' comment.

Lucy waved away the proffered forkful of dark glistening meat. 'Doesn't it bother you? They're all these high-fliers and you're stuck back here, working at the same old school.'

He spluttered at that, going red in the face as he tried to cough, laugh, and swallow at the same time. Followed by a big gulp of fizzy water. 'Dear Lord, no. Quite the reverse!' Argyll sat forward. 'There isn't a single one of them who wouldn't sell their firstborn's kidneys to have my job. And to put that in context: Spoony? The Republican Party are *probably* going to nominate her to be their next presidential candidate.'

'No.'

'Honestly! We've got seven crown princes with us, right now. We've got the sons and daughters of diplomats, captains of industry, heads of state, *world leaders*, and I get to mould and shape them. I get to help forge the future of the whole planet – every – single – day.' He raised his water in a toast. 'And when Gabrielle Simpson is President of the United States, I'll be able to walk right into the Oval Office and tease the leader of the free world about how she used to run around the playing fields dressed as the Mighty Spoonwoman, Dread Avenger from the Mysterious Cutlery Drawer of Fate.'

Lucy shook her head. 'You posh people are all weird.'

They lingered over dessert, the candles burning low in their holders, the murmur of other diners like whispers in a warm, dark forest.

Argyll had finished his shiraz and moved on to some sort of sticky pudding wine with his raspberry posset. He'd also loosened his tie, undone his top button, and was all smiles and rosy cheeks. Which meant, by Lucy's reckoning anyway, that he was well and truly lubricated.

Hopefully, just enough to be useful.

He beamed at her again. 'How's your crème brûlée?'

'Delicious.' She scooped out another wobbly spoonful. 'Argyll, you keep all the files on prospective pupils, don't you?'

'You want to see how you did on the tests? Well, I can tell you, you did very well indeed, Lucy Roxburgh McVeigh. *Spectacularly* well.'

'Actually, I was thinking more about someone else's test results: Benedict Strachan.'

The sound of other people eating and drinking seemed to get louder in the silence that followed. The scrape of cutlery on plates, the icy *ping*-and-chime of glasses, the whispers in the dark forest.

Argyll frowned across the table. 'Can I ask why you want to see them?'

OK – time to turn on the charm and a sincere look. 'Benedict's just got out of prison. He's scared, he's paranoid, he's alone, and there's a very real risk he's going to hurt himself or someone else.' She even threw in a poignant shake of the head, for good measure. 'When he pushed me in front of a train last night, he told me . . . I know it sounds crazy, but Benedict thinks if he can kill another homeless person, and get away with it this time, somehow everything will magically be OK, and his life will go back to the way it should've been.'

'He pushed you in front of a *train*?' Argyll raised his eyebrows and huffed out a breath. 'Bloody hell. Right, well, definitely. Clearly this is in his best interests. I mean if he's going to *kill* somebody. Of course. Pop past tomorrow and I'll give you a seeing to.' A grimace. 'It! I'll give *it* a seeing to. See to it. I'll see to it.' Loosening his tie a little further. 'They must've turned up the heating in here . . .'

'You're working on a Saturday?'

'Well, a boarding school never really shuts, does it? Not even for Christmas.' He polished off the last of his posset, cheeks bright as cherries. 'Some of our parents can be a bit . . . hands off.' The smile was back, but there was something sad about it now. 'Still, nothing wrong with that, am I right? Never did *us* any harm. Teaches self-reliance and initiative when you don't have someone fawning over you the whole time.' Deep breath. 'Anyway, maybe it's time to have a nice large brandy!' Looking around to get the waitress's attention.

She put a hand on Argyll's arm. Gave it a little squeeze.

Not a huge amount of affection, but all he'd be getting tonight.

It banished all traces of gloom from his smile, as if she'd given a Labrador a custard cream. Shaper of the free world, indeed.

If he thought being left at school over Christmas taught self-reliance, he should try being abandoned in the care of psychopaths, because your mum's dead and your dad's having a nervous breakdown. But he didn't need to know any of that: he was going to get her Benedict Strachan's file.

And that was all that mattered.

34

'You sure we can't give you a lift?' Argyll beamed up at Lucy from the taxi's back seat.

'It's fine, I'm parked just down the road.' Pointing in the vague direction of her hideous van as the rain battered against her St Nick's brolly.

'In that case, it only remains for me to say, "Thank you for a lovely evening!"' He patted his driver on the shoulder. 'Isn't she pretty?'

The taxi driver didn't reply, just pulled away from the kerb and headed off down the hill.

Lucy clomped her way to the Bedford Rascal and climbed in behind the wheel. Sagged there for a minute. 'Pfff . . .'

It wasn't that there was anything *wrong* with Argyll – he was actually quite nice, to be honest – but spending that long with another human being she wasn't working with? Bit of a strain. But then let's face it: it was a long, long time since she'd been out on a 'date'. And the food *had* been delicious.

She rummaged in her mum's handbag, pulled out the new phone and turned it back on again. Three messages, and two texts.

Buzzzzzzz-ding.

Make that three texts.

UNKNOWN NUMBER:
> Thank you for being a delightful dinner companion, I had
> a wonderful time!
> Really looking forward to seeing you again tomorrow!

My fondest regards,
Argyll

God, he didn't hang about, did he? 'My fondest regards' wasn't exactly romance on toast, but it was a definite improvement on 'All the best, and with warmest wishes'. And she'd never been called 'delightful' before.

She added Argyll to her contacts list – so at least now the phone would know who he was – then called up her voicemails.

YOU HAVE – THREE – NEW MESSAGES AND – ONE – SAVED MESSAGE.

MESSAGE ONE:

> Sarge? It's me: Duncan. Just wanted to make sure everything's OK and Lover Boy hasn't tried anything. Drop me a text or something when you get home, so I know. OK? Good. Right. By-eeee.

Bleeeeeeeep.

MESSAGE TWO:

> This is a message for DS McVeigh from PC Tim Dawson, night shift? DI Tudor got me to do all the PNC stuff on Dr John Christianson? Yeah, anyway, he said I had to keep you in the loop. So, I've been onto the Land Registry and they've got no record of him owning property in Scotland, other than the house on Birrel Crescent. And I couldn't find anything when I did a PNC, so I had a word with the DVLA. They say he's never been the registered keeper of a red-and-white Mini. Maybe he's borrowing or renting it? Anyway, probably worth someone checking the car-hire places when they open in the morning. Cheers.

Bleeeeeeeep.

It didn't help that she hadn't got a sodding number plate either time she'd seen the car.

MESSAGE THREE:

> Detective Sergeant McVeigh? Abid Hammoud, from the CCTV team, we spoke earlier? I'm kinda stunned, but we managed to find your Audi TT. Give us a shout and I'll walk you through it.

*And don't worry about the hour: we're pulling an all-nighter, on
a people-smuggling ring. OK, bye.*

Bleeeeeeeep.

Just because they knew where the car was, didn't mean Benedict Strachan was anywhere near it. Was worth a go, though.

She fastened her seatbelt and called Abid back. 'Where's the car?'

*'Your Audi TT's tucked down a little alleyway off Lomas Drive. I managed
to pull the footage from a police van doing a sweep for drug dealers. Can you
believe it?'*

Lucy started the engine. 'Still there now?'

*'That, I can't tell you. It was definitely there at twenty-six minutes past two
this morning, and I can't find it on any of the ANPR cameras in the area since.
Which means it's either still there, or the driver knows the network well enough
to avoid every single camera. Difficult, but not impossible.'*

'Excellent work.' Pinning the phone between her shoulder and ear as
she hauled the van around in a juddering four-point turn. 'While I've
got you: I need you to find a red-and-white Mini for me. Didn't catch the
number plate, but I *can* tell you it's got a dented roof and a cracked rear
windscreen. Or it did when it scurried away from Ballrochie at about
quarter past three this morning, heading east.'

*'OK, that's going to be a challenge . . . Erm . . . Look, leave it with me and
I'll see what I can do. Not promising anything, though. OK.'* And he was gone.

She put the brakes on, just before the narrow, cobbled road turned
into Shand Street, and dialled Control, wedging her phone in between
the wheel and the instrument panel before heading off again. 'It's DS
McVeigh. Who's Duty Inspector tonight?'

'Let's see. OK: we've got Inspector Fred Murchison down as—'

'Good enough.' Accelerating down the hill. 'Tell him we've got a possible location for Lucas Weir, AKA: Benedict Strachan. I'm on my way
now. On my own. Off-duty. With no backup. After he tried to kill me,
last night. So, you know, *maybe* someone would like to get a couple of
unmarked cars over there ASAP?'

'Not asking for much, are you?' A groan. *'Give me an address and I'll see
who's free.'*

Should think so too.

*

By the time the Bedford Rascal had made it as far as Lomas Drive, there was an unmarked Vauxhall cruising along behind her.

The road straddled the uncomfortable middle bit between Castle Hill and Cowskillin, not quite posh enough to be the former, and not quite post-war-housing-estate enough to be the latter either. The twin monoliths of Willcox Towers loomed on the right – both blocks twenty storeys high, their concrete façades painted green, blue, and red, as if that would make them any less horrific. They were set back behind a row of terraced buildings that featured kebab shops, all-night bakeries, and a lap-dancing club, lights glowing in the flats above.

A small street led between a bookie's and a vape shop. Lucy drove the van into it, peering through the windscreen as Willcox Towers grew larger and larger.

No sign of Ian Strachan's Audi TT.

A right turn at the end put her in front of the tower blocks on a street lined with cheap hatchbacks and knackered estate cars, where someone had sprayed a string of bollards with pink graffiti, so they looked like oversized knobbly willies.

On the other side of the road, a long row of lock-up garages was punctuated by a series of narrow alleyways. Which looked a lot more like Abid Hammoud's description of where the Audi had been planked. The streetlights didn't reach that far, though, leaving each one a featureless tunnel into darkness.

Lucy parked the Bedford Rascal across the front of two garages, opposite a half-dozen big council communal bins, grabbed her brolly and a torch, then climbed out into the rain.

That unmarked Vauxhall pulled in behind her and a couple of bruisers in cheap suits and heavy waterproof overcoats got out. If either of them was bothered by her standing there, all dolled up in a maxi dress and strappy leather wedges, they kept it to themselves.

The bigger of the two marched over. 'You McVeigh?' She must've barely fitted into the pool car – easily a head taller than her colleague, with broad shoulders and greying hair half trapped under a flat cap. She poked herself with her thumb. 'DC Linton, and this is DC McKeeler.' Hooking the thumb in his direction.

McKeeler bristled his soup-strainer moustache and nodded at Lucy, pulling out a pair of huge Maglite torches. 'Sarge.' He clicked them on and played the twin beams down the nearest alleyway as raindrops bounced off his big bald head.

'But you can call us Bonnie and Tim.' DC Linton's smile wasn't very warm. 'No jokes about how he should be called "Clyde", eh?'

Fair enough.

Lucy pointed. 'CCTV on a police van spotted a red Audi TT down one of these alleys. Driver is Benedict Strachan, may or may not still be in the area. Consider him violent and uncooperative.'

A grunt from McKeeler. 'Great. Drugs?'

'Yup. And he's probably got a knife, too.'

'Right then.' Linton cricked her head from side to side, rolling those massive shoulders. 'Better get to it, hadn't we?'

They searched the nearest alley, then did the next one along, Lucy tottering about on her stupid wedge shoes. Bloody things were eating her feet – crunching on the bones, gnawing at the flesh. And there were probably a whole heap of blisters forming under the straps, too. Should've listened to Charlie and taken a pair of sensible shoes with her after all.

Probably would have, if he hadn't been such a dick about it.

By the time they'd searched alley number four she was seriously hobbling.

The three of them slogged on through the rain, torch beams roving across potholed tarmac and sodden brickwork.

Linton squelched her way into alley number six. 'Maybe he stashed the Audi in one of these lockups?'

'God, I hope not.' Lucy limped in after her. 'Can you imagine how many warrants we'd need?'

McKeeler slid his torch across a stack of soggy cardboard. 'I wouldn't leave an Audi TT anywhere near Willcox Towers: be lucky if there's anything left of it by now. Whole thing: stripped down for parts.'

'Come on, Tim' – Linton marched down to the end of the alley – 'it's nowhere *near* as bad as Mason Court, or Millbank Park.'

'Oh, don't get me wrong, I wouldn't leave a dog unattended for fifteen minutes in Kingsmeath and not expect the poor thing to be up on blocks by the time I got back.'

A five-foot-high mound of glistening black-plastic bags filled a big chunk of alley number seven, pretty much blocking it, their burnt-rubber-and-bin-juice stench barely dented by the deluge. Greasy rainbows shone as Lucy's torch danced around the stinking puddles.

'You know what I think?' McKeeler wiped something nasty off his shoe, using the edge of a pothole as a scraper. 'I think the car's long gone.'

Lucy sidestepped the worst slick of manky liquid, because, let's face it, her wedges were open-toed. 'Probably.'

Linton squeezed past the mound of garbage. 'No point wimping out now, though.'

Even if he *had* stashed the car, Benedict Strachan would be long gone by now. He'd somehow managed to drive the thing over here from his mum and dad's house, ditched it, then gone off in search of somewhere safe to lie low and work on his plan.

Which meant it was probably worth looking into squats and abandoned properties in the immediate area. Or was it? Anyone with half a brain was bound to know the police would find the car eventually, and put a fair bit of distance between themselves and it. Mind you, as that was the *obvious* thing to do, maybe the *clever* thing was to stay local, because no one would expect that.

Which left her right back where she started.

'No car.' Linton was back again, squeezing her way past the bin bags and brushing a hand down the front of her raincoat as if there was something sticky on it. 'Looks like you're gonna need those warrants after all.'

'Sodding hell . . .' Lucy stood out on the road, rain thrumming on her umbrella, feet aching like someone had been playing Spanish Inquisition with them. 'Thanks for the backup, anyway.'

McKeeler shrugged. 'Least we're out in the fresh air.'

'True.' A smile from Linton. 'It was this or a late-night raid on a puppy farm out by Fiddersmuir, and those places always depress the living hell out of me. And the *smell*!' Pulling her chin in. 'Sometimes I think the bastards running them use the stench as a deterrent. How hard is it to clean up a bit of dogshit and put down a squirt of Jeyes Fluid?'

'Preach.' He held up a hand till his partner high-fived it.

'Suppose we should really get back to the ranch . . .' Not really oozing with enthusiasm, there. 'Maybe, if we hurry, we can make the raid?' Linton scuffed a foot along the tarmac. 'Yup. Hurry, hurry, hurry.'

Never let it be said that Lucy McVeigh couldn't take a hint. 'If you like, you could check Willcox A and B – see if there's any squats, or unoccupied flats someone could break into? Benedict Strachan might've stayed local.' She pulled out her phone. 'I can email you a photo, in case anyone recognizes him.'

'Yeah, we could take a shufti, couldn't we, Tim?'

'Always like to help out, when we can.'

After a bit of sodding about with email addresses, Lucy sent the pair of them Benedict's last official police photo, then watched them stride across the road, past the willy-bollards, and into the lobby of Willcox A.

It was worth a try, anyway.

She slumped. Rubbed a hand across her face. Didn't bother hiding or suppressing the jaw-creaking yawn that shuddered its way through her. Been a *long* day. Shame it couldn't have ended on a high note.

Still, no point hanging around till Bonnie and not-Clyde had finished. Might as well head home. Couldn't do anything about the warrants till tomorrow anyway.

Headlights swept around the corner as she limped over to her Bedford Rascal, and by the time she'd got there a crappy old flatbed truck had pulled up alongside – its sides blistered with mud that even *this* monsoon couldn't shift. The driver's door clunked open and out climbed the huge form of DCI Ross.

Perfect. Just in time to witness her disaster.

He was wearing one of those big, waxed duster coats that almost reached his ankles, and a wide-brimmed leather hat, like something out of a western. Ross thumped his door shut and lumbered over. 'DS McVeigh.' Looking her up and down, no doubt taking in the long floaty dress, make-up, and strappy wedges. 'If I'd known this was a formal crime scene, I'd have worn my tux.'

'Boss.' Standing up straight. 'Thought Murchison was Duty Inspector tonight?'

'You called *me* about Benedict Strachan yesterday, remember? I take people trying to kill my officers pretty seriously.' Then he pursed his lips and frowned at the embarrassing-pink Bedford Rascal. 'Are those sausages doing what I *think* they're doing?'

'I'm afraid you've had a wasted trip, Boss. We've searched the alleyways and there's no sign of Ian Strachan's Audi.'

His shoulders curled a bit. 'Wish you'd said that before I traipsed half-way across town.'

'Didn't know they'd called you.'

The two of them stood in the rain.

A little old man hobbled out from the lobby of Willcox B – bent over a walking stick and carrying a small white bin bag.

A scooter whined past, its driver leaning forward, as if that was going to make the thing go any faster.

Water gurgled from an overflowing gutter.

What sounded like a couple of cats having a barney.

Well, this wasn't an awkward silence at *all*.

Ross stuck his paws in his coat pockets. 'DI Tudor's put you up for a commendation, by the way. For IDing the Bloodsmith. I, on the other hand, am going to recommend promotion.'

Twice in one day?

She smiled. 'Thank you, Boss.'

The little old man had made it as far as the communal bins, opposite Lucy's awful van, using the tip of his walking stick to hinge the lid up far enough to chuck in his rubbish. When it hit the bottom, the whole bin rang like a gong.

'That was some great policework, Lucy.'

She faked a modest shrug. 'It was a team effort, really. Me and DC Fraser. He's . . .' She stared across the road at the bins.

The little old man was hobbling his way back towards the tower block.

'Lucy? Are you—'

'Sorry, hold on, I'll just be a minute.' She limped across the road in her stupid wedges. 'Excuse me?' Luckily the old geezer was even slower than she was, so she caught him by the main doors. 'Hello? Excuse me?'

He glared at her with rheumy eyes. 'I DON'T WANT ANY OF YOUR BLOODY DRUGS!' Waving his walking stick in her face.

She batted it away and pointed back the way they'd come. 'Police. When's bin day?'

'Same day it always is: tomorrow. Saturday. I haven't done anything wrong!'

Lucy hurpled back to the bins.

'THIS IS HARASSMENT! YOU'RE NOT ALLOWED TO SEARCH MY RUBBISH WITHOUT A WARRANT!'

Six bins: two with blue lids – they would be for the recycling; four with black – for general landfill waste.

The nearest bin's black lid was partially melted on one side. She grabbed the lip and threw it open. Then did the same with the next one along. And the one after that.

DCI Ross stalked across the road to watch as she flipped back the last of the black lids. 'I'm *assuming* you haven't gone insane, Detective Sergeant?'

'Look at them; they're all empty.'

He peered into the nearest bin. 'So?'

She hauled up one of the blue lids: the bin was stuffed full of tins and cans and paper and cardboard and plastic containers. The other blue bin was too. 'Bin day's tomorrow, but out of two whole tower blocks, the only thing anyone's throwing out is recycling?'

'Granted it's a bit odd, but why would that . . .? Lucy?' He followed her across the road, past her Bedford Rascal, and most of the way down the row of garages. 'I'm starting to rethink my assumption about your sanity.' They stopped at the alleyway blocked with bin bags. DCI Ross stared at the pile, then at Lucy, then at the heaped-up rubbish again. 'OK, now I see it.'

'Someone's emptied the communal bins and piled everything up here.' To hell with worrying about stinky bin-water on her bare toes. She sploshed through the greasy foetid puddles and hauled a black-plastic bag off the mound – tossing it behind her. Then did the same with the next one, and the one after that.

Ross joined in, the pair of them flinging manky bin bags away until a partial avalanche revealed a swathe of red metal. It wasn't shiny any more, but as the last couple of bags slithered off they exposed the four interlocked chrome circles at the front of the bonnet.

Ian Strachan's Audi TT.

Lucy chucked a couple more bags away, revealing the driver's door. 'If you're ditching a car, you ditch it. You park it somewhere remote and you torch the thing.'

To be honest, it was amazing Benedict Strachan had managed to drive his dad's Audi this far, given he'd never had a driving lesson in his life. Unless that was a course they offered in prison these days? With elective modules on ram-raiding and skills for the modern getaway driver.

A cold hard grin twisted DCI Ross's face. 'He hid it, because he's planning on coming back.' One of those massive hands thumped down on Lucy's shoulder. 'How about we bury the car again, then get a wee surveillance operation set up to watch it? And when Benedict Strachan returns for his dad's car, we nab him.'

And with any luck, they'd do it before he killed anyone else.

— there is no God, no redemption, no forgiveness —

only pain

35

'. . . *but I think it's pretty clear there's no love lost between the pair of them.*'

'*Thank you, Nina. Xavier, you've got a story from the* Daily Standard *for us?*'

Lucy polished off the last crust of toast and dumped her plate in the sink. Glanced up at the clock: quarter to seven. 'Sod.'

'*Yeah, buckle up, cos they're using a* lot *of alliteration this morning: "Randy Rhynie's Russian Rumpy-Pumpy Row!" And we've got three pages featuring some* pretty explicit *photos of the Business Secretary, two members of the Russian embassy staff, and what looks like an illegal substance—*'

She clicked off the radio, unplugged her new phone from its charger, and hurried for the door. Maybe if she cut down Granite Drive instead of taking the scenic route along the River Wynd? At least it was Saturday, so rush hour should be pretty much non-existent.

Grabbing her keys from the bowl – and that set she'd found, so it could *finally* go in the Lost and Found – she stuffed them into her overcoat pocket, grabbed her new brolly from the stand, hauled open the front door, and—

'DS McVeigh, are you all right?' It was sodding Charlie, from Professional Standards, standing on her top step, face creased up with concern, one hand raised as if he'd been just about to knock. He lowered it. 'I tried calling, but there was no answer.'

Of course not, because her bloody phone had run out of battery before she'd even got home last night.

'What are you *doing* here?'

'They had to pull the unmarked car; some raid on a puppy farm went a bit . . . sour. Soon as I found out: came straight over.' Turning to point at a manky little Fiat Panda, parked on the other side of the road. 'Why didn't you pick up?'

She thunked the door shut and locked it. 'Told you: I don't need a babysitter.'

'Might rain today.' He hooked a thumb at her overcoat. 'Probably better take the waterproof.'

Patronizing dick.

'It's in the *wash*.' Which is what she got for chucking bin bags about for a large chunk of last night. She stomped across the drive to Dad's Bedford Rascal. 'Don't you have someone else to annoy?'

'Nope. Chief Inspector Gilmore says you're my top priority. So, where are we going?'

'*We're* going nowhere. I'm going to work.' But by the time she'd unlocked the driver's door, the little sod was already sitting in the passenger seat, smiling his bland little smile as he pulled on his seatbelt.

'Don't worry, I can pick up my car later.'

'AAAARGH!' Lucy's scream echoed back from the woods opposite, borne on a cloud of pale-grey angry steam.

Lucy put her foot down, wheeching across the roundabout, onto Kingside Drive, heading for Dundas Bridge.

'So . . .' Charlie stared across the car at her, 'yesterday we found out who the Bloodsmith is, today we find out where he's hiding?'

She tightened her grip on the steering wheel. 'That's the general idea, yes.'

'And I suppose you'll want to go after Benedict Strachan again?'

Lucy forced the words out through gritted teeth. 'Please, I just want to get to work. In *silence*. OK? Can we do that?' Up and over the slate-grey water, still running high from nearly a week of solid rain.

All the way into town and he'd barely shut up once. As if he was actively *trying* to make the spiky headache, clawing away at the back of her eyes, as bad as possible.

Charlie drummed his fingers on the dusty dashboard, because God forbid he wasn't annoying for two sodding seconds. 'I don't see him as the kind of guy who does things on the fly; Benedict's more of a plotter and planner. And I get the feeling he'll have done most of that while he was still inside – working out how to get away with it this time.'

She slowed the van as they made landfall in Castle Hill, coasting down to the roundabout, the ruins looming high on the clifftop above. 'We've got door-to-doors, we've got lookout requests at every police station from Inverness to Edinburgh, we've got "Have you seen this man?" posters going up today, what else are we supposed to do? Can't just magic him up out of nowhere.'

'Odds are Benedict spent last night picking his target and working out the best route of escape.' Charlie's brow furrowed. 'Biggest concentration of rough sleepers is around St Jasper's Lane, isn't it? Lots of CCTV down there: we might get lucky?'

She shook her head, waiting for a gap to leap into, round the roundabout onto the dual carriageway. 'Loads of those small streets don't have any cameras. If I was him, I'd be looking to pick someone up on Wool Lane, Needle Street, Porter Lane . . . maybe Waites Avenue? Or there's all those little alleyways off Archers Lane.'

'True.'

'That way he's got easy access to Camburn Woods. Loads of places to get rid of a body in there.' Lucy took a left at the lights, along McLaren Avenue. 'And it puts a hefty buffer zone between the murder and where he's stashed his dad's Audi. Be a long walk – through the woods, all the way to Lomas Drive – but he could be driving out of town in . . . twenty minutes?'

'Probably more like half an hour, if he's *really* moving. And he'll still have to dig the car out, remember?' More drumming fingers. 'Or maybe he's hunting in the forest?' The deep green mass of Camburn Woods reared up ahead, spreading out on the right as they drove past the halls of residence. 'Must be two or three illegal camps in there, sort of small shanty villages. Wouldn't be hard to wait till the wee small hours and pick someone off?'

'Hmmm . . . Don't know.' She slowed to let an auld mannie in pyjamas and an overcoat shuffle across the road, pulled along by a wee Westie terrier on the end of a tartan lead. 'Benedict's spent the last sixteen years in prison: he's used to rules and routine. Out here, in the real world, it's all new and strange and scary. He's paranoid; he panics. So he's going to want somewhere he's familiar with. Somewhere he knows.' Man and dog made the opposite pavement and disappeared into the trees. Lucy sped up again. 'I think he'll try the same area as last time. We should focus on where he killed Liam Hay.'

A smile. 'Hey, look at us: working together.' Charlie reached across and gave her a gentle punch on the shoulder. 'We make a good team, DS McVeigh.'

God help her . . .

Lucy parked the Bedford Rascal in the same spot as yesterday, locking the van and marching off, leaving Charlie to scamper after her like the Dunk always had to.

If they were going to be a 'team' it wouldn't hurt the boy from Professional Standards to learn his place.

He caught up with her far too quickly, not even breathing hard. 'So, when you get your hands on Benedict Strachan's file from Old Nick's, do you think it'll back up your theory? About him being a creature of habit?'

'How did you know about—'

'You told me, on the way over, remember?'

Did she?

Must've done. She'd been too busy fuming at the irritating sod to pay attention – that was the problem. Dr McNaughton was always banging on about that. *Anger dulls the senses, Lucy . . . Being angry with people means you can't pay proper attention to what they're saying, Lucy . . . Being angry will never make you happy, Lucy.*

At least he was right about that last one. It didn't help the headaches, either.

They turned the corner onto St Jasper's Lane and she nipped into the small Co-op for a packet of aspirin, one of paracetamol, and something to wash them down with.

'So . . . ?' Charlie was waiting for her outside, hands in his pockets, as if they were out for a casual stroll.

She popped two of each pill from their blister packs, chasing them with a swig of Lucozade, then picked up the pace, swinging around onto Peel Place. 'I already *know* Benedict's a creature of habit. When I interviewed him for my thesis, that was about the only thing he was honest about.'

'You're probably right. We could . . .' Charlie's eyebrows went up, eyes widening as he stared down the road. 'Oh dear.'

It looked as if every news agency on the planet had descended on

O Division headquarters: outside-broadcast vans, bristling with satellite dishes and antennae; dented estate cars from the smaller channels with just a single cameraman and a presenter; grubby hatchbacks and saloons, their owners out enjoying a fag in the sunshine, with a couple of heavy-duty cameras hanging around their necks; men and women with mobile phones and domestic video cameras, filming themselves as they pulled serious faces and read their scripts. As if having a YouTube channel made you an investigative journalist.

They filled the space in front of DHQ, spilling down the steps and out onto the tarmac, where a couple of uniforms in high-vis did their best to keep the road clear so the police could go about their daily business of keeping Oldcastle from eating itself.

Nearly every one of the patrol cars that slid by the crowd of reporters whacked its lights and siren on as it passed, either to show off in an attempt to get on the news, or because someone up top had told them to spoil as many takes as possible.

Lucy and Charlie nipped across to the opposite side of the road, not making eye contact with anyone, ducking behind the war memorial.

He peered around the side. 'Any sign of her?'

'Any sign of who?'

'Your nemesis, AKA: Sarah Black. She's bound to be here some-where . . . Yup, there she is: eleven o'clock. Today's banner is "POLICE KILLER MURDERED MY LITTLE BOY!" all in caps, with a photo of Neil Black on it.'

No doubt peddling her lies to anyone gullible enough to listen. 'Shite-faced old bag.'

'Yes, but . . .' Charlie grimaced. 'What she's *doing* is crappy, no two ways about it – harassing you, the name-calling, the spurious complaints – but she's not doing it for fun, is she? She's doing it because her son's dead and she can't cope with the thought that she raised a monster.' Both shoulders came up in a what-ya-gonna-do-about-it gesture. 'You killed her little boy; she's got to blame someone.'

'I didn't *want* to kill him, OK? I had no choice! *He* did. He got himself a rape kit and he went hunting for someone to use it on. The only person to blame for Neil Black's death is Neil Sodding Black.'

Charlie squeezed Lucy's arm. 'I know, but that doesn't make it any easier on his mother.'

'Screw her.'

'Lucy, she's only human.'

'SO WAS GILLIAN!' Shoving him away to bounce off the war memorial, the sunny morning wobbling at the edges, breath burning in her throat. 'And screw you, too. I get enough analysis from that prick McNaughton; I don't need any from you!'

She marched out from behind the statue, leading the bronze figures in a charge down the street towards the back entrance to Divisional Headquarters. Them with their bayonets fixed, her with the St Nick's umbrella grasped like a cudgel. Scrubbing the tears from her cheeks.

Charlie appeared at her side again. 'Hey, at least it's not *all* bad.' Pointing back at the crowd. 'Look, it's whatshername, Craig Thorburn's mother.'

'Judith.'

She was wrapped up in a heavy coat and scarf, standing in front of the O Division sign, holding a placard in the shape of a heart – not a schmaltzy Valentine's one, the proper anatomical human kind. Gesticulating wildly as she talked to someone from *Sky News*. Glancing at the camera every couple of seconds, as if she didn't really trust it.

'At least you know *she's* got your back, right?'

Lucy curled her lip and kept on marching. 'Can't believe Judith Thorburn's up this early; probably still drunk from last night. It's a miracle she sobered up long enough to make a placard.'

'Wow.' Charlie stopped, letting the distance grow between them. 'What the hell happened to make you so cynical?'

Neil Black.

When everyone had a mug of instant coffee and an off-brand Jaffa Cake, DI Tudor brought Morning Prayers to order. 'All right: settle down, settle down.'

It took a moment or three, but finally Operation Maypole shut its communal cakehole and faced front. The whole team was in this morning, each group gathered beneath their dangling signs. And, for a change, most of them were actually smiling. And they weren't alone: a dozen Uniform stood at the back, while a handful of support staff loitered by the filing cabinets. Extra resources, drafted in to help catch Dr John Christianson.

Tudor perched on the edge of a desk, at the front of the room, beneath the pull-down screen. 'Now, you can probably all guess from the circus outside, we had a massive breakthrough yesterday, thanks to our very own DS McVeigh and DC Fraser, who—'

A cheer went up, as if they were at a football match and the home team had just fouled the opposition striker. There was even a scattering of applause.

Lucy buried her face in her mug, but the Dunk stood and gave everyone a bow.

When the noise died down again, Tudor nodded. 'That's right, they did a great job. Excellent work. What's less great is that someone leaked that fact to the press *last night*!' Scowling out at the assembled hordes. 'Do I really have to give you lot the "Don't talk to the media!" speech again? Because DON'T TALK TO THE SODDING MEDIA!'

Dead silence.

'Jesus Christ, people, this is an inquiry into *seven* murders; what about that do you not take seriously?'

There was some shuffling of feet.

Tudor let the embarrassment fester for a long moment, then nodded. 'We are now a zero-tolerance operation. Understood? Good. Someone kill the lights.' He plucked a remote from the desk beside him and pointed it at the back of the room.

Two plainclothes shut the blinds while someone else clicked the switches, plunging them all into gloom.

A face appeared on the screen behind Tudor, partially covering him and casting a shadow.

'Dr John Christianson.'

That familiar high forehead, with a fringe of brown hair curling around it. It must've been an old photograph, because Christianson had lost a fair bit of weight since then. This Christianson didn't have the hollow cheeks and sunken eyes – the bags under them were barely visible. His beard and moustache were a lot neater in the photo, too, and he was smiling. Wearing the same little round glasses, though.

'Christianson lectures in psychology at Dundas University, where he does paid studies on students and members of the public. That's how he selects his victims – signs them up for research into loneliness, picks the ones he likes, and butchers them.'

A posh Inverness accent cut across the room. *'It's really rather clever, isn't it?'* Then Assistant Chief Constable 'Freaky' Findlay Cormac-Fordyce sauntered over to perch on the opposite edge of Tudor's desk. 'Hope you don't mind, Detective Inspector, I snuck in just before the lights went down.'

Difficult to tell if Tudor was going red in the gloom, but probably. 'Not at all, Boss.' He folded his arms, legs crossed at the ankle.

Yeah, because that didn't make him look sulky and defensive *at all*. No, no, no.

'Excellent.' Findlay beamed out at them all. 'As I was saying, it shows how intelligent our killer is: he performs a psychological analysis on each individual before deciding whether to kill them or not. In a way he's not "selecting" them, he's making them active participants. He's recruiting them. And he only recruits the ones he thinks no one will miss – hence the focus on loneliness.' A smile. 'His case files make *fascinating* reading.'

And that was pretty much it – ACC Cormac-Fordyce took over the rest of the briefing, all except for the admin bit at the end, when he gave them what was probably meant to be a rousing motivational speech instead, then made his excuses and sodded off. Leaving a boot-faced DI Tudor to sort out who was on which team and what they were meant to do today.

Lucy and the Dunk sat there, in an ever-dwindling pool of personnel, as everyone else was given an assignment and sent on their way. Eventually, they were the only ones left. Well, them, DI Tudor, and Charlie – loitering by the coffee machine, helping himself to the not-quite Jaffa Cakes.

She stood. 'Something wrong, Boss? Well, other than . . . you know.' Tilting her head towards the door the ACC had swept out of. 'What about me and—'

'The man's an *arsehole.*' Scowling in the same direction. 'Waltzes in here, like he's Lord of the Flies. Oh yes, I'm in "sole charge" when they think it's going down the crapper, but the minute we make progress, it's—'

'Only how come me and the Dunk didn't get a job?'

Tudor's whole face pinched – the muscles in his stubbled jaw clenching and unclenching, as if he was trying to grind his teeth into powder.

Then a long, shuddering sigh. 'I haven't given you two a job, because unlike some *senior officers*, I learn my lessons. You went off dancing to your own tune yesterday, and I gave you a bollocking for it, but you're the ones who made the only breakthrough we've had in over a year. So I'm cutting you free, Lucy.'

He was *firing* them? Shuffling them off to another operation? How was *that* fair?

'Boss?'

'You and the Dunk are now investigators without portfolio – you can look into anything you think warrants looking into. If you find something: shout and we'll come running. I trust you.' He pulled his shoulders back. 'Now get out there and find me the Bloodsmith.'

36

'Well, that was unexpected.' The Dunk leaned on the handrail, staring out at Kings River as the wind whipped it against the tide – seagulls scudding sideways across a sapphire sky. The ash from his cigarette whirling away after them. 'Who'd have thought?'

Lucy picked a stone from the path and hurled it out into the churning grey water. 'Thanks, Dunk. It's *great* to know you're so completely shocked that someone thinks we're not idiots.'

'Yeah, but . . . "investigators without portfolio". Makes us sound like Holmes and Watson, doesn't it? Am I going to have to blog about everything we do and be really condescending about the local plod now? Because, clearly, Holmes is a posh twat and Watson is a doctor – which means he's got a profession-based promotion to second-division posh twatdom – while the police are just working-class hoi-polloi thickies who need the gentry to come in and teach them how to do their jobs.'

Another stone went flying. 'You finished?'

'Barely even started.' A sniff. 'Think DI Tudor's our Lestrade, now?'

Charlie hung back, sheltering in the lee of a notice board announcing upcoming attractions at Kings Park and Dundas House. Fiddling with his phone and, wisely, keeping his mouth shut, because engaging with the Dunk when he was like this only ever made it worse.

'You *do* know this means we've got even *more* pressure on us to find the Bloodsmith?'

'Yeah.' The Dunk leaned even further forward, till his chest was up against the rail. 'I noticed that, too.' A sigh. 'So, where do we start, Holmes?'

Lucy's phone *buzzzzzzz-ding*ed in her pocket. 'How about we go back to Dr Christianson's house and see what we can dig up? Might be some clue where he's hiding himself.' She pulled out her mobile. Two unread text messages – the one that had just come in, and one from last night.

'Worth a try.' The Dunk straightened up and pinged his dogend away into the river, because when you smoked, the world was your ashtray. 'Search team *must've* finished with it by now.'

According to the timestamp, that first text had arrived just after midnight.

BENEDICT STRACHAN:

> Tell Them I can do it properly this time!
> Tell Them they'll be proud of me!
> Tell Them I kept their secrets!

Sod. That's what she got for not spending the extra cash on a phone with a better battery.

Text number two.

ARGYLL MCCASKILL:

> I'm still thinking about our date last night.
> I very much enjoyed myself, and sorry if I got a little
> squiffy, I was a tad nervous.
> Not too squiffy to remember my promise, though. If you
> would like to pop past this morning, I'll give you a copy
> of the information you requested.
> Or perhaps we could have lunch together?

Squiffy? What kind of grown man used words like 'squiffy'? Still, at least he hadn't signed off with anything like 'fondest regards' or 'yours sincerely' this time. *And* he was going to give her Benedict Strachan's file.

Question was: did she need to take the Dunk with her?

Now there was a romance killer.

Not that she was *after* any romance. But it might put Argyll off co-operating if the Dunk was there. So *really* she was helping the investigation by leaving him behind.

Lucy thumped a hand down on the Dunk's shoulder. 'I think you're right about Dr Christianson's house. But first, let's get some background done: bit of context so we know what we're looking at. Head back to the ranch and pull everything you can on him. Not just PNC stuff, either: the full Facebook, Google, Twitter, LinkedIn, and anything else you can find.'

'No point, Sarge' He sparked up another cigarette, cupping the lighter's flame against the wind. 'Tudor's already got Emma's team on research. They'll be doing all that.'

'Her IT guy's DC Steve Johnson, isn't he?'

The Dunk stiffened. 'That prick?'

Lucy shrugged. 'But he'll probably do a decent job of digging up anything important about Dr Christianson, won't he? You know, what with him being *so* good with computers. No way you'd be better at it, on account of him being such a genius and everything.'

'Yeah, but . . .' A long drag on the cigarette. A shuffle of the feet. 'You see, Sarge, Christianson: he's been targeting you, right? At your house, slashing your tyres, following you around all day? He's doing that for a reason.'

'If he *really* wanted to hurt me, he's had plenty of opportunity to try. Instead he's stuck with being a pain in the arse. Probably because he knows I'd kick his for him.'

'Is it worth the risk, though?'

'Don't be daft, I'm *fine*.' She pulled back her shoulders. 'Now, can I count on you to dig up something useful, or can't I?'

'Course you can.' Chin up, like a good little soldier.

And yes, strictly speaking, she was just getting shot of him for a couple of hours, but he liked all that computer nonsense, so what was the harm?

'Meantime, give me the keys to the pool car. I want to go check something out.'

'You're like a bloody limpet!' Lucy clenched her jaw as the pool car weaved its way through Auchterowan, following the diversion signs – which seemed to bypass the main square via the most meandering route known to man. As if they'd done it on purpose, so everyone would have to experience as much of the town's neatly-laid-out-two-storey-sandstone-Scottish-vernacular bollocks as possible. Every now and then, glimpses of the farmers' market responsible appeared down a side street, all gay and multicoloured and twee.

Bastards.

'I'll take that as a compliment.' Charlie stretched out in the passenger seat, hands behind his head, irritating bland smile on his face as usual. 'Limpets are an important part of the coastal ecosystem; they—'

'I take it back, you're not a limpet, you're a *barnacle.*' AKA: a huge drag on her arse.

That's what she got for not locking the car soon as she got into it.

One more hard left and they were back on the road leading north out of town, following the signs for St Nicholas College.

She glowered at him. 'I'm trying to get information out of this guy, and I don't want you hanging around, spooking him. You stay in the car and you *don't* interfere.'

The sandstone houses gave way to fields and drystane dykes. Happy clean sheep in the fields, unlike the soggy miserable things that had milled about outside Dr Christianson's house.

Lucy put her foot down as they left the town limits. 'I mean it, Charlie.'

'I'll be a ghost. They won't even know I'm there, promise.'

Why did that sound sodding unlikely?

Argyll must've left word that she'd be coming, because the broken-nosed porter took one look at Lucy and waved the car through.

'It's *huge.*' Charlie sat forward, gawping at the school's façade – towers and turrets glowing in the sunlight, as if they'd been burnished. 'How much do you think this place costs to run? Must be a fortune; no wonder the fees are crippling.'

She parked in the same spot as last time, but instead of under-prefect Skye McCaskill, it was Allegra Dean-Edwards waiting for her. She'd brought a great big lump of a boy with her – unruly blond hair, puppy-fat cheeks, and the kind of easy smile that implies not all the lightbulbs are working to full brightness. They were both wearing their school uniform, complete with academic gown and two white epaulettes. No brolly this time, though.

Lucy unfastened her seatbelt. 'Stay – in – the – car!'

A nod from Charlie. 'Like a ghost.'

She climbed out into the sunshine. 'Allegra.'

'Detective Sergeant McVeigh, how nice to see you again. When the assistant headmaster said you might be visiting us, I *insisted* on being allowed to escort you.'

Lucy thumped the car door shut, sealing Charlie inside. 'That's very kind.' Which was a *massive* lie, but Allegra didn't need to know that.

The three of them headed off through the archway, into the quad.

'Who's your friend?'

'Ah, yes, indeed.' The big lump stuck out a huge hand for her to shake as they marched along the path. 'Hugo. Lovely to meet you, et cetera, pleasure's all mine.'

Allegra shot her companion an indulgent smile. 'Hugo's my "academic brother"; the school pairs us up to—'

'I know what an academic brother is.' Lucy pointed at the ancient oak tree, now sporting a handful of small orange flags among the black and red ribbons. 'They've started Trencher Day early this year.'

See? I know how the school works just as well as you do, you precocious little shite.

'Yes. It's getting so *commercialized* these days, isn't it?' Precocious *and* sarcastic.

They turned onto the path to the Moonfall Gate.

'So what do you want to be when you grow up, Hugo?'

'Aha, "To be or not to be, that is the question!" as mine dear papa would say.'

'Hugo's going to follow in the family footsteps and run for Parliament, aren't you, Hugo?' It didn't sound as if Hugo had much of a say in it. 'He's going to lead the country, one day.'

'Indubitably!'

The Moonfall Gate loomed over them, its ancient stones carved with the faces of mythical beasts.

'Which country?'

Allegra frowned as they stepped out the other side, sounding genuinely surprised at the question. 'You know, I haven't decided, yet.'

They walked onto the playing fields in silence.

Given there were only thirteen kids accepted every year, nearly all of them must've been out here this morning. That would be, what, seventy-eight children in total? Half a dozen of them did laps of a professional-looking track, while a small troupe of five children, all dressed up in white karate outfits, went through a synchronized repertoire of moves and a very large man shouted things at them in Mandarin. Off in the middle distance, a trio of horses and riders headed out towards Holburn Forest for a hack. Leaving just enough kids for one game of cricket, one of rugby, and a five-a-side football match – the only spectators being a handful of teachers in their school uniforms.

Bit different from the rectangle of half-dead grass round the back of Moncuir Academy . . .

Here's what you could've won.

Allegra broke the silence, leading the way towards the nearest rugby pitch. 'I see you've managed to identify the Bloodsmith, Detective Sergeant McVeigh?'

'I . . .' That was a bit creepy, especially when the investigation hadn't released *who*'d been responsible for IDing Dr Christianson. Perhaps she just meant 'you' as in 'Police Scotland'? 'We did.'

'You're too modest. One of the victims' mothers was on the news this morning, telling everyone how brilliant you are.'

Urgh . . . Judith Thorburn strikes.

'We have to do a project in first term: "Inspirational characters in real life from whom we can garner important life lessons." I'd like to do mine about you, if you'd be happy with that?'

Hugo lolloped along at her side. 'I'm doing Alexander the Third of Macedon. Chap might've been a bit of a woofter, but he'd still conquered half the known world by the time he was thirty.'

Oh joy, just what society needed: another half-wit, homophobic, overprivileged tosser destined for greatness. As if there weren't enough of those already.

Yeah, Lucy was *definitely* spending too much time with the Dunk.

Allegra pointed towards the small knot of teachers watching the rugby match. 'Do you want to let the assistant headmaster know we have his guest, Hugo?'

'Yes. Indeed. Won't be a tick.' And he was off at a lumbering jog.

Lucy waited until he was out of earshot. 'So . . . boyfriend?'

A full-on laugh rang out into the sunshine. 'No. Hugo is many things, but my "boyfriend" is *not* one of them.'

'He thinks he is.'

'Hugo has connections. Leveraged properly, he really *could* go all the way to Bute House or Number Ten. With the right person to guide him.'

Over on the rugby pitch, a large girl with pale-brown hair scored a try.

'And let me guess: you're the right person?'

This time Allegra's smile looked genuine. 'As the saying goes: "If you'd be the power behind the throne, you must first find someone to sit in it."'

An eleven-year-old Machiavelli. How lovely.

'So, DS McVeigh, how *did* you find out who the Bloodsmith is?'

'I followed the evidence.'

They'd reached the edge of the pitch, where the large girl was lining up to convert her try. A *poooomph* and the ball sailed over the bar and between the goalposts, eliciting a cheer and a round of applause.

'Can I ask you a personal question, Detective Sergeant, as you asked about my relationship status with Hugo?'

'Depends.'

Now they were closer, the figure of Argyll McCaskill was easy to pick out from the other two teachers. One was a dumpy man with a florid face and a flat cap; his colleague had her hair in a shiny shoulder-length bob with a fringe that nearly covered her eyes. All three wearing their dark-grey suits and academic robes.

'When you left here, on Thursday, I looked you up online.'

Lucy could feel her shoulders being dragged down. No prizes for guessing where this was going. 'Did you now.' Picking up the pace a little.

'Not everyone would've survived if they'd been in your position. I'm pretty sure ninety-nine percent of them would be dead, because they lacked the intelligence and fortitude to do what had to be done.'

'It wasn't a *game*.' Not looking down at her.

'No, but it *was* a test: can you triumph against overwhelming odds, or will you let this horrible little man kill you?' Allegra skipped ahead, till she was in front of Lucy, then turned so she was going backwards at a matching pace. 'That's why I think you'd be great for my project. It's not enough to be a smart and confident woman in today's world, you have to be willing and *able* to take up arms against the predatory toxic masculinity and insidious rape culture endemic in our society.'

Ignore her, maybe she'll go away.

'You faced the ultimate expression of male violence against women, and you didn't just endure, you *crushed* it.' Allegra held up a hand, fingers splayed, then clenched it into a fist. Just like Gillian did on that horrible night. 'That's why I think you're so inspiring.'

The trio of spectators were just up ahead – Hugo standing off to one side, grinning away like a bear. He was already nearly as tall as Argyll. No doubt about it, when that kid finally finished growing, he'd be massive.

Lucy frowned at Allegra. 'Killing someone isn't inspiring, it's tragic.'

Allegra shook her head as they came to a halt. 'If it comes to kill-or-be-killed, always plan to be on the side that doesn't die.'

'Detective Sergeant McVeigh?' Argyll raised a hand. 'How nice to see you again.' As if this was all a big surprise and he hadn't sent Allegra and Hugo to fetch her.

'Assistant Headmaster McCaskill.'

'Excuse me.' He turned and frowned out at the pitch. 'WILKINSON! PASS THE BALL, FOR GOODNESS' SAKE, BOY! THERE *ARE* FIFTEEN PEOPLE ON THE TEAM, NOT JUST YOU!' He rolled his eyes and shared a wry smile with Lucy. 'We try teaching our students to be team players, but I tell you: it's an uphill struggle with some of them.'

Lucy and Argyll stood side by side as the game lumbered on in a scrappy, messy, not-a-lot-happening fashion – both teams being blissfully free from the twin burdens of skill and talent.

'So . . . you coach rugby now?' Lucy looked him up and down. 'Bit overdressed for it, aren't you? Thought a Saturday-morning kickabout would be more of a hoodie-and-jogging-bottoms deal.'

'That's the joy of being on the faculty – you always have to set a good example. And without wishing to be my own brass section, I understand it's important to impress the female of the species with tales of sporting prowess, so: there isn't a single activity going on today that I haven't coached over the years.'

One of the younger kids grabbed the ball from the grass at his feet and promptly dropped it again, making his whole team groan.

'Horse riding, football, athletics, karate, *and* cricket?'

A smile. 'Especially cricket. And I won trophies in my martial-arts days, thank you very much.' The smile vanished and he clapped his hands a couple of times. 'COME ON, DUNWOODY, RUN! YOU'LL NEVER GET ANYWHERE IF YOU DON'T PICK UP YOUR FEET!' Back to Lucy. 'So, Benedict Strachan.' A grimace curdled his features. 'I had a look at his file. Surprised he got as far as the entrance exam, to be honest. Not really our sort of student at all. OH, DO WATCH WHERE YOU'RE GOING, FITZROY-SMITH! Honestly, that boy's got the coordination of a drunken wildebeest. Of course we've come a long way since then; our analytical tools wouldn't let a substandard candidate like that through the preliminary round. He was *clearly* unstable.'

'Clearly?'

'As in: someone should have called social services. Going by his entrance essay, Benedict Strachan was a very disturbed little boy. Would you like to see?'

Damn right she would.

37

Argyll waved at the woman with the shiny bob. 'Mrs Blenkinsop, can you take over, here? I've promised Detective Sergeant McVeigh a tour of the facilities.'

'My pleasure, Assistant Headmaster. YOU THERE, FARQUHARSON JUNIOR, HANDS OUT OF YOUR POCKETS, GIRL! THIS IS A RUGBY GAME, NOT A PRIMARY-SCHOOL DISCO!'

The sounds of unenthusiastic running around faded into the background as Lucy followed Argyll back towards the school buildings. Leaving Allegra and her minion behind.

'Your Miss Dean-Edwards wants to do me as her first-term project. Apparently, I'm an "inspiration".'

'Well, you did make quite an impact on her with your first visit. That speech about not playing clever buggers with the police? She's applied your advice to her schoolwork, too.' He took hold of the front of his academic robes, like a barrister about to argue a case. 'It's only been a day and a half, and she's like a different person. You know what we were talking about the other day? About her playing chess in her head, and being a bit . . .' Pantomiming a shudder again. '*Completely* changed. Normally you'd have to break someone like Allegra down, then rebuild her from scratch, but you managed it in, what, half a dozen sentences?' He pulled one shoulder up. 'That sounds fairly inspirational to me.'

Hadn't stopped Allegra being a creepy little madam, though. Even if Argyll couldn't see through her sheep's clothing to the wolf beneath.

They walked back through the Moonfall Gate into the quadrangle.

'This way.' Leading her across to the same ancient tower as last time.

'Ten past nine's a bit early for lunch, but perhaps I could tempt you to a spot of brunch in the Teachers' Lounge afterwards? Our head chef worked at the Peat Inn, Moor Hall, *and* Le Gavroche.'

'I'm supposed to be working a murder inquiry.'

'Ah . . .' He wilted a little. 'Yes, of course, I quite understand. Priorities and all that.' Forcing a smile. 'The *Bloodsmith*. It was on the news this morning.'

Urgh . . . Why did he have to have those big brown puppy-dog eyes?

And it wasn't as if he'd been anything other than nice and kind and decent.

Lucy huffed out a long breath.

Come on, take a chance for once.

She glanced up at that disappointed face. 'But maybe we could take a rain check for when this is all over and life can return to normal? Or, at least, as normal as Oldcastle ever gets.'

'Yes, please!' There was a pause, then pink rushed up his cheeks. 'Actually, that might have come across as a little less cool and laid-back than I'd been hoping for.' He opened the door to the admin tower for her. 'Can we forget that bit and pretend that I was all suave instead?'

'Your secret's safe with me.'

There was no one on the reception desk to watch the pair of them climb the stairs past rank after rank of ex-pupil portraits, up to the second floor. Its small landing was festooned with yet more photos – arranged around a single door: 'RECORDS R–Z ~ STAFF ONLY'.

Argyll unlocked it. 'Now, you understand that I shouldn't really be showing you any of this? I shouldn't even be letting you *in* here. But I'm trusting you, OK?'

Two people in one day: first DI Tudor, now him. It was weirdly touching.

'Thank you' – giving Argyll's arm a small squeeze – 'I appreciate it.'

'Just don't tell anyone.' He pushed the door open, revealing a wall of . . . well, they were *like* filing cabinets, but instead of being shoulder height, they stretched all the way up to the high ceiling, forming an impenetrable barrier a couple of paces in. They weren't made out of beige-painted steel, either: they were crafted from wood and burnished to a red-brown sheen. There were more on the wall to either side of the door, creating a filing canyon with a marble-tiled floor.

Lucy followed him inside, craning her head back to take in the upper drawers. A black metal rail ran the length of the stack, just beneath the ceiling, with a steep ladder attached at the top by rollers. She let out a low whistle. 'I thought it'd be all computers in here.'

'St Nicholas College is very careful about its students' personal data. Too careful to leave it plugged into something that can be hacked from the other side of the world, or stolen on a USB stick.' There was another bank of ceiling-height cabinets against the end wall, and Argyll walked into the narrow valley between the two rows, running his finger along the panelled wood. It wasn't *quite* wide enough for the pair of them to walk side by side, so Lucy had to tag along behind.

The whole place smelled of cedarwood, beeswax furniture polish, and the faint smoky-sweet tang of pipe tobacco.

At the end of the row there was a ninety-degree left turn as the stacks followed the inner walls of the tower.

'Bit of a maze.'

He nodded. 'Our founding fathers had some interesting ideas about how to keep information safe.' Halfway down this side there was an opening through into another layer – more ceiling-high cabinets facing each other across a narrow strip of marble. '*Technically*, it doesn't qualify as a maze, but it does take a while to get your head around how to find anything. And every one of the four record rooms is laid out differently, because the aforementioned founding fathers were sadists.'

They were going back the way they'd come, past more and more wooden drawers, each one bearing a small hand-written label. Argyll took a left, a right, another right, a left . . . until finally they arrived at a small seating area complete with antique desk and modern office chair. It even had a view: a thin slice of the playing fields visible through a narrow window set into the thick tower walls.

'If you'd like to take a seat, I'll fetch Benedict's file for you.' Argyll pulled the chair out for her, then disappeared off into the stacks again.

Lucy wandered over to the nearest filing drawer and read the label. Then the one next to it: nothing exciting, just names. Only they didn't seem to be in any sensible order: 'SINCLAIR, HELEN' was wedged in between 'TANAKA, ICHIKA' and 'VOLKOVA-KOVALEVSKAYA, MIRO-SLAVA', with 'TEMPLETON-BAIN, DAVID (III)' next in line. You'd have to be *psychic* to find anything.

There didn't seem to be any distinction between boys and girls, though – no pink drawers and blue drawers – so that was something. Even an establishment as fusty as St Nick's had dragged itself into the twenty-first century.

Unfortunately, they were all locked. But that was OK. She was only here for Benedict Strachan's file.

Mind you, it'd be interesting to see what *hers* contained. And even more interesting to see what the school had to say about everyone's favourite Russian-embassy-staff-shagging idiot, Business Secretary Paul Rhynie. Bet the tabloids would love to get their hands on that.

And this floor was R to Z, so his file was bound to be in here . . . somewhere.

Lucy turned on the spot – the cabinets lining this small work area were only a fraction of the stacks that filled the place. Given the labyrinthine layout and completely random filing system, who knew how long it'd take to find Rhynie's school records?

She went back to the desk and sat in the office chair, setting its wheels squealing as they rolled on the polished tiles. Frowned out the narrow window. Couldn't quite see the rugby pitches from here, so no idea if creepy Allegra and her minion were still out there, watching the match. Or if she'd taken Hugo away to coach him in the grift and graft of British politics.

The Dunk would have a field day with that. Class warfare writ—

'Here we go.' Argyll reappeared, holding a manila folder in both hands. 'Now, before I give you this, we need to go through the school rules.'

'OK.'

'One: no food or drink in the record rooms. Two: only St Nicholas College staff allowed in here. Three: no files are to be removed from this room by anyone other than the headmaster or his duly appointed representative. Four: no files are to be removed from school grounds under *any* circumstances, and that includes copies – electronic or otherwise.'

She raised an eyebrow. 'Not even with a warrant?'

'Then we're into a whole different set of rules, policies, and procedures.'

Of course they were.

'So, if I find something that helps me catch Benedict Strachan before he kills again . . . ?'

'You either didn't find it here, or you get a warrant and come back so we can make it official.' Argyll held the file against his chest, crumpling his school tie. 'I can't *begin* to describe how much trouble I'd be in if anyone found out I was doing this.' Then he placed the file on the desk in front of her. 'But, like I said, I'm trusting you.'

'Understood.' Lucy opened the folder.

There was a fair bit of paper inside: maybe seventy or eighty pages? She slid it all out and flicked through the sheets. They'd kept every test Benedict had done as part of the entrance procedure – the same ones she'd taken, the year after – IQ test; EQ test; aptitude test; personality test; history, maths, science, and English tests. All of them filled out in black biro and an eleven-year-old's handwriting. Each one came with an evaluation by one or more staff members, commenting on Benedict as a prospective student and boarder.

She sorted it all into piles, pretty much covering the desktop. 'His mum and dad only live in the Wynd, why not commute?'

'We don't accept day-boys, or day-girls. If you come to St Nicholas, you're here full-time. It's the only way we can be sure our students get the full benefit of their education.'

Bet they said the same at Jonestown and Waco.

Lucy started at the beginning – the aptitude test.

Strange how the memory of taking it was so clear: what felt like hundreds of boys and girls, all crammed in with her, sitting in the draughty Grand Hall at their little wooden desks on their hard wooden chairs while a big clock *tick-tick-tick*ed down the terrifying seconds until their fate was decided. The scent of panic, deodorant, and linseed oil filling the air till it was so thick you could chew it.

Argyll looked over her shoulder. 'Ninety-six percent of all applicants fail the first test. When I reviewed Benedict's this morning, it was obvious he was struggling with issues.' Pointing. 'It's not so noticeable on the multiple-choice questions, but where he has to give actual written answers it's clear there's an undercurrent of tension to them. As if he's doing his best to hide some fairly unpalatable opinions, but he's proud of those opinions at the same time, if that makes sense?'

She frowned down at the test.

DESCRIBE A HORSE:

Horses are ungulates, but unlike rhinoceroses or giraffes, their evolution has been efficiently bent to the will of man, giving them an advantage over the more lowly creatures in their clade. Even though their numbers have not increased under human patronage to the same extent as pigs and sheep, their utility to mankind has largely saved them from consumption (with the exception of a small number of less intellectually advanced cultures, such as the French and Belgians).

'You got all that from this?'

'When you've been reviewing student applications for as long as I have, you get a sense for these things. That talk about "bending evolution to the will of man", and the casual racism towards French-speaking nations, all dressed up as scientific fact. It's got "red flag" written all over it, for me.' A shudder. 'Next thing you know he'll be asking the school library if they've got any books on eugenics, and taking an unhealthy interest in racism, antisemitism, and vivisection.' Argyll poked one of Lucy's piles of paper. 'You should read his "What I did over the summer holidays" essay. If that doesn't give you the heebie-jeebies, I don't know what—'

Vivaldi's 'Four Seasons' twiddled out from beneath Argyll's academic robe.

'Sorry.' He answered it, turning to face the stacks for a cheery 'Good morning, Myung-Hee, how can I help you?' Then one hand came up to massage his forehead and the smile disappeared from his voice. 'I see . . . Yes . . . OK . . . No, you did the right thing. I'll be there right away . . . Yes . . . Bye.' Argyll slipped the phone back in his pocket, stared up at the ceiling, and sagged. 'Someone's broken their arm on the football field, and given who their father is . . .' He pursed his lips. 'Well, let's not go into that, but I have to pop out for a minute and supervise. Are you going to be OK in here, on your own, bearing in mind you're *really* not supposed to be here at all?'

'I promise not to burn the place to the ground.'

He blinked at her, chin pulled in as if that might actually have been a possibility. 'Good. Er . . . No burning things.' And then he was off, the *clicker-clack* of his brogues on the marble tiles fading as he navigated the *technically*-not-a-maze. Then, finally, the faint hollow thump of the records-room door closing.

Right – first things first.

Lucy pulled out her own phone and fired up the camera, spreading Benedict's essay out to make it easier to—

'*What are you doing?*'

Shit.

She flinched hard in her chair, spinning around, setting the thing squealing.

'Oh, Detective Sergeant McVeigh . . .' Charlie closed his eyes and shook his head. 'What did the assistant headmaster *specifically* tell you?'

She whittled her voice down to a razor-edged whisper. 'How the hell did you get in here?'

'He said no copies to leave this room. That includes pictures on your phone, and you know that.'

'Nearly gave me a heart attack!'

'He trusted you.'

'I'm trying to catch Benedict Strachan before he kills someone else, OK?' She turned back to the desk, holding her mobile up to get a whole sheet of A4 on the screen. 'Watch the door.'

'What if he asks to check your phone?'

'Fine.' Lucy held out a hand. 'Give me yours, then.'

'Oh, no. I'm having nothing to do with this. Argyll *told* you how much trouble he'd be in if anyone found out he'd helped you!'

Back to the essay. 'Am I breaking any laws? No. So help me do my job and go watch the door.' The photo app made that annoying fake shutter sound, clicking away as she took both sides of every sheet. Then did the same with the teachers' comments.

'Is this what you do when someone tries to get close to you? You don't just push them away – you shove them down the stairs!'

Next up, the official evaluation: *click, click, click, click.*

'Come on, DS McVeigh, don't do this to him.'

'You're not watching the door, Charlie. You want to help, or not?'

Emotional Quotient test: *click, click, click, click, click.*

'God's sake . . . Apart from anything else, he's expecting you to *read* this stuff while he's away. What are you going to do when he gets back and asks you about it? Scroll through your phone?'

Yeah, Charlie maybe had a point about that.

She didn't need the maths test, or the multiple-choice bits, or the IQ test, as long as she had the teachers' notes – prompting another flurry of clicks.

She glanced up at him. 'How *did* you get in here?'

He hooked a thumb towards the nearest stack of filing drawers. 'I took the lift, like a civilized person. It wasn't locked.'

So much for the founding fathers' cunning plan to keep everything up here secret.

'Then you can sod off back the way you came, before someone catches you.'

'You're a very difficult person to save from themself, you know that, don't you?' Charlie gave a long rattling sigh, frowned at her like a disappointed parent, then turned and walked away, disappearing through the gap between two sets of filing cabinets. '*Don't say I didn't warn you . . .*'

Good riddance.

Lucy returned everything, except the 'What I did over the summer holidays' essay, to the folder. Sat back in her chair and read.

'Sorry, that took longer than I thought.' Argyll bustled into the small working area, bearing a wicker hamper – opening it to pull out two china mugs; a thermos; and a collection of sticky-looking pastries, safely cling-filmed to a plate. All of which got arranged on the desk. 'Thankfully, His Highness is going to be fine. Clean break, nothing complicated. I think our resident doctor was hoping for something more dramatic. He was an army surgeon in Iraq, and I always get the feeling he rather misses the excitement.'

Lucy eased her chair back on its squealing wheels and nodded at the hamper. 'What happened to rule number one?'

Argyll actually had a very nice smile. It went well with the whole boyish-charm thing he had going on. 'If you're going to break the rules, you might as well go to town.' The thermos top twisted off with a soft *poooom*, letting the bittersweet brown scent of coffee ooze out into the room. 'So, what did you think?' Not looking at her as he filled both mugs.

She picked up the essay. 'It's . . . *disturbed*. Disturbing? Thanks.' Accepting the proffered coffee. 'That kid had some serious issues. Still does.' She took a sip – rich and warm and just sharp enough to perk up a half-nine slump.

'He's got an IQ of one-seventy-five, so he's clearly an *exceptionally* bright kid, but some of the things he comes out with? I mean, take the anecdote about his neighbour's dog. It's obviously meant to be amusing, but—'

'Comes off as incredibly sinister. Yes. And the part where he's patrolling the neighbourhood to' – Lucy made air-quotes – ' "keep everyone safe", and ends up watching that couple having sex in a Ford Mondeo? Then "coincidentally" finds someone else at it, in their own home, with the blinds open. He's a peeper.'

'I'd put money on the man in the Mondeo being his father, and the woman not being his mother. You know what politicians are like.' Argyll unwrapped the pastries. 'Everything's lovely, but I can *particularly* recommend the millefeuille and the framboisier.'

Lucy helped herself to a custard slice. 'And the story about his mother falling down drunk, and his dad yelling at the neighbours . . .' It was tasty, but the crumbs of puff pastry went all down her top. 'It's a bit disloyal, isn't it? Think he's trying too hard to impress? Or maybe it's just genuine contempt for his parents?'

'Whichever it is, it's not something we consider a virtue at St Nicholas College. Throw in the flirtation with eugenics and racism and, as I said, I'm surprised his application wasn't rejected then and there.' Argyll nibbled on an eclair. 'The big question is: did any of that give you an idea of how to catch Benedict before he hurts someone else?'

Good question.

38

Argyll walked her to the car, hands clasped behind his back as if he was scared he might touch her by accident. 'It's been lovely seeing you again, Lucy.'

Wonder what would happen if he actually *had* tried physical contact. Maybe she'd be OK with it? Or maybe she'd put him into a full hammer-lock-and-bar, before smashing him against the pool car and slapping the cuffs on?

Kinda hard to tell . . .

Charlie was sitting in the passenger seat, frowning out at the pair of them. A disapproving maiden aunt in a cheap suit.

Wonderful.

'Thank you for your help, Argyll. And the picnic, of course.'

'Which we've *sworn* never to talk of again, on account of it being against the rules.'

'So we have.'

They stood there, both scuffing their feet on the gravel, while Charlie gave them the evil eye through the windscreen.

'Lucy, I wonder if—'

'If we find anything—'

A little light nervous laughter, as pink rushed up Argyll's neck and set his cheeks ablaze. 'Sorry, after you.'

You know what? Sod Charlie. 'Maybe I'll give you a call next week, if you're free?'

'Great! Well, I have a few things on, but I can *definitely* shuffle them around. And there's always Fandingo's, if you didn't like La Poule

Française? Or I could cook? I'm told I do a very passable *canard et échalotes au vin*?' All said with an earnest face, and that floppy fringe threatening to droop into his eyes at any moment.

Had to admit there was something weirdly appealing about him. Like a very posh, slightly awkward Labrador.

'We'll see.' Lucy leaned in and kissed him on the cheek, before turning and marching over to the pool car, where Charlie was clearly seething. Good. She thumped in behind the wheel and waved through the windscreen at Argyll.

He stood motionless, cheeks blazing.

More than 'slightly' awkward, then.

Lucy started the car, reversed, turned, and headed back down the long drive, past the porter's lodge – barrier up, its pugilistic operator nowhere to be seen.

Charlie shoogled around in his seat till he was scowling at her. 'Well?'

Argyll was still there, a tiny figure in the rear-view mirror, but he'd finally recovered enough motor control to wave at the departing car.

Lucy gave Charlie a haughty sniff. 'None of your business.'

'Possibly.' He transferred his scowl to the mirror. 'You know fine well Assistant Headmaster Argyll McCaskill is sweet on you. Think he'll be so keen if he finds out you betrayed his trust?'

She turned left, onto the main road, and put her foot down. 'I'm doing what needs to be done.'

'But then, betrayal's the order of the day, isn't it? I imagine, when DI Tudor said you could investigate whatever you liked, he *probably* thought you'd be out looking for the Bloodsmith, not wasting the whole morning on Benedict Strachan!'

'I've got DC Fraser working on background, OK? This is just me making good use of my time till he's done.'

The road was lined with hedgerows and trees, thickets of gorse spilling out their vivid-yellow blossoms.

'Benedict Strachan isn't your responsibility, Lucy, he's—'

'You *want* him to kill someone, is that it?'

A bus stop was nestled in at the side of the road, just up ahead, complete with ugly, rectangular plastic shelter. An old lady peered out of it at the pool car, as if hoping they were the number forty-seven.

'Of course I don't want him to kill—'

'Then get off my bloody case!' Lucy waggled the steering wheel from side to side as the car slowed. 'What the hell?' It drifted down to a walking pace, kangarooed forward in a teeth-rattling lurch, then stalled.

Lucy started the engine again. 'Why can't they ever service these damn things properly?' She put the car in gear and— 'Sodding hell.' The Vauxhall jerked to a halt again, six feet short of the bus stop.

'Have you tried pumping the clutch?'

She drummed her fingers on the steering wheel. Then tipped her head to one side. 'Charlie, when you left the car unattended for ages, even though I *specifically* asked you not to, did you check everything was OK before you got back in?'

'Why would I check the car?'

'Because I wouldn't put it past that creepy little madam, Allegra Dean-Edwards, to stick a potato up the exhaust pipe or something. Just to screw with us.'

He looked over his shoulder, as if he could somehow magically see through the back seats and car chassis. 'Does that even work?'

'Will you just *check*, please?'

'All right, all right.' He undid his seatbelt and climbed out into the sunshine. 'Because I'm fairly certain the whole potato-in-the-exhaust-pipe thing's an urban myth.'

The second his door closed she flicked on the central locking, cranked the engine back to life and put her foot down. Leaving him standing there in the middle of the road.

Sucker.

Who the hell did he think he was, lecturing *her* about leading Argyll on? Maybe she actually liked Argyll, had he thought about that? Of course not, he was too busy scrambling up on his moral high horse. It wasn't Lucy's fault life was complicated.

And yes, she'd probably get a bollocking for abandoning Charlie, but it's not as if she'd left him in the middle of nowhere, is it? There was a bus stop, right there.

Lucy clicked on the radio, found something cheery to listen to, and sang along.

Charlie would just have to find his own way back to DHQ.

*

In the same borrowed office as last time, Lucy pulled the room's manky chair over to the desk, sank into it, and powered up the saggy grey computer.

It'd taken some doing – a lot of fiddling, even more swearing, and a blistering headache – to get her new phone connected to the fancy printer on the fourth floor, but she now had her very own hard copy of everything she'd photographed back at St Nick's. It sat in neatly stacked piles as the computer chugged and bleeped away to itself.

She knocked back a couple of paracetamol, then logged in. Ejected the CD tray and slipped in the disk PC Manson had dropped off for her yesterday. The one with Benedict Strachan's interviews on it, and, with any luck, some CCTV footage too.

Clicking on the CD revealed nothing but video files. So no transcripts. And none of the files were named for what they actually were; instead each was marked with the case number followed by a hyphen and a bunch of random digits. Hopefully, ordering them by their last-modified date would put them into some sort of useable order.

She clicked on the oldest file first and a window popped up on the screen, showing grainy, night-time footage, taken from about eighteen feet off the ground. Going by the kebab shops, chippers, and pizza places, it was Harvest Lane – at 03:12:06, according to the timestamp in the bottom right corner. No sign of anyone, just the rain-slicked tarmac, shuttered shops, and a couple of lonely streetlights casting their sickly yellow glow over proceedings. A car slid past in complete silence, its headlights blowing the image out for a moment, but when that passed, two figures were clearly visible, walking across the screen. Not tall enough to be adults, both dressed in dark hoodies, dark baseball caps, dark joggy-bots, and bright-white trainers. Benedict Strachan and his unknown accomplice. They hurried through the shot and off the other side.

End of footage.

Well, that was worth the wait . . .

She called up the next file in line. The camera was a little further along Harvest Lane: a bookie's, another chip shop, and a tattoo parlour filling the screen – seen from a weird top-down angle that distorted everything. On came Benedict and his mate, shoulders hunched, walking fast, keeping their heads down. Looking about as suspicious as it was possible to be. They took a right at the junction, fading into the gloom between streetlights.

Her screen went blank again.

The third lot of footage was from Campbellmags Way, opposite Hallelujah Bingo – its shutters down and suspiciously free of graffiti for that part of town. Quarter past three in the morning, but the canopy above the doors was all lit up, the glowing white backboard boasting, in its red plastic moveable lettering: 'GREAT BIG PRIZES TO BE WON EVERY DAY!' The only thing out of place was the bundle of rags heaped up in the doorway, not much bigger than a coffin.

Right on cue, the two hoodies bustled into view. They crossed the street, stopping in front of the pile of debris. Stood there, looking up and down the road. Checking the coast was clear, even though there was a dirty-big security camera pointed straight at them from the other side of the road.

Idiots.

Then one of them rushed forwards and swung a trainer at the pile. Then another.

The second hoodie joined in, throwing punches as their mate kicked and stomped.

Jesus . . .

They were just children.

And it wasn't debris, it was a *person*. Liam Hay, thirty-one. Former bus driver for Oldcastle City Council, before depression and supermarket-brand vodka got their claws into him. Father of two – Pamela, seven, and Alex, nine – though he didn't have visiting rights. Ex-husband of Tracy Hogarth, who hadn't bothered turning up to identify Liam's body.

Benedict and his accomplice kept at it for nearly two minutes, then staggered onto the pavement again. Backs heaving, breath pluming above them in swathes of pale grey.

An arm flopped out of the doorway.

One more quick check to make sure no one was watching, and they snuck forward, grabbed hold of their victim and dragged him onto the road, leaving a trail of newspapers and bits of clothes and a sleeping bag and cardboard sheeting behind.

They hauled Liam up, then half carried, half dragged him around the corner of Hallelujah Bingo, onto Brokemere Street, out of view.

Next file: the camera was pointing along Brokemere, past a baker's, a dry cleaner's, the entrance to a set of flats, and a little place that did tailoring alterations. A small convenience store sat right at the very top left, its signage disappearing off the edge of the screen so only 'AMILY STORE' was visible.

Benedict and his accomplice wrestled Liam Hay along the pavement, then into the small alley that separated Angus MacBargain's Family Store and the tailor's.

Then nothing.

A speck of rain drifted by the camera. Then another one. And another. Until a slow steady fall turned the streetlights into glowing spheres of septic yellow.

Four minutes later, the two children lurched out onto the road again. One of them was clearly pumped: bouncing on the balls of their feet and punching the air. The other looked as if someone had just chained a couple of breeze blocks to their bowels.

Four minutes to stab someone *eighty-nine* times.

They stood on the tarmac, staring back into the alley, then the pair of them hurried away down Brokemere Street and vanished.

And that was it.

The next file wasn't CCTV footage, it was an interview room in what would've been Oldcastle Police Force Headquarters, before the big Police Scotland merger came along.

Benedict Strachan was framed in the middle of the shot – a small, hunched figure with deep dark bags under his eyes, spots on one side of his mouth, blond hair cut in a sensible short back and sides, freckles standing out like blood spatter against his pale skin. Bottom lip wobbling as he pulled off his glasses and rubbed away the tears.

He clearly hadn't been assigned a duty solicitor – the woman sitting next to him was far too well dressed for that, in her sharp suit and ninety-quid haircut.

Two police officers were sitting on the other side of the interview-room table, but because of where the camera was positioned, only the tops of their heads were showing – one fat and balding, one with a thick thatch of dishwater brown.

The dishwater-brown one did the time, date, and introductions in a hard no-nonsense tone, then she dropped into a much softer voice for, *'Do you understand why you're here, Benedict?'*

He nodded. Wiped at his eyes again.

'I'm afraid you have to say something; it's for the tape. In case someone can't see, OK?'

A sigh rattled out from the woman in the fancy suit. *'Can we get on with it, please, Detective Sergeant Massie? My client is well aware of his situation and his rights. He has prepared a statement, so if we can skip the—'*

'Come on, Phillipa' – the bald one poked the desk – *'you know how this works. We ask questions; Benedict gets the chance to put his side of the story.'*

'For clarification of all doubt, Detective Inspector Morrow, my client will be answering every single one of your questions with "no comment". So, if you want to go through the charade of asking them, go ahead and we'll see how much of each other's time we can all waste, shall we?'

Morrow patted DS Massie on the shoulder. *'In your own time, Rhona.'*

'Where were you last Friday, Benedict, at around three in the morning?'

Benedict looked up at his solicitor.

She nodded at him.

He blinked at DS Massie, then forced out a strangled, high-pitched, *'No comment.'*

And that's how it went for the next twenty minutes. Every single question, from *'Why did you kill Liam Hay?'* to *'Who was with you that night?'* and even *'Do you like Star Wars?'* was met the same way: *'No comment.'* Lucy had interviewed professional criminals who were less disciplined about it than Benedict Strachan was.

'Now, are we all done, DI Morrow? Can my client read his statement?'

'Urgh . . .' Morrow slumped in his seat. *'Might as well.'*

'All right, Benedict, like we practised.' She reached into her pocket, produced a sheet of paper, and handed it to him.

Benedict cleared his throat and read aloud, sounding every bit as young and scared as he looked. *' "My name is Benedict Samuel Strachan and last Friday morning I killed a homeless man. I did not know his name at the time, or who he was, but I now know him to be Liam Hay and I want to ex . . . express my deepest sympathy and regret to his family . . ."'* A huge sniff rattled out of the speakers as snot varnished Benedict's top lip. *' "I had no . . . no reason to do what . . . what I did. I am sorry. I never wanted to hurt anyone, but I have killed Liam Hay and I understand that I must face the consequences of my . . . actions."'* He took off his glasses and scrubbed his sleeve across his eyes.

'You're doing fine, Benedict. Get your breath.'

He could barely speak now, rattling it out between sobs. ' *"I do not know why I killed Liam Hay, but in order to . . . save his family . . . save his family the trauma of a trial . . . I . . ."'* Staring at his solicitor as if she was asking him to swallow a rancid toad.

'Almost there.'

' *"I wish to plead guilty to the murder of Liam Hay. I will not be making any . . . any further statements . . . or answering any further questions."'*

His solicitor plucked the statement from his trembling hands. *'Good boy.'*

Of course, DI Morrow and DS Massie tried to get him to ID his accomplice, or say where the kids had got the knives from, or where they'd ditched them, or why they'd stabbed Liam so many times . . . but Benedict Samuel Strachan wouldn't deviate from *'No comment.'*

The next video file wasn't any help – just DI Morrow and DS Massie, sitting opposite Benedict and his solicitor the next morning, trying to get him to say anything else and failing.

Lucy watched the first five minutes, then clicked the video through to triple speed, making everyone sound like chipmunks. She did the same with the last two sessions, then sat back in her chair, frowning at the blank screen.

Clearly Benedict hadn't written that statement himself, so it was probably the work of his expensive-looking solicitor. Only, normally, when a family shelled out a small fortune for someone like that to represent their kid, or wife, or husband, the lawyer did everything possible to get them off. Even if it meant bending the rules, twisting the truth, and threatening all sorts of legal repercussions if the accused wasn't released immediately.

So why had Benedict's lawyer just sat there and encouraged him to read out an unforced confession? OK, so the investigation had the kid's trainers with Liam Hay's DNA on them – a quick scrub with washing-up liquid not being all that efficient at removing microscopic traces of blood. Probably didn't want to throw out a brand-new pair of Nikes, or risk chucking them in a boil wash. And yes, they *also* had a whole bunch of circumstantial evidence against Benedict, and a witness statement from someone who'd been walking their dog down Brokemere Street that night, but *surely* a hot-shot solicitor wouldn't have let that get in the way.

Why just let him confess?

She opened up the last chunk of footage again and when DS Massie did the introductions, Lucy copied down the solicitor's name: Phillipa McKeever. Definitely heard of her somewhere before, but then if she was a high-flying criminal-defence lawyer, that wasn't exactly surprising. Might be worth giving her a shout – see if she remembered anything about Benedict and the murder – but given her interview-room performance, the chances of Ms McKeever breaching client confidentiality were about the same as the Dunk buying a pair of red trousers, becoming best friends with a merchant banker, and joining the Conservative Party.

And the confession wasn't the only thing . . . off about all this. The Benedict in the videos didn't really match the picture she'd got from his answers to the St Nicholas College tests. You'd think a kid who'd written an essay like that would've been less terrified. More defiant. More like a cold-hearted little monster and less like a scared little child.

More like Allegra.

39

'Thought you'd be in here.'

Lucy looked up and there was the Dunk, standing in the office doorway, holding two wax-paper cups that exuded the burnt-toffee scent of canteen coffee.

He eased the door closed behind him. 'How'd you get on?'

'Not sure. You?'

'Dr Christianson's not posted to any of his social media accounts since he took his leave of absence from the university. Before that: two, three tweets a day, half a dozen retweets, update on Facebook, couple of pictures on Instagram. After: tumbleweed.' The Dunk put one of the cups on the desk, then produced a Penguin biscuit from his leather jacket. 'Here, I definitely didn't pilfer these, either. They . . . Eww!' He snatched the biscuit back. 'Nope. Your hands are *filthy*.'

'Don't be daft, they're—'

'Manky. No chocolate biscuit till you wash your hands. We're not animals, Sarge.'

'There's nothing wrong with them. See?' She turned her hands palms up to show him . . . but he was right. Every single one of her fingertips was covered in little black smears, as if she'd been squashing spider legs. A tentative sniff didn't reveal anything. 'OK, maybe they could do with a *bit* of a wash.'

'Go. Before your coffee gets cold.'

Yeah . . . Might as well. In case it *was* something nasty.

She pointed one of the offending digits at her illicitly obtained printouts. 'While I'm away, read that lot.' Lucy left him to it while she headed for the ladies. No idea how she'd managed to get her fingers so dirty. It looked like biro, or something. But she hadn't used one. Well, unless . . .

What if she'd spaced out again? Only this time Dr McNaughton hadn't kicked it off with his horrible questions, which was worrying. Or maybe there was a biro on her borrowed desk, and she'd simply been fiddling with it, without realizing, while she'd watched the CCTV and interviews? That made a lot more sense.

Nothing to worry about at all.

She stomped her way to the stairwell, through the door, and into the toilets.

Someone sobbed quietly in one of the cubicles.

Probably best not to interfere, so Lucy washed her hands, scrubbing at her fingertips with her nails until at least some of the black ink shifted.

Whoever it was, they were still crying by the time Lucy had finished with the wheezy hand drier and thumped back into the corridor again, pulling out her phone and bringing up 'DCI ANDREW ROSS' on her contacts. Might not be a good idea to phone him out of the blue, but a text wouldn't hurt.

> Hi Boss,
> Did anything come back from the trace on Benedict Strachan's phone, or the obs on his dad's car?

SEND.

Lucy shoved back into her borrowed office. 'Well?'

The Dunk was slouched against the filing cabinet – beneath that photo of the Queen and the auld wifie – frowning away at a handful of A4 sheets. 'Give us a chance; you've only been gone five minutes.'

She gathered up the remaining printouts and slapped them against his chest. 'You can read the rest in the car.' Grabbed her overcoat and was out the door in twenty seconds, flat.

He caught up with her on the way down the stairs. Clutching both wax-paper cups. 'You think our Dr Christianson's holed up somewhere local, or further out?'

'Nothing in his social media about a caravan, or a mate's flat, or something?'

'Nope. Holidays are either taken in Corfu, where he's got a timeshare, or Brighton, where he's got a mate who writes crime novels. But he's not been to anywhere more exotic than Marks and Spencer since his wife died, five years ago.'

'Oh aye?'

'Been a homebody ever since. Does this big "I'm so sad and lonely" routine every year on the anniversary of her death.'

They made the last turn and clattered down the final flight of stairs.

'Suspicious?'

'Natural causes.' Holding out one of the cups. 'You want this or not?'

It tasted terrible, but better than nothing. 'Let me guess: his wife died of some sort of heart condition, waiting for a transplant match.'

'Nah. It'd be nice and neat, what with him hacking out his victims' tickers, but it was an aneurism. Dropped dead in the Asda car park.'

Lucy barged through the doors into the—

Froze.

Charlie from Professional Standards was standing at the other end of the corridor, hunched forwards, phone clutched to one ear, his free hand over the other, shutting out the screams echoing around the custody block. He was partially turned away, which meant he *probably* hadn't seen her yet.

Fingers crossed . . .

Lucy did a quick about-face and slipped into the locker room instead.

The Dunk hurried after her. 'Sarge, why are we—'

'Just keep moving, OK?' They clattered out the other side, into the corridor, wheeched past the muster room, and up a narrow staircase to the ground floor.

'Sarge, much as I love cloak-and-dagger stuff, it's—'

'Would you rather spend the rest of the day dragging some dick from Professional Standards around with us? Because that's what's on offer.' She entered the security code and pushed her way into Reception. Keeping up the pace till they were out through the main doors.

He was starting to go puce. 'Sarge, can we—'

'Shhhhh . . . !'

Eleven o'clock on a Saturday morning and the assembled media seemed to be half asleep. Certainly, none of them were awake enough to notice as she led the way across the front apron and down the steps onto Peel Place. Heading straight for the opposite side of the road and speeding up again. Putting a bit of distance between them and the cameras.

She didn't slow down until they'd made the turn onto Guild Street.

Where the Dunk promptly limped to a halt and partially collapsed against the wall of an all-night bakery. Grabbing at his side. 'Oh Christ . . . Argh . . . Oh Jesus, Mary, and buggery . . .'

Lucy gave him a minute. Drinking her horrible coffee while he wheezed. 'Where's Christianson's wife buried? We need to check: see if he's dug her up, trying to get his new hearts to fit.'

'Stitch . . .'

'Dunk!'

'Argh . . .' He levered himself upright, still clutching his side. 'Why do we always have to go everywhere at a bloody sprint?'

'Where – is – Christianson's – wife?'

'The North Sea. He scattered her ashes from the Aberdeen to Orkney ferry. Does the trip every year, writes a poem about how much he misses her, and posts it on Facebook. Told you he made a big thing of it.'

'Oh.' Well, at least they didn't have to worry about his wife's decomposing corpse mouldering away somewhere, like Norman Bates's mother.

The Dunk limped after Lucy all the way to her ugly-pink Bedford Rascal. He stopped on the pavement, face pinched, shoulders dipped, like a kicked puppy. '*Please* tell me we're not taking the Shagging Sausages Mobile.'

'It's this or we're lumbered with Professional Standards.' She unlocked both doors. 'Take your pick.'

'Urgh . . .'

Dr Christianson's house had been a lot tidier when Lucy had last set foot in here. The search team had left their usual trail of devastation: every drawer and cupboard ransacked, their contents left strewn about as if a hurricane had ripped through the place.

The Dunk clunked the front door shut behind him and grimaced at the mess. 'Where do we start?'

'Master bedroom, then work our way out from there.'

It was a tip, too.

'How?' The Dunk did a slow three-sixty, scowling at everything. 'How does *anyone* make this much mess?' Clothes were all over the floor, along with a few dozen books, and a couple of cuddly toys. He curled his lip and pulled on a pair of blue nitriles. 'You sure we can't just pretend they did a good job, and we don't have to go through everything again?'

'You're quite right, Dunk, because never in the history of O Division has a police search team overlooked something glaringly obvious that ended up being crucial to solving the case. They're the poster boys for professionalism, competence, and efficiency. What *was* I thinking?'

'Fair enough.' He plucked a pair of jeans from the carpet, going through the pockets before folding them neatly and laying them on top of the chest of drawers. 'One down . . .'

Lucy donned gloves of her own, and clambered inside the built-in wardrobe, going up on her tiptoes to peer over the top shelf. Empty. She stuck her hand out and bashed at the roof, then the sides, then the back. All sounded solid enough, so no hidden compartments. She did the same with the rest of the wardrobe, knocking and listening. Having a bash at pulling out the baseplate. Failing.

The Dunk seemed to be specializing in trousers, so Lucy went through the shirts and jumpers – the search team had chucked the hangers into a clattery pile in the corner, so everything she searched got hung up in the wardrobe.

'These chinos are hideous.' He went through the pockets of a perfectly normal pair of trousers. 'You know what I think?'

'Not everyone has to look as if they crawled out of a 1950s poetry recital, Dunk.' A cashmere hoodie went on the next hanger. It was in a pale shade of pink, with the sweet musky scent of a feminine perfume. Maybe it belonged to Christianson's late wife? Lucy's dad was probably not the only one who hoarded things like that.

'I was talking about Benedict Strachan's essay. It's . . . you know?'

'Of course I do, Dunk. I'm psychic, didn't you realize? I can tell exactly what you're thinking at any moment in time.' A couple of plain white shirts got hung up, too. 'Which is depressing.'

'If I'd handed in something like that at school, I'd be hauled up before the guidance teacher quicker than you could say "psych evaluation", "trouble at home", and "call a social worker".' Another pair of chinos got rummaged through.

'True.'

'So how come *none* of the teachers' notes scream, "DO NOT ACCEPT THIS HORRIBLE, FREAKY, *CREEPY* LITTLE KID INTO OUR NICE POSH SCHOOL!"? They're all talking about his sentence structure and good use of grammar, while completely ignoring the fact he's clearly psychotic.'

Lucy hung up a couple of feminine jumpers. 'You finding anything?'

'Only that Christianson's got terrible taste in clothes.' The Dunk made a disgusted gurgling noise. 'Cargo pants. Seriously?'

She searched all the pockets on a trio of denim shirts and added them to the wardrobe. 'Starting to think we're wasting our time here.'

'Can you imagine reading that essay and thinking, "Yeah, this kid's going to fit right in. Bet his roommates are going to have a ball with this one. No way they'll all end up murdered in their beds."'

More shirts. 'What did you think about the dog story?'

'Exactly.' The Dunk shuddered and added another pair of trousers to his pile. 'I wouldn't let Benedict Strachan babysit a dead hamster, after reading that.'

The last shirt joined the collection, then a couple of tank tops. 'His dad was a local politician: maybe the old man put a bit of pressure on so they'd admit Benedict?'

'Nah, posh twats like that don't take well to threats, especially from jumped-up little Hitlers like Ian Strachan. Bribery's more their thing. Bet he promised them favours with business rates and planning permission, that kinda thing.'

Lucy closed her now-full wardrobe and moved on to the bedside cabinet. Hauling the drawers all the way out to check underneath for anything secret taped there. Nope. 'If you had all of Oldcastle to hide in, where would you go?' Scooping up an armful of scattered socks and pants and stuffing them one at a time into the gaping drawers.

'Me? Jane Cooper's swanky apartment. I'd burrow myself in there like a tick on a dog's neck and never come out.'

'Yes, but we *know* about Jane Cooper, so Christianson can't do that.' She stuffed the last loose sock into the drawer. 'Help me flip the mattress.'

The Dunk did – the pair of them working their way around the outside, searching for little hidden compartments. Finding sod, and indeed, all.

'OK, well, maybe he's got another victim we haven't found yet?'

Lucy went through the discarded duvet cover and pillowcases. 'Risky. If someone reports them missing: next thing you know, Operation Maypole's kicking your door in.'

'There is that.'

They pulled the chest of drawers away from the wall, but it didn't have a false back, or anything trapped behind it.

The Dunk shoved it back into place again. 'Want to check under the carpet? Search team yanked it up anyway . . . ?'

'Not really, but we might as well be thorough.'

Fifteen minutes later they were giving the spare bedroom the same treatment, leaving it 2,000 percent tidier than it'd been before they started. Then the bathroom – including taking the front panel off the bath, and the medicine cabinet from the wall, after a judicious bit of unscrewing. Then the airing cupboard. Then the kitchen, living room, downstairs toilet. Then the attic. Until, finally, they both stood, clarted with dust and little shards of fibreglass insulation, in the garage.

The SEB had taken all the victims' boxes away, along with the jars of blood from the freezer. They'd left the lid up, though, so everything else in there was busy defrosting. Lazy sods. Lucy thumped it shut again as something angry growled in the gloom. 'Was that you?'

'Starving, Sarge.' The Dunk cupped his stomach in both hands. 'Got to be *well* past lunchtime by now.'

She checked her phone: quarter past two, and DCI Ross had got back to her.

> No movement on Ian Strachan's Audi. No sightings of
> Benedict Strachan either. No reports of murdered
> homeless people. 2 more days then I pull the obs.

Two days? Surprised he was prepared to stick with it that long. The operation must be costing him a fortune.

'Give the hall a quick rummage, would you? I need to make a call.'

She left the Dunk to it and marched back through the house, out into the back garden.

The search team had trampled the knee-high grass into submission, the flowerbeds all dug up till there was nothing but churned earth left. Maybe they thought Christianson had buried his victims' hearts out here? When it was obvious he must've taken the things with him.

Well, unless he'd cooked and eaten them . . .

Lucy pulled up her contacts and scrolled through to 'BENEDICT STRACHAN', pressed the call button as she paced the length of the garden. If he had any sense, he'd have ditched the phone by now, but you never knew.

A harsh electronic voice grated out at her: *'THE NUMBER YOU HAVE CALLED IS NOT AVAILABLE. PLEASE LEAVE A MESSAGE AFTER THE TONE.'*

Bleeeep.

'Benedict? I need your help, OK? Your mum's in trouble and I need you to help me help her. You don't want her to go through what you did, do you? In prison? It's—'

'Ahem.' A voice, right behind her. *'Thought you could give me the slip, did you? Again?'*

'JESUS!' She nearly dropped her phone, spinning around, free hand curled into a fist – ready to fly.

Charlie from Professional Standards stood there, wearing his bland little smile. Only now it had a sad edge to it. Like Argyll's smile, when he'd talked about his parents. 'Hello, Lucy.'

'STOP SNEAKING UP ON ME!'

He frowned at the house. 'I take it you didn't find anything?'

She jammed her phone back in her pocket. 'Seriously – you keep doing that, and sooner or later someone's going to knock your sodding teeth out!'

' "Violence is the last resort of a gentleman and the first resort of a rogue." Can't remember who said that.' He wandered down to the bottom of the garden, looking out over the rough fields and glum sheep. 'I'm worried about you, Lucy.'

Oh, here we go.

'Well, you don't have to, because—'

'Dr McNaughton thinks you're struggling. He thinks you're starting to unravel.'

She stiffened her back, folded her arms. Heat surging up her spine. 'Dr McNaughton is a prick.'

'He is.' A shrug. 'Doesn't make him wrong, though.'

High overhead, a buzzard wheeled its way across the sky.

The sheep murmured.

Charlie didn't move.

'God's sake, I'm *fine*! Better than fine: I identified the Bloodsmith, didn't I?'

'A long time ago, in a housing estate very much like this one, there lived a little girl called Lucy McVeigh. She was . . . troubled.'

'Oh, spare me your schlock psychology.'

'I did my homework, Lucy. They like us to be thorough in Professional Standards, you know that.' He nodded out at the sheep. 'This little girl had a next-door neighbour who was mean and grumpy all the time, and *he* had a dog. A big dog. A big dog whose name was Maximus, but Lucy called him Mr Bitey. Because that's the kind of dog he happened to be.'

'I don't have to listen to this.' She turned on her heel and stomped back towards the house.

'So, Lucy poisoned Mr Bitey.'

She stopped.

Silence.

'I did *not* poison someone's dog!'

A sigh. 'The neighbour wanted to press charges, but there wasn't enough evidence to do anything about it. Then, a couple of months later, Lucy's mother died. Coincidentally, she'd consumed a large quantity of rat poison, too.'

'You're lying.' The heat turned to ice, spreading out through Lucy's lungs. 'Mum had cancer; she wasn't poisoned!'

'Lucy's dad told everyone his wife had been depressed for months. Which was *sort of* true. She was pregnant, you see, so they thought it must've been antenatal depression; she couldn't cope, so she took her own life. But she didn't, did she?'

'Shut up.' Lucy's hands coiled into fists. 'Shut – your – lying – mouth.'

'Like I told you: I did my homework.' The soggy lawn squelched beneath his feet. 'When I said you identified with Benedict Strachan, I meant it. You and Benedict are a lot more alike than anyone else can ever know. That's why you're so obsessed with him. He's you.'

Everything trembled. Each word forced out between clenched teeth.

'I am *not* obsessed. We are *nothing* alike.' Spittle glowing in the sunlight. 'And I *didn't* kill my mother!'

'The only difference is: you got away with it.'

Her right fist lashed out, hard and fast, smashing straight into Charlie's nose, lifting him up off his feet and sending him sprawling on the trampled grass, blood spurting out in gobbets of bright red.

40

Lucy stormed through the kitchen, every muscle in her back twitching, jaw aching. Blood beating a thunderous rhythm in her throat and head.

'Sarge?' The Dunk stood in the doorway, holding a pile of junk mail. 'Are you OK? Only you look like you've seen a ghost.'

'AAAAAARGH!'

He jumped out of the way before she mowed him down.

'Sarge?'

'YOU CAN TELL THAT PRICK HE CAN SHOVE HIS INSIGHTS UP HIS ARSE AND SET FIRE TO THEM!' Thumping her way down the hall and wrenching the front door open.

'Sarge, are you all right?' Chasing her down the path to the kerb.

'No, Dunk, apparently I'm some sort of sodding monster!' Lucy clambered into her ugly-pink van and slammed the door shut again. Stabbed the key into the ignition. 'Lying BASTARD!'

'Sarge?'

She cranked the engine and jammed the Bedford Rascal into first, letting the gears scream in protest, because why should *she* have all the fun?

'Sarge!' The Dunk thumped his palm against the passenger window. 'You forgot to unlock my door!'

The van juddered into a messy three-point turn as the Dunk retreated to the safety of the pavement.

Behind him, Charlie emerged from Christianson's house, blood streaming down his face, arms waving about, as if that was going to make her heel, like a good doggie, so he could spout his crap again.

The Dunk looked back towards the house and Charlie gave him an exaggerated women-what-ya-gonna-do? shrug. Patronizing dick.

'Sarge!'

She put her foot down.

So Dr McNaughton thought she was *unravelling*, did he? Thought it was *OK* to go *blabbing* to Professional Standards and breach patient *confidentiality*? Thought he could *lie* about her being mentally ill? Thought she'd let him get *away* with that?

Well, he was in for a great big sodding shock.

Lucy blinked. Frowned. Then climbed out of the van onto rainbow-slicked setts. Wincing as an electric drill screeched hole after hole through her skull.

How . . . ?

She was on Woronieck Road again, down by Queen's Quay, where the dilapidated warehouses and boarded-up businesses were. Back in the same part of town where she'd chased Dr Christianson through that Polish meat-processing plant.

'Bastard . . .' That's what happened when you wound someone up to breaking point. When you lied to their face and dragged their dead mother into some sort of twisted fantasy. And if she was having an aneurism or a stroke, right now, it was bloody Charlie's fault.

Probably way too soon to have another lot of painkillers, *especially* a double dose, but she swallowed the last four paracetamols in the pack, shuddering as they caught halfway down.

Bet he was back at DHQ, squealing bloody murder to his boss at Professional Standards. *Look at my nose, look what she did to me! She's unhinged. Unbalanced. She can't be trusted. You have to suspend her. Throw her off the force!*

The air was thick with the iodine-and-diesel scent of the river, a sharp iron tang coming from somewhere upwind.

Her right hand throbbed – still curled in a fist – and when she forced it open, that set of keys sat in her palm. The ones she was meant to hand in to Lost and Found. All seven of their outlines pressed into the aching skin.

Well . . . maybe *she* should make a complaint about *him*. Go back to DHQ *right now* and tell everyone what an utter lying piece of shit Charlie was. See how *he* liked being on the receiving end of a Professional Standards investigation for a change.

Off in the distance, the *clang, clang, clang* of someone pounding metal with a big hammer rang out like a funeral bell.

Deep breath.

Lucy hissed it out.

Who the hell did he think he was, *lying* about her mother like that?

It was his own bloody fault she'd broken his nose. Lucky she hadn't broken his jaw as well.

Lucy turned and thunked back against the van's side.

Covered her face with her hands and groaned.

They were going to fire her, weren't they? Do her for assault, and fire her.

And all because of sodding Charlie.

'AAAAAAAAAAAAAAAARGH!'

She lowered her hands. Sagged.

The Bedford Rascal was parked outside what looked like an old chandler's warehouse – all the windows boarded up with mouldy bloated chipboard. A 'FOR SALE' sign drooped on rotting supports, sticking out from an upstairs window frame.

The only difference is: you got away with it.

Was it supposed to be some sort of *joke*?

Ha. Bloody. Ha.

The chandler's door was one of those steel-reinforced ones, peppered with rivets. The kind beloved of drug dealers on housing estates everywhere. And above it, carved into the red-brick frontage, was a lion's head. The weather and years had blurred its features, but it was still clearly a lion, its mouth open in a silent roar . . .

Lucy looked down at the keys in her hand. At the chunky silver one with 'DO NOT DUPLICATE' embossed on it; at the one that looked a bit like an anvil; the rectangular security key with dimples recessed into its straight blade; the three Yales, each with a different coloured plastic cap; and the old-fashioned barrel key – its thick round bow stamped with a crude lion's head; all bound together on a brass ring.

The lion was pretty much identical to the one above the door.

OK . . .

Well, that was self-explanatory, wasn't it? Someone with access to the chandler's dropped their keys, and she found them when she was here three days ago. No mystery there.

Lucy walked over and frowned at the door. It was far too modern to take an old-fashioned barrel key. But its Yale lock didn't accept any of the three colour-coded keys on the ring.

Still, no point giving up now.

She made her way along the front of the building and down the narrow alleyway that lay between it and another derelict warehouse. The gloom stank of old fish and motor oil, so strong she could taste it at the back of her throat.

A door lay at the end of the alley, partially hidden by a rusting display rack – like the ones dumped outside the printer's she'd chased the Bloodsmith past. Didn't take much to lever it out of the way.

That old lion-headed barrel key slid into the lock and turned, smooth as if it'd just been sprayed with WD40. *Click.* The door's hinges didn't even creak when she pushed it open, letting out the damp-grey fug of mould and mildew, laced with something sharper. Something unwell.

'HELLO? I FOUND YOUR KEYS!'

Lucy stepped through into a gloomy brick-lined corridor, where the only light oozed in from the alley behind her. She pulled out her phone and brought up the torch app, following its hard white circle deeper into the corridor. A couple of doors hung open, the rooms beyond filled with nothing but darkness, dust, mouse droppings, and mould. The corridor doglegged around to the right, ending in another door. This one was locked, but it took the same key as outside, swinging open on a wide flight of stone stairs, leading down.

No dust on the floor here – it'd been used recently.

She opened her mouth to shout, 'Hello?' again, then closed it. Maybe not the best of ideas to advertise her presence till she found out what she was dealing with here. Instead, Lucy crept down, and down, and down, until she had to be about the same level as the river – maybe even below that – where a third locked door awaited.

Yeah . . .

This probably wasn't the best situation for a lone police officer to be in. The sensible thing would be to give the Dunk a call and get some backup over here.

For what?

To help return a set of lost keys? Not exactly a number-one priority for Police Scotland, was it? Don't be such a wimp.

The lion key fitted this door, too, and it swung open on a long, low room that—

'Christ . . .' Lucy shrank back, free hand clamping over her nose and mouth as the stench of raw sewage and rancid BO stampeded out of the gloom.

She gagged.

Spluttered.

Blinked away the tears that sprang into her eyes.

Ducting and wires criss-crossed the ceiling, glinting in the torchlight. But someone had set up a kind of play office in the middle of the room, complete with a threadbare couch, a little coffee table, and a dead pot plant, all of which looked as if they'd been dragged out of a skip.

She stepped into the room, Cuban heels echoing back from the bare brick walls.

Something clinked and rattled in the darkness, beyond the torch's reach.

Lucy's stomach clenched. 'I'M A POLICE OFFICER!' Putting a bit of force behind it, as if that would cover up the tremble in her voice. 'ON THE GROUND NOW! HANDS WHERE I CAN SEE THEM!'

Assuming it was a human being making the noise and not a huge dog, of course.

Maybe backup wasn't such a bad idea after all?

A thin, croaking voice rustled out from the shadows. *'Lucy . . . Have you . . . Please, I'm so hungry . . .'* Coming from the same direction as the rattling.

She inched further into the room, torch held out in front of her. 'Who's there?'

A different voice this time, but right by her ear. *'Who do you think it is?'*

'AARGH!' She whirled around, free hand swinging a fist.

Thunk.

The blow reverberated up her arm as the person she'd hit went sprawling on the filthy concrete floor.

'POLICE! STAY DOWN!'

The torch beam caught a dark-grey suit and mousy blond hair. Charlie.

He rolled over onto his back and smiled up at her. 'We've been waiting for you.'

There wasn't a single mark on him – no sign of the broken nose she'd given him at Dr Christianson's house, not even a scratch where she'd punched him just now.

Charlie sat up. 'That wasn't very *professional*, DS McVeigh.' He stood, suit clean and neatly pressed, not so much as a smudge or crease on it. 'But it's all right, I'm not going to report you. I'm here to help.'

'Who the *hell* are you?'

'Have to admit I'm a bit hurt by that.' He wandered through the circle of torchlight, heading deeper into the room, towards those rattling noises. Disappearing into the darkness. *'Don't you want to see what all this has been building up to?'*

He was off his bloody head.

Seriously, properly insane.

And quite possibly dangerous.

Why the hell hadn't she brought an extendable baton down here with her? Or a can of pepper spray, or CS gas, or any sodding thing? Unless . . . She dug her hand into her overcoat pocket and yanked out the rape alarm DI Tudor had given her – the hundred-and-fifty-decibel one. Pointing it in the direction Charlie had gone, like an invisible sword.

Edging her way forwards, keeping the torchlight moving side to side like a search beam.

'Charlie? Are you feeling OK?'

His voice came slithering out of the pitch dark. *'Never better, DS McVeigh. Or do you think I should call you Lucy now? After all, we've got to know each other so well over these last few days . . .'*

Should've got backup. Why the hell didn't she call for backup?

She cleared her throat and kept moving. 'It's you, isn't it? You set all this up. Dr Christianson isn't the Bloodsmith, *you* are. You killed seven people and pinned it on him!'

'Six people, Lucy. Six, not seven.'

The torch beam hit something pale. A bare foot, its skin a grubby shade of charcoal. Then the whole body came into view. It was a man, stark naked, so thin he wasn't much more than a skeleton wrapped in tight pallid skin, peppered with bruises. Sharp cheekbones sat above a big, ragged beard – the hair around his high forehead long enough to curl down to just above his shoulders. Watery brown eyes squinting behind cracked round glasses. A twisted nose that looked as if someone had taken a hammer to it. He flinched back from the light, one bony hand coming up to shield himself from the glare. 'Please . . .' The knuckles were all swollen and twisted, the fingernails misshapen and caked with dried blood.

Thick chains were shackled around his wrists, another one around his neck, all bound together with a big padlock, the trailing edge leading to a loop of iron set into the floor next to a filthy stinking drain.

Lucy stared.

It was Dr John Christianson. A battered and starved version of him, but it was definitely him.

'How . . . ?'

Charlie appeared from the gloom behind him. 'Too much?'

The ragged figure reached for her with those distorted claws. 'Please, Lucy, I'm so *hungry* . . .'

'But you've been *following* me!'

'Lucy, I need you . . . I need you to listen to me.' Christianson pressed his misshapen hands together, as if in prayer. 'I'm sorry. I'm really, *really* sorry for everything I've done. I confess: I killed those people and I'm so, *so* sorry for saying you're unwell. You're not, I was *wrong*, I can see that now. It's all my fault.'

Lucy pulled her chin in. Took a shaky step closer. 'Are you two in this together?'

'But you came back! I didn't think you'd come back, you didn't leave me any food, and I'm so hungry . . .'

The stench was thick enough to chew. 'Came *back*?'

'You have got food, haven't you? I've been good! I've done everything you wanted!'

Lucy opened her mouth, then closed it again. 'I don't understand.'

Charlie stood behind the thin, grubby, starving Christianson. 'He's telling the truth, Lucy. You don't need to punish him any more. You just need to remember.'

She stared. 'You're supposed to be Professional Standards! How could you *do* this?'

'Lucy, please, I . . . just a little food. *Please!*'

'Dr Christianson has told you what he did to his victims, what he did with their hearts, many, many times, but soon as you walk out that door you forget, don't you? And the next time you come back, you . . .' A frown. ' "Torture" is such an *emotive* word, isn't it?'

'Jesus . . .'

'Lucy, I'm begging you: I've confessed, I've told you everything, please, just arrest me. Please. Arrest me and put me in prison. I'll plead guilty!' Tears made tracks through the grime on his skeletal cheeks, disappearing into that unkempt beard. 'I won't tell *anyone* about this. I won't, I *swear*!'

'He's even been trying to help you.' Charlie thumped his hands down on Christianson's naked shoulders. 'Talking through your issues and your problems; getting you to confront what happened with Neil Black. And, OK, he's only done it because he's terrified of you, and you hurt him if he doesn't, but he really *has* done everything he can. It's time to let him go.'

'*Please*, Lucy!'

'This is . . .' She backed away and the torchlight slid off the pair of them. 'You're . . . This is crazy. You're trying to make me think *I'm* crazy. Well, I'm not!'

'Poor Lucy.' Charlie stepped out of the darkness. 'If I tell you how you caught him, would that help?'

She stayed where she was, staring off into the gloom as Christianson moaned and sobbed.

Charlie smiled his bland little smile. 'Once upon a time, there was a brave detective sergeant, called Lucy McVeigh . . .'

41

Jane Cooper's flat is far too big and far too posh for one person. It must've been lovely, when she was alive, but the six months it's lain unoccupied have given it an abandoned, dusty air. Desperation just beginning to mingle with the first gritty hint of mildew.

Doesn't help that the SEB team left nearly every surface covered in a thin patina of fingerprint powder, the cupboards and wardrobes as gutted and empty as their owner – their contents scattered around the bedroom. Also like their owner.

Lucy wanders from the bleached remains of the bedroom to the ransacked study, to the bathroom, then the kitchen, before ending up in the living room with its impressive views over the sun-sparkled river.

She huffs out her cheeks. This is a complete waste of time.

Yes, but it's been fifteen months and they *still* have no clue who the Bloodsmith is. So a little clutching at straws isn't exactly unexpected.

Her footsteps echo, making the house sound even more empty. Well, not *empty*, empty: all of Jane Cooper's stuff's still here. Scattered all over the place by a search team that never tidies up after itself.

A small table lies on its side in the living room, tipped over and abandoned, the single drawer hanging out.

Lucy puts the thing back on its feet, scooping up the leaflets, and notepad, and pens, and various unidentifiable plastic things drawers like that always accumulate. And even though the search team will have been through every single one of them, she examines each piece before placing it back into the drawer and sliding it shut again.

Then frowns.

There was a leaflet . . .

She opens the drawer and pulls out the bits of paper, chucking away fliers for takeaways, and opera performances, and bookshop events, until she gets to the leaflet asking for people to take part in a study on loneliness. It's got a name scrawled on it, in blue biro: 'DR CHRISTIANSON', along with a local telephone number. Worth a go.

She calls it.

'Oldcastle Dundas University, Psychology Department.'

'I need to talk to a Dr Christianson?'

'One moment.'

After all, what did she have to lose?

'I'm sorry, Dr Christianson's working from home today, can someone else help you?'

'Don't suppose you can give me his address, can you?'

Lucy double-checks the address, then climbs out of her pool car into the blustery afternoon. The university might have a policy against telling random strangers where faculty members live, but a PNC search doesn't have any such qualms. Which is why she's standing in a nice cul-de-sac, on the edge of Castleview, that backs onto the glorious emerald riot of sunlit fields and trees.

She marches across the road and rings Dr Christianson's bell. Stands there with her face warming in the afternoon sun and waits for him to answer.

Finally, a man appears, dressed like a geography teacher, even though he's working from home.

She shows him her warrant card. 'Dr Christianson? Police. I need to have a word with you about someone who might've participated in one of your studies.'

He blinks at Lucy's ID, then at Lucy, then nods, turns and heads back inside, leaving the door open for her. 'I'm just making tea, if you want one?'

It's a nice enough kitchen, if you like faux-farmyard chintz – the welcoming scent of baking bread wafting out of the oven as Christianson busies himself brewing a pot of tea. 'I'm not sure if I'll be able to help you – I keep all my notes at the office. What was the name you were interested in?'

Lucy pulls her gaze away from the fields beyond the neat back garden. 'Cooper. Jane Cooper.'

'Cooper, Cooper, Cooper . . .' Topping up a little milk jug with a carton from the fridge. 'Doesn't ring a bell. But, as I said, all my notes are—'

'In the office.' The worktop is clarted with clichéd tat – ceramic cows and metal chickens and biscuit jars in the shape of cats. There's even a bowl moulded to look like a cabbage leaf, hosting a handful of coins, an electronic fob for the Skoda estate parked outside, and a small bundle of keys.

'Can I ask why you think this Jane Cooper was on one of my studies? Oh, and do you want a biscuit? I've got chocolate-covered ginger snaps – homemade, not bought?'

Seven of them, held together with a brass ring. One's a high-security key, with a straight blade and dimples recessed into it, like the key to Jane Cooper's swanky apartment. One has 'Do Not Duplicate' on it, like the key to Adam Holmes' cramped little rented flat. Three Yales, each with colour-coded caps – Abby Geddes, Bruce Malloch, and Craig Thorburn's homes all have Yale locks . . .

A sigh from behind her. 'I'm sorry.'

Lucy tenses – Dr Christianson's reflection in the kitchen window has a metal pan in his hand, raised like a hammer.

By the time she spins around, it's too late . . .

She wakes up choking, head pounding like it's full of dynamite and rock salt, concrete rough against her cheek.

'Unngh . . .' Lucy shoves one hand against the floor, sending pins and needles screaming up her whole arm as she flops over onto her back. Letting free a cry of pain that echoes against the exposed ducts and pipework suspended from the ceiling.

Her glasses are scratched, the pads digging into the side of her nose, but that's nothing compared to the searing agony as her brain tries to batter its way out of her skull.

Everything's the wrong way around.

What happened to the kitchen?

She'd been in a kitchen, hadn't she? At someone's house? Now she's in a large, low room with a manky couch and coffee table sitting in the middle of the space, beneath a single spotlight. The rest of the place is barely visible in the gloom, but it's far too big to be a garage.

'*Ah, you're awake. That's a shame.*' Someone fumbles with her jacket, hauling it off her. '*Shhh . . . It's OK. It'll all be over soon.*' A face swims into focus: high forehead fringed with brown hair, a beard, little round glasses. Dr Christianson. He grabs the hem of her stripy top and tugs it upwards, turning it inside out as he pulls it up over her arms and head, till she's lying there on the dusty concrete floor in jeans and bra.

'Don't . . .' The words are heavy and slippery in Lucy's mouth. 'Don't touch . . . me . . .'

'It's all right, Lucy, I know what happened to you from the papers, but I'm only taking off your clothes to make it easier to cut you open and remove your heart, OK? It's nothing sexual.' He folds her top and places it on her jacket, beside her boots and socks. 'And after that, you'll be *free*. No more worries, or troubles, or pain. No more being alone.' He squats down beside her again. 'Now, let's get those trousers off, and—'

'NO!' Her fist smashes into his face, hard enough to snap his head back like a gunshot.

He crashes into the manky couch, sending up a plume of dust that glows in the spotlight, both hands trembling in front of his face as blood courses from his ruined nose. 'Unnnnnnnnngh . . .'

And she's on top of him, pinning him to the dirty upholstery, fists raining down like mortar shells. 'DON'T TOUCH ME! DON'T EVER TOUCH ME!' Until he's nothing more than a rag doll, twitching each time a blow lands, bright-red bubbles popping between swollen lips.

Lucy scrambles off Dr Christianson and into her clothes again. Running, barefoot, out of the long low room, up a flight of stairs, down a mildew-stinking corridor, bursting through an old wooden door into the warm fresh air. Folding over and vomiting, one hand clutching her stomach, the other braced against her knee – holding her upright.

When she finally wipes away the last spiralling string of yellow-green saliva and straightens up, she's not in Castleview any more. She's standing outside an old brick building, looking across Kings River at MacKinnon Quay, with its collection of brightly coloured boats and ships. While the sound of an angle grinder screeches from a workshop, somewhere nearby.

Lucy huffs out a sour breath.

Then smiles a cold hard smile.

Turns around.

And heads back inside.

Charlie held his arms out, as if he was about to take a bow. 'And they all lived unhappily ever after. The end.'

'*Please, Lucy, I'm so hungry.*'

She stared into the gloom. 'Oh God . . .'

'So, you see, you've been coming here for ages. Asking the same questions, over and over. And Dr Christianson does his best to help you get better, even though you won't let him use his real name. He has to be Dr McNaughton, because that was your childhood therapist, remember? The one who spent all those years trying to fix you after Mum died? Who taught you that trick about smiling in the mirror?'

'I've been keeping him *prisoner*?' Backing away.

'*Arrest me! Please. Make it stop . . .*'

'Don't you think he's suffered enough, Lucy?'

Charlie was right: she *is* a monster.

Never mind getting fired, she'd go to jail for this. Or a psychiatric institution. Probably both.

'*Please, Lucy . . .*'

'You have to arrest him, Lucy. I know you can't trust him – he can promise to keep it secret, but when they get him alone he'll tell them all about what happened here. But that's OK, isn't it? This way you can get the help you need, and his victims' families can finally bury their loved ones.'

The dark room danced and swayed, then warm tears spilled out onto her cheeks.

'You owe it to the six people he killed.'

'Seven.' Scrubbing them away with the palm of her hand. 'He killed *seven* people.'

'Oh, Lucy . . . He's been chained up in here for nearly eight weeks, how could he murder Malcolm Louden?' Charlie pointed towards the back wall. 'It's six people. See?'

She let the torchlight drift upwards till something glinted in the darkness. More than one something. Stepping closer brought the beam near enough to pick out six large glass jars, like the ones pickled onions came in, only instead of little white spheres, each one of the six held a single human heart, surrounded by cloudy yellow-pink liquid. 'Oh Jesus . . .' She backed away.

Charlie followed her. 'I know it's hard, Lucy, but it's the right thing to do.'

'Lucy, don't go! Please don't go!'

'Who *are* you?' She pinned Charlie in the torch's glow.

'You know who I am.'

She jabbed the rape alarm at him. 'WHO ARE YOU?'

'I'm you.'

'Sarge?' It was the Dunk's voice, right in her ear. *'Sarge, you still there?'*

Lucy blinked. Where the hell . . .

It was a quiet residential street, the kind of place that had neat little gardens out front and bigger ones out back. The sound of small children playing somewhere nearby. Magpies cackling. A lawnmower humming. The sweet smoky scent of a barbecue in full swing.

'Sarge?'

'What? Yeah. Sorry.' When she turned around, the view dipped down towards Montgomery Park, with Kings River in the middle distance and Castle Hill on the other side. Which made *this* Blackwall Hill. She locked her knees to stop them giving way. 'Got a bit distracted there. What were we talking about?'

A sigh huffed out of the phone. *'You* abandoning *me at Dr Christianson's house. Are you sure you're OK? Only you've been acting even weirder since Benedict Strachan pushed you in front of that train. When you hit your head?'*

Lucy rubbed a hand across her eyes.

Maybe that's all this was: some sort of delayed concussion? She *didn't* have Dr Christianson locked up in an old chandler's warehouse down by Queen's Quay, and Charlie wasn't in on it. Because that really *would* be crazy. Benedict Strachan shoved her off the platform, she fell and bashed her head on one of the train tracks, and now she was . . . suffering from concussion. That's all.

Should've gone straight to A & E for an X-ray or an MRI. Could be walking around with a fractured skull and swelling on the brain for all anyone knew. It would certainly explain a lot. Like assaulting a member of Professional Standards.

'Sorry. For abandoning you. I wasn't . . . How angry was he?'

'Sarge?'

'Never mind.' She'd find out soon enough anyway. Concussion or not, Charlie was hardly going to look kindly on getting punched in the face. 'Where are you now?'

'*Back at the station. Got a bus.*'

You'd think Charlie would at least have given the Dunk a lift, but there you go. Probably too busy planning his revenge.

'Sorry.'

There was something . . . familiar about the street: the way it curved around to the right; the post box sitting at the bottom, where the road joined onto a cul-de-sac; the stubby two-storey houses with their pink-grey pantiles and faux-mullioned windows.

'*DCI Ross is looking for you. Says they got a couple of pings off Strachan's phone, but he's only turning it on for brief flashes, so they can't track him in real time.*'

'Right.'

Was this the street she grew up on? Well, until they took her into 'care', when Dad couldn't cope. Which meant she hadn't been back here since just after her sixth birthday.

'*And Tudor keeps asking for updates. Seems like our "roving brief" comes with a* really *short leash.*' He put on a nonchalant voice. '*You coming back anytime soon?*'

'Probably.'

'*Only, I was thinking, we know Christianson did a heap of psychological studies, right? What if they weren't all done at the university? What if he did some of them in the community? Might be some place he's still got access to.*'

'Thought you were bored of Operation Maypole and wanted a transfer.'

'*Yeah, but that was when we weren't getting anywhere. Now you and me have figured out who the Bloodsmith is, Tudor thinks we're the terrier's testicles. Imagine what it'll be like if we* catch *him? They'll probably put up a statue.*' Pause. '*So, what do you think? Worth chasing up other places he might've carried out studies?*'

She wandered uphill, towards number nine. 'Good idea. You should definitely speak to his department head and get back to me. And if she gives you any crap about it being Saturday, dangle the possibility of a post-mortem report in front of her.'

'*Sneaky. Like it.*'

'Thanks, Dunk.' Lucy hung up.

Number nine hadn't changed *all* that much. The tree in the front garden was much, much bigger, and the new owners had painted the door British Racing Green, and put a satellite dish up, but other than that: identical.

No point asking the people who lived there any questions, but the neighbours either side would surely know something.

When she rang the bell for number seven, it was answered by a flustered-looking woman in a hijab and 'KISS THE COOK!' apron, flour dusting one olive cheek.

'What?'

Lucy flashed her warrant card, keeping a finger over the name, just in case. 'Police. How long have you lived here?'

'Ten, eleven years? Is this about that racist wanker at number twenty-four again? We're *not* running an illegal sweatshop! You can come in and check if you like.' Throwing the door wide. 'You should be arresting him, not harassing us. We're not the ones getting stoned every weekend and playing heavy metal full blast at all hours!'

'OK' – backing away down the drive – 'number twenty-four. We'll definitely look into that. Sorry to bother you.'

'Good.' And the door thumped shut again.

A bright-yellow Volvo estate sat on the driveway outside number eleven, the boot partitioned from the back seats by a thin metal grille, the black carpet in there all furred up with white hairs. Lucy marched past it and rang the front-door bell.

Barking erupted on the other side of the door, hard and loud enough to make her retreat a couple of paces. God knew how big the dog was, but it sounded *huge*.

The clamour went on and on and on and on, until finally a fat old man in an Oldcastle Warriors top opened the door. Squinting at her through beer-bottle-bottom glasses that magnified his eyes like a manga character. No hair on his head, but plenty sprouting out the neck of his football top. 'Yes?' Then he turned his back on her for a moment. 'MINIMUS, QUIET! DADDY'S TALKING TO SOMEONE!' Scuffing around to face Lucy again. 'Sorry about that: she gets very excited when we have visitors.'

Lucy gave her warrant card another brief flash. 'Police. Have you lived here long?'

'Oh, years and years. We bought this place in . . . must've been eighty-two. Of course, back then it was all shiny and *new*. We were the very first family to move in.' A sigh. 'Our eldest's in Singapore now, married a local lass, and oh – my – God, you wouldn't believe how gorgeous our grand-kids are. Cute as buttons.'

'Great.' She jerked a thumb towards number nine. 'Do you remember a family, next door? Mother, father, little girl? Name of McVeigh.'

He stiffened. 'Oh, I remember Lucy McVeigh, all right.' Baring his teeth. 'Little horror burned down our shed, stole things from my garage, and she *poisoned* my Maximus! Killed him, stone dead! But would your lot do anything about it? No, they wouldn't. "She's just a child, Mr Denholm", "She didn't mean it, Mr Denholm." Rubbish!' Jabbing a finger at the house next door. 'She wasn't "just a child", she was a nasty, vicious, vindictive little *monster*.'

'I . . .' Lucy retreated a couple more steps.

'Then her mother "committed suicide", and if you believe that, I've got a monorail to sell you. I'm not surprised her father had a nervous breakdown.' He folded his fat little arms over his big fat chest. 'Best thing that ever happened around here was when those social workers came round, carted her off, and stuck her in a home. If there was any justice, it would've been borstal. For life.'

Inside, the dog launched into another barking fit.

Mr Denholm jerked his chin up, setting his jowls wobbling. 'So, what did she do, kill someone else? Because she killed that woman's son, didn't she? Neil Black. Smashed his head in. Is she on the run? Because if she is, and she shows her face round here, I'll set the dog on her!'

Lucy sat in the driver's seat of her dad's stupid Bedford Rascal, blinking at the phone in her hands. The screen wobbled and distorted, then a tear splashed against the display, and when she wiped it away the con-tacts list scrolled – down and down, getting slower till 'DR JOHN MCNAUGHTON' appeared.

She'd . . . had an episode, that's all.

Imagined all that stuff in the warehouse basement.

McNaughton would understand. He was a dick, but at least he'd try to help her.

She tapped his name, then the call button. Scrubbed a stripy forearm across her eyes as the phone rang. And rang. And rang.

None of it was real, and he'd help her. Like he always had.

Because he was a good man.

Deep down.

'ANSWER THE BLOODY PHONE!' Trembling, the new handset gripped tight in burning fingers.

More ringing.

Then a soft click, followed by a shaky woman's voice, old and kind. *'Hello?'*

'I need to speak to Dr McNaughton.'

Silence.

Lucy shifted in her seat. 'Hello? I said I need to speak to—'

'You again?' The voice lost its kindness and grew some claws. *'How many times do I have to tell you? Brian died six years ago. STOP CALLING THIS NUMBER!'* And the line went dead. The old woman had hung up on her.

Dr *Brian* McNaughton, not John. Of course it wasn't. She *knew* that. She'd seen him once a week for four years. Dr Brian McNaughton. The only man who ever really cared about a broken, damaged, twisted little girl.

Lucy clutched the phone to her chest, curling forward till her head grazed the steering wheel. Teeth clenched. Breath ragged in her throat. Pulse throbbing behind her eyes as the tears fell.

Oh God. It was all true . . .

42

'Penny for them.'

Lucy didn't need to look up to know who it was. 'Charlie.'

'Mind if I join you?' He squatted down, then sat, wiggling forward on his bum until he was right beside her, on the edge of the damp concrete walkway, legs dangling over the river, forearms resting on the middle railing. 'Something smells nice. When did you last eat?'

The scent of potatoes and garlic wafted over from the Tattie Shack as Shaky Dave got ready for the sneaky-chips-on-the-way-home-from-a-day's-shopping crowd.

A quick glance made sure this was the Charlie without a broken nose.

'You're not real, are you?' Staring out across the sun-flecked water at the blade of granite rearing up into the sky with the Old Castle's remains perched on top like a carrion crow. 'Benedict Strachan shoved me off the train station platform, I hit my head on the track, and now I've got some sort of brain damage . . .' A humour-free laugh barked out into the sunny afternoon. 'And Christianson battered me over the head too, didn't he? Two months ago.' Just before everyone started complaining about her acting strangely. Before the headaches and the blackouts. 'It's like scrambled egg in there. That's why I'm seeing things, because apparently having *blackouts* wasn't enough. It had to get worse.' Curling her lip. 'You're nothing but a delusion.'

'According to Dr Christianson, I'm an externalized projection of your psyche, remember? Or one element of it, anyway.' That bland smile of his clicked on. 'Your very own Jiminy Cricket.'

'Lovely.' She let her forehead thunk against the top rail. 'I've gone insane . . .'

'The human mind is a remarkable hunk of machinery, Lucy. Yours has been finding ways to help you cope with everything that's been going on. Why do you think you kept seeing Dr Christianson, out in the wild? It was showing you who to look for.' Charlie gave her shoulder a squeeze. 'And it's why *I'm* here. To help you.'

'And what about Dr Christianson? He a figment of my imagination, too?'

'Oh, no: he's real. Battered, bruised, broken, and starved half to death, but definitely real.'

She pressed her forehead against the rail, increasing the pressure until the skin throbbed. 'You were right, I'm a monster.'

'Come on, Lucy: you had a troubled childhood; you reacted the only way that made sense to you. It's not your fault things turned out the way they did.' A shrug. 'Did you kill Mr Denholm's dog with rat poison? Yes. But it was a horrible big brute of a thing, remember? Always lunging at the fence whenever you were out playing in the garden. Snarling and growling and barking its head off. You called it "Mr Bitey" for a reason, Lucy. That animal wasn't safe around children.'

A small bitter laugh snapped out of her. 'It certainly wasn't safe around me.' Deep breath. 'Did I really kill my mother?'

'What can you remember?'

Lucy took off her glasses, screwed her eyes shut, and pinched the bridge of her nose. 'I don't know. Fuzzy images of her shouting at me the whole time. Yelling and throwing things.' A sharp knot tied itself at the base of her throat. 'Is that why Dad had his breakdown? Because I killed her? He was . . . We used to be so close before Mum died, but he could barely look at me afterwards.'

They sat there in silence, listening to the clatter of pots and pans, and the tinny strains of something coming from a transistor radio in the distance.

Her voice was so small she could barely hear it. 'I'm going to prison, aren't I?'

'We need to tell DI Tudor where the Bloodsmith is, before it's too late. When the Dunk speaks to Dr Christianson's boss, she'll give him a list of all the outside venues the good doctor used for his research. He'll find out that the chandler's warehouse was part of a study on "sensory deprivation and its impact on fear-response mechanisms".' Charlie pointed across the water, off to the left, in the general direction of Queen's Quay, *just* visible beneath the rising arch of Dundas Bridge. 'And when DC Fraser goes charging round there to solve the case, what's he going to find?'

Nothing good.

She buried her face in her hands. 'God . . .'

The sound of a small child's laughter wafted over from Montgomery Park, behind them. It was joined by the crackle and fizz of chips frying in hot fat, coming from Shaky Dave's Tattie Shack, the mournful screams of wheeling seagulls, and the *lub-whump-lub-whump-lub-whump* of blood pounding in her ruined head.

'Come on, Lucy, it's the right thing to do. Tell them where he is, tell them you've been having blackouts and seeing things. You won't go to prison: you'll go to a hospital where they can *help* you.'

'What about the real you? The one I punched in the face?'

'There is no real me. Well, there used to be, but that was a long, long time ago. The Bloodsmith, and me, we're all in here.' Tapping Lucy on the forehead.

Next stop: padded cell, straitjacket, and all the tranquillizers she could eat.

Maybe it would be a relief?

Say goodbye to all of this . . .

Mind you, there was another way to do that.

After all, it wasn't as if anyone would miss her.

She rubbed at her aching skull. 'If you're me; if you can remember all this stuff that I can't – Dr Christianson, he confessed to everything? He's *definitely* the Bloodsmith?'

'One hundred percent.'

That was something, at least. What she'd done was horrible, but it had stopped him killing anyone else. Surely that counted?

'Why did he do it?'

The pans clattered. The seagulls shrieked. A truck rumbled by.

Then, finally: 'That's . . . complicated.' Charlie wriggled in place. 'Hold on, maybe this will help.' Grunting and straining, as if he was trying to herniate himself.

She turned, grimacing at him. 'What on earth are you . . .'

His face twisted and changed, getting longer and thinner as the hair receded up his forehead and turned brown, his dark-grey suit fading into a corduroy jacket and chinos. Until she was sitting next to the Bloodsmith. That bland smile turned into something far more lupine. 'Hey, Kiddo.'

'Jesus . . .' Flinching back.

'It's OK, I won't hurt you.' A wink. 'You want to know why I killed all those people? Well, why the *real* Dr Christianson killed them.'

Up close, he smelled of malt whisky and old cigars.

And he sat there, Mr Hyde to Charlie's Dr Jekyll, as if this was all perfectly natural and normal. As if she wasn't losing her mind.

Lucy blinked. Swallowed. Turned her head to look at the river instead. *Anything* other than him.

The Bloodsmith sighed. 'I wish there was an easy-to-understand explanation: a nice clean line from "A" to "B", but in real life there are all these tiny little steps in between that build and build and build, till you end up so far away from "A" that you can't even see it any more. Our motivations are *always* complicated. Truth is, he . . . I miss her.'

Lucy kept her eyes on the water. 'That's *it*?'

'Well, there's more to it than that, but deep down inside there's this aching void where she used to live.' The Bloodsmith's voice caught a little, thickening with pain. 'I know nothing is ever going to make that go away, but the human heart is full of love, Lucy. Sometimes it's constructive, sometimes it's not, but it's all love.'

'He . . . you killed seven people!'

'Six. Malcolm Louden was someone else's fault, remember?' There was a sad smile as he wiped away a tear. 'I don't *want* to kill them. I just don't want to feel like this any more. Why do you think I keep begging for help? Right up there, in three-foot-high letters, belting it out again and again, "HELP ME!"' The Bloodsmith sagged against the railing. 'And you keep *erasing* it.'

Lucy's phone *buzzzzzzz-ding*ed in her pocket.

She sat back and stared at him. 'What about the kidneys, the livers?'

'I assumed, if I could make you believe I was some sort of lunatic cannibal, it would skew your investigation in the wrong direction. Simple misdirection.'

At least their rambling forensic psychologist had got that bit right in her reports.

'Thought you *wanted* to be stopped.'

'Like I said: it's complicated.' He gave himself a little shake and wiped his eyes again. 'Anyway, do you want some chips? I think we should get some chips. Been a long time since breakfast.' The Bloodsmith wriggled his way back from the edge and stood. 'You must be starving.'

'I can't really tell . . .' But she got up anyway, brushed the grit off her jeans. Then followed him over to Shaky Dave's Tattie Shack and stared at the menu as a smirr of drizzle drifted down like a cold breath.

The man behind the counter was one of those big, Buddha types, with a short-sleeved shirt and a semi-white apron stretched across his barrel chest and stomach. Both hairy arms were solid with oriental tattoos. He smiled a wide indulgent smile at Lucy. 'What can I get you?'

'Chips?' She glanced at the Bloodsmith. Cleared her throat. 'Please.'

'One Kingsmeath salad, coming right up.' Shaky Dave plucked a couple of large tatties from underneath the counter and used one to point at the menu. 'You want them skin on, skin off, duck fat, dripping, vegetarian, dirty, cheesy, spicy, gravy, curry sauce, beany, or pickle-frenzy?'

'Whatever's best?'

'Excellent choice.' He grabbed a pen and a tiny pad, printed '#1 PFC&C' on it, tore off the top sheet and handed it to her. 'Normally I've got books of raffle tickets, but needs must. I'll give you a shout when your order's ready.'

He set to work with a knife as Lucy and the Bloodsmith made their way to the picnic tables – out of earshot.

They didn't sit.

'I know Charlie wants you to turn yourself in, Kiddo – let the police know what you've done with Dr Christianson. I'd like to make a counter-offer.' He bit his top lip, creases lining that high forehead of his. 'Yes, you *could* hand him in, and end up in a secure ward for the rest of your life, but what if we found some way to make him disappear instead? As long as you're in there first, with the Dunk, when you "discover" the chandler's warehouse, you can probably style out *some* of your DNA being there, but it probably wouldn't hurt to douse the place in petrol and set fire to it first. Singe away as much trace evidence as possible, even if dank, subterranean, brick dungeons don't burn very well.'

She stared out across the water again. 'I can't kill him.'

'Sure you can. It's like falling off a bicycle.' The Bloodsmith perched his bum on the edge of the picnic table. 'And you don't have to stab him, or anything physical like that. Poison would work just as well. It's not like he won't wolf down anything you give him, is it? And I'm sure your dad has something lurking in that old shed of his that would do the trick, sneaked into a couple of sandwiches.'

'I *can't* kill him!'

'If you don't, they're going to find him, and he's going to talk. Time's running out, Kiddo. You need to woman up.'

'*NUMBER ONE! PICKLE-FRENZY CHIPS AND CHEESE!*' Belted out across the car park, followed by the ridiculous *ding* of a hotel-reception-style bell.

'Trust me on this: Charlie is wrong. You need to kill Dr Christianson.'

'*. . . last track of the day. This is for Marion Taylor, from Baskerville and Morrison Accountants, in Logansferry, who's retiring after thirty-four years on the job. Good for you, Marion!*'

'You know, there's something that's just occurred to me.' The Bloodsmith sat in the passenger seat, peering out of the rain-spattered windscreen as they took a left at the roundabout, onto St Jasper's Lane. 'If I talk to you while you're interacting with other people, it's probably going to get a bit distracting, isn't it? Confusing, even.'

'*We've got the news coming up at five, then you lucky people better buckle up, because it's Crazy Colin's Weekend Drive-Time Club!*'

'I shall remain silent.' A tiny pause. 'Unless I have anything pertinent to add to the conversation, of course.'

'Charlie never talked this much.'

'True, but when he does it's all tedious moralizing, isn't it?'

'*Till then: happy retirement, Marion. Here's Catnip Jane and "Monster In Me" to play us out!*' A heavy guitar riff made the Bedford Rascal's speakers vibrate, completely out of time with the windscreen wipers' groan-and-thump.

'I'm a *much* better conversational companion.'

She suppressed a sigh, joining the queue of traffic backed up at the pedestrian crossing outside WHSmith.

He pointed. 'You're getting grease all over the steering wheel, by the way.'

That was the trouble with pickle-frenzy chips with cheese – very tasty, but they left their mark on everything. There was a thing of hand sanitizer squirrelled away in the door pocket of her Kia Picanto, a legacy of the Plague Times, but that was sod all use here. She peeled her right hand off the wheel and sooked at the fingertips, getting sharp vinegar and warming herbs, balanced on a raft of duck fat and smoked sea salt.

She went to have a sook at the left hand, too, then pulled back and frowned at the fingertips. In addition to the chip residue, two of her fingers were covered in black smears. More ink.

The Dunk would love that.

Must've been from the scrawled-on bit of paper Shaky Dave had handed over to mark her order.

Ah well, at least biro wasn't poisonous.

She sooked the last remnants of lunch off her fingertips.

Then sat there, gob hanging open. 'Wait a minute . . .'

A horn blared out from behind them as the cars in front disappeared off up the road.

'Lucy? We should be moving now.'

The biro on Shaky Dave's order note: it hadn't had time to dry properly before he handed it over. How long did biro take to dry – not the strokes, they were almost instantaneous, but the blobby bits where the pen's nib had rested a little too long – fifteen minutes? Half an hour, tops. It certainly wouldn't still be wet after sixteen-plus years.

She'd *assumed* there was a pen on the desk, when she'd watched the footage of Benedict Strachan's CCTV and interviews. But what if, instead, those smudges on her fingertips had come from the essay he was supposed to have written?

This time, the car horn behind them was joined by three or four others.

'Lucy?' The Bloodsmith patted her on the shoulder. 'Crossing's clear, we can go.'

'Right . . .' She accelerated away.

If the ink was still wet on Benedict Strachan's essay from *sixteen years ago*, something was very, *very* wrong at St Nicholas College. But then that was a big "if", wasn't it?

The song on the radio crash-bang-walloped to a halt.

'It's five o'clock, you're listening to Castlewave FM, and here's the news read by Gabrielle Downie . . .'

What if she was imagining it? Maybe it was yet another one of her delusional symptoms? The result of a cracked skull.

'The Metropolitan Police have confirmed that the journalist who broke the Paul Rhynie sex scandal was found dead at his London home this morning. Patrick Howden had been a vocal critic of the Business Secretary's handling of various contracts awarded to . . .'

Maybe she should drive straight round to Accident and Emergency? Get herself admitted for some antipsychotics and an MRI scan.

'. . . confirmed that Howden's death is not being treated as suspicious. United States now, and tensions are running high after an explosion at the campaign headquarters of right-wing think tank "The 1791 Patriot Association" killed four and left dozens wounded. The think tank's links to white supremacists are seen by many as . . .'

There was a way to check, though – the photos she'd taken of the essay. If they were all smudged, that would mean something, wouldn't it? Or would it just prove that Benedict Strachan was a messy child? Maybe.

'. . . appealed for calm. This afternoon Assistant Chief Constable Findlay Cormac-Fordyce confirmed that local police are looking for a Dr John Christianson in connection with a series of murders in the city . . .'

The Bloodsmith sucked a breath in through his teeth. 'They're going to find out about that chandler's warehouse sooner rather than later, Kiddo. I know you don't like it, but we need to get this done.'

But why would anyone fake the 'What I did over the summer holidays' essay written by a little boy sixteen years ago?

43

Lucy sat behind her borrowed desk, working her way through the print-outs of Benedict's essay. Slow and steady. Ringing every smudge with a swoop of red biro. Not that it necessarily meant anything. Just because the pages had a few smudges on them, didn't mean it was *her* that had smudged them. They could've been smudged years ago. There was no way to tell.

She slumped back in her seat.

Stared up at the manky ceiling tiles.

That sodding headache had returned, pulsing away as though something horrible was trapped inside her skull, *breathing*. And she was all out of painkillers. Didn't matter that she'd already had much more than the recommended daily dose of paracetamol and aspirin.

Just have to struggle on, till she could buy some more.

She picked up the essay again. Skimmed through the bit about the neighbour's dog for the fourth time since getting back to DHQ. How could anyone read that and not realize Benedict Strachan was a monster? But he wasn't the only one, was he?

OK, so perhaps she could *maybe* believe she'd poisoned Mr Denholm's dog, *accidentally*, when she'd been little, but her mother? It couldn't be true – if Mum had been poisoned, it would've left a trail, wouldn't it? An investigation: interview notes, post-mortem reports, door-to-doors, findings and conclusions.

She powered up the office computer and logged in. Sent a search creaking its way through the system. Sat back and waited for the results to come in. And waited. And waited.

Urgh . . .

Where was the Dunk when you needed him? He could always get this sodding stuff to work.

'*Ahem?*'

She sagged. 'What *now?*'

The Bloodsmith settled onto the edge of her desk and rummaged through the printouts of Benedict's essay. 'One thing occurs to me that you appear to have overlooked, Kiddo.' He held up the first sheet of A4. Three or four smudges around the outside of the page were ringed in red. 'Want to take a guess?'

'I never thought losing my marbles would be this annoying.'

He rolled his eyes. 'I'm a manifestation of your subconscious, remember? So if I'm sitting here, annoying you, it's because you're trying to tell yourself something.'

A long breath rattled out of her. 'Go on then.'

'How many smudges do you see on this page?'

'Four. I circled the bloody things.'

'Exactly. Four smudges, all around the outside of the paper.' He placed the printout in front of her and held up the next one. 'What about now?'

'Three.'

'Well done.' That sheet went beside its mate. 'And this one?'

She snatched the third printout from his hands. 'Are you finished?'

'OK.' He nodded. 'Let's approach this another way: remember when Benedict came in here, on Wednesday, and he was really struggling to smooth out the article he'd torn from the newspaper?'

'Well, it can't have been easy – they broke his left arm, and he's left . . .' She looked down at the sheet of paper, crumpled up in her fingers. 'Benedict Strachan's left-handed.'

'And if there's one thing we know about the world, it's that it's really not set up for left-handed people. When right-handed people write, their hand moves *away* from the letters they've just put down; a left-hander's has to drag its way across everything they've written. But we're supposed to believe an eleven-year-old Benedict can write twelve sides of A4, in a timed exam, and not smudge at least *some* of the words in the middle?'

'Benedict Strachan didn't write this.' That's why it felt so out of character: the frightened little boy in the interview room didn't fit. It wasn't him. She sat back in her chair. 'Son of a bitch.'

The Bloodsmith poked her in the shoulder, voice bitter as battery acid. 'Argyll *lied* to you. All that nonsense about how *troubled* Benedict was, about the *eugenics* and *racism*, when he'd faked the whole thing!' Another poke. 'Argyll thinks you're an idiot. Thinks you'll believe his *lies*.' Poke. 'Bet he's laughing at you, right now. He's sitting in his office, *laughing*, telling all his friends how he put one over on stupid, moronic, gullible old Lucy McVeigh.' Poke. 'Are you going to let him get away with that?'

The poking finger came up again, but Lucy slapped it away. 'Bastard.' She dragged out her phone. One unread text message, a missed call. Neither was from Argyll, so she went straight to her contacts and found his number. St Nick's assistant headmaster was about to get a nasty shock.

'That's right: call him.' The Bloodsmith smiled his wolf-like smile. 'Tell him we're coming for him. Tell him we're going to make him suffer, the way we made Dr Christianson suffer. Tell him—'

'Shut up.' She jabbed the button, setting it ringing.

Argyll must've been hovering over his phone, because he picked up almost immediately. *'Lucy? How lovely to hear from you so soon. Did the lure of my canard et échalotes au vin prove too much to—'*

'Were you in on it?'

Silence from the other end of the phone.

The computer finally chugged out a response to her query.

'In on what, Lucy?' Doing his best to sound reasonable. *'I've no idea what you're—'*

'Bet you thought you'd been so clever.'

Turned out there *had* been an investigation when Mum died – the screen was full of links to file numbers and document IDs. Sodding hell. The police didn't investigate when someone died of breast cancer, they did that when there were suspicious circumstances. They did that when someone was murdered.

What if Charlie was right?

'Lucy, are you feeling OK? Sometimes, after a blow to the back of the head, people can get a bit . . . confused about things.'

She copied the case number into her notebook, turning her voice into a snarl. 'You did a great job, really convincing.'

'Have you seen a doctor, because I'm worried—'

'But you forgot one thing, Argyll: Benedict Strachan's left-handed.'

Silence.

She gathered up her printouts, stood, and powered down the computer.

'I'm sorry, Lucy, but I don't understand what that has to do with anything. He pushed you in front of a train; what if your head injury is worse than you think? Have you been feeling dizzy, or sick at all?'

'You lied to me!' Grabbing her overcoat off the rack by the door.

'Lucy, I don't know what you think has happened, but I can assure you, I've not done anything – I wouldn't do anything to hurt you. That's why I think you maybe need to get some help. I've got friends at Castle Hill Infirmary; we could get you seen right away. It's—'

She hung up and thumped out through the door, storming down the corridor.

How stupid did he think she was?

Round the corner, onto the stairs, heels chattering against the concrete steps.

She reached the bottom, just in time to see the double doors through to the custody suite bump open and the Dunk bustle in, water dripping from his dark-grey leather jacket.

'Hi, Sarge.' He took off his soggy bunnet. 'Spoke to Professor Rattray: she's on a weekend break in Birmingham and, shockingly enough, forgot to pack details of where Christianson did every single one of his research studies. But . . .' Dragging it out. 'She said there might be someone knocking about at the department, you know, if they had a deadline on, so I headed up there.' The Dunk gave himself a shake, like an oversized black terrier.

Lucy did her best not to look as if she was holding her breath. 'Any joy?'

'Nah. Place was locked up tighter than a millionaire's wallet. We're out of luck till the university opens on Monday morning.'

Thank God for that.

The Bloodsmith emerged from the stairwell, hands in his corduroy jacket pockets. 'Which means we've got thirty-eight hours till DC Fraser here speaks to someone at the Psychology Department and finds out about the chandler's warehouse.'

The Dunk raised his eyebrows at her. 'We off out again?' Sounding hopeful that the answer would be no.

And let's face it, she didn't want him tagging along.

'Shift finished thirty minutes ago, Dunk. Got one wee job for you, then you can sod off home.' She dug out her notebook and flipped back a few pages. 'Phillipa McKeever was Benedict Strachan's solicitor: Puller, Finch, and McKeever Advocates. I want to know why she let him confess to Liam Hay's murder. Why didn't she even *try* to get him off? You know the drill.' The notebook went back in her pocket. 'And as it's Sunday tomorrow, let's call it . . . half ten start?'

A smile split the Dunk's fat wee face. 'Cheers, Sarge.'

Behind him, the Bloodsmith shot out his wrist and tapped a finger against his watch, one eyebrow raised. Was that going to give them enough time to sort out Dr John Christianson?

'Actually, let's make it noon, Dunk. Pretend we're civilized human beings for once.' Hooking a thumb over her shoulder at the stairs: 'Off you go.'

He scurried away up the stairwell, leaving soggy little footprints.

'So, where are we going, Kiddo? Off to fill some jerrycans with petrol and burn away any trace evidence?'

'Yes, because what we *really* need at this point is footage of me filling jerrycans at a petrol station just before a fire breaks out. I'll top up the van on the way to R & P: we can siphon some out when we get home.' It was a shame the Bedford Rascal was bright sodding pink, so not all that great for clandestine operations, but there was nothing she could do about that.

Sometimes you just had to work with what you had.

There was no sign of PC Manson in the Records and Productions Store. Instead, a small dumpy constable with a Lego-bob haircut wheezed his way out of the darkness and thumped a cardboard file box down on the table. Wiped a hand across his sweaty forehead. 'OK. Pfff . . .' Then sank into a folding chair. 'Surely it's the right box *this* time!'

Lucy slid the thing through the hatch in the chain-link fence, pulled the lid off, and peered inside. The case numbers actually matched. 'We have a winner.'

'Thank Christ for that . . .' He wafted a couple of evidence bags in front of his face, as a makeshift fan.

She emptied the contents out onto the table. Probably best not to start with the post-mortem photographs. Instead, she flipped to the two-page summary included with the Procurator Fiscal's official decision, skimming through the usual police arse-covering doublespeak to the important bit:

> . . . and while the toxicology report shows Harriet McVeigh had a significant quantity of brodifacoum, difenacoum, and fluoxetine in both her stomach and bloodstream [see Appendix A], the possibility of self-harm can not be ruled out in this case. The deceased's husband has repeatedly stated that Harriet was still in considerable distress following the death of her son earlier in the year and interviews with doctors at the Blackwall Hill Medical Centre confirmed that she was being treated for clinical depression [with the selective serotonin reuptake inhibitor, fluoxetine].
>
> The rodenticides brodifacoum [more commonly known as 'Formula "B"'] and difenacoum were both present in the family home, due to an ongoing rodent problem that Kevin McVeigh was unable to bring under control.
>
> Allegations made by the neighbours [see Appendix D] appear to be malicious and part of a sustained campaign of harassment against the McVeigh family, after an acrimonious boundary dispute some years before.
>
> It is considered highly likely that the stress of losing her son, along with a difficult pregnancy and antenatal depression, drove Harriet McVeigh to take her own life . . .

Lucy read the report twice. Then placed it back in its folder. And returned it to the box.

Stared off into the gloomy warehouse.

The stress of losing her son?

All these years she'd been told she was an only child and that Mum had died of cancer, but there it was in black-and-white official police talk. Her mother really *had* been poisoned.

The Bloodsmith placed a hand on Lucy's shoulder – warmth leaching through into her skin. 'They didn't find any grounds for prosecution.'

'She was pregnant . . .'

'I know.'

The fat little constable looked up from his fanning. 'What?'

'Nothing.' Lucy put the lid back on and slid the box through the hole again. 'Thanks.'

'Are you sure you don't want to read the PM report, Lucy? How about your dad's statement? That might tell you something?'

'No. I've seen more than enough.'

The PC nodded. 'Glad to be of service.' Then he groaned himself out of his seat, picked up the box, and humped it off into the darkness from whence it came, leaving her alone with her delusions.

'Lucy, the important thing is that no one said *you* did it, did they?' A shrug. 'Well, that fat onanist Denholm did, but no one believed him. Perhaps, after we've dealt with Dr Christianson, we should consider paying him another visit. Teach him to mind his own business and not slander people . . . ?'

Her voice was barely more than a whisper. 'I killed her.'

'There's no proof you—'

'I killed Mr Denholm's dog with rat poison! You think it's a *coincidence* Mum died of the same thing? I killed her.'

'You were only five, Lucy. After all this time, does it really matter? What would it change?' The Bloodsmith wrapped his arms around her and held her tight, her forehead pressed against his chest. 'Shhh . . . It's OK.'

'I'm a monster.'

A light kiss brushed the top of her head. 'You're amazing. You're smart and funny and clever and you don't give up. Whoever you were, that's not who you are *now*.' There was a pause. 'Unless you want it to be, of course?'

No. She didn't.

Lucy spat a bitter mouthful of saliva-and-unleaded out into the back garden. She'd parked Dad's Bedford Rascal in the garage, shutting the door so the neighbours couldn't watch as she filled three ancient metal jerrycans from the van's fuel tank.

The Bloodsmith nodded. 'Excellent job. Now, all we need is something to act as a fuse and we'll be ready to go.'

She went into the house, returning with an empty bottle that used to contain elderberry and pomegranate cordial. Filled it up from one of the jerrycans, screwed the top on tight, and tied a rag around its neck. Then loaded it and the jerrycans into the van, snapped off her blue nitrile gloves, and headed back inside.

Sitting on the kitchen worktop, her phone launched into its bland ringtone – the name 'Argyll McCaskill' glowing in the middle of the screen. She didn't answer it. Marched through the hall and into the lounge instead.

She stood in the middle of the room, with its massive murder board, staring at the victims and the suspects and the notes and the Post-its and the hours and hours of work and study and worry and trying to figure out what was going on and who the Bloodsmith was, when all the time she had Dr John Christianson locked up in a chandler's *sodding* warehouse.

The Bloodsmith stalked in after her. He dug Dad's secret stash of cigars out from under the sofa. Rolled one back and forth in his fingers. Sniffed it. Smiled. 'My favourite brand.' Then lit the thing, puffing out a thick veil of pungent smoke as he watched her like a cat watches a wounded bird. 'You're very quiet, Lucy. Are you feeling all right?'

'No.' Grinding her teeth. Hands clenched into aching fists. 'It's all lies, isn't it? All of it.'

'Lucy, you—'

'I'm driving around in that crappy Bedford Rascal because you slashed my tyres. Only you didn't slash them, did you? Because you're not *real*. It was *me*.' Getting louder with every word. Blood pounding in her throat. Headache screaming. 'I did it. *I* slashed *my own* tyres; I cut the sodding telephone line, what, just to *sabotage* myself? BECAUSE LIFE WASN'T *HARD* ENOUGH?'

He tried to take her hand, but she jerked it away.

'Lucy, I know it's confusing, but you need to—'

'AAAAAAAAAAAAAAAAAAAAAAAAAAAAAAAAAAARGH!' She snatched at the nearest suspect and tore his photo from the wall, throwing it to the floor and grabbing the next one, and the next, ripping them down in handfuls now, hurling everything to the carpet at her feet. Then the victims and the post-mortems and everything else, stomping it into the faded Axminster and screaming and crying and yelling till there was nothing left but the pockmarked wallpaper and an aching throat.

Lucy swayed there, breathing hard.

All of it, nothing but a waste of time.

She bent and picked the photo of Mum and Dad from amongst the drifts of suspects and the dead. The glass was cracked into a jagged mosaic, but there they were, still smiling away behind it.

'Lucy?' The Bloodsmith settled onto her father's couch.

'All this time, he told me she died of cancer. Lying to the police about her being suicidal, when he must've *known* it was me. No wonder he could barely look at me after . . . after the funeral.'

'He must've loved you very much.'

She sank down into the other settee, the photo on her knees, both parents smiling up at her. 'I used to hate him. Why wasn't he there for me? Why did I have to get put in a home with those *bastards*?' A harsh laugh barked out of her. 'Can you imagine what it must've been like, trying to raise the child that murdered your wife? I'm surprised he didn't smother me in my sleep . . .'

'Lucy, you need to forgive yourself.'

'The world would've been a better place if he had.' Scrubbing the tears from her eyes with the heel of her palm. 'It's all lies and shit and horror.'

'Come on, Lucy, don't—'

'I CHAINED A MAN UP IN A BASEMENT AND TORTURED HIM!'

The Bloodsmith got up and knelt in front of her. Taking her hands. Cigar poking out the side of his mouth. 'You're just doing what you need to survive. That's all. You didn't have any option.'

'There's *one* other option: I don't have to kill Dr Christianson.' She pulled her hands free and stood. Lurched out of the room and up the stairs. Thumped through the tears and into the bathroom.

It wasn't anything fancy – a bit old-fashioned, with a nice big enamel bath and clean white tiles. Even if the grout was going a bit grey and mouldy in places. A row of glass bottles and plastic containers were lined up along a low shelf above the bath. Lucy grabbed one, cranked the taps on full, and tipped in a good glug of 'relaxing' bubble bath, leaving the water running while she stomped back downstairs to the sideboard, where Dad's bottle of eighteen-year-old Glenfiddich had lain for the last half-decade, gathering dust, awaiting a special occasion that never came.

Well, this was its lucky day, because today was going to be very special indeed: the last will, testament, and breath of Lucy Roxburgh McVeigh.

44

'Lucy, are you *sure* this is what you want to do?' The Bloodsmith perched on the toilet lid, legs crossed, brow furrowed, as if this was some sort of therapy session and she was lying on a couch instead of in a hot bath.

'I told you to get out.' Glaring at the bubbles that covered nearly every bit of her that poked out of the water.

'Lucy, it's all very dramatic – the bottle of whisky and the razor blades – but if this is a cry for help, no one's coming to save you.' He took a long draw on his cigar. 'It's just us in here, Kiddo.'

She picked off the foil that covered the bottle's cork. 'I don't *want* to be saved.' Pouring a stiff measure into one of Dad's good crystal tumblers. The ones she was never allowed to touch. 'Leave me alone.'

'Come on, Kiddo, things aren't that bad. OK, so you're not who you thought you were, but nobody is. We're all different versions of ourselves every—'

'Please!' She screwed her eyes tight shut. '*Please*, just leave me alone.'

The silence stretched.

Then, 'OK. If that's what you really want.' A sigh, then a creak – that would be him getting up off the toilet. 'But if you change your mind . . .'

Now the only noise was the faint effervescent susurrus of tiny bubbles popping. And when Lucy opened her eyes, she was the only one there.

The tumbler was heavy in her hand, the rich scents of warm peat and sharp ethanol mixing with the lavender-and-honey bubble bath. Been over a year since she'd last touched alcohol. Not much point staying teetotal any more – wasn't as if she'd be around tomorrow for the hangover.

She knocked back a mouthful, setting her throat and chest on fire. *Hooooo*ing out a breath that tasted of baked apple, cinnamon, and oak. Maybe she should've gone for a splash of water in it?

Bit late to worry about that now.

She reached out and grabbed the pack of razor blades from the top of the cistern. Dad never did hold with those 'new-fangled' plastic disposable ones; instead each double-edged blade came in its own wax-paper wrapper. She was pulling one free when there was a knock on the door.

'*Lucy?*'

It swung open and Charlie wandered into the bathroom, smiling his bland smile, hands in his pockets.

She screwed her face up. 'Great.'

'Thought you could use a bit of Jiminy Cricketing. You know, now that He's gone.' Charlie pulled the tails of his suit jacket in at his waist and climbed into the other end of the tub, sending a frothy tsunami sloshing out over the edge and onto the tiled floor as he sat. Dark-grey suit turning black as the water soaked into it.

'Why can't you both just leave me alone?' Knocking back another mouthful.

'Because I'm here to *help*.' He scooped up a double handful of soapy water and doused his head with it. 'What's killing yourself going to achieve? What if the Dunk doesn't find out about the chandler's warehouse, because the Psychology Department hasn't kept its records properly? Are you *really* happy about Dr Christianson starving to death, all alone, in the dark?' Charlie plucked a bottle of Alberto Balsam from the glass shelf, lathering it into his wet hair.

'He killed six people. Gutted them. Stole their blood and their hearts!'

'Because he's ill, Lucy. Because he's grieving. Because he's lonely. Not because he's evil.' Charlie used the palms of his hands to scoop his hair up into a tiny Mohican. 'Have to say, this is a bit of an improvement on last time we shared a bath.'

'What?'

'We used to share a tub all the time, remember?'

She shrank away from him. 'Who *are* you?'

'I'm Charlie, silly. Your brother. Who died.'

The deceased's husband has repeatedly stated that Harriet was still in considerable distress following the death of her son earlier in the year . . .

'My *brother*?'

'Who died. In a tub, just like this one, back at the house on Blackwall Hill.' He flattened his mohawk. 'Have to admit, I'm a bit hurt, Lucy. How could you forget your twin brother?' Rinsing the soap out of his hair with another double scoop of water. 'If nothing else, I'm the first person you killed; that should get me some sort of recognition, right? In the bathtub? You knelt on my chest and held me underwater till I drowned? There was me, struggling to get free, and you're laughing and giggling. But then you've always loved a bath, haven't you?'

'Oh God . . .' She covered her mouth with her hand. 'I'm sorry. I'm so, *so* sorry!' Breath coming in sharp ragged gulps. 'You were right: I'm a monster!' She chucked back another mouthful of whisky, half choking as it went down the wrong way mid-sob.

'I was your imaginary friend for ages and ages, until Dr McNaughton convinced you I wasn't real.' Charlie's bottom lip scrunched up in a pout. 'Not sure what hurt more: being cast aside, forgotten, or drowned. Maybe it's . . .' He tilted his head to one side. 'Did you hear that?'

'Everything that's happened, everything I've worked for, everything I *think* I am, it's a lie.'

'Will you shush for a minute?' He half raised himself out of the bath – suit, shirt, and tie dripping as he stared at the bathroom door. 'I think there's someone in the house.'

She held her breath.

A creak sounded, out in the hallway. As if someone was climbing the stairs.

But she'd locked all the doors and windows.

What if it was Sarah Black and her idiot son – the one with the builder's van?

Well, who else could it be?

They must have broken in. To her house.

They'd finally worked up the balls to come for her.

And she was stark naked, in the sodding *bath*.

There was a dressing gown, hanging on the back of the bathroom door – Lucy clambered out of the bath, reaching for it as the handle turned.

The door swung open, and in stepped a large man dressed nearly all in black. Only the neck of his white T-shirt broke up the gloomy ensemble. His shaven head gleamed in the light, topping off a hard face with puffy eyes and a sharp nose. Not a local accent – something a bit more like the posher areas of Edinburgh: 'She's in here.'

It wasn't Daren Black.

Maybe they really *had* hired a thug to come and kill her.

A second figure appeared behind him – a woman, dressed nearly identically, with her hair trapped under a black knitted cap. 'Lucy McVeigh?' The woman stepped forward. 'I'm Dr Meldrum; this is my associate, Dr Lockerby; we've come to take you to Castle Hill Infirmary. You've had a serious head injury and it's gone untreated for nearly forty-eight hours. There's a very real risk the impact has triggered swelling on your brain. That can cause long-term damage to your memory and make it difficult to think straight. Have you had any symptoms like that?'

Lucy scrambled back into the bath, covering herself with her hands.

'If the pressure builds too much it can lead to delusions, paranoia, and if we don't do something about it as quickly as possible, it can be fatal.'

Charlie frowned. 'Actually, that would make a lot of sense. *Especially* after Christianson battered you over the head, back at his house. That's when it all started going wrong, didn't it? When you started having blackouts . . .'

'How did you get in?'

'The important thing is that you come with us right now, Ms McVeigh. I'm going to grab you some clothes, then we'll get you to the hospital.' Dr Meldrum ducked back onto the landing, leaving Lucy alone with Dr Lockerby.

He nodded. 'Don't worry, we'll take good care of you.' Slipping his right hand into his pocket.

'Lucy, this is a *good* thing! They can help you get better: no more seeing dead people.'

She shook her head. 'You don't understand, there are things I've got to do . . .'

Lockerby took a step closer. 'It's all right, Ms McVeigh, there's no need to get yourself all upset.' That hand of his – the one in his pocket – he had a knife, didn't he? Or a gun. Or maybe a syringe of something lethal.

'Or maybe you're just being paranoid, Lucy, like Dr Meldrum said?'

She glanced from the pocket to the man's face and back again. 'You need to step outside, so I can get dried and dressed.'

'Sorry, can't do that.' His eyes drifted to the bottle of whisky, then the open packet of razor blades. At the lone blade, removed from its wrapper, sitting on the edge of the bath. 'What if you slipped and fell, or collapsed because of your condition?'

'Please, I'm naked. I need to get my clothes on.'

'Just stay in the bath please, Ms McVeigh. My colleague won't be long.'

What sort of doctor talked like that? Why were they both dressed in black? And why did this feel more like a home invasion than a house call?

'Where's your ID?'

'You look stressed.' Charlie put a hand on her bubble-covered knee. 'Hey, come on, it's going to be fine. I'm sure they aren't—'

'I want to see your ID.' She jerked her chin up. 'Now.'

Lockerby looked back over his shoulder. Then shook his head. 'There's no need to be rude, Ms McVeigh. We've all got jobs to do, right?'

'Jobs like breaking into lone women's homes and making them disappear?'

He raised his eyebrows at her. 'What makes you say something nasty like that?' Then his tongue darted out and moistened his top lip. 'You psychiatric types like a bit of drama, don't you. That's why you kick off the whole time.' Stepping closer. 'You like when things get a bit rough.'

Lucy's eyes drifted down to Lockerby's other hand – the one not hidden in his pocket. It was gloved. Not a medical nitrile glove, but black leather.

'It's OK.' Charlie stood up, water cascading off his sodden suit. 'Come on, Lucy, nice calm breaths. It'll all be all right. You want help, don't you?'

Dr Lockerby loomed over the bath, grinning down at her. 'But that's all right, because I like it rough too.'

She grabbed the eighteen-year-old Glenfiddich and lunged to her feet, bringing with her a great swathe of water that crashed down on the tiled floor as she raised the bottle high and battered it down onto Lockerby's head.

He staggered backwards, feet skidding in the soapy water, sending him crashing into the towel rail, then down to the floor, one arm and both legs flailing.

She clambered out of the bath, wielding the whisky like a cudgel.

He got his arm up in time and the bottle hammered down into the wrist, hard enough to send a shock reverberating all the way up to Lucy's elbow.

Lockerby's hand sagged at the end of the crumpled joint. 'You BITCH!' His other hand flashed out of his pocket, but it was too slow to stop the bottle raining down again. Bouncing off the crown of his head with a resounding *clunk*. 'Gmnnnn . . .' One eye rolled up in its socket.

One more thump and a sickening crack muffled out into the room. Lockerby keeled over, blood trickling from his nose as he lay there, on his side in the puddle of bathwater, left leg twitching, lips opening and closing like a drowning fish.

A clatter sounded on the landing and Dr Meldrum charged in through the door again, one of Mum's floral dresses clutched in her leather-gloved hand. 'What the bloody . . .' Eyes wide as she took in the scene. 'Sandy!'

'WHO ARE YOU?' Lucy swung the bottle, but Meldrum jerked backwards, getting *just* enough distance to let it fizz through the air millimetres from her nose.

Meldrum surged forwards, both fists up and curled, held tight in front of her face like a professional boxer. The first jab was so close it brushed Lucy's cheek, but the second landed with a resounding clatter, jerking her head sideways.

Another fist smashed into her bare stomach, folding her in two. Then a knee flashed up, catching Lucy on the jaw and jackknifing her back into the side of the bath, setting it ringing like a muted bell as burning nettles scorched their way through her stomach, face, and spine.

Lucy slid down onto the drenched tiles, groaning.

Charlie stared at her over the lip of the bath. 'What the *hell* just happened?'

Dr Meldrum took off her right glove, pulled out her phone, and thumbed at the screen for a moment. Holding it to her ear as she knocked the whisky bottle out of Lucy's numb fingers with the toe of one black boot. 'Yeah, it's me . . . Uh-huh . . . No: listen. I think she's killed Lockerby . . . No, I'm not "joking"! She battered his head in with a whisky bottle . . . Uh-huh . . .'

'Lucy, I don't think they're real doctors.'

You don't sodding say.

Dad's eighteen-year-old Glenfiddich was almost empty now, its saved-for-special contents glugging out onto the swamped bathroom floor. Five years it'd lived in the sideboard and this was all it got.

'I'm not kidding, Lucy. You have to get up and do something!'

'Well, how am I supposed to know? This was meant to be a simple job, and now I'm standing here, up to my ankles in soapy bloody water while—'

Lucy launched herself forwards with a bellowing scream, bare feet squealing on the wet tiles as she sprinted the four paces from the bath to the doorway, slamming into Dr Meldrum.

The phone went flying as they careened across the landing, then a rattling boom filled the air as Meldrum's back hit the handrail. She bounced, pushing forward, a fist slashing up like a sledgehammer into Lucy's ribs.

Lucy's knees buckled, and large, gloved hands grabbed her shoulders.

Next thing, she was sailing through the air, crashing into the door to the spare room and collapsing onto the carpet. Breathing hard, each inhalation rubbing gravel between her ribs.

Charlie hunkered down in front of her. 'Lucy, you don't have time for this, you need to run away or she's going to kill you!'

'Unngh . . .' Lucy struggled onto her hands and knees, crawling to the top of the stairs.

'Go on then!' Meldrum grabbed a handful of Lucy's hair. 'Don't let *me* stop you.' Yanking her forwards and up, over the top step, sending her tumbling downwards, end over end, steps cracking into Lucy's back and arms and legs and arms and head and—

Thud: she hit the floor at the bottom. Rolled once, before coming to a jarring halt against the sideboard, knocking over the umbrella stand and the bowl with the keys. Then slumping over to lie, flat on her back, just inside the front door. Gasping for air.

Everything ached. And stung. And throbbed. Skin burning, even though it should be cold down here, stark naked and dripping wet.

Charlie paced back and forth across the tiled hallway floor. 'Please, Lucy, you have to get up. She's coming!'

45

Heavy boots thumped down the stairs. Taking their time. 'You shouldn't have done that.'

Lucy's bare heels squealed across the cold tiles, pushing her backwards, towards the door, hands scrabbling through the fallen walking sticks and keys and brollies.

'Sandy was an arsehole' – Meldrum stood over her, scowling down, hands flexing – 'but he deserved better than—'

Lucy's right fist punched sideways, each one of the Bedford Rascal's keys poking out between her knuckles, slamming into the side of Meldrum's right knee. Hard enough to stab two of them straight through the black fabric of her trousers and deep into the joint.

'AAAAAAAAAAAAAAAAAAARGH!' Both hands clutching the knee as blood and clear fluid welled up through the puncture wounds.

Lucy's other hand wrapped around the shaft of Dad's metal walking stick, swinging it to batter off Meldrum's head.

She collapsed to the hall floor, still trying to protect that ruined knee as Lucy struggled upright and brought the stick down on Meldrum's back. Shoulders. Legs. Head.

Teeth bared. Spitting out each word as if it was rat poison: 'YOU – DON'T – COME – INTO – MY – HOUSE!' The stick smashing down with every word until the so-called 'doctor' went limp. Lying there, cheek pressed against the skirting board, eyes closed.

'Oh, thank . . . thank . . . God . . .' Lucy staggered over to the sideboard, leaning heavily on the thing, breathing hard, one arm wrapped around her ribs, wincing with every inhale. Then froze. 'Urgh . . .' She lurched into the kitchen and over to the sink, grabbing hold of the taps and holding on as the post-adrenaline slump evicted the contents of her stomach in half a dozen bitter-spattering heaves. Leaving her slumped against the draining board.

A small round of applause clattered out behind her, and when she turned, there was the Bloodsmith – still puffing away on one of Dad's stinky cigars.

'You did good, Kiddo. You did good.' He smiled his wolf smile, nodding towards the kitchen doorway and the unconscious figure in the hall. 'Now, all we need to do is wait till she wakes up and ask her some questions she's *probably* not going to enjoy a great deal.' A small frown. 'Your dad does have pliers, doesn't he?'

And a lot more besides.

It couldn't be the most comforting of feelings – waking up naked, gagged, and tied to a dining chair that had been positioned in the middle of a large plastic dustsheet, beneath the harsh glare of a single bare lightbulb, in a cold dark garage. Nice and roomy, now that the Bedford Rascal was out on the driveway.

Dr Meldrum's eyes creaked open, then snapped wide. 'Mmmmmnnn NgngnnnnnPhhhh!' Struggling against her bonds as Lucy dragged another chair over and clunked it down in front of her. 'Mmmmmmm MmmmmGhggggghhhhhh!' Tears welling up as the pain kicked in.

It was quite the role reversal: Lucy in black jeans, a black Foo Fighters' hoodie, black gilet, and old black trainers; Meldrum stripped bare – her clothes rolled up and laid in a circle around the chair. The only concession she had to modesty was the bloodstained bandage wrapped around her right knee. Which had to be *really* sore.

The Bloodsmith stepped onto the plastic sheet, walking behind Meldrum and placing his hands on her shoulders. 'It's OK, Lucy, you can do this.'

'I . . . I don't know if . . .' Deep breath. 'I don't want to hurt her.'

'Mmmmmffggnnnn!'

'You need to know who sent her to kill you.' A wink. 'Come on, we'll make a game of it, it'll be fun.'

'Can't we just call it in?'

'Mmmmnnn! Mmmmngh ggg nnnn!' Meldrum's eyes flashed from side to side, as if she was trying to spot who Lucy was talking to.

'Lucy, Lucy, Lucy. When your colleagues get here, what are they going to think about . . .' Pointing upwards, in the vague direction of the bathroom. 'Battering *one* man to death is unfortunate; *two* begins to look a bit like a pattern. And while they're questioning you about what happened, the clock's ticking. Your little friend's going to find out about the chandler's warehouse, and then where will you be?'

Lucy sagged. 'I really don't want to do this.'

'Mnnnggggnnnh!'

'You've got no choice, Kiddo. It's her or you.' He gave Lucy a warm, paternal smile. 'Now, remember, it's important to set the scene before you start. Helps put our guest in a cooperative frame of mind.'

'OK . . .' Lucy pulled on her dad's old butcher's apron, then a pair of blue nitrile gloves. She pointed at the circle of clothing, arranged around the plastic sheeting. 'It stops the blood from spreading.'

Meldrum's struggles got a *lot* more pronounced.

'Excellent.' The Bloodsmith nodded. 'Now show her your tools.'

Lucy untied the canvas bundle and unrolled it on the garage floor. 'My father was a butcher. He was very good at it. I used to watch him taking carcases apart.' Dad's knives sparkled in the artificial light. 'I know it looks like a lot, but they all do different things, and it's important to pick the right one.'

At which point, Dr Meldrum went dead still. Eyes wide. Air hissing through her nose in short sharp panicky breaths.

'That's my girl. You've got her attention now.'

Lucy selected a long, curved blade from the set and sank into the empty chair. 'Before we get started, I want to tell you a few things. First: I know you and your friend came here to kill me tonight, so don't insult my intelligence by pretending otherwise, OK? Two: you're going to answer all my questions, honestly, and truthfully, because if you *don't* I'm going to start removing bits of you. Three: feel free to scream and shout all you want. You've seen where I live. We're in the middle of nowhere and all my neighbours will be in bed with a mug of Horlicks and their hearing aids switched off by now.' She held up the cimeter knife. 'Any questions?'

'Mmmmnnnngph.'

'Good.'

She undid the gag, and sat back as Meldrum coughed and spluttered.

'We . . . we didn't come here to kill you, I *swear*! We're *doctors*, we genuinely are doctors. Call Castle Hill Infirmary and ask! They'll tell you!'

'Who sent you?'

'Ms McVeigh, you're not well, OK? You've had a serious head trauma and you didn't get treatment for it. This, all this, thinking we're here to kill you, talking to people who aren't there, it's a sign something's gone very, very wrong.'

'She's not cooperating, Kiddo. There have to be consequences for that.' He leaned forward and patted Meldrum on her bandaged knee. 'But start off small. If you go in cutting and stabbing, you've got nothing to escalate to. Even a tiny bit of pressure can focus the mind wonderfully, if you know where to exert it.'

'Ms McVeigh, *please*, ask yourself why would anyone try to kill you? It makes no sense. But swelling on the brain can cause paranoia that—'

Lucy slapped her hand down on Meldrum's knee, fingers curling around the joint, nails digging into the bandages as she squeezed.

A bellowing scream ripped through the air.

She let go and Meldrum slumped against the ropes, sobbing.

'Good girl! That wasn't so bad now, was it? You're a natural.'

It took a bit of doing – swallowing down the knot in her throat – but she managed. 'Who sent you? Was it Sarah Black?'

'I'm a . . . I'm a doctor . . . at Castle . . . Castle Hill Infirmary . . . Please, I'm only here to help you. Please . . .'

'This isn't *The Thirty-Nine Steps*; you can't just keep pretending to be someone you're not and suddenly everyone will believe it. Now: who – sent – you?'

'Please, I'm a doctor . . .! I *swear*, I'm a— AAAAAAAAAAAAAAA AAAAAAAARGH!'

The Bloodsmith stalked around the outside of the plastic sheeting. 'You know what I think? I think Sarah Black had nothing to do with this, Kiddo. I think they came here because you were asking awkward questions about St Nicholas College.'

'Is that true?' Lucy let go of the bandaged knee. Fresh blood darkening the fabric. 'Did Argyll send you? He said he had friends at CHI, are you one of them?'

'I . . . I don't know anyone . . . anyone called Argyll, I promise! I swear on my mother's grave, I'm a doctor and I came here to help you and you killed Sandy and it's all horrible and I wish I'd stayed at home . . .' Naked body jerking and wobbling as she sobbed and wailed. 'I didn't *do* anything . . .'

Why did everyone always say that?

The Bloodsmith shook his head. 'She's lying, but it doesn't matter – we worked it out anyway. Argyll McCaskill sent her and her friend to kill you, because you found out he'd faked Benedict Strachan's entrance exam. And for some reason, that's an exceedingly big deal . . . You know, I'll bet they've still got the real one on file. A place like that never throws anything out. We could find out why it matters so much?'

Lucy pulled off the bloody nitrile glove and dropped it on the plastic dustsheet. 'We're done here.'

'Oh, thank God.' Meldrum hung forward against the ropes. 'Please, I need . . . I need to go to the hospital! Please . . .' Tears falling into her lap.

'The only trouble, Kiddo, is now we've got three bodies to get rid of, instead of one: Christianson, Lockerby, and her.'

Lucy unfurled an old tarpaulin on the bathroom floor. It was a bit paint-stained and manky, but it would do. She rolled Dr Lockerby onto it, then scrambled away from him as he groaned. He was still alive . . .

She grabbed the whisky bottle, ready to batter it down again, but he didn't move. Didn't even breathe. Lucy lowered her makeshift weapon and reached out two fingers, pressing them against his neck, just below the jawline, where the jugular would be. Holding them there. And feeling nothing.

Must have been air shifting in his lungs when she moved the body.

This was all so much more *difficult* and *worrying* and *horrible* than she'd thought . . .

'Come on, Lucy, you can do this.' The Bloodsmith parked himself on the toilet lid again. 'Think of Dr Lockerby as a Christmas present no one really wants.' Miming wrapping a parcel.

OK.

When you looked at it *that* way, it only took ten minutes to get Lockerby rolled up in the tarp, the ends folded in, halfway through, to keep everything inside, like a burrito. She secured the bundle with bands of duct tape, going through nearly a whole roll, just in case.

'Oh, and you probably don't want to leave this lying around, Kiddo.'

A finger came down to point at a small rectangular black object wedged between the toilet brush holder and the wall.

The thing Dr Lockerby had been trying to pull out of his pocket, just before she caved his skull in.

It was a digital camera, the old-fashioned kind that didn't come attached to a mobile phone. Turning it on made a little screen on the back light up, displaying the last picture taken: a middle-aged woman, lying pale and still in a hospital bed, hooked up to tubes and wires. Her hospital gown had been pulled up around her middle, showing off her genitals.

Lucy pressed the button to bring up the next photo and it was a different woman, only this time the gown was up around her neck. And the photo after that—

'Urgh . . .' Lucy turned the camera off again.

Now she didn't feel anywhere near as bad about bashing his brains out.

The full moon hung low on the horizon, swollen and yellow, wearing a hazy shroud of mist as Lucy hauled the tarpaulin-wrapped bundle into the back of her Bedford Rascal. It was amazing how much heavier a dead body was than a live one. Suppose all the layers of tarp and duct tape didn't help, but there was no point letting anything leak out inside the van. Trace evidence was a sod to get rid of, and it wasn't as if she could afford to torch her only form of transport.

Mind you, if you thought about it, she didn't *have* to use her own vehicle, did she?

Lucy went back into the house and rummaged through Meldrum's clothes till they gave up a BMW fob, with a couple of keys attached. Then marched out onto the road, held the fob up high, and pressed the button.

A set of hazard lights flashed down the road, not far past where the 'WELCOME TO BALLROCHIE' sign lurked – as if four houses counted as an actual place.

She limped over there and climbed into a new-looking mid-range shiny-black Beamer. Leather seats. Swanky. The engine purred into life and she drove it back to the house, reversing up the drive, past the Bedford Rascal, and up to the garage door.

Just gone nine and there wasn't a light on in the houses opposite. She hadn't been kidding about Horlicks and hearing aids. So there was no one to watch her wrestle the body out of the van and into the BMW's boot. Took a bit of effort to get Dr Lockerby in there, and it left no space for the jerrycans, so they'd have to go in the rear footwell.

Lucy headed back inside.

House was a bloody mess – all that soapy water had soaked into the upstairs-landing carpet, probably ruining it. The hall was a tip. A huge, splintered crack ran across the spare room's door. There were scuff marks all the way down the stairs. And the bathroom looked as if a bomb had gone off in it.

Pfff . . .

She grabbed her overcoat from the rack, locked the front door from the inside, picked up the bulging bag-for-life from the kitchen, and headed through the linked door to the garage. Where 'Dr' Meldrum was still tied to her chair, shivering in the gloom, her breath steaming out through the cloth gag in wispy tendrils of white.

Lucy squatted down in front of her. 'We're going for a little drive.' Resting her hand on that bandaged knee. 'You're going to be well behaved, aren't you?'

Meldrum closed her eyes and nodded. 'Mmmmfff!'

'Good.' Lucy produced a pair of cuffs. It didn't take much to get Meldrum, bound and gagged, in the back of the car, lying there covered with the plastic dustsheet.

The garage door rattled down again, and when Lucy turned, Charlie was standing by the car, watching her. No sign of the Bloodsmith.

'You coming?'

He dug a toe into the gravel driveway. 'You don't seem to want a Jiminy Cricket any more.'

Lucy tilted her head, then pointed. 'In the car.'

There was some feet-dragging, but eventually he climbed into the passenger seat with the bag-for-life in the footwell – along with a rucksack stuffed with a few choice items from Dad's toolkit. There wasn't any point asking him to fasten his seatbelt, so she started the BMW up and pulled out onto the road. Clicked on the radio and fiddled with the buttons till it latched onto the local radio station and a jaunty ballad filled the car.

Charlie frowned at her in the dashboard light. 'You seem to be taking all this remarkably well.' He shook his head. 'Lucy, this isn't you, OK? You don't have to be like . . . this. I'm begging you: go to the hospital. You're not well; they'll help you get better.'

The song jollied along to itself.

'Lucy? I said—'

'I don't have any choice, OK? The tide's *way* up above my head and there's nothing I can do to change that. Either I swim with it, or I drown.'

Lucy stuck to the speed limit, all the way from Ballrochie to Woronieck Road, because it *probably* wouldn't look too good if she got pulled over driving a vehicle without the owner's permission, an abducted woman in the back seat, and a corpse in the boot. Traffic Division tended to take a dim view of that kind of thing, even in Oldcastle.

She parked in front of the chandler's warehouse, strapped on a head-torch, opened the back door, and pulled Dr Meldrum out onto the pavement. 'If you struggle or make any sort of noise, it's not going to end well, understand?'

A wide-eyed nod.

Took a while to haul her down the alley, in through the door, along the corridor, and down the stairs – every thump and jolt eliciting a moan, sob, or whimper – but eventually Lucy got her new guest into the long, low, stinking room.

'Is this really such a good idea?' Charlie followed her in, arms folded tight as Lucy dragged Meldrum across the stained concrete to the filthy grate where Dr Christianson was shackled.

Christianson barely moved, just lay there and groaned as Lucy hand-cuffed Meldrum's wrists to the thick length of chain.

You'd think she'd resist, or complain, or kick off, but Meldrum just sat there, staring, shrinking back from what was left of the psychologist. 'What did you *do* to him?'

Good question.

Lucy left them to get acquainted while she levered Lockerby out of the boot and dragged his body down into the room. Dumping him on the couch in the faux therapist's office. The next round trip brought the bag-for-life and one of the jerrycans, and a final visit fetched the last two cans of petrol. Setting all three in a line by the door.

'*You don't have to do this, Lucy.*' Charlie stepped out of the shadows.

'You could hand them both over to the authorities and tell Tudor what's happened. He'll *understand*. Hell, show him Lockerby's camera and they'll probably throw a parade in your honour. But the important thing is: they could help you get better.'

She nudged Christianson's manky body with the toe of her trainers. 'Can you hear me?'

His filthy, twisted hands came up to cover his face, hiding it from the torchlight. 'Please . . .'

'I'll make you an offer, John. Someone sent your new roommate and her friend to kill me. Get her to tell you *who*, and why they want me dead, and I'll think about letting you go.' Lucy opened the bag-for-life and poured out a half-dozen clingfilmed sandwiches in front of Christianson. 'Two egg mayonnaise, two cheese and pickle, one ham and mustard, and a peanut butter.' A trio of bottled waters bounced and spun on the manky concrete. 'You've got till I get back.'

She locked up, heaved the rusting display unit back over the door, and limped out onto Woronieck Road again. Taking in the scents of diesel, rotting seaweed, and old fish.

MacKinnon Quay's lights blazed away on the other side of the river, the sweep of Castleview rearing up the valley behind it. The first drop of rain kissed her cheek. Then another, and another. Getting heavier as she slid in behind the BMW's wheel, turned the blowers up full, and pulled away from the chandler's warehouse.

Charlie fidgeted in the passenger seat. 'You know it's not too late to call this off?'

'I know.'

'Only, what if . . .' Deep breath. 'Benedict Strachan was always going on about a mysterious "Them" being after him. And now you've been attacked by Dr Meldrum and Dr Lockerby. What if Benedict's *not* paranoid and "They" are connected to St Nicholas College?'

She smiled across the car at him. 'That's what I'm counting on.'

46

The Bloodsmith checked his watch. 'How much longer?'

'Soon.' Lucy stretched out in the heated leather driver's seat as the rain drummed on the BMW's roof. It really was a lovely car; shame she'd have to torch it when they were done.

They'd parked on a narrow track, near the end of the golf course, partially shielded by a thicket of gorse bushes. The clubhouse was in darkness, but there were a few lights in the middle distance, flickering as the rain swept between here and the back of St Nicholas College.

He hissed out a lungful of thick grey cigar smoke. 'Don't let the boy get to you, Kiddo. You're doing what you have to do.'

'Do you have any idea how much secondhand smoke I'm getting off that thing?'

'From an imaginary cigar, smoked by a man who doesn't exist?'

Fair point.

Lucy reclined her seat all the way. 'Charlie's disappointed in me.'

A shrug. 'That's the trouble with having an externalized manifestation of your superego: it'll always try to make you walk the straight, narrow path. Whereas *I* represent your id, getting you to trust your instincts, take *chances* in life, and *live* a little. That's why I'm more fun.'

She risked a gentle prod of the ribs where Dr Meldrum had punched them. Stung a bit, but nowhere near as bad as they could've been.

The rain drummed.

The silence grew.

Lucy cleared her throat. 'Before Neil Black, I was this normal happy person with friends and a great job and a social life. Now I'm . . . I don't even *know* what I am.'

The Bloodsmith's voice softened. 'Can I give you a little unsolicited advice? Neil Black was a rapist scumbag and you did the world a favour, smashing his head to a pulp. Don't *ever* give him credit for "breaking" you, because he didn't. Oh, he may have primed the pump, and Dr Christianson opened the floodgates, but they didn't make you like this, Kiddo. You've *always* been this way.'

'Is that supposed to make me feel better?'

'They forced the real you into remission – shackled you with psychotherapy and drugs, beat the real Lucy out of you every Sunday after church, till you learned to pretend you were the same as all the other people. And, eventually, you started to believe it too. But they couldn't kill *you*, Kiddo; you came back.' He patted her on the shoulder. 'I'm proud of you.'

Welcome to the asylum.

'It's—' Her phone sang its generic ringtone song and, when she pulled it out, 'THE DUNK' glowed in the middle of the screen. She pressed the button, forced her voice to be plain and normal. 'Dunk.'

'Sarge? Sorry, I know it's late. Look, I couldn't get anyone on the phone at Puller, Finch, and McKeever Advocates, cos it's Saturday. But I've just had a wee brainwave and googled Phillipa McKeever.'

'Phillipa . . . ?'

'McKeever. Benedict Strachan's solicitor? Yeah, only she's not actually a solicitor, she's a QC. A proper, full on, Queen's Counsel, and she's representing an eleven-year-old in a murder case, but doesn't even try *to get him off? Even worse, she's a nouveau-posh twat – they made her a "baroness" in 2019.'*

Lucy buzzed her seat back up. 'Thanks, Dunk.'

'You know what I think? I think someone spent a lot of money making sure Benedict Strachan took the fall for killing Liam Hay. My guess is it was his accomplice's family. Think they'll give us a warrant to see Baroness McKeever's files?'

Not a chance in hell.

'Worth a go, I suppose. Don't hold your breath, though.'

The Bloodsmith raised his eyebrows and tapped his watch.

Time to go.

'Are you OK, Sarge? Only you sound kinda . . . you know.'

'I'm fine. Been a long day, that's all.' Bit of an understatement. 'You did good, Dunk. See you tomorrow.' Lucy hung up, put her phone on silent, and slipped it back into her pocket. 'Shall we?' She pulled on a baseball cap and grabbed her rucksack from the passenger footwell. Donned a pair of nitrile gloves and flipped up her hoodie's hood. Climbed out into the rain.

The Bloodsmith joined her, not bothering with waterproofing, because, as he said, he wasn't real.

They crossed the boundary from the golf course onto the school's playing fields.

'What if they've got security cameras, Kiddo?'

'It's dark, it's raining, I'm dressed completely in black, and you don't exist.'

They squelched their way across two football pitches and the athletics track. The baseball cap's bill kept the worst of the rain off her glasses, but things were still getting hazier.

'When we get in there, I don't want you distracting me, OK?'

'I wouldn't dream of it.' Sounding slightly offended.

The last playing field gave way to a manicured strip of parkland, complete with picnic benches and trees to lounge under. Then they were hurrying past the dorms and along the back of the school – stables in the far corner, then the gym, then a science lab, then the Moonfall Gate. Lucy crept through it into the quad, sticking to the outer wall, where the shadows were thickest.

Lights glowed pale yellow in a handful of the upper windows, misty in the drifting rain, but there was no sign of life.

'There's going to be some sort of fancy security system.' The Bloodsmith wandered out onto the gloomy path, puffing away on his cigar, hands in his pockets, as if they were out for a Sunday stroll. 'Can't just break the glass with a rock this time.'

She stopped in front of the admin tower's thick wooden door. Swung the backpack off her shoulders and went rummaging inside. The lock was old-fashioned, like the one back at the chandler's warehouse, so nowhere near as secure as something more modern, but also nothing like as predictable. Maybe the cordless drill—

'I know it's going to make me sound a little glass-half-full' – the Blood-smith pointed – 'but have you tried the handle?'

'Yes, because they're going to leave the admin tower unlocked, aren't they? After all, it's only full of all their top-secret files, why would they bother locking that?'

'Humour me.'

'Fine.' She pulled on the handle: it clicked, then the door swung open without so much as a creak.

The Bloodsmith pulled his chin in. 'Does that worry you as much as it worries me?'

Lucy gathered up her backpack again. 'Want to call it quits and go home?'

'What, and wait for the next pair of thugs to come knocking?'

'Yeah, me neither.' She slipped into the reception area and eased the door shut behind her.

No sign of any traitorous little red lights, winking in the darkness, and she hadn't seen any motion detectors or security cameras the last two times she was in here, but that didn't mean anything: these days you could buy a spy-cam off the internet that was smaller than a thimble. Still, too late to worry about that now.

She gave her glasses a quick dry-and-polish with a clean hankie, then pulled on the headtorch and clicked it to the lowest setting, tiptoe-ing up the stairs, past photo after photo of the great and the good, to the second floor. 'RECORDS R–Z ~ STAFF ONLY'. She tried the handle, but the door was definitely locked this time. It was a more modern lock, too.

If this was a film, she could've poked about inside it with a kirby grip for thirty seconds and it'd pop open, but down here in the real world . . .

She dug the cordless drill out again and fitted a 6-mm metal bit into the chuck, then placed the point an inch below the keyhole and started her up nice and slow. Put a bit more speed into it when the drill had made a decent dent in the metal plate. Keeping her head back, out of range of the tiny flying curls of metal. The glasses would protect her eyes, but no point getting them scratched.

'Look on the bright side, Kiddo, at least we know it's not a trap. If it was, they'd have left this one unlocked as well.'

The drill was well into its stride now, squealing its way through the lock's cartridge, juddering every time it hit a spring, before jerking forward into the next one.

Then there was no resistance at all – must have drilled through and out the other side. She put the drill back in the rucksack and pulled out Dad's ancient flathead screwdriver. Turned it around the wrong way and chapped the wooden hilt on the lock's face, four or five times, till a collection of little metal pins tumbled out of the drilled hole to click and ping against the marble floor.

'Here we go.' She turned the screwdriver the right way around and slid the flat head into the keyhole and turned. *Clunk.*

This time, when she tried the handle, the door swung open. The whole procedure had taken about seventy seconds.

Lucy stepped into the dark canyon between the opposing walls of filing cabinets, headtorch sweeping the polished wood like a searchlight.

Now for the tricky part: figuring out where the hell Benedict Strachan's file was hidden in the school's byzantine non-alphabetical filing system . . .

'This is taking far too long.'

Lucy scowled down from the top of her ladder. 'You're not helping.'

The Bloodsmith shrugged in his pale spotlight, making a show of checking his watch. 'It's after midnight and we're still no nearer finding Benedict Strachan's file, Kiddo. At this rate they'll be doing morning assembly and we'll still be in here.'

She read her way across the next three drawers.

'WAITIMU, NKASIOGI', 'WALKINSHAW, PETER', 'VOIGT, BARDUWULF'. Moved down two rungs.

'TULLOCH, GORDON', 'RUKHMABAI, BHAVNA', 'SYMINGTON-BROWN, MARTIN'.

He was right: this was going to take forever.

'YUNG, TALIA', 'YOO, CHIN-SUN', 'WESTWATER, COLLIN'.

But what other choice did she have? There was no sodding logic to the system, at least none that she could see. It was all random.

'ZAKHAROV, PAVEL', 'RHYNIE, PAUL', 'TILFORD-SMITH, ROBERTA'. And she was still *at least* twelve foot off the ground.

'WRIGHTSON, BORRIS', 'VELÁZQUEZ Y GALDÁMEZ, CATALINA', 'YEADON, SAMUEL'.

Hold on.

She climbed up a couple of rungs again.

'RHYNIE, PAUL', as in Paul Rhynie, the Business Secretary?

Might as well, as she was already up here.

It was a bit of a balancing act, getting the drill out of the backpack without falling off the ladder, but at least the 6-mm bit was still attached, and the drawer locks were much less robust than the door's had been. Thirty seconds and she was in.

The drawer was a good two-and-a-half feet deep and full of hanging files, each with its own named divider.

She pulled one out and laid it on top of the others.

The Bloodsmith gave a big, exaggerated sigh. 'Do we *really* have time for that?'

'Still not helping.'

It was full of newspaper clippings about Paul Rhynie's rise to power: mostly bits from the *Financial Times* featuring contracts he'd awarded, many of which had a gold star stuck to them. No idea what that was supposed to signify. The next file contained handwritten notes, detailing a whole raft of deals that looked about as legal as a pallet-load of cocaine. And speaking of cocaine – the one after that held about half a dozen grainy hidden-camera photographs of the Business Secretary and a leggy blonde in a hotel room somewhere, snorting up before getting down to some pretty hard-core sexual activities. 'Wow.'

Tucked in right at the back was a hanging file with an old manila folder in it, 'ENTRANCE EXAM' written on the front in a child's careful printing. Inside were Rhynie's IQ and aptitude tests, along with the obligatory rambling essay entitled, 'WHAT I DID OVER THE SUMMER HOLIDAYS, BY PAUL LYNDON RHYNIE (AGED 11½)'. The IQ score was 116, so slightly better than average, but not exactly setting the world on fire. According to the assessment, what young Paul *did* have was a very rich and well-connected family, so the examiners had approved his application to join St Nicholas College.

The Dunk would've had something to say about that.

The last thing in the folder was a lumpy white C4 envelope with a black border around it.

Lucy tipped the contents out.

'Bloody hell . . .'

Four glossy eight-by-ten photographs, taken with a telephoto lens; a single sheet of A4, covered in the same handwriting as the essay; and what looked like a grubby striped tie in a ziplock plastic pouch.

> *My name is Paul Lyndon Rhynie and I hereby confess to the*
> *murder of Melissa Allenson, by strangulation. I acted alone*
> *and am solely responsible for my actions . . .*

'Holy *shit!*'

It was all there: dates, times; how he'd found her soliciting down by the docks in Logansferry and convinced her he was lost and there'd be a reward if she helped him find his way home; how he'd assaulted her in the car park of a disused cash-and-carry; strangled her with one of his father's regimental ties; doused the body in lighter fluid and set fire to it . . .

The first photo showed two boys talking to a woman, beneath a street-light, in front of a blank brick wall – 'PIERSON ROAD' visible on a sign above her head. The boys were dressed in hoodies and anoraks; she was in a grubby duffel coat, high-heeled boots, and a painfully short skirt. There was something . . . artistic about the image, as if it was destined for a gallery or a coffee-table book.

The next picture *wasn't*. It caught the moment in the disused car park when both boys tackled their victim to the ground. They were garrotting her in the third photo. And in the last one, they stood over her body as blue and yellow flames licked along her back.

Lucy stared.

So Paul Rhynie was lying when he said he'd acted alone. He had an accomplice, just like Benedict Strachan did.

The grubby tie.

She held it up, focusing her headtorch's light on the ziplock bag. There were scorch marks and smears of red on the green-and-yellow fabric – lipstick? Had to be, blood would've dried to a powdery brown by now.

The tie wasn't the only thing in there: something glittered at the bottom of the bag. An earring.

There was more than enough evidence here to put Paul Rhynie away for eighteen years to life.

Lucy stuck everything back in the folder, then stuffed the whole thing into her backpack.

Frowned.

Surely it couldn't *just* be Paul Rhynie. It would be too huge a coincidence if the first file she looked at was the only one full of incriminating evidence. So she drilled through the next drawer along: 'TILFORD-SMITH, ROBERTA', skimming past the clippings and notes to the 'ENTRANCE EXAM' folder at the back. Another set of photographs and another signed confession.

> *I, Roberta Tilford-Smith, do hereby confess to the unlawful*
> *killing of one Luke Appleton, at four thirty pm, on the*
> *sixteenth of July 1975, in the public toilets near the Clifton*
> *Suspension Bridge, Bristol. I alone am responsible for Mr*
> *Appleton's death . . .*

The photos were in black and white this time, showing her and another girl stabbing a tall thin man in a suit. He had his trousers and pants around his ankles.

The Bloodsmith thumped on the ladder. 'I think I can hear someone coming, Kiddo.'

So, including Benedict Strachan's victim, the body count so far was one homeless person, one prostitute, and one pervert. All people that society wouldn't miss too much. People the police might not put a lot of effort into finding.

Jesus.

The drill screeched through another lock.

'I'm serious, Lucy, we need to get moving!'

'Will you shut up for two seconds?'

> *My name is Pavel Ivanovich Zakharov and I hereby confess*
> *to the murder of Mikolaj Lewandowski, a homeless man, in*
> *Vorontsovsky Park, Obruchevsky District, Moscow. I acted*
> *alone and take full responsibility for this man's death.*

It was as if they were all working off some sort of template confession, always making sure to claim they acted alone. Bet their accomplices' confessions would be exactly the same: everyone covering up for each other.

'*Ahem.*'

'For God's sake! All right, OK? I get the . . .'

She looked down, but it wasn't the Bloodsmith standing at the bottom of the ladder, framed in the dim glow of her headtorch – it was Argyll and the headmaster. The pair of them staring up at her with a mixture of sadness and disappointment. Even though it was after midnight, they were both wearing their dark-grey suits and academic robes.

Lights flickered on, flooding the place with a warm white glow, sparkling back off the brass fittings and marble tiles as Argyll held up a file. 'Is this what you were looking for?'

She licked her lips.

Sod.

47

Lucy threw Pavel Zakharov's confession down at them. 'So, what, this is your blackmail bank?' Grabbing a handful from the other open drawer – clippings and notes detailing Roberta Tilford-Smith's accomplishments and dodgy business dealings. 'There have to be thousands of these in here.'

'Ah, dear Lucy' – the headmaster clasped his hands behind his back and frowned up at her as if she'd just said something stupid in class – 'nice though it is to see you again, I have to admit that I'm a little surprised to find you *here*. Rummaging through our records. Having clearly broken in to conduct an illegal search without a warrant.' The frown became a pained expression. 'You will, I hope, understand if that rather taints what might otherwise have been a pleasant reunion.'

'Really?' She hurled the notes and clippings at his fuzzy-bald head, but they scattered on the way down, fluttering to the marble floor around him. 'Because I got the feeling you didn't like me very much. Especially when you SENT A PAIR OF THUGS TO KILL ME!'

There was a moment's silence, then an indulgent sigh. '*Thugs*, Lucy? I'm sure I don't know any—'

'Dr Lockerby and Dr Meldrum. And in case you're wondering, it didn't end well for them.'

'Oh dear. That *does* sound unpleasant.' He turned to his assistant. 'Argyll?'

'I'm disappointed, Lucy. I know you've had a serious head injury, but this . . . wanton destruction is beneath you.'

'Oh, I'll give you wanton bloody destruction!' She clambered down the ladder. Slammed her palm against one of the locked drawers. 'Want to explain why every file I've looked at has a murder confession in it?'

'I trusted you, Lucy. I let you read Benedict Strachan's file, if you promised to obey the rules, but you didn't, did you? You took photos on your phone, even though I *expressly* forbade it. And don't bother denying it; did you really think we wouldn't have security cameras in here?'

'In what way is that even vaguely comparable? I'm talking about murder!'

'If nobody follows the rules, we end up with chaos.'

'ARE YOU EVEN LISTENING TO ME?'

The headmaster put a hand on Argyll's shoulder. 'Perhaps I could interrupt, for just a moment?' His voice was like golden syrup: 'Lucy, I don't want you to think I was eavesdropping, but I couldn't help overhear you talking to someone as we came in. I'd hate to think of them running about the school at night, in the dark; they might injure themselves. Where are they, and how did they manage to avoid our security cameras?'

She blinked. 'He's . . . waiting outside the school gates, with the rest of my backup. Patrol cars, Operational Support Units, dogs, firearms team.'

'Excellent.' The headmaster clapped his leathery hands. 'I *do* love an imaginary insurance policy. We know you don't have any of those things, Lucy. So, I'm going to ask you again: where is your mysterious friend?'

'Going for help. They'll be here any minute now.'

'No they won't. Argyll, perhaps you'd be so kind as to locate DS McVeigh's elusive friend for me?'

Argyll pulled out his phone and poked at the screen, wandering off a couple of paces as he held it to his ear. 'Vanessa? Sorry to disturb you so late, but I'm afraid we have an intruder on school grounds. Can you get the house leaders to wake everyone up, please? . . . That's right: we need every building and classroom searched. Oh, and there will be *house points* for whichever group catches our unexpected visitor . . . Thank you.'

The headmaster nodded. 'There we are; he'll be found, safe and sound. Now, you were saying something about a pair of doctors trying to kill you?'

'Don't pretend you didn't know.' Jabbing a finger at Argyll. 'Ask *him*.'

'And you were able to defeat these doctor assassins? How very resourceful of you.' A sigh. 'I genuinely had hoped we could be friends, Lucy; your test scores really were quite remarkable. But I'm afraid your interest in St Nicholas College has caused some of our parents to feel concerned about the safety of their children. I do hope you'll understand.'

'*Understand?*'

'I'll just be a moment.' He produced a mobile of his own, selected a contact and listened to it ring.

Argyll gathered up the fallen pieces of paper. 'This was none of your business.'

'You've got four floors full of crimes and scandals and corruption and BLOODY MURDER CONFESSIONS!' She snatched one of the newspaper clippings from his hands – a photo of Roberta Tilford-Smith in all her angular fake-tanned glory, smiling away as she posed with some grim-faced fat bloke, both of them in hard hats and high-vis jackets, beneath the headline 'DEVELOPERS TEAM UP TO BUILD NEW PANDEMIC QUARANTINE FACILITY'. This one had two gold stars on it. 'She stabbed a man to death in Bristol, and you're giving her "good girl" stickers?'

The headmaster turned his back on them. 'Hello, Shauna? It's Arnold, from St Nicholas College? . . . Oh, fine, fine, thank you. How are Gerald and the little ones? . . . Oh, how lovely.'

'Don't be ridiculous.' Argyll snatched the clipping back and shuffled everything into a neat pile. 'The stars are a merit system based on one ex-student assisting another, and, in this case, the school. There's no need to pretend you don't know that's how the world works.'

'Listen, Shauna, I've got a little favour to ask. Apparently there's been some sort of a fracas at Detective Sergeant Lucy McVeigh's home in Ballrochie . . . That's right, the old grieve's house. Would you be a sweetheart and send a team in to tidy up for me? . . . Oh, I'm not a hundred percent sure, but bodies, blood, incriminating evidence, that sort of thing.'

Lucy blinked. 'How the *world* works?'

'Honestly, Lucy, you sound like a broken parrot.'

'Yes . . . Yes . . . Oh, that does sound helpful, thank you.' The headmaster turned and peered at Lucy. 'And I think we'll need a bit of cleaning at the school as well . . . Two of them . . . Sometime in the next half-hour would be best . . . That's right; if it's not too much trouble? . . . Wonderful.'

'So, let me guess – you "mould" these children, you "guide" them, and they all get into Oxford and Cambridge, and they become bigwigs in business and politics, and then you *own* them.'

Argyll grimaced. 'You make it sound so . . . exploitative. We help them become their best possible selves and they very kindly look after St Nicholas College, but not because we "own" them; they do it because we're *always* here for them. Their parents farm them out to nannies and boarding schools, but we support them. We *care*.' He pulled one shoulder up, the smile on his face the same sad one he'd worn in the restaurant. 'We're the only family they know.'

'All right, thank you, Shauna. Give my love to Gerald and the kids . . . OK . . . Bye.'

'You make them *kill* people before they start here!'

'We need to know they're ready!' Argyll stared at the ceiling for a moment, then tried what he probably thought was a reasonable voice. 'There are certain traits that indicate whether someone is suited to positions of high power or not; we select the candidates that best align with those traits through rigorous tests and examinations and assessments, and we weed out anyone who isn't suitable. We're not asking random children to prove they've got the gumption to succeed at that level!'

The headmaster put his phone away. 'My dear Lucy, remember, *you yourself* were deemed worthy. If your father had been able to afford the fees, I'm sure you would've passed your final exam with flying colours.' His face softened. 'All those wasted years "getting better" in psychiatrists' offices, suppressing everything, when you could have come *here* and been seen and appreciated for who you really are.'

Argyll stepped closer. 'You're one of us.'

Lucy backed away. 'Who did *you* kill?' Waving a hand at the floor-to-ceiling stacks of filing cabinets. 'It'll be in here somewhere, won't it? Your confession and the photos and the incriminating evidence.'

Closer. 'You shouldn't have come here, Lucy.'

'Yeah, but you screwed up, didn't you? With your little forgery of Benedict Strachan's essay – oh, whoever you got to do it did a bang-up job, except for one thing: they weren't left-handed.'

Argyll brought his left hand up, moving it across his body, fingers twitching as if he was writing with an imaginary pen. The wrinkles deepened on his forehead. 'The letters should've been smudged.'

'That and the ink hadn't dried properly.' She flashed up her stained fingertips.

'You're right. I should've known better.' He lowered his left hand, the right one disappearing into his academic robe. 'But sometimes one has to improvise. I'm sorry, Lucy, I really am.' When the hand reappeared, it was wrapped around the handle of a knife. Not a big, flashy hunting knife, nothing showy or shiny – it was short and brutal, the kind of knife you used to kill people. 'But I'm afraid you've left us no option.'

'I'll take that backpack, please.' The headmaster held out his hand. 'You have something in there that doesn't belong to you, and rules *are* rules.'

Damn.

She slipped the straps from her shoulders.

Argyll spun the knife, so the blade pointed downwards from his clenched fist. 'St Nicholas College has stood here for over three hundred years. What we've built is simply too important to let anyone ruin it.' He twisted his wrist, till the blade lay back along his forearm. Which meant he actually knew what he was doing. And that was *never* a good sign. 'Try not to worry, though, I'll make it as quick and painless as possib—'

Lucy's backpack slammed into the side of his head. The cordless drill and other bits and pieces gave it a decent amount of weight. Enough to bounce him off the wall of filing cabinets before he clattered to the marble floor.

The headmaster only had time to open his mouth before she barged past him, knocking the old man flying as she sprinted her way through the almost-maze of stacks and out onto the landing.

The Bloodsmith was waiting for her.

'Where the hell have you been?' She hammered past him and down the stairs, taking the steps two at a time as the school's PA system *bing-bong*ed into life.

Argyll's voice echoed out from hidden speakers, the words hard and clipped. *'All pupils and teachers: block every exit from the quad! There are now* two *intruders loose on school grounds. One of them has just assaulted the headmaster.'*

'You might want to pick up the pace there, Kiddo. He doesn't sound happy.'

Lucy skidded her way around the first-floor landing and onto the next set of stairs, bouncing off the wall on her way, setting a handful of portraits flying. Clattering down the final flight to the soundtrack of their glass shattering and the frames splintering.

Her trainers squealed on the reception floor as she ran for the main door, shoving through it into the rain. Every window in every building shone with light, but it was still dark out here, the paths and that twisted old oak tree shrouded in the blue-grey gloom of a stormy night.

The Moonfall Gate was closest; all she had to do was get through it before anyone tried to stop her. Easy.

She accelerated, trainers splashing along the path, knees up, elbows out, the backpack swinging from one hand like a big black pendulum.

Almost there . . .

Then *clack*, and the whole quadrangle was flooded in bright white light.

Almost there . . .

It was less than two dozen feet away. This was going to work.

She made the turn into the Gate and—

'Bastard!'

The thing was packed with children and teachers, standing shoulder to shoulder. Most of them were still in their pyjamas, but a few had made it into their school uniform. Some had armed themselves with hockey sticks or cricket bats, others with hammers or knives.

Lucy staggered to a halt.

Main gate.

She turned and sprinted down the path . . . Slowed. Then came to a standstill. Lungs burning, back heaving, ribs complaining, breath rising like smoke into the downpour.

The main gate was clogged with bodies, too.

They advanced, completely silent. And when she turned, the other lot were doing the same. Fanning out until they formed a big circle around her, closing in with the security lights blazing away behind them. Tightening their ranks. Their silhouettes bristling with makeshift weaponry. Seventy-eight children, thirty-two adults, all staring at her as if she were some sort of science experiment that hadn't *quite* worked.

She turned on the spot.

They were everywhere. Just standing there in complete silence.

Then two of them stepped to the side, and Argyll strode into the circle.

He stopped a dozen feet from Lucy. 'Thank you, all: good job.' Cricking his head from side to side, limbering up. 'Everyone *not* in Raxton House, I need you to keep searching – there's another one, like her, somewhere on the school grounds. I – want – him – caught. Off you go.'

The teachers, support staff, and most of the kids slipped away into the buildings and out through the gates, leaving a dozen children behind. Some were clearly seniors, the others a mix of ages all the way down to the two first-years: Allegra and Hugo. They spread out, re-forming the circle.

Argyll held both hands in the air, the knife's blade a dull glint in the spotlights. 'I'm sorry it had to come to this, Lucy, but I'm afraid I have to make an example of you.'

Yes, she could charge the circle, batter through one of the smaller kids and run for it, but that would mean turning her back on Argyll and his knife, and there was no way in hell she was risking that.

He circled left, half crouched, keeping both eyes firmly fixed on Lucy as he hauled in a deep breath. 'FIDES!'

The circle of children belted out a reply: *'FAITH!'*

'SILENTIUM!'

'SILENCE!'

'POTENTIA!'

'POWER!'

Argyll attacked, the knife slashing through the air – so dark it was nearly invisible.

48

Lucy staggered backwards as the blade sizzled past, barely an inch from her face – but it hit one of the backpack's straps and sliced straight through it. *Jesus*, that was sharp. The return stroke caught her across the upper arm, before she could get her feet under her. Pain sparked like a firework, all the way from shoulder to elbow. 'Son of a bitch!'

Argyll kept circling. 'Dean-Edwards: what does Sun Tzu teach us about knowledge and the enemy?'

Allegra took a single step forward. 'If you know the enemy and know yourself, you need not fear the result of a hundred battles!'

Lucy swung the backpack at his head again, but he dodged it, then lunged forward, the knife searing across her shoulder – sending the backpack sailing free to crunch into the sodden grass. 'AAAAARGH!'

'Know the enemy! Very good.'

A dozen children glared at her.

'Ooh . . .' The Bloodsmith sucked on his teeth. 'Not looking good, is it?'

She squeezed her burning shoulder with her good hand, the palm already slick with blood. 'YOU'RE ALL UNDER ARREST!'

'Nice try, Kiddo, but I get the feeling that *isn't* going to work.'

Argyll feinted left, then right again. 'To truly know your enemy, you must know what they fear most.'

Lucy scrambled away from the blade. 'I'M A POLICE OFFICER, AND I'M ORDERING YOU TO PUT THE KNIFE DOWN!'

'Come on, the man's a trained killer. You're going to *die* if you don't do something.'

Argyll lunged again, but this time she got her arm up in time to block his wrist, keeping the blade away, but it left her side exposed and his knife-free fist slammed into her bruised ribs.

All the air *whoomph*ed from her lungs and Lucy staggered.

He danced back. 'So we must ask ourselves, what does Detective Sergeant McVeigh fear?'

Lucy dropped into the defensive pose they taught at Officer Safety Training: one leg forward, both knees bent, elbows in, hands up, palms out, ready to—

He dropped into a squat and swept her legs out from under her, sending her crashing into the wet grass. She clambered upright, but he'd skipped out of reach again, bouncing away as if he was standing on a tiny trampoline.

The bastard was *playing* with her.

'DS McVeigh here was held prisoner by a rapist. I know because how, Farquharson Junior?'

The knife flashed – her left shoulder exploded in shards of broken glass. 'AAAAAAARGH! You utter—'

His fist battered into the side of her head and the soggy grass rushed up to greet her again.

'*Google, sir?*'

'"Google, sir"! Your first weapon in any war is knowledge; I *googled* her. So what do we think Detective Sergeant McVeigh fears the most?'

She struggled to her knees, both arms barely working.

The Bloodsmith knelt beside her. 'I believe in you, Lucy, and not just because I'm a figment of your imagination. I believe in you because I know who you *really* are. And I need you to believe in you, too.'

'Come on, children: she was held prisoner by a *rapist*, what – does – she – fear?'

That big pre-teen buffoon, Hugo, put his hand up. 'Rape?'

Oh Jesus . . .

'Listen to me, Kiddo.' The Bloodsmith brushed the rain-soaked hair from her eyes. 'You need to embrace the real you. Not just the good you – the careful one who always does the right thing – you need to love the *other* one too. The Monster.' He cupped her face in his hands, staring into her eyes. 'Because you're not the same monster you were when you were little – you're a whole *new* monster. You've got power, remember?'

'Correct.' Argyll raised his foot and placed it against her chest, shoving her onto her back. 'And what our enemy fears will bring them to their knees!'

'And if you don't use that power, he's going to slice you open like a frog in science class and this bunch of little weirdos are going to cheer as he hauls out your innards.' The Bloodsmith patted her on the blood-smeared shoulder. 'Dig deep, Kiddo.'

Argyll stooped over Lucy, grabbed her overcoat and tore it open, sending buttons flying.

'GET OFF ME!' Scrabbling in her coat's pocket.

'You see, children? See what fear can—'

'GRAAAAAAAGH!' Lucy swung the rape alarm like an ice pick, stabbing it into his ear and pulling the pin with her thumb.

DI Tudor had only been partially right about it being mono-directional. A barrage of high-pitched wailing screeched out, hard and sharp enough to make Lucy flinch back into the wet grass. And she was only getting a fraction of its full volume.

Argyll *screamed*. Tumbling away, one hand clamped to his ruined ear as blood oozed through his fingers. That was what a hundred and fifty decibels got you.

'Now would be the time, Kiddo.'

Lucy leaped on his back, her weight forcing him into the ground. Fingers clenched around the rape alarm like a knuckle duster as she slammed her fist into his face. Again and again and again. Getting stronger with every punch. Bellowing a scream of fury as the blows rained down.

He struggled over onto his side, but she stayed on top of him. Yelling and punching with both fists now, bright-scarlet droplets sparkling like rubies in the harsh spotlights. The knife fell from his fingers and she snatched it up, slamming the hilt into his face over and over and over. Keeping going till there was nothing left but mush and blood and shattered bones, and Argyll McCaskill wasn't moving any more.

She sat back on his chest, breath rasping in her throat. Arms aching.

Rain pattered down against her burning shoulders as she stood and stared at the small circle of pale quiet faces.

Lucy hauled in a deep, snarling breath. 'COME ON! WHICH ONE OF YOU MOTHER*FUCKERS* WANTS TO BE NEXT?'

A couple of the older kids looked as if they might have been thinking about it, but their gaze drifted to what was left of their assistant head-master and then they wouldn't meet her eyes any more.

Didn't think so.

Lucy threw back her head and howled her rage and glory out into the dark sky. There was a small pause, then Allegra joined in, followed by Hugo, and one by one the other kids took up the cry, until all twelve of them were baying at the storm like a pack of wolves.

The King was dead, long live the Monster.

'Here. You look like you could use this.' The headmaster returned from his desk, holding out a tumbler with a very generous measure of whisky ambering the glass.

'I don't . . . You know what? Sod it.' Took a bit of doing – what with her knuckles being all bloody and cracked and swollen and stinging like an *utter* bastard – but she accepted the tumbler and knocked back a good mouthful. Hissed out a fiery, smoky breath. Shuddered as all the hairs on her arms clambered to attention. Well, where they weren't matted down with blood. Hopefully the whisky's analgesic properties would kick in soon, and dull the stabbing, throbbing aches currently rampaging up and down her body.

Look on the bright side, though: the blistering headache she'd had for the last two months was finally gone.

Lucy winced her way into one of the two matching sofas. And if she left it covered in nasty dark-red stains, tough.

The headmaster's office was warm and comfortable, pulling steam from her sodden clothes. He'd turned the lights down low, leaving most of the room in darkness, transforming it into a cave. A place to tell stories about the vicious beasts that roamed the world outside.

Even if it was obvious that the two most dangerous animals in the place were right here, having a drink together.

He placed a manila folder on the coffee table in front of her. 'I believe this is what you were looking for: Benedict Strachan's entrance exam. The *real* one.'

She grunted and fumbled out the 'What I did over the summer holi-days' essay, trying not to get too much blood on the thing. It was nothing like the version Argyll had shown her in the records room. No creepy story about a dead dog, no peeping on screwing couples, no drunken mother, no father flying into a rage . . . Just a little boy proud of the experiments he was doing with the new chemistry set he'd got for his birthday, and fizzing with excitement about a trip to the Science and Natural History Museums in London.

Lucy flipped through to the aptitude test.

> DESCRIBE A HORSE:
> *60 million years ago, Hyracotherium (more commonly known as Eohippus: the 'Dawn Horse') evolved in what is now North America. It was the size of a small Border collie and was primarily a forest browser, presumably to minimize its exposure to predators . . .*

So much for the casual racism and eugenic tendencies that Argyll had been so worried about. Benedict had even dotted his 'i's with little bubbles.

Lucy put the essay back on the table and picked up the black-bordered envelope instead. 'Doesn't exactly seem like the kind of kid who'd stab a homeless man eighty-nine times.'

'I don't know why Argyll felt the need to mislead you, Lucy. If he'd come to me . . .' A sigh. 'Still, that's all blood under the carpet now, isn't it?'

'He wanted us to think Benedict was always bad news. That him killing Liam Hay was inevitable and nothing to do with St Nick's.'

The headmaster sank into the sofa opposite, holding a glass of his own. 'I keep telling people: the cover-up gets you into trouble *far* more often than the crime.' A sad smile. 'But no one ever seems to listen.'

She slid the envelope's contents out. One photo showed Benedict and his mystery friend attacking Liam Hay in the doorway of Hallelujah Bingo; the rest had been taken in the alleyway beside Angus MacBargain's Family Store. At the bottom of the pile was the confession:

> *I, Benedict Samuel Strachan, do hereby and of my own free will take full and sole responsibility for the murder of Liam Hay, a homeless man (of no fixed abode), in Castle Hill, on Sunday the 18th of May . . .*

He hadn't dotted the 'i's with little bubbles this time, and the paper was crinkled, as if someone had spilled drops of water on it.

The first photo proved he was definitely involved, but the rest?

Lucy held two of the pictures up. 'None of these show Benedict stabbing Liam Hay.' In both, his unnamed accomplice was slamming a knife into Liam's torso, face a mask of glee, while Benedict stood in the background, one hand over his mouth, eyes wide and shiny.

He probably hadn't stopped crying till long after he wrote his 'confession'.

'To be honest, Benedict didn't really fit the psychological profile necessary to succeed at St Nicholas College, but his father had power over the planning authority and the school had just been gifted a large parcel of land in Shortstaine ripe for development.' The headmaster shook his head. 'Our Board of Governors overruled my objections and insisted Benedict be entered for the final exam anyway. "Greed and hubris are oft the downfall of weak men."'

She went back to the photo of that gleeful face, the blade hammering down. 'It was his academic brother, wasn't it? The other boy. You pair them up and send them out to kill people.'

'It lets them know they can always trust their fellow students. Because they have to.' A smile. 'Friendships forged at St Nicholas College are for life, Lucy.'

'Who was he: Benedict's academic brother? Who *really* killed Liam Hay?'

'I'm afraid I can't tell you that, Lucy. It violates our data-protection policy.'

'Of course it does.' She knocked back the last of her whisky, a nice warm pressure growing behind her eyes, wrapping her aching flesh in a soft cosy blanket. 'What happens now?'

'That's a very good question.' The headmaster levered himself out of the sofa and carried his glass over to the front of his office, gazing down through the window at the quad. 'I see Shauna's people have arrived. I shall have to send her some flowers as a thank-you.'

Lucy groaned her way upright and limped over there.

Caught in the harsh-white glare of the quadrangle's floodlights, two figures in the full white SOC get-up were zipping Argyll's battered remains into a body bag, while two others treated the ground with backpack sprayers that were probably full of trichloroethylene. Getting rid of any nasty contaminants and signs of blood.

'So Argyll just disappears.'

'It's disappointing, to be honest. I wanted to retire in a couple of years, and now I have to train up a new assistant head. And I genuinely *liked* Argyll. He was a good man.'

'He tried to kill me!'

'That's . . . unfortunate. But he paid the price for underestimating you, didn't he? And now, instead of a prime spot in the St Nicholas mausoleum, a brass plaque in the quad, and his painting in the Noble Hall, he'll be dismembered and hidden away in a number of unmarked graves, never to be spoken of again.' The headmaster placed a warm papery hand on her forearm. 'And there's no need for you to worry about repercussions, Lucy; Shauna's people are *very* discreet and extremely thorough. There won't be any forensic traces to link you with the remains.'

'And you expect me to *trust* you? What about the dozen witnesses?'

'Witnesses?' A smile deepened the wrinkles around his mouth and eyes. 'You asked if we keep all these files to blackmail our students, but how could we? If we release them to the world, don't you think people would ask why we kept them secret for so long? Our destruction would be mutually assured.' He plucked the empty glass from her hand and topped it up from a small decanter. 'I reviewed your file again, Lucy, and after tonight's events I'm more certain than ever that you would've made an *excellent* addition to our family. So, I have a proposition for you.' He returned the filled tumbler. 'Would you like to join the faculty here at St Nicholas College? I really think your . . . unique perspective on things might well prove instructive to our pupils, and you'll find our salary rates are *very* generous.' He clinked his glass against hers, then drank. 'Or, if full-time academia doesn't tempt you, perhaps you'd consider becoming a visiting professor?'

Charlie emerged from the shadows. 'Oh, he has *got* to be joking! Work here? Covering up murders and corruption and God knows what else? Are we supposed to be OK with that?'

Yes, but given how well connected the school was, going against them would probably get her chopped into little pieces and disposed of 'discreetly', like Argyll.

'Lucy, no!' Charlie threw his arms out. 'How can we let them get away with *murder*?'

Why not? They'd been getting away with it for years. Decades. Maybe even centuries.

At least, if she was on the inside, they wouldn't touch her. And *she* had the power, now. Be nothing stopping her taking that job with ACC Cormac-Fordyce, getting the promotion, *and* becoming a visiting professor. And it probably wouldn't hurt to have the great and the good owing her favours because she hadn't burned this whole rotten place to the ground.

'You can't be serious. This is horrific, you *can't* be part of it!'

Besides – her eyes slid to the crumpled backpack with its one working strap – she had a government-backed insurance policy.

'Lucy?' The headmaster waved a hand in front of her face. 'Are you all right? You zoned out for a bit; perhaps you've got concussion? Let me get the doctor to look at you – he's very good. Former army surgeon in Iraq, you know.'

'That's not a bad idea.' Charlie looked her up and down. 'Those cuts need stitching, and if you go to A & E they'll have to inform the police you've been in a knife fight. And then you've got all *that* to explain.'

'Lucy?'

She nodded. 'Thank you.'

'My pleasure, I assure you.' The headmaster pressed a button on his desk phone, setting it buzzing. 'Vanessa, would you ask Major Redpath to come to my office, please? I have a young lady here that needs his attention.'

'*Yes, Headmaster.*'

'Thank you, Vanessa.' He pressed the button again. 'Now, where were we? Ah yes, you were about to accept my proposition and join us here at St Nicholas College!'

'It's been a long night.' Lucy put her glass down. 'I'll have to think about it.'

'Of course. One should never rush a lady.' He fiddled with a letter opener, avoiding eye contact. 'Don't take too long, though. As I say, certain of our parents get nervous when there's a potential threat to their offspring. And some of them have a whole country's security services at their disposal, not to mention a somewhat *casual* approach to extradition and human rights.'

'Understood.'

'Excellent.' The headmaster clapped his hands together. Pursed his lips. Frowned. 'There is just *one* more thing: Shauna tells me that when her people went to "tidy" your home, they couldn't find the two doctors you say tried to kill you. So, I was just wondering . . . what did you do with them?'

— we go in darkness —

(on the count of three)

49

Huddled under the brolly, Lucy checked her watch – just visible between her jacket sleeve and the black leather gloves – only wincing slightly as the movement pulled at the stitches in her shoulder. 'Three, two, one . . .'

On the other side of the road, a huge guy in the full Method-of-Entry gear smashed his big red door key into the chandler's warehouse door, popping the ancient lock right out of the wood and sending the whole thing *woom*ing in to bang against the brick walls.

'*GO, GO, GO, GO!*'

The six-person team swarmed inside, extendable batons drawn. They were followed by the Dog Unit – PC Clark being dragged into the building by PD Bawheid, the huge Alsatian's paws scrabbling on the paving stones, desperate to find someone to bark at, and, if at all possible, bite.

Not a bad way to spend a Monday afternoon.

The big OSU Transit van was parked next to the Dog Unit's smaller one, Lucy and the Dunk's pool car behind that, and last, but not least, DI Tudor in an old Jaguar – rusty rather than antique – with his phone clamped to his ear. Doing a lot of listening by the look of things, and not enjoying it much.

The Dunk puffed out his cheeks, gazing up at Lucy. 'Sarge?' He'd got himself a brolly from somewhere – a bright-green-with-pink-spots one, which didn't really go with his traditional black beatnik outfit. Puffing away on a fag as the rain drummed down. 'Are you *sure* you're OK?'

'No, Dunk, I'm at death's door. That's why I've organized this massive raid on a random building down the docks: because I'm suffering from a serious head injury.' Which didn't seem quite so worrying, now the permanent headache was gone. Maybe it wasn't scrambled eggs up there, after all?

'Only you look like you fell asleep at a six-year-old's birthday party, and they all coloured your face in with blue, green, and purple felt-tips.'

'Told you: I tripped on a loose stair rod. House needs some new carpets, anyway.' What with Shauna's people having ripped the old ones out, after dousing them in trichloroethylene to get rid of any blood or DNA from Dr Lockerby and Dr Meldrum.

He shuffled his feet and went back to staring across the street. 'Do you think this is our boy? I think it's our boy. I can feel it in my doodahs.'

The Bloodsmith leaned against the car roof, immune to the downpour as he lit up a big fat cigar. 'Well, he's not wrong there. Just twenty-four hours too late.'

DI Tudor climbed out of his Jag, turned up his collar and hurried over, ducking in under Lucy's brolly.

'Any news?'

'Only just gone in, Boss.'

Another *BOOM* echoed out from inside – that would be them battering down the door at the top of the stairs.

'I've had DCI Ross, Superintendent Spence, *and* ACC Cormac-Fordyce crawling up my fundament all morning. "Why haven't you found him yet, Detective Inspector?", "You've known who he is since *Friday*, Detective Inspector!", "Do I have to come down there and do it myself, Detective Inspector?"' He spat out into the rain. 'Bunch of bastards.'

The Dunk stood on his tiptoes and peered down the alley. 'This could be it, though, Boss.'

One final muffled *BOOM* marked the door through to the long, low, subterranean room.

'Let's hope so, for *all* our sakes.' Tudor raised an eyebrow as he stared at Lucy. 'What's with the black leather gloves? Planning on assassinating someone later?'

She shrugged. 'Just feeling the cold, Boss. You know, after I fell down the stairs. And everything.' It certainly didn't have *anything* to do with the scabs puckering the skin across her swollen knuckles.

Tudor checked his watch. 'What's taking them so long?'

Two minutes later, all six members of the Operational Support Unit lumbered out into the rain again.

'Please God, let this be it . . .' Tudor marched over there, Lucy and the Dunk hurrying in his wake. 'Anything?'

'Not any more.' Sergeant Niven's voice was solid Kingsmeath, half the vowels flattened and nasal as he parked the big red door key on his shoulder as if it barely weighed a thing. 'But someone's gone to a lot of trouble covering their tracks.' He clicked on an oversized torch, turned, and led the way back inside, motioning for them to follow. 'You smell that?'

The harsh acidic tang of bleach hung in the corridor, mingling with a fug of scorched plastic and tarry soot. It got thicker as they turned the corner and thumped downstairs. By the time they stepped into the long, low room, it was choking.

Lucy cupped her hand over her face, eyes watering. 'Dear God . . .'

The whole room was blackened and charred. A small pile of carbonized rubbish smouldered in the middle of the place. None of it recognizable as a manky couch and coffee table.

'Whoever it was, they didn't want us finding anything. You can get the FSSER down here, but I'd put cash on this place being cleaner than a priest's conscience.'

Lucy stiffened. 'Those are dirtier than you'd think.'

While DI Tudor dug out his phone again, and organized a forensic team, she did a circuit of the room, stopping to nudge the length of chain where Dr Christianson used to live, setting it rattling. 'Dead end.'

'Sod.' The Dunk drooped. 'Really thought I'd got him, there.'

She patted him on the shoulder. 'Never mind, it was a good bit of detective work. We were just a wee bit too late.'

Thank God.

The call came in at twenty past five, as the Operation Maypole office was emptying out for the day. Everyone heading off to the Bart for a post-not-achieving-anything drink.

'*DS McVeigh? Yes, hi, it's Abid Hammoud. You wanted to know about a missing red-and-white Mini with a dented roof and cracked rear windscreen?*'

Lucy sat up at her desk. 'Hold on.' Pulling out her notebook, then snap-snap-snapping her fingers at the Dunk. 'OK.' Pen poised.

'*You will not believe how much of a struggle we had, especially without even a partial number plate to go on, pretty much impossible really, but I had a brainwave and expanded the search parameters—*'

'You found it? You found the Mini?'

'Erm . . . Yes. Red-and-white Mini, dented roof, cracked rear windscreen, spotted by a traffic camera on the A9402, about three miles south of Short-staine. It was turning onto a single-track road, which is a dead end, so there's no way out but back the way it came. And there's no sign of it leaving. I'll email you the map coordinates.'

'Thanks, Abid, you're a genius. Can you throw in a screengrab, too?'

'Will do.'

She scribbled down the details, hanging up as the Dunk scuttled over from the coffee machine.

'Got you a latte.'

She ignored the proffered mug. 'No time. Get a car, we've got a sighting.'

Even with the siren going, it took a good thirty-five minutes to fight their way through rush-hour traffic and onto the single-track road – the Dunk driving hunched over the wheel, teeth gritted, elbows out, but not quite brave enough to put his foot flat to the floor.

He slowed, killing the lights-and-music as the road twisted through a small patch of woods. 'Aren't we going to need backup, here?'

'Probably. But I want to check it out first. Don't want a repeat of this afternoon.'

He wilted a little at that. 'Yeah, probably best.'

The road curled around to the left – the grey bones of a standing circle reaching out through the earth on the hill above them – then right – past the tumbledown skeleton of an ancient croft – over a crumbling bridge and into a big chunk of Forestry Commission pines, where the tarmac ran out, leaving the car's tyres growling over muddy yellow gravel. Rain pounded down on the road, but a pale-grey mist clung to the tree trunks on either side, haunting the forest floor, beneath that dense green canopy of needles.

Lucy pulled out her phone and checked the screengrab Abid Hammoud had sent through: a red-and-white Mini, its rear windscreen covered with what looked like bin bags and duct tape, a long narrow dent creasing the back end of its roof.

Definitely the car she'd bashed with Dad's metal walking stick.

Which . . . wasn't really possible.

Had to hand it to them: St Nicholas College's cover-up squad were good at their job.

She zoomed in on the Mini's number plate, copied it down into her notebook, then forwarded the email on to Monster Munch. Gave it a minute, then called her.

'Operation Maypole, DC Stockham speaking?'

'Monster Munch? Just sent you a screengrab from a traffic camera. I need you to run a PNC check on the Mini's number plate.'

'Urgh . . . Bad enough I get lumbered with the crappy back shift, without people piling on extra work.' A rough sigh, followed by the noise of a keyboard click-clattering away. Monster Munch's voice dropped to a gossipy whisper. *'Tudor's still here and he's got a face like a walloped backside. Superintendent Spence was in with him for half an hour, and just between you and me, he's torn Tudor a new one. God, you should've heard the shouting – it was like Christmas at my mum and dad's house. Right, here we go . . . Number plate belongs to a Volkswagen Touran, registered to one Julie Wilkinson, seventy-two, who's been dead for three months. So she's probably not the driver.'*

The St Nicholas team were very, *very* good indeed.

'Thanks.'

'You hear about Tudor's wife? Vow of chastity is what I heard, which is a polite way of saying—'

'That's great, got to go.' Lucy hung up.

The Dunk glanced across the car at her. 'Anything?'

'Christianson nicked the number plates off some dead old lady's people carrier.'

'So we couldn't trace him through the car. He's a sneaky bastard, I'll give him that.'

The further they went on the forestry road, the worse the potholes got. Water surged out in dirty arcs as the pool car wallowed through them. Rain thrumming on the roof, windscreen wipers grunting and groaning, blowers howling – filling the interior with the twin scents of pine and dust.

'There!' The Dunk bounced up and down in his seat. 'You see that?'

As if it was hard to miss.

The track widened out into what was probably a turning circle – access to the rest of the woods blocked by a padlocked metal gate. Sitting in front of it was the burned-out carcase of a small car. It sat on four grubby alloys, the tyres turned to ash, paintwork scorched to a pebble-dashed brown. All the plastic trim had gone, and so had the headlights, windows, and windscreens, the interior reduced to its metal framework . . .

'Sodding hell.' The Dunk pulled up a good dozen feet away and killed the engine. 'I'll call it in.' Digging out his phone as Lucy grabbed her umbrella and winced her way out into the downpour.

She popped the brolly up, holding it tight in her aching gloved fist, and limped over there.

The driver's charred remains were slumped behind the wheel. Not that there was a lot left of it, or him. His torso was more or less intact, if scorched to a cinder, but there was no sign of his head, or his arms – just a few blackened lumps.

Lucy peered inside.

A second body lay curled up in what would've been the boot. It was just as bad as the driver.

'Lucy?' Charlie waved at her from the gate. 'Over here!'

On the other side of the five-bar metal gate, someone had set up a row of large glass jars. Each one held a human heart, suspended in a pink-tinged liquid, a drift of brown making a layer at the bottom of the jar.

There'd only been six, back at the chandler's warehouse, but now there were eight. One for each of the Bloodsmith's *real* victims. And she'd put good money on the other two belonging to Dr Meldrum and Dr Lockerby.

Yes, but if that was the case, they were short a body, because the one in the driver's seat *had* to be Dr John Christianson, didn't it? Why would the headmaster set all this up and leave that thread messy and unfinished? And Lockerby was already dead, so you'd be daft not to stick him in the boot. Which left . . .

Malcolm Louden.

'Old Nick's is cleaning house, isn't it?' Charlie squatted down in front of the jars. 'No one's going to look for who really killed Malcolm Louden. If it's all solved, why would you bother?'

And *of course* they'd have his heart, just lying around at the school, ready to add to the real Bloodsmith's collection. It would be the physical evidence tying Allegra Dean-Edwards and her academic brother, Hugo, to Malcolm Louden's murder.

All they'd had to do was write 'HELP ME!' on the wall in his blood, after they gutted him, and everyone blamed the Bloodsmith. The *one* secret Operation Maypole had managed to keep was the thing that let Allegra and Hugo get away with murder. Because nothing was ever really secret when you had the kind of reach St Nicholas College did. Especially with ex-pupils like Assistant Chief Constable Cormac-Fordyce in charge of Police Scotland.

Which raised the question: what did St Nick's do with Dr Meldrum?

Charlie leaned back against the gate. 'Maybe they made her "discreetly" disappear, like Argyll?'

The Dunk came scurrying over from the car, pink-and-green brolly trembling in the downpour. 'They're on their way, Sarge. What have you . . . ? Holy *crap*! Are they what I think they are?' He stared at the jars. 'We did it. We solved the whole sodding thing! Hoooo-rah!' Doing a little victory dance in the rain.

At least someone was happy.

50

'All I'm saying is it wouldn't hurt us to have the patter of tiny feet about the place, would it?' Charlie scuffed along the pavement, hands in his pockets, dirty-blond hair caught in the glow of a streetlight like a small fuzzy halo.

Brokemere Street was quiet for a Wednesday night, the kerb lined with parked cars and wheelie bins. Tenements ran the length of the road, the ground-floor shops dark and shuttered, lights glowing in the flats above. Only two businesses were still open: Angus MacBargain's Family Store – its blue-and-white signage shining like a beacon, while its window promised '40% OFF MCEWAN'S EXPORT!', 'ALL TAMPONS ~ 2 FOR 1!', and 'GUARANTEED £6M JACKPOT THIS FRIDAY!!!'; and the sex shop that had replaced the tailor's, on the other side of the little alley-way where Liam Hay had been stabbed eighty-nine times.

Its windows were blacked out, an LED sign pulsing red in the gloom: 'XXX!', 'ADULTS ONLY!', 'FETISH!', 'BONDAGE!', 'TOYS!', 'LUBE!', then back to 'XXX!' again.

The Bloodsmith lingered on the corner, washed in the scarlet glow. 'I'm not sure we're quite ready for that level of commitment, yet.'

Lucy limped into the alleyway. If her arms were another three inches longer – and she could extend the things without grimacing in pain – she could probably touch both sides of it at the same time.

It was cleaner than you'd think, for a narrow lane running between a convenience store and a sex shop. No piles of garbage, or old cardboard boxes. No stacks of plastic wrapping.

She stopped outside the loading door to Angus MacBargain's.

A rectangle of concrete was raised out of the tarmac, just big enough for a dead body. There was something on the other side of the plinth, tucked in beside the wall, nestling up to the bricks.

She wrestled a pair of blue nitrile gloves over her black leather ones, and clicked on the little torch from her pocket. Played its soft white beam over whatever was hidden there.

The Bloodsmith appeared at her shoulder. 'Told you.'

It was a bunch of flowers. Nothing big and flashy, just the kind of thing you could pick up from a supermarket for a couple of quid. Or steal from a graveyard for free. Her ribs screeched, bruising and scar tissue growling, as she bent over and retrieved it. Turning it in her squeaky blue fingers.

There was a card, tucked into the foliage. Two words, in wobbly, smudged letters: 'I'M SORRY.' But then writing wasn't easy, with your dominant hand in a cast.

Charlie was waiting for them, out on the pavement. 'Was he right?'

'Of course I was.' Swaggering past, puffing on his cigar. 'For who knows better the secrets of the human heart than one who's carved *six* of them from his victims' chests?'

Lucy rolled her eyes. 'He's going to be impossible all night now, isn't he?'

'Probably.'

She hobbled after the pair of them, up to the end of the street, then around the corner, and onto Campbellmags Way – enveloped in the seductive scents of garlic, vinegar, and hot grease wafting over from the takeaways on Harvest Lane.

Sixteen years after that grainy CCTV footage had been taken, and Hallelujah Bingo was still there. It hadn't aged well, though. The canopy over the main entrance was propped up by scaffolding that didn't quite manage to stop it sagging on one side. A barrier of weather-bloated chipboard ran around the outside of the poles, projecting out onto the pavement and blocking off the old doors. Fliers and posters lay in thick layers on the barricade, advertising festivals and concerts and bands and DJ rave parties that had happened ages ago, overlaid with badly spelled graffiti tags and half-arsed attempts at sub-Banksy stencilling.

The lights that had once bordered the canopy were cracked and darkened, the red plastic letters on the sign set forever at 'TO LET / MAY SELL'.

The Bloodsmith rubbed his hands together. 'Now, who'd like to place a small wager that I'm right about this next bit, too? Charlie? No? How about you, Kiddo?'

'No one likes a show-off.' She dug out her phone and scrolled through the contacts as she crossed to the opposite side of the street, stopping under the CCTV camera that still watched the derelict bingo hall. OK, so it was a bit late to be calling a senior officer, but DCI Ross *did* say he wanted to be kept up to date.

'Hello?' The sound of some sort of sitcom chortled away to itself in the background.

'Boss? DS McVeigh. Just wondered if there was any update on your surveillance op: Ian Strachan's Audi?'

'At ten to eleven on a Wednesday night?' There were rustling noises, followed by a muffled thump, shutting off the canned laughter. *'Are you about to have another breakthrough, like you did with Operation Maypole? I'll have to watch out; you'll be after my job next.'*

'Do my best, Boss.'

'There's been no movement on the car since we found it. Meanwhile, nobody's murdered one of our homeless population – that we know of – and the residents of Willcox Towers are complaining about all the rats hanging round the huge pile of bin bags we won't let the council clear up.'

That was good to know.

'Believe me, Lucy, if it'd been anyone else, I'd have cancelled the obs days ago. But you seem to be on a streak at the moment, so I'm willing to let it run till the end of the week. After that, I'm pulling it, the council are taking the rubbish off to landfill, and Ian Strachan's Audi's getting towed.'

'Thanks, Boss.'

'Unless you can get me a result sooner than that . . . ?'

'I'll give you a shout when I know.'

'You do that.' And he was gone.

She put her phone away. 'Right, boys, shall we?'

Charlie pointed. 'This looks promising.'

There was a door set into the chipboard-and-graffiti barricade, with a big Yale lock on it, presumably to allow access for the selling agents and anyone mad enough to consider buying a dilapidated bingo hall that had been falling apart for *at least* the last dozen years.

There wasn't a handle, and no sign of hinges, so it had to open inwards. Lucy gave it a gentle push, just in case.

'Before you do what I think you're going to do, Lucy, are we all remembering that there's a security camera right across the road, pointing this way?'

'Come on, Charlie, live a little. Boot it in, Kiddo.'

She stepped back, took a deep breath, gritted her teeth, and slammed her heel into the chipboard, just left of the lock, putting her weight behind it. The thing sprang open, bounced off one of the scaffolding poles and juddered closed again. But the lock was buggered now, so Lucy gave it a shove, clicked on her torch, and limped inside. Wincing with every step.

Might not have been a great idea: kicking a door in, when most of her body was one big paisley-patterned bruise. Still, too late to worry about that now.

Rancid yellow light seeped in through the gap between the barricade and the drooping canopy, leaving the interior wrapped in monochrome gloom, the shadows solid black.

She ran her torch across the floor till the beam caught a large bundle of rags, huddled against the boarded-up doors.

A pale face stared out at her from the folds of a manky sleeping bag, eyes red-rimmed and watery, pupils like stitched-on buttons. His skin was greasy grey, smeared with dirt, a week-old beard matted around the corners of his chapped-lipped mouth.

He scrambled backwards, legs struggling in the sleeping bag's depths, arms shoving at layers of drooping cardboard and filthy newsprint. 'Oh God, oh God, oh God . . .' His shoulders pressed against the side of the doorway, but he kept on going till he was sitting upright, both arms covering his face. 'PLEASE DON'T KILL ME!'

Lucy let the torchlight drift away from Benedict Strachan's face. 'I'm not going to kill you, you idiot.'

'I'M SORRY, I COULDN'T DO IT! I COULDN'T! I TRIED, BUT I COULDN'T!'

'He doesn't half go *on*. Whinge, moan, whimper.'

'Leave the poor guy alone, he's just scared.'

'Will you two shut up?' She propped herself up against one of the scaffolding poles, hissing breath through her teeth, till the screeching pain settled into a burning ache instead. Doing her best to ignore how Benedict's rancid BO and rotten breath were strong enough to flavour the air. She even managed a smile for him. 'You're safe now.'

'Please don't kill me . . .'

'No one's going to kill you.' She held up the little bouquet of flowers. 'You didn't murder Liam Hay, did you? It was your accomplice. It was never you: you were just a wee boy, pressured into playing along and too scared to say no.'

'I tried . . .'

'And they let you take the fall, didn't they? Whoever your academic brother was, he got away with it. He got to attend St Nick's, and university, then off to some high-powered job, while you rotted in prison. And he's never given you a minute's thought since.' Lucy creaked her way down till she was right in front of Benedict. 'So why are you protecting him? Tell me who he is and I'll make sure he pays for what he did to you.'

'I . . .' Benedict blinked at her, then looked away.

'Come on, he's a powerful man now, isn't he? And he's *never* lifted a finger to help you.'

A shudder, then both shoulders curled up and in, head drooping. 'I . . .'

'He's had a life of *luxury* and *privilege*, and what have you had? Sixteen years in a crappy prison cell, people spitting at you in the street, your own father turned against you. While *he* sits in a gilded boardroom *laughing* at you.'

Silence.

Come on, come on.

You can do it.

All she needed was a name.

Benedict's tongue slithered across his cracked lips. 'I . . .' Deep breath. 'I, Benedict Samuel Strachan, do hereby and of my own free will take full and sole responsibility for the murder of Liam Hay . . .'

So close.

Lucy used the nearest scaffolding pole to pull herself upright again. 'Benedict Strachan, I am arresting you under section one of the Criminal

Justice, Scotland, Act 2016 for breaching your release conditions.' She gestured. 'On your feet.'

He did what he was told, quiet and meek as she slapped on the cuffs, finished the official script, and marched him out into the night.

51

Lucy checked her make-up in the bedroom mirror. Not exactly ready for the cover of *Vogue*, but it would do.

Three weeks and the bruising had completely gone. If it wasn't for the puckered scar tissue where Argyll's knife had slashed across her arm and shoulders, you wouldn't know anything had happened. And, according to St Nick's ex-army surgeon, they'd fade over time. Till then, she'd just have to avoid sleeveless tops. Not exactly a hardship in Scotland, in October.

For some reason, the person in the mirror didn't look like a stranger any more. And this time, when Lucy pulled on that therapist-mandated smile, it spread much, much easier. More naturally. Even if it did have a distinctly lupine edge to it now.

'I'm proud of you, Kiddo.' The Bloodsmith gave her a round of applause as she slipped her old warrant card out of its wallet and replaced it with the new one: Detective Inspector Lucy McVeigh.

Charlie was perched with his backside on the windowsill, basking in the dawn's anaemic glow. 'Are we sure we're doing the right thing?'

'No.' She pulled on her suit jacket. 'But I'm doing it anyway.'

He followed her downstairs. 'Now, on the subject of the pitter-patter of tiny feet, can I suggest—'

'Oh, give it a rest, Charlie!' The Bloodsmith was waiting for them at the front door. 'Lucy's got an exciting new position and a career to take care of. We don't need another mouth to feed.'

She grabbed her raincoat and backpack, unlocked the front door, and stepped outside. Half seven and the sun had just scraped its way above the horizon, turning the fog a *slightly* lighter shade of grey. Her breath hung in the air as she scrunched across the frosted gravel, pointed her key fob at the Kia Picanto – setting its hazards flashing – and climbed inside. The engine started first time.

The Bloodsmith stretched out in the back seat. 'I know this might sound controversial, but I rather miss the old Bedford Rascal, with its creaky gears and rattling suspension and humping sausages down the sides.'

'They're not *humping*, they're dancing!'

'Oh, Kiddo, everyone knows they're humping. Shagging. Making the sausage with two backs. Isn't that right, Charlie?'

He pulled on his seatbelt. 'I just think having something *real* for Lucy to focus a bit of love and affection on would be good for her. She can spend as much time as she likes with you and me, but we're not real. It's not the same.'

Lucy reversed out of the drive. 'Are you going to bang on about this all the way there?'

'Probably. You should give in now: it'll save you a lot of bother.'

'Don't listen to him, Kiddo. Stand firm!' The Bloodsmith produced one of his stinky cigars, lighting up and filling the car with imaginary smoke.

Charlie scowled. 'You're *not* smoking that filthy thing in here.'

'Yes I am.'

'Would you two *please* just—' Her phone launched into its blandest ringtone and she pulled it out, pinning the thing between her shoulder and her ear as she accelerated. Not exactly legal. 'DI McVeigh.'

'*Lucy? It's Findlay.*'

'Boss. I'm leaving now; should be with you in a couple of hours, road-works permitting.'

'*Excellent; the team's buzzing to meet you. We've got a rather interesting case just come in, on Mull. Have you heard of the Rammach Brotherhood? If not, I won't spoil the surprise, but let's just say they won't be getting a Michelin star anytime soon. Not unless they start awarding those for cannibalism.*'

The Bloodsmith rubbed his hands. 'Yummy.'

'Doesn't sound like one of ours, Boss, so I'm assuming . . . ?'

'*A certain highly respected technology tycoon and peer of the realm's daughter joined the Brotherhood six weeks ago and hasn't been heard from since.*'

That was more like it.

'I'll be there soon as I can.'

'And I've been giving a little thought to your dilemma, vis-à-vis Sarah Black and her less-than-delightful family. Now that you're officially part of the St Nick's family, I think I have a few ideas that might tickle your fancy.'

A smile tugged at Lucy's cheeks. 'Thank you, Boss.'

'Welcome on board, Professor *McVeigh.'* Then ACC Cormac-Fordyce hung up.

Charlie held up a hand. 'So, back to my perfectly reasonable suggestion that—'

'Put the radio on, Kiddo, let's drown the bugger out.'

'I'm not saying she should get married and have kids, I'm saying we should get a dog. We could call it "Lucyfer". Ooh, or how about "Mr Bitey"?'

'We are *not* having a dog called "Mr Bitey". Tell him, Lucy: it's just asking for trouble.'

'Well, I don't hear you coming up with any better suggestions.'

'Here we go!'

Lucy tightened her grip on the steering wheel. 'If you two don't play nice, right now, I'll go to my new police shrink, get them to prescribe a whole shedload of antipsychotics, and *then* where will you be?'

Silence.

The Bloodsmith cleared his throat. 'Sorry, Lucy.'

'Yes, sorry, Lucy.' Charlie shifted in the passenger seat. 'But he started it.'

Oh, for God's sake.

Lucy clicked on the radio and turned it right up.

It was going to be a long, *long* day . . .

And last, but not least, some thank-yous

With every book I've ever written, I've been lucky to call on some extremely talented people for help, so I'd like to take this opportunity to thank: my police specialist, Inspector Bruce Crawford; my excellent editor, Frankie Gray; Imogen Nelson, Sarah Adams, Bill Scott-Kerr, Kate Samano, Richenda Todd, Josh Benn, Eleanor Updegraff, Tom Chicken, Laura Garrod, Emily Harvey, Gary Harley, Louise Blakemore, Julia Teece, Louis Patel, Leon Dufour, Marie Goodwin, Alison Barrow, Phil Evans, Richard Ogle, Sarah Scarlett, Lucy Beresford-Knox, Larry Finlay, and all the brilliant team at Transworld; and, of course, Phil Patterson, Guy Herbert, Leah Middleton, Sandra Sawicka, and the gang at Marjacq Scripts.

While we're here, I also want to thank all the librarians and booksellers out there who do such a great job getting books of all shapes and sizes into people's hands. You are magnificent. And let's not forget you, the person currently reading these acknowledgements. In an ever-stupiding world, we need as many readers as we can get to fight the tide. Thank you!

Lastly, I have to doff my cap to Fiona, and our beloved little girl, Grendel, who we both miss every day. Lastlier, let's finish up with a nod to Onion, Beetroot, and Gherkin. They didn't help in the least, but haven't interfered too much (except for Beetroot).

Stuart MacBride is the *Sunday Times* No.1 bestselling author of the Logan McRae and Ash Henderson novels. He's also published standalones, novellas, and short stories, as well as a slightly twisted children's picture book for slightly twisted children.

Stuart lives in the wilds of north-east Scotland with his wife Fiona; cats Gherkin, Onion, and Beetroot; some hens; some horses; and an impressive collection of assorted weeds.

For more information visit:

StuartMacBride.com
Facebook.com/StuartMacBrideBooks
@StuartMacBride